PRAISE FOR
THE QUEEN OF PARIS

"The book is exceedingly well researched, bringing German-occupied Paris to life. Despite Chanel's alliances with Nazis during World War II, the reader is left with a deeper understanding of her motivations, her power, and her allure."
—*HISTORICAL NOVELS REVIEW*

"Coco Chanel comes alive in the pages of *The Queen of Paris*... as thoroughly as she ever did in even a brilliant biography like that by Edmonde Charles-Roux...The result is a fictional portrait of Coco Chanel so oily and convincing that she'll linger in the reader's mind long after they finish the book."
—*OPEN LETTERS REVIEW*

"Empathetic yet unsparing, *The Queen of Paris* is an engrossing historical novel that reveals another room in the House of Chanel."
—*FOREWORD REVIEWS*

"Through meticulous research, Ewen vividly brings the enigmatic Coco Chanel back to life... Multilayered and compelling."
—SONIA VELTON, author of *Blackberry and Wild Rose*

"*The Queen of Paris* brings Paris alive during World War II with exacting and fascinating details as Ewen explores the constantly evolving complexity of Chanel's enigmatic character...The most engrossing novel I've read all year. I loved this book. I wish I had written it."
—BEV MARSHALL, author of *Right as Rain, Hot Fudge Sundae Blues, Walking through Shadows,* and *Back Home*

"Ewen spins fact and rumor into compelling fiction with a novel about brilliantly talented, supremely self-absorbed fashion designer Coco Chanel... A well-imagined, highly entertaining tale."
—TOBY DEVENS, bestselling author of *Happy Any Day Now*

THE QUEEN OF PARIS

Pamela Binnings Ewen

THE QUEEN OF PARIS

A novel of
COCO CHANEL

BLACK STONE
PUBLISHING

Copyright © 2020 by Pamela Binnings Ewen
Published in 2021 by Blackstone Publishing
Cover and book design by Alenka Vdovič Linaschke

Printed in the United States of America

First paperback edition: 2021
ISBN 978-1-79995-641-9
Fiction / Historical / World War II

1 3 5 7 9 10 8 6 4 2

CIP data for this book is available
from the Library of Congress

Blackstone Publishing
31 Mistletoe Rd.
Ashland, OR 97520

www.BlackstonePublishing.com

To my father,
Lt. Walter James Binnings
Captain, PT Boats 279 & 281
Pacific Theater, WWII

"Give them fast boats,
for they intend to go in harm's way."

*I, Coco Chanel, have discovered
the first rule of survival:
Trust no one but yourself.*

℘rologue

Paris, Place Vendôme
Fall 1944

Once, all of Paris lay at my feet, and Europe, too. The world was mine. Even after I closed the House of Chanel in 1939 in a fit of pique, my luminous No. 5 still sold, until Pierre stole it away. No. 5 was perfection. It infused my legend, lit my world like a brilliant star held in the weightless universe by the sheer grace of unknown powers. That perfume bore my name, making me famous and, until now, rich beyond my dreams. Like me, No. 5 has staying power—the *sillage* of it, the persistence—a ghostlike scent that lingers in the air even after substance disappears. The problem is that such fragrance triggers memories—for me, and others—and not all of them are good.

I've done terrible things. But really, I had no choice. And I always understood the risk. Still, I never thought this moment would come. The Germans have left Paris and there will be no last-minute absolution, not for me. Just ask the howling mob below in the Place Vendôme. Yesterday I watched from my rooms

1

in the Hôtel Ritz, peering through the lace curtains while vicious thugs stripped a beautiful young woman of her clothes. I think I knew her. But where is her SS lover now? There she stood, naked, while they shaved off her lovely hair. The rabid crowd cheered when they burned a swastika upon her forehead.

Oh—I still hear her screams.

There are people down in the streets today—I cannot believe my eyes—a string of women tied together with a rope. They're called "horizontal collaborators," the *collabos*. They weep, they beg, they plead. But with the Nazis gone, this is the time for vengeance.

This is the purge.

Next they will come for me. I tremble like a coward thinking of it. When they come I'll walk instead of being dragged, even though there's no one left to care. I am Mademoiselle Chanel, after all. Perhaps they'll forget about me. Perhaps I'll call downstairs for a cup of tea. Perhaps it will be my last.

Life is strange. You would think a star as bright as No. 5 could have lifted me up into the light instead of pulling me down into this darkness. It all began with Pierre's betrayal, I suppose.

Or perhaps my descent began earlier, with André.

Part One

Chapter One

France, the region of Provence
Spring 1940

Cannes, old and dense, still the rococo queen of the Côte d'Azur, is a palette of muted pastel this early May morning. Spring has arrived in Provence and the light is radiant, glazing the town in an apricot glow. Across the boulevard, the sandy beach is white, and flecks of gold sparkle in the green sea. On the Côte d'Azur you'd never know that the iron fist of the Reich already grips Czechoslovakia, Poland, Norway, and Denmark. But the gossip around town is that they're headed this way.

Gabrielle Chanel—Coco to most—does not believe this is true. She sits at a shaded table off the boulevard across from the sea with a cup of tea before her, as she does almost every morning when she's at La Pausa, her villa on the coast. She glances about, breathing in the fresh salt air. It's good to get away from Paris for a while, away from the tension of the war, of guessing what comes next, and away from the hoards invading Paris from towns and farms close to the German border. When they realize the migration is all for nothing, they'll run back home and then Paris will return to normal.

Coco is not worried; merely annoyed. France declared war on Germany nine months ago, and nothing's happened since. Not here on the Riviera at least. This is a phony war, Coco thinks. Even the Duke and Duchess of Windsor remain in residence not far from here, in Cap d'Antibes. If a German invasion were imminent David would be the first to flee despite his friendship with the German führer. The former king of England—Edward VIII, known as David to his inner circle—makes no secret of his admiration for Hitler. And, after David abandoned his throne for the woman he loved, the führer hosted him in Berlin with all the trappings of the throne. But facing a real war is something else. David isn't nearly as tough as Wallis; the duchess's pleasant manners and polished exterior hide a needle-sharp spine, which, when necessary, carries the venomous sting of a scorpion fish. Coco has seen Wallis cut other women dead when they get too close to David.

Still, most men and, initially, many women fall for Wallis's camouflage. Even Hitler's difficult foreign minister von Ribbentrop fell in love with her. At least that was the rumor. He'd sent Wallis a bouquet of red carnations every morning in the months before she and David married, even as Britain roiled with the scandal of David's abdication.

Coco wrinkles her nose, musing—why carnations instead of roses?—while her eyes roam over the wide boulevard to her left, to the beach on the other side and then out across the water. Through the shimmering haze of sun she glimpses the silhouette of a schooner anchored far offshore. She shades her eyes, peering at the boat. For a moment she'd thought it was the *Flying Cloud* out there, one of Westminster's yachts. But, of course, that is impossible.

The last time she was aboard the *Flying Cloud* was on a spring day just like this one, years ago. The yacht belonged to the richest man in England, Hugh Richard Arthur Grosvenor, the Duke of Westminster—Bendor to his friends. She'd been standing on the main deck that morning enjoying the view, the harbor water still as glass, watching the dozens of smaller boats anchored between the *Flying Cloud* and the beach. Bendor walked up behind and kissed the nape of her neck, surprising Coco. And then, leaning on the railing, he'd looked out over the harbor and said he had something important to discuss. She knew immediately what was going on.

So you say—

At last he would ask the question. She would make him wait for her answer, she'd decided, after her own years of waiting. After all, this is a woman's prerogative. He should have to suffer for the delay, at least a little.

Filled with pleasure and a sense that her future was now secure, she'd stood quietly beside him while he'd gathered his thoughts. But after the first words, she'd had to turn away while he cheerfully announced that he'd asked a lovely English lady to be his wife and the lady had agreed. Bendor had rested his hand on her arm, saying he looked forward to introducing them. Ah, yes, the mistress and the future wife.

Humiliation had washed through her in that instant and every muscle in her body had tensed while she'd absorbed the news. Bendor was marrying someone else instead of Coco! Her lover was marrying a rose of England. A woman who, unlike Coco, was born on the right side of an invisible line. The same line which had barred Coco from attending public galas and private parties on Westminster's arm. The same line which kept her from entering the paddock at the racecourses with him, or the duke's boxes at the opera and ballet.

Her hand trembles now as she picks up the teacup again, recalling the moment. Bendor's look had been happy and expectant as he'd waited for her congratulations, while her thoughts spun and hot fury coiled in her chest. She'd braced her arms on the ship railing, taking quick breaths, fighting to calm the rage. She remembers settling her thoughts on the simplest things while minutes passed—the sun warming her shoulders, bathers racing across the very same Cannes beach then splashing through the shallows.

Without a second thought, she'd reached back to the spot where he'd kissed the nape of her neck and lifted the long ropes of pearls from around her throat in one fell swoop—large creamy pearls, priceless pearls, gifts from him. Emitting a sound from the back of his throat, Bendor, suddenly realizing, had reached out in the same instant that she'd leaned over the railing and dropped the necklaces into the sea.

He'd let out such a roar.

Westminster's eyes had bulged and he'd simply panicked, whirling about, shouting, "All hands on deck! All hands must come to dive!" Even as the clamor began—whistles blowing, the sound of shoes running, Bendor howling—she'd dropped the emerald bracelets from her wrists, too, and, as if in a dream, she'd watched them follow the pearls into the deep, dark water below.

She smiles to herself now, sipping her tea. Time does not heal all wounds, but that was all so long ago.

"Mademoiselle!" She starts as a shout from the distance breaks into her thoughts and the *Flying Cloud* disappears.

Coco looks up, squinting through the sunshine at someone hurrying down the pavement toward her. Charles Prudone! What is he doing here? The managing director of the House of Chanel should be attending to business at the Maison in Paris, not charging down the Boulevard in Cannes. Her line of couture may be finished, but there is still a small staff on rue Cambon selling perfume and cosmetics. She leans back, waiting. Really, she's never seen the director move this fast before.

"I hoped I would find you here," he gasps as he reaches her, bracing against the edge of the table.

Lifting a brow, she smiles. "Good morning, Director Prudone." His suit and tie are rumpled, she observes, as if he'd slept in his clothes last night. His face is flushed, his breath comes hard and shallow. "Please sit." She indicates the chair. "What brings you to Cannes?"

"I've brought a letter, mademoiselle." From across the table he hands over an envelope. "It's marked urgent, so I took it upon myself to catch the overnight express. I've just come from the station." She takes the envelope, studying the return address. The sender is Georges Baudin, general manager of the perfume plant in Neuilly, which produces her fragrances.

"The letter was delivered yesterday." Monsieur Prudone whips a handkerchief from his pocket and wipes his forehead. Lifting his hat, he drops into the chair.

In silence Coco slits open the envelope and pulls out the letter. She scans the page, then, pressing her lips together, begins again, reading slowly. Impossible! Her heart skips a beat. She looks up, gazing past the director. This cannot be true.

Suddenly aware of Prudone's fixed attention, she steadies her hand, folds the letter in half, and slips it back into the envelope. She watches a yellow cat sitting on the pavement behind the director. The cat twists, licking its shortened tail, slowly, as if time does not exist.

But time does exist, and if what this letter says is correct, she must take action at once. The cat stretches then leaps to the curb, startling Coco just as a flash of green appears in the corner of her eye and an automobile flies around the corner. She drops the envelope onto the table as the feline darts under the wheels, tires squeal, the horn blasts, and the car streaks by.

Prudone turns, following her eyes. But by now both the automobile and the cat have disappeared. Coco fixes her eyes on the spot, but the street is deserted, and pristine.

The director stares at her. "Are you all right, mademoiselle?"

She nods. He waves to the waiter even as the man appears at her side with a clean white linen napkin folded over his arm. The waiter lifts his brows, bending toward her.

She points. "A cat was just there, in that very spot when the automobile raced around the corner." She turns to him. "Have I imagined this?"

The waiter merely straightens and smiles. "Was it perhaps a large yellow cat with only half a tail, mademoiselle?"

She nods, still stunned. "Why yes, I believe you're right."

The man folds his arms over his chest. "Then you have witnessed one of La Bohemian's finest tricks. Disappearing." Jutting out his bottom lip, he shrugs. "She escapes every calamity. It's a Gypsy's trick, like magic."

With a sigh Coco glances back down at the letter lying before her. She could use a little magic right now.

"Shall I bring another pot of tea? This one must be cold."

"No, thank you." She waves him off. "I am fine."

The waiter turns to Prudone. "Something for you, monsieur? An aperitif? Tea?"

The director shakes his head, glancing at his watch. "Not today. I don't have the time." As the fellow hurries off, he turns back to Coco. "The letter. Have I brought bad news?"

"Yes, Monsieur Prudone, this is indeed bad news. But you were correct to come. This is an urgent matter."

He opens his mouth to speak, but she lifts her hand. "Silence, please. I must think." Her response must be swift and fatal to Pierre. She should have known Pierre Wertheimer would pull a trick like this, now that he's moved from France to America. He'd left to escape the German threats of war, so he'd said—and now comes this letter! From the day they'd created Société Mademoiselle together to sell No. 5, back in 1924, she's had to fight to protect her rights to her perfume, and her name.

What a fool she was. But she was only beginning to gain success with her dresses at the Paris Maison when they met, and she'd just created No. 5, and Pierre, with all his money and his huge perfume companies, wanted to invest. And his company, Lenthal, owned the factory right outside of Paris, which was ready to produce and distribute her perfume right away. The idea of a partnership between them had seemed a dream.

They made a deal—and she'd ended up owning only 10 percent of the shares of Société Mademoiselle, abandoning control to Pierre and his brother Paul. She was a novice in the business of perfume in those early days, focusing her energy on building her name in couture, leaving the details of the agreement to Pierre. And, he—so debonair, successful, and rich—had seemed so wise. He handled all the contracts, all the legal threads in the final documents, and she'd not understood he would not have her best interests at heart.

From under her lashes she studies the director. She will need his assistance, and for that she must confide in him. She trusts no one. Still, he has been with her for years. He understands the value of discretion, especially in the competitive world of fashion—couture and perfume. And he is fully aware that discretion is a constant condition of employment.

Coco clasps her hands, fixing her eyes on him. "I must take you into my confidence, Director Prudone." She waits for a beat. When he nods, she continues. "It seems that my business partner is a thief."

"Pardon?" His eyes grow wide. "Are you speaking of Monsieur Wertheimer?"

"Yes. Yes!" She takes a breath, struggling to tamp down fresh fury.

A deep line forms between the director's eyes. He leans forward as if someone may be listening and lowers his voice. "But I understood that Monsieur Wertheimer and his brother and their families moved to America a few months ago." He tilts his head to one side. "New York City, as I recall?"

"Yes. They immigrated." After Hitler invaded Poland, Pierre had thought the writing was on the wall for Jewish families. He thought the phony war was real. She picks up the envelope, using it to fan her face.

The director stammers, "But what ..."

"According to Monsieur Baudin, Pierre has taken—no, Pierre Wertheimer has *stolen* my formula for No. 5 from the factory."

"Stolen!" Prudone looks away. "I've always thought him a gentleman. Are you certain there is no mistake, mademoiselle?"

"Yes, Monsieur Prudone. I am quite sure. It appears Alain Jobert, Pierre's right-hand man, arrived at Neuilly from New York two days ago bearing a written power of attorney and instructions from Pierre to hand over the formula for Chanel No. 5." Pausing, she fingers her pearls. "Monsieur Baudin seems to believe he had no choice but to comply. Alain Jobert then left with the formula for my most precious perfume in his briefcase."

Prudone's expression at last acknowledges the full meaning of her words. The formula has been stolen. The No. 5 formula has never left the vault at Neuilly, because a perfume formula, like even the best chef's recipes, depends entirely on secrecy. Only three people hold the combination to that vault: Coco, Pierre, and Georges Baudin.

Of course, trusting no one, Coco also has her own copy of the formula in her vault at the Maison.

Prudone shakes his head. "Monsieur Wertheimer a thief! Mademoiselle, how is this possible without your consent?"

"Not so difficult to understand. Alain Jobert is sometimes quite intimidating." Her smile is bitter.

"But everyone knows No. 5 is yours. The formula is yours."

"Yes," she spits out the words. "But as Monsieur Baudin reminds me in this letter, Pierre Wertheimer controls the company."

Prudone wears a puzzled expression as his voice softens to a conciliatory lull. "The theft will be futile, mademoiselle. The world knows you created No. 5. Why the perfume even bears your name. And No. 5 has always been produced at Neuilly. What use would Monsieur Wertheimer have for the formula in America?"

Indeed, that is the question.

Suddenly the picture becomes clear. Pierre is planning never to return to France. He would only dare to lift the No. 5 formula from Neuilly for one reason: he plans to produce the perfume in America. This is his opportunity to get rid of her complaints once and for all. He's moving their business to New York, leaving Coco behind. He will never return to France. He will cut her out while she's trapped in Europe by the threat of war. Regardless of the outcome with Germany, he will abandon her.

No. 5 has always been produced at Neuilly. Why else was Pierre so sly, so secretive, sending Alain instead of talking over the change with her? Absorbing the full import of her partner's betrayal, Coco slams her hand down on the table and Prudone flinches. No one knows how dependent she's become on the perfume's revenues. Yes, she has savings in the form of gold and investments locked up in her vault in Geneva. But since closing her line of couture last year after the workers' strike, No. 5 has become her primary source of income.

She lifts her chin. "No. 5 is mine, Monsieur Prudone. The formula is mine. I am the creative partner in the company. No. 5 was only my first fragrance, but it is the finest. I composed it after years of planning, and months of work in dank chemistry labs in Grasse."

Pierre has done it this time. Why, even if she desired to revive her couture line, because of Hitler's rampage in other parts of Europe, it is almost impossible to obtain supplies and fabric at this point. Since France declared war on Germany, even fabric mills in France have been requisitioned for the phony war. She clicks her tongue against her teeth thinking of the lost silks and wools and linens.

It wasn't the war that shut you down. It was your temper, Coco. Well, that was not my fault.

They had *forced* her to close the House of Chanel, her little hands—her seamstresses—joining the communist mobs in the workers' strike last year, demanding more than they'd already wrung from their mademoiselle. Ah, that was a bad time, thugs tearing down precious monuments, attacking businesses and employers like her—she who took those girls off the streets and trained each one, paying good wages. How dare they turn on her, her little hands, barring her from the doors of her own Maison!

Is it any wonder she fired the lot?

They said she'd acted for spite.

Although, truth is it was also a good business decision, at the time. Revenues from No. 5 were already eclipsing sales of her dresses.

And now? This theft is just one more in a line of Pierre's attempts to thwart her at every turn in the business. For years they've battled over her perfumes—every detail of design, distribution, marketing, sales. She may not own the most shares of Société Mademoiselle, but the company's only assets are Coco Chanel's perfumes and a few cosmetics. Her creative talent is more important than the number of shares she owns. This theft, this attempt to cut her out of the business—this is the final straw. She will not allow Pierre to win.

And with this, a thought strikes. A plan so logical she almost smiles.

Société Mademoiselle is a French company, governed by French law—not laws of the United States. And this French company owns the rights to produce No. 5, not Pierre. She presses her lips together. Any fair court in France would rule that with Pierre in America indefinitely and Coco in France, it is mademoiselle's business to protect the companies' most valuable assets.

She will take the case to court at once. She will argue moral and legal necessity for control of the company. No. 5 is a French treasure. And, as the director acknowledged, both the company and perfume already bear her name. Yes, this plan will work for one reason if no other—because with Hitler on the march, Pierre will not dare return to France to fight in court.

Across the table, Director Prudone waits in silence, his brows knitted as his eyes roam the vista behind her.

"Monsieur Prudone?" Her voice is silk as she leans toward the director.

"I am at your service, mademoiselle."

"We must get right to work." Step one—halt production of her perfume in America. First, she will purchase all remaining supplies of jasmine in Provence, cutting off Pierre. Jasmine grown in Provence is an essential ingredient in No. 5. Foreign-grown jasmine diminishes the scent. Synthetics will destroy it. Step two—she will utilize the jasmine purchased to produce the fragrance at Neuilly. She will sell the perfume throughout Europe until politics on the continent are settled. And then, she will compete with Pierre worldwide. After all, No. 5 *is* Chanel.

And step three—if necessary, she will fight this claim in court.

She watches him from under her lids. For now, she will tell the director only so much as he needs to know. "As my emissary, you will go to Grasse this afternoon. You will purchase on my behalf all quantities of jasmine still available on the market in this region."

He frowns. "Grasse?"

"Yes, Grasse—the perfume capital of the world." Coco flicks her hand in a northerly direction. "It's not far, thirty minutes or so from Cannes. As you know, for No. 5 we use only the best jasmine, which grows only in this region. Most flower growers here sell their crops to the chemists in Grasse. Now we must hurry. The jasmine harvest begins soon and we are late to market. Fortunately, Grasse is a small town. You must visit every perfume-company representative."

"But, mademoiselle ..."

"I must have all jasmine stock still available for sale. What's left of our supply from last year is stored at the factory in Neuilly. If Pierre has only just now got around to the idea of stealing the formula and producing No. 5 in New York, it's likely he's not yet thought to obtain a new jasmine supply. We will beat him to it. With harvest just months away, already he is late."

She adds, "Is this clear?"

Prudone lifts his hat with a little shrug. "I had thought to return to Paris this afternoon, mademoiselle. In order to return to work at the Maison tomorrow morning."

"No, no, no. You are needed here instead." She waves toward the confection of white hotels on the boulevard behind him. "Book a room at the Majestic on my account and hire a car and a driver. This business is more important."

"But Monsieur Wertheimer ..."

"No. 5 is mine, Monsieur Prudone. The formula is mine." She runs her thumbs under the collar of her blouse, crisping and straightening it. "The perfume was my original inspiration, signifying Chanel to every woman in the world and generations to come. I will not allow Pierre to take that from me."

Prudone dips his chin to his chest. She takes this as agreement.

"*I* chose each ingredient for No. 5. There are over seventy in that formula, Monsieur Director, blended by the chemist to my exact specifications." She taps the tip of her nose. "I have a talent for sensitive smell, you know."

Again, he nods.

"I have the Nose, monsieur."

"You are an artist."

She's never thought of herself as an artist. But with this perfume, perhaps. "No. 5 is an icon. It is France."

And without it, expenses will soon exceed revenues and my funds will dwindle.

Prudone blows out his cheeks, then exhales. "I understand. Of course, No. 5 is an icon. Yes, I shall go to Grasse. But what will you do with all the jasmine after we purchase it, mademoiselle?"

She gives him a little smile. "I have decided to take charge of Neuilly and the business. I will produce No. 5 without Pierre. Right now my immediate concern is assuring an adequate supply, in case the phony war with the Germans becomes real."

"This may be somewhat difficult. Summer crops are likely sold."

Coco gives him a hard look. "Purchase what you can on hand. And if crops are committed, offer to buy out their existing contract prices. You have my authority to offer double the amount they're receiving." Prudone frowns, but she presses on. "Remind them to consider the future. Remind them that you represent the House of Chanel. And they've nothing to lose because my offer guarantees immediate profit in an uncertain time."

"And Monsieur Wertheimer?" Prudone shakes his head. "Ah, this will cause talk, mademoiselle."

"If anyone mentions Pierre, you may inform them that Pierre Wertheimer is in America and I am here, and there is an ocean and a war between us. I am the one they will deal with now."

After a brief hesitation, he nods. "Perhaps *this* is the real war, mademoiselle."

She cocks her head. "Perhaps all of life is war, Monsieur Director."

She sits back, smoothing the fingers of her gloves one at a time. "Have the Grasse sellers prepare their contracts for my review tomorrow. I must have the jasmine right away."

But still the director hesitates. "Mademoiselle, we are discussing the purchase of acres and acres of flowers. I am not certain shipping such quantity at this time is possible—cargo trains have been conscripted by government for the war effort."

She props her elbows on the table. "I see I've neglected your education, Monsieur Prudone. Of course, we don't ship the actual flowers. The fragrance is extracted from blossoms by the chemists in Grasse." She lets out a little laugh. "I must give you lessons on perfumes. The final product, the oil taken from the flowers—the absolute—is stored after extraction in small glass kilo flacons. One kilo of jasmine absolute contains the oil from many acres of blossoms." She lifts a shoulder. "Transport to Neuilly is not a problem."

Prudone blushes. "Of course. I should have known."

"Without couture sales, Monsieur Director, you must surely understand the importance to the Maison of taking this step." Her voice turns hard. "Be certain that Grasse also understands. Grasse must realize that Mademoiselle Chanel demands loyalty in exchange for our business."

"Yes, mademoiselle."

Think twice, Coco. Pierre believed in you from the beginning when you were still a risk, when the House of Chanel was new and untested. Do you remember when he presented to you a gift of the first bottle of No. 5 produced after Société Mademoiselle was formed?

That first bottle is still in her safe on rue Cambon.

It was years ago and Pierre has changed. If she does not act quickly, he will destroy her. She will not allow that to happen. She will never go back to the old life, to what she was.

The old fear tugs at Coco. Gabrielle, the child she once was—abandoned, kneeling, scrubbing the stone floor in the corridor of the abbey atop the mountain at Aubazine, her hands raw. She can almost smell the yellow soap. Can almost feel the frigid cold on the north side of the building where the charity girls lived. The stones in the long corridor formed patterns of flowers with five petals. Five is her lucky number. The sisters told her that when she'd washed every stone, she may eat. The Lord

18

says that only clean, good girls may eat. She was Gabrielle then, an orphan. Not yet Coco.

Five, five, five—even then she knew the number would bring her luck.

She shivers, feeling again the cold in that corridor. She's certain she is making the right decision. Money is security. No. 5 is her security. Pierre has left her no alternative but to fight for what is hers. Never again will she scrub floors for food and a bed.

"Mademoiselle?"

Prudone's voice rouses her. Again, she is Coco, and the walls she's built over the years since Aubazine rise around her.

"Enough fine points," she says, impatient now. "Go on to Grasse, please, Monsieur Prudone. You will stay here in Cannes until the contracts are signed. We'll stay as long as this takes."

"Yes, of course." Picking up his hat, Charles Prudone rises.

"Come to my villa at ten o'clock sharp in the morning. That should give us time to sign and return the contracts."

As he walks off, something soft brushes against her ankle. Pushing back the chair, she peers down at the yellow cat, who looks up through agate eyes—green and amber swirls of light. Coco leans down, scooping up La Bohemian into her arms. Cradling the cat, Coco whispers, "Good, my sweet. You are safe," and then she allows the feline to settle into her lap. Scratching the silken fur between the ears, she notices the waiter hurrying back to her.

"I am sorry, mademoiselle," the waiter says, reaching for the cat.

Coco shakes her head. "No. Leave her. We understand each other."

"No one understands a cat." The waiter chuckles. "And this one is clever. She hides her thoughts like a good thief."

"Perhaps I will take her home with me."

He jerks his chin in the direction of the Boulevard hotels. "She lives in the alleyways over there, behind the kitchens. She is feral, mademoiselle; she would not stay. La Bohemian craves the freedom of the streets."

Coco strokes the contented cat. La Bohemian is soft and warm. But the waiter is right. "I will take your advice, monsieur. The cat will remain free." Her tone is reluctant. "But, bring us a bowl of cream before I leave."

Chapter Two

La Pausa, near Cannes
Spring 1940

Coco sits in the courtyard that evening, warmed by the soft breeze, the night air fragrant with scents of lavender, mimosa, and hyacinth. The sea breeze cleanses thoughts of the letter Prudone brought from Paris. Earlier, when the pain of Pierre's theft was still raw, she'd sent her regrets to Wallis and David in Cap d'Antibes. Too late to abandon a dinner party given by the Duke and Duchess of Windsor, she knows. One is not expected to inconvenience the former king of England. But c'est la vie. Until she has the contracts from Grasse in her hands, she will not rest.

The villa nestles in a grove of olive trees on a rocky promontory overlooking the Mediterranean. La Pausa is her refuge. It is partially a gift from Westminster before his marriage. Only partially because, although he bought the property, Coco designed the house and supervised construction down to the smallest detail, even to the beaten wood and false patina of age on each shutter, giving the place an aristocratic look, like Westminster's worn but beautifully tailored tweed jackets. Like the home Papa would have built, if he'd ever had any luck—if he'd returned.

In the moonlight she fingers the long strands of pearls, replacements for Westminster's gifts now lying under the sea. Maman always wore a strand of pearls fit close around her neck, until she died of that hacking cough.

After Maman passed, Papa let Coco's young brothers out for work on a farm. She can still see their little legs beating as they ran behind the old farmer, following him through the fields while Papa's cart moved farther and farther away. She'd watched until they were mere specks in the distance.

And then Papa left too.

He abandoned Antoinette, Julia-Berthe, and Gabrielle, left all three sisters at the abbey in Aubazine. He'd promised that he would come back for his children, as soon as he'd earned money to care for them. The memory of that night shrouds Coco in gloom even now. In the back of the cart on the long trip to the orphanage, he'd told his girls where they were headed. She'd burrowed down in the hay with her sisters at the news, huddling close. Papa gave them apples to eat along the way. Still, Antoinette and Julia-Berthe had wept for hours. But Coco had held her misery inside.

At twilight, in the town of Limoges, Papa had stopped the cart before a shop. A sign hanging on the door promised "Fair prices for your china, silver, jewelry." For a long time Papa sat very still, holding Maman's pearl necklace in the palm of his hand as if weighing it. And then his face contorted, and she'd thought he might cry. Instead, he jumped down from the driving seat, straightened his back, and, curling his fingers around the necklace, he'd walked into the shop.

Coco remembers the sudden rush of hope she'd felt while staring at the door. Papa had changed his mind! He would sell the necklace for money to build a home for them, someplace warm, with room for a garden. She remembers the happy glow moving through her as she lay in the straw, imagining the new future. They would have a cow and grow vegetables. They would go to school, and in the afternoons the boys would work and the girls cook and clean. And Papa would peddle his wares in village markets, and he would come home every night.

But minutes later he burst through the door, his shoulders drawn around his neck, his brows low over thunderous eyes. She'd hunkered down in the hay. Papa had a temper. As he untied the mule, he'd shouted, "Shylock!" She felt the cart rocking with his weight as he scrambled to the driving seat.

"Ten francs!" he'd muttered, snapping the reins. "Ten lousy francs for her pearls."

Not enough to pay for a house.

Julia-Berthe lifted her head. "Papa, what's a shylock?"

"A shylock's a thief, a Jew."

"Go back, Papa!" Gabrielle sat up, calling out as desperation gripped her. "Tell the man they're worth more."

"Hush, girls." Papa's voice was tight, strangled. "It's no good." He snapped the reins. "Listen to Papa. When you're poor, no one cares. The poor suffer; this is something you must understand. Make up your minds to fight for everything you want in life. That is the only way to survive." He spat back toward the shop and the cart rattled down the street.

The lights in the village were behind and the road grew narrow. Except for the mule's heavy step and the wooden wheels bumping along the rutted dirt road, the world around them was dark and silent as they headed up the mountain to the abbey. Huddled with Antoinette and Julia-Berthe, she'd suddenly understood that Maman was gone forever, and that Papa would leave them at Aubazine just as he'd left the boys behind. Coco understood that this moment was a turning point.

She gazes across the villa courtyard, feeling the same hollowness inside she'd felt on that night. It's strange, looking back—she does not allow herself to do this often. But she can almost see Papa shuffling down the hallway and through that door. She'd watched him, still hoping he would change his mind. He'd never looked back.

She and Antoinette and Julia-Berthe soon learned they were considered charity girls in the abbey. Charity girls were different from the other students, forced to earn their stay. She'd struggled to help both sisters, but in the end they weren't strong enough—nor hard enough. Both died years later by their own hands. And her brothers—what can you do? They're still alive and penniless, and on occasion they write to her and sometimes she sends them money. For a while she'd had hopes, but finally she'd realized that the family no longer exists.

The truth is, since the night Papa left, she's known she was on her own.

Coco lights a cigarette and rests her head against the chair, watching smoke curl into the darkness. She's done all right on her own. Back then she was still Gabrielle, dependent upon others. Now she is fully formed—she is Coco. She has built a new life and Gabrielle remains in the past. The truth of that poverty, that misery, remains her secret.

Except for one person. She'd given herself to him, almost from the moment they met, body and soul. The sound of the sea below the cliffs at La Pausa relaxes her, pulls at her, allowing dangerous memories to flow. The rhythm of the waves is soothing, almost hypnotic—the warm water tumbling in and washing back out. Boy Capel, the only man she will ever love. Oh, how she'd trusted him.

No. She throws the cigarette to the ground, rubbing it out

under the toe of her shoe. She has enough problems to deal with tonight without thinking of Boy Capel. Rising, she crosses the garden to the covered walkway surrounding the courtyard, a cloister reminding her of the abbey nuns gliding up and down the walkway, praying their rosaries.

She enters the bedroom through tall glass doors open to the breeze. Alyce has just turned down the bed. Seeing Coco, she smiles and quickly leaves. Coco undresses and slips into a white silk gown, which Alyce has laid out on the bed; one of Coco's favorites with thin ribbon straps and otherwise unadorned.

Crossing to the dressing table, she sits before the mirror. Alone now, she poses—turning slightly to the right. Photographers say her profile is classic—her nose small and perfectly shaped, her jaw a bit too square, but strong. Her neck long and slender. The olive complexion inherited from Papa—which she claims is really sun color—is a bit darker than society prefers, but it compliments her wide black eyes under flaring brows, and the short dark curls framing her face. Boy once said she was not pretty in an ordinary sense, but that she was beautiful. She's still trying to puzzle that one out. She smiles and picks up the brush, then, rising, she moves close to the mirror.

When did those fine lines appear at the corners of her eyes?

Coco turns off each lamp in the room except one on the bedside table. As she slides between the cool silk of her slip and the lavender scented sheets, she reaches for the book she'd left last night on the table. Colette's newest. She sighs, propping it against her knees. Colette is a fine writer, but a difficult friend.

Her mind wanders from the story, her thoughts returning to Pierre's betrayal. In the past when she and Pierre have battled over differences regarding Société Mademoiselle and her perfumes, each time they had managed to salvage their friendship in the end. In fact, she's often wondered if perhaps Pierre might be a little bit in love with her. Several times, even at times she'd won her case in court, he'd send a bouquet of her favorite white camellias.

Images of the day they met rise in her mind, mellowed as a lovely painting, an impression. A sunny day at the racetrack. Red, white, and blue flags fluttering in the breeze, the deep jewel-toned colors everywhere, the rich scent of salt air from the sea on the Normandy coast.

Pierre was distinguished, tall and slender, with dark hair and a high forehead. Always smiling. She'd admired his style—the fashionable waistcoat, the neat tie and light wool overcoat, his derby pushed back at a slight tilt. But his eyes took prominence: deep set, but with a friendly sparkle, crinkling at the corners. And fierce dark shadows underneath.

She sighs at the memory. She's always found Pierre's eyes impossible to read. Was he a true friend back then, or her rival?

She slams shut Colette's book, tossing it aside, and turns off the lamp.

When Charles Prudone returns from Grasse, she will sign each contract, sealing Pierre's fate. And no French judge will deny her claim to sole ownership of Société Mademoiselle after her lawyers set the bill of particulars before the court.

But, as always when problems loom, Gabrielle rises, hissing in her mind. *Pierre will fight you, and what will we do if with all his money he wins the case? We will be poor again.*

Calculations spin through her head, one after the other. There's the cost of her suite at the Hôtel Ritz, but the Ritz is her home. And the cost of keeping La Pausa, and of maintaining what's left of business at the Maison.

Coco clucks her tongue. *I will not allow Pierre to win.*

Rolling onto her back, she stares at the ceiling. If only Boy Capel were here right now. Boy would comfort her; he would hold her in her arms. He would whisper that he loves his little

Coco and she would not have to fight so hard all the time. He would whisper that Coco is his only, forever love.

Boy's long dark lashes brush her cheek. His breath tickles her neck. As her eyes begin to close, the breeze rustles through the room and the pale moon shines down on the lovers. Wrapped around each other they sink into the spell—Coco and Boy. Once again, Boy Capel is her lover, father, brother, friend, confidant. Her protector.

Chapter Three

Compiègne, Château de Royallieu
1904

The day I first met Boy at Royallieu, Étienne was in a hurry to get to the stables and barely stopped in the château hallway to make the brief introduction. He walked on, but Arthur Capel, known to everyone as Boy, just stood there, mute, studying me. Without a word he tipped up my chin, his green eyes searching mine while I stared back at him, this man cut from stone by the creator and browned from the sun, like me. It seemed he could see into my mind, into my soul. I was vaguely aware of Étienne's voice, greeting someone in the courtyard. Above, a maid's footsteps echoed as she moved along the hardwood floors. But these sounds seemed to be outside of us, Boy Capel and me. I was intoxicated.

At last he spoke, cutting through the intensity of the moment. "So this is little Coco." He stepped back, slipping his hands in his pockets, his manner turning nonchalant. "You are the sprite, and as lovely as Étienne has bragged." When he smiled, his eyes danced. "I've heard you were the most popular chanteuse in Moulins, and that you led him on quite a chase."

After I'd left the abbey at the age of seventeen, Étienne had wooed me from a cabaret stage in the village of Moulins, not far from Aubazine, sweeping me off to his estate at Royallieu, about forty-five kilometers northeast of Paris. Étienne was tall, handsome, and married—although his wife lived elsewhere. He was rich, and I was young and poor, just a girl. In Moulins, I left behind a sewing job in a tailor's shop and singing at night for tips at the cabaret La Rotonde.

Oh, the excitement of those evenings—the sparkling lights and music and dancing. Soldiers garrisoned at Moulins all came to La Rotonde, and other young men from town, cheering when I strutted around the stage singing. I loved it, the men and boys, the smell of leather and smoke and wine, and the musty wood of the old oak stage. Coco, they called me, from a song I sang. And the name stuck. I told myself I was no longer poor Gabrielle.

At Royallieu, for the first time since Maman died, I felt secure in one place. Thanks to Étienne, now I had my own room, my own space, and a lovely big bed with silken sheets and piles of pillows, and the pleasure of sleeping late. In that first spring when I arrived at Royallieu, I lazed in the mornings, gazing through open windows at the broad fields of Étienne's estate, bright with new green grass and rolls of golden hay, and the stables nearby, built of the same ancient gray stone as the château. I breathed in the clean scents of cut grass, of potpourri and lemon wood polish and fragrant yeasty bread baking in the kitchen below.

My stomach had rumbled the entire time I was at the abbey. Now, I could eat an entire loaf of that bread if I wanted! All this because Étienne Balsan had chosen me. I was his *petite amie* and this was my new home. Étienne said I could live at Royallieu as long as I wanted—forever.

Étienne's stables were renowned throughout Europe. He was *almost* French aristocracy, learned, if not by blood—old money through and through. He taught me how to sit a horse, navigate a table set for thirty, how to pretend to love someone I secretly thought of only as a friend. He kept many houses and mistresses, and somewhere there was his wife, but she was no bother. I knew that I was special. When his other women visited the château, they wore long dresses with tight corsets squeezing their waists. They made up their faces, wore their hair in complicated twirls under their hats, and rode sidesaddle. I wore Étienne's old cotton shirts, his jodhpurs, and a cast-off jacket of his that I tailored to fit. My dark hair was long back then, and when we rode, I let it fly unbound in the wind. We raced. I rode like a banshee, he teased. I was Coco, his lover, but also his friend. Already I was wise enough to know that friendship often outlasts love.

It was Boy Capel who captured my heart at Royallieu. He was always elegant, no matter the time of day or the situation. He wore a trim mustache and his hair brushed back over his ears in a new and modern way. Boy was an Englishman with grace and wit and money earned from Newcastle coal and ships and rail, a fortune made by his own hands, not like Étienne's, which came from his father. Boy was charming, smart, rich, single, and an athlete. He was a five-goal polo player with stables of ponies and, like Étienne, with strings of women. He was also shrewd, and ambitious—something I lost sight of. I was drawn to Boy from the moment we met. Still, I fought the emotion at first, thinking, *well, here's another rich man fond of pretty coquettes.*

After that day we met, Boy came to Royallieu almost every weekend. We began as friends, but something else under the surface connected us. I felt it and I sensed Boy felt this too. I knew there was a depth to this man that he'd not yet revealed.

The château was filled with Étienne's friends every weekend.

From sunup until late at night we filled our time—long breakfasts, then riding, card games, gambling, farces and charades, picnics, dinner and dancing and cocktails on the terrace, and plenty of laughter. Men brought their mistresses on these weekends, never wives. Boy always chose me as his partner in the games and we almost always won.

My favorite times came on warm evenings when the other guests wandered off and Boy and I sat alone together. He was a natural teacher and I was enthralled as he talked about such things as the science of the stars and moon and planets, how everything in the universe is perfectly balanced. I loved hearing him speak, his voice so controlled, low and modulated while he talked of other dimensions in time and space. He taught me the names of the constellations and told their ancient myths, stories of gods and lovers and tragedy. Often we talked of music, or art, or history, and always, always he'd bring the conversation around to philosophy and another world he called the spiritual world.

I felt stupid sometimes. I was a Catholic and familiar with musings on the afterlife, but Boy spoke of another kind of spirituality. At first, I pretended to understand. Then, one night I asked him to explain.

He stood, walked to a low stone wall edging the terrace, and snapped a jasmine flower from its vine. "Look," he said, holding it up as he turned to me.

It was a common flower. He handed it over and I took the blossom and sniffed the fragrance. As he returned to his chair, he watched me, smiling. "You love the scent, the shape, the color?"

I nodded.

"Does the flower bring memories?"

I closed my eyes, sniffing the fragrance again, and on the spot I was carried into the past—into a haze of yellow sunshine. I could almost feel the warmth on my shoulders. I sat in the back of Papa's peddler cart with my brothers and sisters, bumping down a narrow dirt road running through a sweet-scented jasmine field. We were off to a summer festival market somewhere in Provence. And Maman was with us, alive and sitting close to Papa on the driving seat in front.

"You see?" Boy's voice broke in.

I opened my eyes and put the flower in my lap as I nodded.

"Nothing ends. Even though the material plants—the original flowers you saw and smelled that day—are gone, the essence of the flowers remains. And even after all these years, the fragrance releases memories imprinted in your mind associated with the scent, bringing back those same feelings of joy, of happiness."

"Yes. Good memories." I mulled this over. "I understand now. Something really does remain of those old dead flowers. You're saying the past becomes the present."

He smiled, pleased. "The material plants decomposed long ago. But the feelings they generate through scent remain. So," he lifted his brows, "where do you think those feelings originate?"

I stared out over the moonlit field and said casually, "From the memories, of course." Slouching down in the chair, I stretched out my legs and clasped my hands behind my head.

He laughed. "That's circular thinking, Coco." I turned my eyes to him, watching as he pulled his pipe from a pocket, along with his gold lighter and the leather bag of tobacco. I loved the smell of Boy's tobacco.

"Well, I guess I've never thought of this before," I said with a shrug. I was curious and waited in silence while he filled the pipe, tapped it on the table, and lit it.

Then, puffing on the pipe, he spoke in a tone that told me this was important to him. "Feelings, like the happiness you experienced from those memories, are not material things like the flower or the table over there. Feelings have no structure, they're ephemeral. But like the memories, they are a real part of each of us."

I sat very still, listening, longing to understand.

"Emotions, feelings, are stirrings from the soul, your inner self. They're created *after* your brain takes in information about the flower—its color, shape, scent." Pipe smoke curled toward the sky as he spoke. "They come from the spiritual world which existed long before we were born and continues after we die. So the human soul, the inner you, Coco, isn't limited by human restrictions of time or space or structure. Those ephemeral parts of you, like the happiness brought up just now when you smelled the jasmine ... you can access those moments any time. They remain always a part of you."

He swooped his hand toward the silver stars. "So, in that way, we are all eternal." Removing the pipe from his mouth, he held it in his hand. "In fact, our souls may even have lived through previous lives on earth."

"Are you a Buddhist then?"

He smiled. "What I'm trying to explain is how things in the universe are connected." He paused, regarding me, and I nodded.

"As for us—human beings hold a higher connection to the spiritual world than other living things, because our feelings cause us to make choices, to act through will. And those actions lead to consequences, which in turn lead to more actions ..."—he rolls his hand—"... and so on and on, through eternity."

"But once I'm dead, my actions cease," I said, thinking I'd got him now.

He shook his head. "We each leave a mark when we act, consequences that roll on. The links to others never end. Everything in the universe is connected through eternity this way."

I watched smoke rising from his pipe, wondering if the smoke would drift through the universe and time forever.

"Do you see my point? Because our actions have effects which never end, we must be thoughtful when we act. Our choices must never be random."

So far, my life has certainly been random, I thought.

He gave me a sideways look. "If you open your mind, Coco, you'll begin to understand. I could give you books to read, if you'd like."

"Yes," I said. "I would like that." How I wanted to understand this idea that Boy believed and loved. Boy Capel was so different from Étienne, from any man I'd ever known.

He set the pipe on the table beside him and knelt before me. He cupped my face in his hands, studying me, as if memorizing. His lips touched mine then, a long, deep kiss sending little explosions of light through me like fizz in good champagne. From that moment on, I knew that I was lost. I was hopelessly in love with Boy.

It was a full month before Boy became my lover. We all have turning points in our lives, a moment that changes everything—your future, even how you feel about the past. Papa's leaving me at the abbey was one such moment. Falling in love with Boy was another. On that day, we rode together across Étienne's fields toward the forest of Compiègne about two kilometers away. Flost, my bay, was restless, wanting to run, but at the edge of the woods Boy slowed his horse to a walk, motioning toward the path entering the cathedral of delicate silver beech trees. I'd ridden there many times. But, as I followed Boy down the shaded path winding through the trees, I felt something wonderful was happening between us.

The air was cool and fresh, heavy with the pungent scent of Scots pine and damp leaves. Pale green light shimmered through the canopy overhead as we rode along. Our silence was broken only by birdsong, with an occasional mournful whistle from a black woodpecker, and the scurrying of foxes and rabbits and other small animals in the bushes. Ruffles of tiny blue, yellow, and scarlet wildflowers grew in the tall green grasses fringing the edge of the path.

"There's a spot I want to show you," Boy said as we reached a small clearing in a patch of sunshine. "Follow me." Nudging his mount to the right, we left the pathway and rode across the clearing and into the trees on the other side. I heard water tumbling in a stream. The horses picked their way toward the sound.

We stopped when we saw it, the clear water shining in the sun as it fell from a rocky ledge into a limestone pool. "Beautiful, isn't it?" Boy twisted in his saddle, looking at me. I rode up beside him. I'd been riding in this forest for over a year and had never come across this place.

We dismounted and tethered the horses to a bush. For a while we sat on a flat rock at the edge of the stream talking and watching the play of water and light, the silver and gold spangles dancing over the bubbles. My heart was pounding in my chest, because, I knew then what would happen. And I wanted him.

Boy placed his hands on my shoulders and turned me to him. Sounds of the forest faded as our eyes met. He cupped my face in his hands, kissing me, his lips gently caressing mine at first, then moving harder as his tongue explored, parting my lips, and I responded, feeling weak under his touch. He lifted me then and I folded my arms around his neck as he carried me to a mossy patch of green beneath a tree, laying me down between roots bulging through the earth. I shivered as he settled beside me, propped on his elbow, as his other hand brushed lightly over my breasts and over my belly, and then I opened my arms to him.

Needing him.

He smiled, and his eyes held mine while his hands worked open the buttons on my jodhpurs—this seemed to take forever— and then, I caught my breath as he slid them off, and I reached up, so hungry, pulling him down on top of me, and we melted into each other in that silent forest, where nothing existed right then but Boy and me.

I was in love with Boy. And after that day, I trusted him completely. Étienne's best friend swore he loved me too, then, and again and again. We kept our affair a secret. Even so, Étienne would not mind the loss of one small mistress, I told myself. Besides, the beautiful famed coquette Émilienne d'Alençon was also in residence at Royallieu. Étienne hadn't come to my room in over a week. But we did not tell him. Not then.

I arrived at Royallieu as a poor girl, and I kept the past to myself, except for Boy. When asked, I would always say I was raised by two strict old aunts in their home near Moulins. I told that story to Boy at first, as with everyone else. When I confessed the truth, after the day we first made love, Boy professed he was stunned that I'd manufactured my past from beginning to end.

Lies, he called my stories.

I called them innocent little deceptions. Boy never did really understand. A lie requires an intention to deceive. My only purpose in hiding my past was survival. I wanted respect, not pity, from my friends.

I told him that. I told him that I only ever lie when a thing is important.

Chapter Four

La Pausa, near Cannes
Spring 1940

After a sleepless night, Coco is impatient for Charles Prudone's return from Grasse. Sitting in her office, she works on the letter she's begun to René de Chambrun, her lawyer in Paris, describing Pierre's theft of the perfume formula. *The time has come for justice,* she writes—she requires his assistance. Obtaining the jasmine is not enough. She must also take control of Société Mademoiselle. Even Pierre Wertheimer, despite his wealth and power in the business world, is not immune from the law.

Yes, she has a good case. She will begin to fight immediately by signing the contracts with Grasse as soon as Prudone arrives. Looking up, she leans her elbows on the desk and rests her chin on her hands. This side of the villa faces the sea. The doors and windows are open to the breeze, which is cool and exhilarating, just what she needs to calm her impatience.

She hears Alyce's voice at the far end of the hallway, followed by Prudone's. At last. Coco straightens in her chair, replacing the fountain pen in its onyx stand, and slips the letter into a drawer. She will travel to Grasse this afternoon with Prudone to finalize the contracts and organize shipping of the absolute oil to Neuilly. Smiling to herself, Coco leans into the chair.

Director Prudone appears in the doorway, hat in hand.

"Good morning, Monsieur Prudone." Coco extends her hand. "Give me the contracts. I'll read through them quickly and we will return together to Grasse for signing." But in the same instant her eyes flick to the hat in his otherwise empty hands. Where is the briefcase? Where are the documents? Confused, she draws back.

Director Prudone's brows pull together. "I regret to admit that I arrive with bad news, mademoiselle."

Coco finds she cannot speak.

"It is as I feared," he says. "With the summer harvest only two months away, we are too late. Every jasmine crop in the area is allocated, they say. Contracts for the season were signed months ago. Supplies are limited to begin with, they say, because of the war mobilization. They are even having difficulty signing up pickers this year."

Turning her eyes to the open doors, Coco gazes over the pale blue water stretching toward the horizon. She can see reflections of the high white clouds today. This beautiful day is spoiled.

"I am sorry, mademoiselle."

She stiffens at the tone of pity in his voice and turns, giving Prudone a cold look. She will not allow it. No one pities Chanel. "Did you visit every perfumery? Did you tell them what I am willing to pay—those old men of Grasse?" He opens his mouth, but she holds up one hand. "I do not believe they would turn down this amount of money. You must not have been clear. Did you give them our highest offer?"

"Yes, mademoiselle. No one budged. Your offer was generous,

of course. But the money seemed to make no difference. They insist all supplies are under contract. They are committed, they say. They have brands to protect, they say." His eyes stray to the doors, as if contemplating escape as he continues. "For some, I even offered more than double the ordinary contract price. I pressed hard. Still they refused."

Coco braces her hands on the edge of the desk, regarding him. There must be some mistake. She should never have sent an underling to do this work. She will return to Grasse immediately. The old men will certainly not refuse a personal request from the woman who created the House of Chanel; from the woman who envisioned No. 5.

"You will return immediately to Paris, Monsieur Prudone," she says, pressing the call bell for Alyce. She is a legend in the world of fashion and perfume. She will handle this problem on her own, as—it seems—she must handle all serious problems in this business. Although the idea of going to Grasse, hat in hand, is almost more than she can bear.

"You are needed at the Maison, on rue Cambon, Monsieur Prudone. I will go to Grasse myself. On the way we will drop you off at your hotel in Cannes."

"As you wish, mademoiselle."

Behind him, Alyce appears in the doorway. Coco orders the car brought around right away.

In the back seat of the black British Daimler saloon with its glossy burgundy hood, Coco instructs Jacques, her local driver, to stop first at the Hôtel Majestic before continuing to Grasse. She presses her lips together, dreading the trip. But it is unavoidable, not only for revenge upon Pierre, but also because once she takes control of the company, she must ensure an ongoing supply of jasmine oil for the Neuilly plant.

Traffic slows as they near Cannes, merging onto boulevard de la Croisette into a parade of barely moving automobiles. Bored, irritated, Coco gazes at the long blocks of hotels, shops, and cafés to her right, and the sea to her left. A shop they pass catches her eye, boasting a sign over the door that this is the House of Besse. Written underneath are the words "Provence Parfums." She peers at the sign over her shoulder. She has never heard of this House.

Beside her, Prudone gazes at the crowds. "What's going on?"

Jacques turns his head as the car inches forward. "The Paris train has just arrived. I hear every hotel along the coast is booked. They say the Germans are really coming this time. What do you think, monsieur?"

"We beat them in 1918 and we'll do it again if they're foolish enough to try. But I suppose I'll have room enough traveling back to Paris today."

"What nonsense," Coco says. "The Germans will not invade; they are our cousins." She forces a smile. Her tone is light, unlike her present mood. "Besides, we have the Maginot Line. Our men are prepared."

The street before the Hôtel Majestic is blocked by lines of automobiles parked end to end and side to side. Fumes choke the air. Jacques removes his cap and rubs his forehead. "We'll have a wait to get you curbside, monsieur." Coco watches chauffeurs and bellboys swinging trunks and bags from the cars, hefting them off toward the hotel entrance. Men wearing bowlers, suits, and ties cluster on the pavement, talking together while their wives, children, and nannies mill around them.

This could take forever.

Prudone turns to her. "I think it best I leave you here, mademoiselle."

"Yes, I suppose. I expect you'll have things in hand on rue Cambon when I return to Paris. Soon, I hope." Coco glances at her watch. "As always, Monsieur Prudone, be discreet. Do not answer questions regarding my business here."

"Of course not, mademoiselle."

The car stops. Coco lowers her voice. "And check the inventory at Neuilly. Use whatever excuse you want, but I'll need to know how things stand when I return. Order whatever we need for the boutique, too. If anyone at the factory complains make it clear that you are acting on my orders."

"Yes, mademoiselle." Prudone steps out and, after closing the door, turns and tips his hat. "Good luck in Grasse."

The road toward Grasse is behind them. Jacques maneuvers the Daimler through the traffic and swings the automobile around to the other side of the boulevard. Coco is silent, thinking of the small perfume shop they'd passed on the way into town—the House of Besse. If the perfumer is local and sells his own fragrances, perhaps he also grows his own jasmine. Perhaps she does not need Grasse. Perhaps such a small farmer would appreciate an opportunity to sell excess product to the House of Chanel.

Jacques glances over his shoulder. "On to Grasse, mademoiselle?"

She leans forward. "Not yet. There's a little shop over there ... just on the left. Yes, there. I want to stop."

On the sidewalk outside, Coco eyes the window displays of perfume. When she opens the door, a small bell rings overhead. The showroom is washed with sunshine and redolent of a clean white scent, like linen drying in the breeze—the essence of Provence.

From a door in the back of the shop a young woman appears. "Hello, madame," she says, smiling, spreading her hands. "May I be of assistance?"

Coco fingers her soft white collar, looking about. The shop

is well stocked. "I would like to try some fragrances. Something with a good jasmine note, but not too sweet." She tilts her chin. "Not a single flower. Something more complex."

The girl smiles, murmuring that she has several items; one in particular. "Please, come with me," she says, heading for a counter across the room. Coco follows, trailing her gloved hand along the glass. While the clerk retrieves bottles of perfume from a low shelf behind the counter, Coco inspects the tips of her fingers. The gloves are clean. She sets her purse on the glass top, waiting.

The clerk places four bottles on the counter and plucks a handful of small strips of blotting paper from a jar on a shelf behind her. As she pulls the stopper from each bottle, she dips a strip into the perfume and hands it to Coco.

Coco waves the strips slowly under her nose, back and forth one after the other. Seconds pass, and she repeats the process, this time waiting longer before moving on to the next strip. Yes, as she'd first thought. It's the last scent that shimmers. Light and not too sweet, with a heart of jasmine and rose. And she detects also hints of ylang-ylang, orange blossom, sage, bergamot, cedarwood, and just a hint of iris. It is a superb composition. Exactly what she needs and, she thinks in surprise, almost as elegant as No. 5. The perfumer has talent.

"I'll take this one." She places her fingertip on the last in the row. "One bottle."

The girl nods, smiling. "That is a good choice. Provence Amour, my favorite. I thought you might like it." She pauses. "The price is twenty francs."

As Coco opens her purse, her tone is casual. "Is the perfumer local?"

The girl pulls folds of white tissue from the shelf behind her. "Yes, mademoiselle." She wraps the bottle and ties it with a thin satin ribbon before handing the package to Coco. "The family has a farm near Grasse."

"So they grow their own flowers?"

"Oh, yes. Besse is an old family of perfumers in this region. Generations of—"

"I would like to meet him, the perfumer."

"I don't know about that." She wrings her hands. "No one has asked before. Monsieur Besse does not often come into town, so I don't know him well."

Coco works to hide her impatience. "I leave Cannes tomorrow for Paris, but I must meet with him before I go. I'll wait while you telephone. Ask, please. I am Gabrielle Chanel, from the House of Chanel in Paris."

The girl's hand flies to her mouth. "Oh, well of course."

"Say that I would like to see him today if possible."

"Yes, madame … ah, Mademoiselle Chanel. I will call immediately." Turning, the clerk hurries to the back of the shop. Minutes pass and, with a sigh, Coco sets her belongings down on the counter. A telephone connection from Cannes to a farmhouse upland could take a while, even these days. From behind the door, she hears the girl speaking low into the telephone.

At last the clerk reappears. Mademoiselle Chanel may visit the perfumery this afternoon if she desires, she says.

"Fine." Coco smiles at the clerk. She has located an independent source of jasmine. Pierre should weep. "I'll need directions. How far away is the farm?"

"About forty kilometers, mademoiselle." On a piece of paper, the girl sketches a map. "Drive north. Not far from Cannes, past Mougins. But before you come to Grasse you must turn west, here—" she taps pen to paper. "The Besse farm is located on the far side of the village Fleur. There's a sign at the entrance. If you reach Bargeman, you've gone too far."

Coco takes the map, picks up her purse and package, thanks the clerk, and leaves. What luck; from the quality of the perfumes, she is certain this farmer processes his own absolutes. He is of the old school, a perfumer who controls each step of composition, from the first to the last. She will purchase all the jasmine absolute he holds in stock and will use it to produce No. 5 at Neuilly.

And Grasse and Pierre be damned.

Chapter Five

Fleur, Provence
Spring 1940

Once Cannes is left behind, the road narrows and soon they enter a forest. The wind blows through the open windows, ruffling her hair. Smoothing her curls, Coco settles back into the soft leather seats, breathing deep, taking in the fragrance of the air, the clean, crisp scents of pine, cypress, and cedar.

Filled with hope after discovering a new source of jasmine in that funny little shop, the earlier melancholy fades. For the first time since receiving the letter, Coco relaxes. She's taking action—she's in control. And there's some consolation in the thought that if she could not purchase jasmine from Grasse at this late date, neither can Pierre.

In the distance, the foothills of the Alps Martine rise, dark silhouettes in the east. They pass sun-washed fields dotted with red-roofed cottages. They drive through vineyards and orchards of shimmering olive trees, and then again into dark woods, miles and miles of thick green foliage. Near Mougins and the turn before Grasse, the road ascends. Here in the rolling hills, rows of men and women move slowly through the fields harvesting flowers. Here the air is heavy with an intense sweet scent.

"May roses," says Jacques.

Even before Fleur comes into view, Coco hears the perfectly tuned village church bells. For an instant the bells recall the abbey at Aubazine. Closing her eyes she wills the thought away, pushes it back into the shadows of her mind where Gabrielle dwells. She is Coco now, she reminds herself. Those days of poverty and anguish are gone, and not even Pierre Wertheimer can drag her back.

The village of Fleur is small, just a few centuries old, Jacques tells her. They pass through a crowded market, each stall piled high with colorful fruit—vegetables, herbs, green and white asparagus, golden apricots, purple plums bursting with juice, jars of swirled honey, bright red strawberries.

"The strawberries come from Spain this time of year." Jacques smiles at her in the rearview mirror. "In a few weeks we'll have our own *garriguettes*. My wife makes preserves and sells them in Mougins. She won't let me in the kitchen when she's working; afraid I'll finish them off before she gets them in the jars."

How she would love to stop. But there's no time.

They drive through a shaded arcade and out onto a cobbled road walled in by heavy, low stone buildings gleaming amber in the sunlight, some with narrow walkways in between. Then, suddenly, they turn, and straight ahead is the village church with the same open wrought iron bell tower seen throughout Provence, designed to withstand the mistral winds. On the right, small shops and an open café face the square. A small fountain bubbles in the center of this grassy area. Turning left at the church, they exit the village of Fleur through a cypress windbreak.

After another half mile, the entrance to the farm comes into view. The words "House of Besse" spiral through arched ironwork over a narrow dirt road. The sun is high, the air crisp, the sky clear and blue. Coco is exhilarated—this farm is the answer. No need at all for Grasse. The car turns under the arch and they drive through the sloping fields of the Besse farm between rows of blooming roses. She takes a deep breath—the air is sweet with the smell of clay and warm earth. And then they drive through new plowed furrows with summer jasmine creeping up. Already the fragrance is intoxicating.

Near the road's end Jacques points to the *mas*, a cottage built with the same amber quarried stone as those in the village. Behind the cottage Coco spots a long single-storied building built from the same stone. The perfumery, she imagines.

They stop before the cottage and Jacques climbs out and opens her door. Coco slides from the car, stretching her muscles. Practical Provence, she thinks, inspecting the house facing southeast to buffet the north wind. Shuttered windows of thick glass are small enough to protect against wind and rain, but large enough to allow light. The curved red clay tiles on the low sloping roof interlock, forming canals for rainwater to drain.

Hearing a noise, Coco turns to see a young woman—a girl—hurrying toward her from the back of the cottage. Spotting Coco, she lifts her hand, smiling. "I heard the motor," she calls. "Welcome to the House of Besse, Mademoiselle Chanel!"

The girl has the look of an excited colt—she's beautiful, slender, with a bounce in her step. Not yet twenty-one, Coco guesses. As she comes to a halt, breathing hard, she pulls her long flaxen braid over one shoulder—strands of gold in the sunshine. Coco is struck by her wide sparkling amethyst eyes, her smooth soft skin, the natural color in her lips and sun-blushed complexion.

"Suzette from the shop called," the girl says, breathless. "We've been expecting you."

Coco extends her hand long enough for their fingertips to

touch, inspecting her with a couturier's eye. These looks are wasted hidden away here in Provence. If Coco were still in couture, she would hire this one as a mannequin.

Then the cottage door opens and an older man emerges. The father, the Besse perfumer, Coco guesses. She watches him, taking his measure as he makes his way down the steps, coming toward them on a narrow dirt path under a string of gaslight lanterns hanging from tree limbs overhead. Behind, in the doorway, waits a shadowy woman—gray hair, features blurred. As she has often done before, Coco wonders why women of a certain age allow themselves to simply disappear.

He stops when he reaches the girl. "I am Uri Besse," he says, nodding to Coco. His voice is brisk, irritable. "And this is Marielle, my daughter."

"Thank you for allowing this visit, Monsieur Besse. I am Gabrielle Chanel."

"I know who you are," he says. He is unimpressed; a blunt, hard-working Provincial irritated at this interruption in his day.

"Come," he says, gesturing. "We will show you where we work." Placing a hand on his girl's shoulder, he steers his daughter toward the long building behind the house, leaving Coco to follow. The woman in the doorway fades away.

As they round the corner of the cottage, the girl stops, waiting for Coco while Uri Besse walks on. "Please excuse my father, mademoiselle. We are preparing for the summer harvest and he's out of sorts. We're having a difficult time finding workers." She shrugs. "All the young men are gone off to fight, if war comes." Marielle slips her arm through Coco's. "But I believe this is what you've come to see—the perfumery."

"It's lovely," Coco says. And after a beat, "Do you sell your entire product from the store in Cannes?"

"Yes, mademoiselle, except for a few foreign clients." The girl gives her a sideways look of pride. "We're a small farm. We've near sixty acres here, but that is more than enough to fill our shelves in Cannes each year."

Coco nods. Yes, as she'd hoped. The store in Cannes was empty; they will have leftover stock.

Uri Besse opens the door and steps aside for Coco and his daughter, ducking in after them. Inside, the ceiling is low, beamed with rough dark wood. The room is dim, chill. Clouds of mingled scents have settled into the stone and wood over many years. As he closes the door, Besse switches on the overhead electric bulb. The only other light comes from a window facing the cottage and the road. A large chiseled oak table sits underneath the window, a worktable.

The girl pulls a tall stool over to the table. "Sit here please, mademoiselle, if you'd like."

Coco ignores the stool. She is a small woman with grace and poise and prefers standing at full height while talking to this unfriendly farmer. If Besse's manners improve, perhaps she'll offer a long-term purchase contract for his jasmine absolute. Although threats of war will soon pass, and the price will drop as well. So why commit?

She places her purse on the table and slips her hands into her skirt pockets, looking about. Uri Besse disappears through a door beside a fireplace at the far end of the room. There is another door, leading to the flower fields, she supposes. Shelves to her left hold vessels with names of ingredients hand labeled on the sides—plant roots, spices, herbs, musk pods, ambergris, civet beans. There are flasks of chemicals, too—she turns to the girl, "Synthetics?"

"Yes, mademoiselle," the girl says, picking up a cloth from the worktable.

To Coco's right, across the room, more shelves hold thick

amber glass flacons which she guesses contain the essential oil reduced from the flowers—the absolute. A small, black iron safe is almost hidden on the floor in the corner under the shelves.

"Papa will be right back," the girl says. "Excuse me, please," and, holding on to the cloth, she moves to the fireplace where a large double copper kettle hangs over the hearth. Marielle chatters about the farm and crops and life in Fleur while she cleans the kettle surface and they wait for her father's return.

At last Besse reappears. With a nod toward the shelves of perfume ingredients, Coco says, "I see that you blend with synthetics, Monsieur Besse. Where did you learn the science, the chemistry … if I might ask?"

The man's thick brows draw together. He stands a foot taller than Coco, and although slightly stooped, he's muscular and weathered. His skin is browned from the sun, his unruly gray hair bristles. "Blending synthetics and plant material is an art, not a science, mademoiselle. A painter need not understand the chemistry of his paints to create art. Neither a perfumer." He rests his hand on the kettle beside him. "Besse men," with a glance at the girl, "and women, have created fragrances for generations."

Coco turns her eyes to Marielle. "Oh, so you compose perfume too?"

"Yes, mademoiselle." With a slight lift of her chin, she adds, "Suzette says that you purchased a bottle of my Provence Amour this morning. It is my creation, my first alone. I hope to work in Paris someday."

"I'm interested in that particular perfume." The girl looks too young to have created the sophisticated fragrance. "Tell me about the jasmine. Which process did you use to obtain the oil?"

Marielle clasps her hands together, smiling. "Of course, we use only the flowers grown in our fields."

"We're in the rose harvest now." Besse interrupts. "And, as

you must know, the formula ingredients for Provence Amour are confidential."

A small farmer must guard his secrets. Still, his tone is rude. In her pockets, Coco's hands curl; she digs her fingernails into her palms. But her voice remains calm. "I am not here to pry, Monsieur Besse."

"Ah. Good then." His hand slides over the curve of the kettle. "For May roses, this is where we separate plant oils from the blossoms and leaves, through maceration. Using heat. The materials simmer in solvents in this kettle before we move them to the extractor in back." He nods toward the door and the room beyond. "The end product, the oil as you say, is the 'absolute.'"

"Yes, I know that much."

"But with jasmine," Marielle interjects, "instead of maceration, we prefer the old way."

"Mari!" Besse breaks in. Coco stares. Provençals are difficult. She is used to more reverence in Paris.

Besse crosses the room to his daughter, clamping his hand upon her shoulder. "Enough. It is time for our visitor to leave." With a glance at Coco, "We have work to finish."

"But I've driven all this way."

His eyes turn cold. "That is unfortunate. Mari spoke to the store clerk in Cannes," he says. "I would have suggested you not waste your time coming, mademoiselle. We are busy. And we don't generally allow visitors." Beside him, the girl flushes.

Coco leans back against the edge of the worktable, fingering her pearls, fighting her growing irritation. "Perhaps you misunderstand the purpose of my visit. I've come on business, if you will hear me out. I wish to purchase jasmine absolute, as much as you have in stock. What is your price, per kilo?"

"We only have one flacon at this time," Mari says. "It holds one kilo. Harvest is not until midsummer."

"Our excess jasmine absolute is already promised, Mademoiselle Chanel." The old man's tone is gruff.

The stiff smile she'd formed disappears. "All of it? Even after harvest?"

"Any amount we do not use."

"You have a contract?"

"I have given my word."

"Who is the purchaser?"

"That is not your business, but I don't mind telling you." His eyes rake over her. "I hear your man was in Grasse yesterday attempting to purchase contracts for jasmine. My friend said he was insistent. But as you must know, we are all used to dealing with Monsieur Wertheimer."

The room is silent. The fragrance is suddenly stifling. She crosses her arms, feeling her heart beating in her chest as he adds, "Perhaps you were not aware that Monsieur Wertheimer has already settled for stock in Grasse, and with us as well."

Coco works to steady herself, understanding that his words also explain Prudone's reception in Grasse. But perhaps it's not too late. She will outbid Pierre, at least here with this one flower farmer. That will send a message. And this is only the beginning.

"I'll pay eighty thousand francs for the full flacon you have now." This is a generous offer, higher than prices in Grasse, higher than a shrewd businessman like Pierre would offer to a small farmer in Provence. "And the same per kilo for your coming summer harvest, all the excess you do not plan to use."

"I find it strange you are bidding against your partner."

"We have different interests at the moment." Coco brushes a small piece of lint from her sleeve. "My offer is enough to invest in your property and expand. Enough to double your acreage and your future production, monsieur."

His hand drops from his daughter's shoulder. "As I said, the jasmine is sold."

"Ninety thousand." Almost twice the market price.

"Put your money away," Besse snaps. "You do not seem to understand, mademoiselle. I have given my word. This is a matter of honor."

"One hundred thousand francs per kilo, Monsieur Besse." He would be a fool to refuse.

He steps back, shaking his head. "I believe our business is finished."

As Besse's words sink in, Coco stares at him, studying the deep lines across his forehead, the vertical creases between the brows, the dark shadows circling his eyes and under the sharp cheekbones. How can he refuse such an offer? Life cannot be easy for a small perfumer with customers on edge waiting for Hitler's next move.

"Please. It is time for you to leave."

Whirling, she hurries toward the door. Outside, Coco strides across the yard, along the side of the cottage wall to the car, her back straight, her head held high.

Jacques scrambles from the car when he spots her, hurrying to the passenger door just as she arrives. She gasps for breath, unable to fill her lungs and, pressing her hands to her chest, she wills her heart to slow as Jacques starts the engine.

Pierre will have the jasmine and he will win. Madonna, Saint Theresa Little Flower, pray for me. Pierre will take everything from me. Reaching for her purse, she pulls a small worn card from the inside pocket. The edges are frayed, but it is a card that she's never without. One which proves she's a Catholic, one which assures that when she passes, a proper mass will be said for Mademoiselle Chanel at the Church of La Madeleine in Paris.

Holding the card in her hands, the pounding in her heart slows. At last her lungs receive the blessed air. Yes, there, now she's breathing, at last. Leaning her head against the cushion she fans her face with her hand. But as the car passes through the gates and onto the road toward the village of Fleur, Coco still feels the sting of the encounter with Uri Besse.

She is fatigued from the happenings of this day; so tired. She must remember who she is—who she has become. She is Chanel. Closing her eyes, she sees herself gliding down the spiral stairs at rue Cambon long ago, on the day she launched No. 5. She's holding up the clear rectangular bottle of amber perfume, her own simple design. In the showroom below reporters' flashbulbs burst into stars.

How she'd worked to come up with a unique quote for the press, something perfect—but sounding impromptu. Something everyone would remember and quote time and again.

And sure enough, when the reporters shouted out their questions, she had laughed and, casually—oh-so casually—the clever quote rolled off her tongue as if without a thought: *A woman without Chanel No. 5 is a woman with no future.*

As with everything else in her life—so carefully manufactured.

But as they drive through the village of Fleur, Coco's smile fades. Because now she must find some other way to protect *her* future.

Chapter Six

Cannes to Paris
Spring 1940

The following morning Coco rests in her compartment on the Blue Train, the express to Paris from the Côte d'Azur. She presses her forehead against the window, staring out at the blur of trees, farms, cows, houses, and small towns rushing by. Ever since receiving the letter from Neuilly she's felt a sense of time closing in. How long before Pierre resurrects the business in America and his theft is a fait accompli? Weeks? Months?

Pulling a handkerchief from a pocket, Coco dabs a tear from her cheek, angry at her weakness. She will not allow this self-pity. This is not the first battle she's been forced to fight with her partner—but this time she will finish him. She drops the handkerchief into her lap with new resolve. She will consider every option.

A mass of humanity greets Coco and Alyce as the train stops at the Gare de Lyon in Paris; a pushing, shoving mass of people desperate to board the train going south. On the platform, Coco instructs the porter with the baggage to lead the way through the buzzing hive. She and Alyce follow in his wake.

Coco's blue Rolls Royce waits outside the station entrance. She chose the automobile colors in tribute to the Blue Train with its blue sleeping cars trimmed in gold. Evan, her driver for many years, opens the passenger door and helps her in, and then Alyce, and he loads luggage into the trunk.

"What is all this commotion, Evan?"

"They say the Germans are coming, mademoiselle."

The streets from the station to the Hôtel Ritz are packed with automobiles and trucks moving slowly toward the southern routes away from the city. When at last they arrive at the Place Vendôme, Evan pulls into a line near the hotel and, leaving the engine running, rests his elbow on the windowsill, announcing that it looks like they'll have a wait. Coco glares at the stalled automobiles waiting to reach the entrance. To her right a wall of men, women, children, pets, boxes, trunks, and bags moves along the pavement toward the hotel at a crawl.

Remembering the crowds in Cannes and at the station, Coco leans forward tapping Evan's shoulder. "Even here?"

"They're from the northern suburbs and towns," Evan says. "Fleeing the Boche."

She groans and falls back. "Can't you do something?" She catches his eyes in the mirror.

"Yes, mademoiselle." Pulling out of line, the Rolls careens ahead of the other cars toward the entrance, cutting into a space in front. Coco ignores the screech of the horn behind her as Evan turns off the engine and hurries to Coco's assistance.

"Hey!" The driver calls out from the car behind them. "You there—who do you think you are!" But as two doormen rush from the hotel entrance to greet Coco, the man halts, slams his fist on the hood.

"Take the automobile around to the garage," Coco commands Evan with a nod to each doorman, ignoring the infuriated driver. "Then bring the baggage up to my rooms."

Inside, entire families sprawl throughout the grand entrance hall—men, women, and children covering every inch of space—the divans and chairs and footstools, some squeezing two or three to a chair. She walks past families squatting on the floors, even on the wide curved marble staircases, stretching out, slumping against their belongings. Coco's eyes sweep over the scene as she calculates damage to the lovely tapestries and woven carpets, the velvet settees and mahogany carved tables, the delicate glass lamps. Blankets, pillows, picnic baskets, children's toys, all are strewn about the main entrance of the Hôtel Ritz.

But she's too tired to complain. Stopping at the concierge desk, she greets the only man she trusts at this moment. "Géraud, I am home."

The head concierge lifts his eyes to her and nods before turning back to the guests before him. Coco is taken aback—no warm smile, no arms spread wide celebrating her return. In this crowd it is as if Mademoiselle Chanel does not exist.

Coco shoots him a hard look. "I'd hate to see what would happen to Paris in a real war," she mutters, pushing through the crowd toward the elevator. Alyce follows. As she presses the elevator bell, she glances at her maid. "I'll have a steaming cup of tea right away. And a croissant ... with marmalade." She's never truly been fond of the bittersweet orange jam that Boy loved, but it's become a habit.

As the elevator grill slides open and the operator greets her, Coco turns back to Alyce, catching the girl in a yawn. Coco flips her hand in the direction of staff quarters. "Never mind, Alyce. Go on to your bed. I'll have someone else bring up the tea."

Chapter Seven

Paris
Spring 1940

An ominous cloud hangs over Paris this morning. The BBC reports that Hitler has turned his eyes to France. For the third time this week, Alain Jobert stands before the barred entrance to BancLeval on Avenue Hoche, looking at the Closed sign posted on the grill gate. Alain has obtained the No. 5 formula for Pierre as ordered, but the remainder of this assignment requires assistance from the missing Henri Leval, Pierre's banker—not least, a new passport for Alain. He'd arranged the paperwork with Henri before leaving New York. If the Germans do arrive before he leaves Paris, he will need a new set of documents, papers with a new name, a less recognizable name.

Both Alain and Pierre had understood the danger of this trip—both are Jews, well known in Paris. But the Germans are moving faster than either had anticipated. Alain's family immigrated to Manhattan seven years ago. And although he is now a citizen of the United States, the problem is that he also remains a citizen of France, still subject to her jurisdiction and laws.

"Get in, get out," Pierre had said.

Already it's the end of the first week in May, and he's still here. So where is Henri Leval?

It seems the banker is stuck in his Geneva office, and with the Boche on the move, there's nothing either of them can do at the moment. Alain has only managed to get through to Henri once by telephone before the lines were cut. Henri did assure Alain that he has the new passport, and he understands the urgency. Perhaps Henri knows something he couldn't discuss over the telephone, as most are tapped.

He pulls a Gauloise from the pack and, bending over his cupped hand, lights up. Straightening, sucking smoke, he begins walking, heading back across Paris in the general direction of the apartment he keeps, about a kilometer distance from BancLeval, just off the Étoile. Now he's stuck in Paris. Coco was on the Côte d'Azur when he arrived, and out of the way—Pierre had timed the mission well. But she's likely returned, and of course the Neuilly plant manager will give up his name in a minute. Coco will raise hell; call it theft. Ignoring the fact that Pierre owns the company and the formula, something she's never fully understood. He has never gotten along with Chanel—her constant interference in the business, her mercurial tempers—but then she's Pierre's problem, not his.

A pretty woman comes into view as he turns the corner ahead. He watches her stride toward him with pleasure, her hips and arms swinging. She's wearing a suit like one of Coco's things— short skirt and jacket, soft fabric skimming her hips and breasts. Coco would approve of the look even if it's a knockoff, especially with the short white gloves and pearls. A red beret covers her hair at a jaunty angle. He catches her eye, but she merely smiles and hurries on. He sighs; how things have changed. A year ago she'd have slowed her pace and given him a look.

Near the Étoile, not far from the apartment, Alain cuts over to the Hôtel Napoleon on Avenue de Friedland. The small bar off the lobby is empty except for the barman. Removing his hat, Alain takes a seat.

"*Bon soir*, Monsieur Jobert." The barman shakes his head while he dries a glass inside and out with a small white towel. "Well, you have picked a fine time to return to Paris."

"I'll be here another week or so."

"I thought you were smart. You should know better. Haven't you heard the news?" He sets the glass down and reaches into the sink for another. "If I had someplace to go, I'd be off by now."

Alain shrugs.

"Still cognac?"

"You have a good memory. And pour one for yourself."

The barman nods his thanks and retrieves the bottle from underneath the bar and sets down two glasses, pouring two fingers each.

Alain lifts his glass. "Santé." The barman does the same, throwing back his head, emptying the glass.

"Dunkirk was bad enough. Now they say the fighting has already begun in Belgium," the barman says. "Radio Paris reports nothing about what's going on, as usual. But the BBC says the Boche are coming through the Ardennes."

"I hadn't heard." Alain sips the cognac and sets it down, turning the glass in circles. "That's bad news. And the Maginot Line won't hold. They'll go around it, or the Luftwaffe will just bomb it to hell."

The barman nods. "Could be a rumor, but noise is the government's leaving Paris." He grimaces. "They won't fight for us, the bastards. You watch. They'll live it up in Tours or Bordeaux and leave us to suffer under the Boche."

Waiting for Leval to return is, among other inconveniences, a bore. A few nights later Alain sits alone on the terrace of Le Dôme, one of his favorite cafés. Rumors of an invasion are flying and already citizens of Paris are beginning to leave, heading south. Tonight the streets are all but deserted while everyone waits.

As he sips his beer, Alain reflects on better times. That last evening with Letty before he'd left New York for Paris on this mission for Pierre. He smiles at the memory as it lifts him from the sounds of explosions in the outer arrondissements. Paris tonight vibrates with fear, a wave of terror simmering beneath the surface of the city streets. He thinks instead of beautiful, spoiled Letty Harlow, and other women in New York who float through his life on their pretty clouds, safe in a country protected by an ocean from the horrors of war. He remembers Letty's fury when he'd announced that he wouldn't be around for a while, and that, no, he couldn't say where he was headed—nor, when he would return.

Three men talking at the next table break into his thoughts. They mention someone he used to know. Hans von Dincklage was a good friend of Coco's, he recalls. She'd introduced the man and his wife to Pierre and Alain several years ago. Officially, Dincklage was Special Attaché to the German Embassy in Paris at the time, but Pierre always said he was fifth column—a Nazi spy—or worse. The wife's name was Catsy. And he remembers that Pierre had said the wife was Jewish. The couple were an odd combination.

He gives the men a sideways glance and relaxes. He doesn't know them, but listens.

"Say, put that down. Did you hear what I said? Hans Dincklage is back in Paris."

"Well I suppose that makes sense." A little chuckle. "He's here to welcome the jackboots. I never liked the fellow."

"The ladies will be happy enough to see him. My wife, too."

Dincklage was tall, blond, and good-looking, as Alain recalls. A bon vivant on the surface. Alain picks up the beer glass and finds it empty. Setting it back down, he lights a cigarette, still listening.

"You're right. Marriage didn't stop Dincklage any. And he spread plenty of dough around."

"He was Gestapo even then in '38 they say."

"Yeah?"

"I don't believe it." The new fellow slurs his words. "Dincklage was all right. He was a pal. Sure knew how to throw a party." He signals the waiter while he talks.

"Listen." The man sitting closest to Alain lowers his voice and Alain strains to hear. "Everyone back then was wise, knew Dincklage was a spy—Gestapo or not. My friend at InterPress got it straight from the Deuxième Bureau." He falls silent as the waiter arrives with a new bottle of wine, sets it on the table and sweeps the empty.

"You never saw the man working, did you?" Everyone seems to agree. "So how do you think he afforded that big apartment? A thousand francs a month at least, and that's before the franc took a dive."

"I hear he kept a villa on the coast in Sanary too."

"Remember that little silver two-seater? That car drove the ladies crazy. Drove my wife a little nuts, I always thought."

"Yes, well, a villa in Sanary's pretty convenient if you're a spy, with our naval bases right there at Toulon."

"Wonder if he's still got that car."

Alain's heard enough. Leaving a few franc notes on the table, he rises. He'd best watch his back if Coco's old friend has arrived. By now Coco knows he's lifted the formula from Neuilly, and she won't hesitate to turn him over to someone like Hans Dincklage in an instant if she learns he's still in town. Worse, Coco knows exactly where he lives.

An hour later in his apartment on rue Beaujon, Alain tucks the No. 5 formula into an almost invisible slot between the lining and the leather side of an old worn valise, down near the bottom, a hiding place he's used before when traveling on business for Pierre. Wearing a pair of cuffed trousers and a decent shirt, he packs some practical brown twill pants, a couple jerseys, a tweed jacket, requisite underwear, and socks. It's June, so he adds his raincoat just in case. Tossing in an old billed cap, he closes the suitcase. Into the valise he stuffs a detailed map of France, and his wireless radio, which will be contraband soon, he's certain. Then, closing and latching the windows, he turns off the lights, slaps his snap-brim hat on his head, locks the door, and walks away.

Within hours, Alain rents a small place in the crowded warrens of the left bank behind the Sorbonne, eight blocks from the river Seine. Two rooms with a bath down the hall on the second floor of a walk-up. He's anonymous here, an American known only as Alain. Neighbors may suspect, but they will not know for certain that he is a Jew. The landlord has little to say, happy to take his money.

Alain drops the suitcase on the floor and places the valise on the table. The place reeks with odors of urine, cheap whiskey, and small animals. The walls are bare, the beige paint chipped. In the front room is one chair, a small table, a cookstove with a pan on top, and an icebox that doesn't work. There's a bare mattress on the floor in the back room. An electric bulb hangs from the ceiling in each room. He flips the switches—both work—and switches them off again. It's dark, no sense in creating a target. One window in each room looks over the street below. Each is covered with cotton strips probably torn from an old sheet, with a large hook on one side to pin the curtains back. This will do until Henri Leval returns from Switzerland, and then he can get out of here.

Removing his shirt, he hangs it on the back of the chair. He lights a cigarette, drags the chair to the window, and pulls back the curtain. Sets the wireless on the floor and turns it on. The evening is hot, but there's a slight breeze. A smoky haze hangs in the air outside, filtering the moonlight, hiding the stars. The city is blacked out, with all lights snuffed.

The wireless crackles to life. Static—then, *Blitzkrieg!*

Alain stiffens, rubs out the cigarette, and leans forward, listening. The BBC reports that on this eighth day of May, German forces have struck like lightning. They came through the Ardennes, crossing into Holland. Alain listens for thirty minutes or an hour, until he's certain—the Boche are avoiding France. At least for now.

But two days later, while Alain is passing time in the Napoleon Bar, his relief vanishes as nearby church bells ring out. They're quickly joined with others, more and more across the city, blending sinister warnings to Parisians. The barman goes still. Their eyes meet as automobile horns begin blaring in unison on the Avenue and the surrounding streets, around the Étoile, and over on the Champs-Élysées. Voices outside join the cacophony. Policemen are shouting, blasting their whistles, and a woman screams just under the barroom window.

Alain turns his head as a commotion erupts in the hotel lobby. Over his shoulder he watches two strangers hurrying in from the street—shouting, gesturing—businessmen in suits and ties, carrying attachés. Together they turn into the bar.

"Have you heard?" the first cries as he drops onto a barstool near Alain. His eyes are wide.

The barman looks at him. "What's the trouble out there?"

The second fellow seats himself on Alain's other side. He slaps his hat on the bar, wiping his brow. "They're heading for our borders—and the lowlands. This is it—war. They'll crush Chartres and then we're next." He lowers his voice. "Paris is next."

"Already crossed the border, I'd bet." The first man yanks a

THE QUEEN OF PARIS

handkerchief from his pocket, patting the sheen above his lip. "Whisky neat, all around," he says, glancing at Alain.

The barman says thanks and reaches for the glasses. "Listen, our infantry will stop them."

"You haven't heard?" The first man spreads his arms on the bar. "The BBC's just announced the news. The government's declared Paris an open city. We're sitting ducks, here for the taking, gentlemen. We are helpless. We'll have no defense when the Boche arrive." He takes the drink from the barman and slugs it down.

Chapter Eight

Paris
Spring 1940

Coco awakes on the day after her return to find Paris covered in smoke. Buildings across the Place Vendôme are etched in gray, shadows in a haze. Throwing aside the blanket, Coco pads over to the windows, pressing her face against the panes. Ash drifts against the glass. Across the plaza hundreds of men, women, and children with luggage and boxes and pets swarm around the taxi post.

"What is this?"

Alyce slips up behind her, peering at the disorderly crowd.

"I do not know, mademoiselle."

Quickly Alyce helps her dress.

Downstairs Coco finds Géraud, as always, at the concierge desk. He never seems to sleep. She stands beside him observing the still-packed entrance hall. "What is happening out there?"

He gives her a grim look. "The government flees from Paris to Tours, mademoiselle. And despite odds, it seems everyone wishes to accompany the tyrants. Shops are closing, groceries, cafés, even our monuments are closed." He watches the doormen at the street door, struggling to hold back another crowd. The Ritz is full.

"The government is moving?" Coco is momentarily stunned. "But, why are they leaving us and where are they going? And why all this smoke? Is the city on fire?"

He turns his eyes to her. "Our brilliant government has decided that Paris will not be defended from the enemy. Infantry are destroying oil supplies on the outskirts of the city." He looks off, blowing out his cheeks. "And diplomats are burning files before they flee."

"Well then, I suppose the phony war is real after all." But she is not afraid—Coco Chanel is beloved in Germany. And in her heart she believes they will never take France; they lost brutally in the Great War.

Still, precautions must be taken. Following a light breakfast at her usual window table in a corner of the hotel dining room, Coco strolls across rue Cambon to the House of Chanel, as she does on almost every day when she's in Paris. A shop girl dressed in a navy-blue skirt suit with a crisp white blouse, as required, holds the door open at her approach.

"Good morning, mademoiselle," she says when Coco enters the Maison, gliding through the cloud of No. 5, which the girl sprays on her arrival. Chandeliers glitter overhead and marbled tiles shine beneath her short heels as Coco passes the glass cases filled with real and costume jewelry, scarves, belts, and rows of gleaming amber bottles of No. 5—all that's left of the Maison's inventory. As she starts up the stairs spiraling between panels of opposing walled mirrors, in peripheral vision she sees her infinite reflection. Inside she smiles. The mirrors confirm that she is real; she exists.

Charles Prudone waits at the top of the stairs wringing his hands. He greets Coco with a slight bow. "It's good to have you back. Have you heard, mademoiselle? The worst is true! They are coming."

"Gather everyone," she says, passing him, heading through the atelier for her private rooms. He trails behind. "I doubt you're right, but just in case, we must prepare."

He says nothing, following behind as she rattles off instructions.

"The metal shutters will be lowered over the windows. Have the girls take everything from the shelves in the boutique. They are to pack everything in tissue and straw. The jewelry, perfume bottles, purses, belts—those must be wrapped precisely three times in the tissue, and then the tissue tucked exactly like this, and then the item must be placed into the straw—just so." She illustrates with her hands.

"After that, everything must be placed in the storeroom." Pausing at the door to her private rooms, she turns to look at him. "When we leave at the end of the day, monsieur, the storeroom will be locked, and you must close and pull the grills over the doors and lock them too." She lifts one finger. "No one leaves until I'm satisfied that we're secure."

"Some of the staff request permission to leave early, mademoiselle. They have families …"

She lifts her brows. "Certainly not. Out of the question. Everyone stays until all three floors are properly cleared and secured." She glares at Prudone. "Is that clear?"

The director puts his hands together, steepling them under his chin. "Yes, mademoiselle."

Turning away, she opens the door. She longs to be alone. Sensing Director Prudone has not moved from the doorway, she hesitates, then turns back to him.

"You push me too far, Monsieur Director!" Her head aches. She frowns. "Well, I suppose if they have small children …"

"Yes, but only a few."

"All right; any girl with a young child to care for may leave now." She fixes her eyes on his. "But the rest must stay and help. Is that understood?"

"Yes, mademoiselle. Of course."

The apartment is blessedly quiet after she closes the door. Sounds from the street below are muffled in these rooms by heavy silk curtains and tapestries. She drifts through the hallway toward the sitting room, touching each Coromandel screen along the way. Most are gifts from Boy.

Sinking onto a long, soft, beige sofa, she kicks off her shoes, leans back against the corner cushions, and swings up her legs. She takes a Gitanes from the silver box on the low table and lights the cigarette. Her rooms at the Ritz are only for her, they are private. But this opulent apartment is her face to the outside world, when she chooses—the place where she meets with reporters, or entertains clients and friends, or transacts business, and sometimes just lazes about.

Coco gazes over this glory with the pleasure of a woman no longer dependent upon any man to live well, but also with the eyes of an impoverished, desperate child still hidden deep inside. For these few minutes her eyes roam over the lovely Oriental furniture, the intricate handwoven rugs from Persia and China, the colorful screens, the profusions of crystal, amethyst, and rose quartz fruits dangling from the chandeliers overhead. Her eyes touch on the lovely things she's collected over the years; the sculptures and paintings scattered around the room; the ornate Venetian masks; the gold, silver, and onyx objets d'art; the jeweled boxes. Here, again, reflections from mirrors enhance the light and beauty of her surroundings. As in Étienne's library at Royallieu, and as in Boy's library, shelves bearing leather-bound books with gold embossed lettering on the spines rise to the ceiling. And most of these books are Boy's. A smile comes as she thinks of him. She's read almost all these books and many more, good books to consume and learn, as Boy taught.

All this glory, this beauty, everything she's spent a lifetime to build is at risk now.

With the turmoil in the city, time is precious. She must not wait for a response to the letter she'd sent to her attorney from La Pausa a few days ago. She will call René de Chambrun this minute and demand an appointment, for tomorrow at latest. She goes to the telephone on the desk, tucked behind a screen in a corner of the room. Lifting the receiver, she waits for the operator's voice, then gives her the number. Coco sits on the edge of the desk, waiting for the connection.

On the telephone, René's secretary says the attorney is in the south of France advising the prime minister and his cabinet on the diplomatic situation. No, she does not know when he will return, particularly with the Germans in the neighborhood. No, not tomorrow—a few weeks perhaps, or longer, and telephone lines from outside the city are already cut.

Slowly Coco sets the telephone onto the receiver. It seems she has no choice but to wait. Pacing back and forth, the reality of the war at last sinks through her.

Every moment ticking by without action is a gift for Pierre Wertheimer. A woman can never take her place in the world for granted. Security is everything. Nothing is more important, even love. She learned that lesson early on with Boy Capel.

Chapter Nine

Royallieu
1905

I tossed my hair, laughing as Flost galloped into the château courtyard just ahead of Boy. "Really, I must find a riding companion to keep up with me," I called back to him.

He was smiling as he dismounted, tossing the reins to a stable boy. "You almost took a flier at the hedge, Coco." He came round my horse and helped me down. "I let you win, impudent girl. But I can see I've done nothing but feed your recklessness. Next time, we'll stick to the ring."

"Dressage? Yes, that should make you comfortable."

"I'm serious." He took my arm, leading me inside. "I don't want to lose you." My heart warmed at his words.

Across the gleaming walnut floor in the entrance hall, the wide marble stairway rose to the second floor. My room was there, and Étienne's, and Émilienne's suite. Beautiful Émilienne, former mistress to royal dukes and even kings. She was now Étienne's lover, and had taken up residence at Royallieu, which was fine with me. I was still Étienne's *petite amie*, his special friend. Seven other bedrooms upstairs were kept empty for guests.

Stairs to the third floor, where the staff resided, were at the far end of each wing of the château, one staircase on each side. As we stood in the entrance hallway, to our left was the ballroom. To our right was the drawing room, behind that a salon, the grand dining room, and then a smaller, more intimate dining area. And in the back were the kitchens and pantries.

This was my home, Étienne had always assured. How naive I was. On that morning, Boy and I turned into the hallway, strolling toward the back of the château, passing open archways into the ballroom. I was surprised to see carpets rolled up today and ladders scattered about. Workers stood on the ladders, balancing on the top steps, while looping ivy garlands around the ceiling. Flowers were woven through the ivy, too, and colorful ribbons, and more flowers hung from the chandeliers. I stopped in a doorway, clapping my hands.

"How lovely," I exclaimed, breathing in the sweet fragrance wafting from the room. A flush of excitement ran through me. If all this was preparation for a ball, the reason was something special.

Boy slipped his hand under my elbow, attempting to nudge me on. But I was rooted to the spot, taking in the beautiful high-ceilinged space with sunlight streaming in through the rows of double glass doors. An army of uniformed maids moved throughout, sweeping, polishing, arranging silver candlesticks on tables, and also crystal and china. The tables were covered with crisp white linens hanging in folds to the floor.

Boy released my arm with a loud sigh, and I slipped my hands into the pockets of my jodhpurs. The jodhpurs were Boy's—I'd borrowed them and cut them down to fit. When Boy noticed, he was amused. "Are we having a party this weekend?" I asked.

"Étienne didn't mention it and I've nothing to wear. I'll have to borrow something beautiful from Émilienne."

"Coco," Boy muttered, turning away. "I'm hot and tired. Let's cool down on the terrace. We'll ring for some cold water and biscuits."

I followed, hurrying to catch up. We walked past the library, then Étienne's study, and out to the terrace. Émilienne was waiting when we arrived, standing near the balustrade watching the stable boys exercise the horses. I noticed today she wore the long green and burgundy striped satin dress I disliked, with a full skirt cinched tight at the waist. It was a dress she usually reserved for traveling. Her hair was tucked under a wide-brimmed hat weighed down under the usual pile of artificial fruit and flowers—a heavy, uncomfortable dress and hat. Wearing one white glove, she tapped the other against the palm of her hand as she turned to us.

"Are you leaving?" I asked, surprised. As I spoke I saw her eyes shift to Boy's. Something passed between them. A spark of jealousy flicked through me.

"When do you leave, Émilienne?" Boy asked without even looking at me.

"Not for a half hour or so," she said.

"Good." He sauntered over to an empty chair, a long chair meant for lounging and sunning.

Émilienne nodded and headed for the door. "I'll wait in the library," she said.

I watched her for a moment, and when she was gone, turned to Boy, arching one eyebrow. "What was that about?"

Stretched out on the sun chair, Boy shaded his eyes with his hand and gave me a strange look. He patted a space beside him. "Come sit with me, Coco. We have to talk."

I heard tension in his voice, the first warning. It seemed a shadow crossed the sun, but I knew how to hide. "You two are as subtle as fireworks," I said with a little laugh. "Are you and Émilienne suddenly in love? Tell me the secret." As I spoke, I walked toward him, but stopped short, and instead of perching beside him, I took a nearby wrought-iron chair, turning it so I could see his expression.

Immediately Boy sat up and swung his legs around so he was facing me. He dropped his feet flat onto the terrace and spread his hands, palms up, pleading. "Darling, please come over here."

I said nothing.

Then, clasping his hands between his knees, he looked straight at me. "Coco …" I braced myself at hearing his tone. "We have a small problem. Étienne's wife, the Countess Balsan, arrives this afternoon with her entourage."

"What! Here?" I gripped the edge of the seat, stunned. When I had first arrived at Royallieu, Étienne clarified that he and his wife lived separate lives; that she stayed in Lyon and had yet to set foot in this château, only one of his many houses. I'd assumed then that, like most society wives, the countess was content to look the other way.

I pulled my feet up onto the chair seat, wrapping my arms around my knees, and stared across at Boy in disbelief. "Is this true?"

He nodded. "Tomorrow night she and Étienne are hosting a banquet and ball in honor of their niece, her sister's child. The girl has just got engaged, Étienne says."

"But why here?"

He shrugged. "Location, I suppose. The niece lives in Paris."

But what about me—was I to meet his wife? I felt stricken. His next words shook me.

"You will not attend the ball, Coco. It isn't allowed."

Society did not allow.

I heard Sister's voice in my head—*Only good, clean girls are allowed to eat, Gabrielle.*

Hurt, humiliated, suddenly feeling cold and alone, angry words clamored for release. But even as I narrowed my eyes at Boy, that inner voice warned if I let our worlds collide—Boy's and mine—everything between the two of us could change. And so, instead of firing off the barrage, I stood, linked my hands behind my back, and walked to the balustrade, hiding the tears stinging my eyes.

I heard Boy rise from the chair, his footsteps coming toward me. I blinked back the tears. Laughter and chatter came from the ballroom, the men flirting with the girls. Boy rested his hands upon my shoulders and turned me around. I ducked my head; he pulled me close and I rested my cheek against his chest. Society's rules are not Boy's fault, I told myself. This is how life is. He loves me. One day we'll marry and make things right.

"What should I do?" I mumbled.

Holding me at arm's length, he looked down with a sad half smile. Gently he brushed curls back from my forehead. "Wait here for one minute, Coco, while I fetch Émilienne. She wants to speak with you."

I nodded. But when he was gone, I turned away, my back to the door as I pressed knotted hands against my quivering mouth.

Minutes later, a quiet voice called my name. I turned to see Émilienne standing in the doorway. Boy was gone. Sweeping her skirt aside, she took a seat. "Boy asked me to speak with you," she said. "He's worried you'll be hurt, and like most men,"—she rolled her eyes to the heavens—"he cannot bring himself to speak the truth. So he's asked me to explain."

I stood there speechless, with the same prescient sense of fear I'd felt one day a few months ago while riding Flost, when at the last instant the bay dug in her heels and refused a jump. Already half out the saddle, the jolt sent me flying over her head. In that split second of air, before I hit the ground, I knew—fully anticipated—the impact of terrible pain to come.

Émilienne saw it in my eyes. "Sit down, Coco," she said, folding her hands in her lap.

I set my jaw, planting my hands akimbo on my hips. I wasn't going to make it easy. "No thanks."

With a sigh, Émilienne leaned back in the chair. "Surely you understand why you cannot remain at Royallieu this weekend, *chérie*, with Étienne's wife arriving soon."

But this was my home, Étienne had promised. Royallieu was where I felt secure.

She shook her head. "Surely you are aware that we ladies of the demimonde and those of society can never meet. You and I are not received by our lovers' families and friends."

I blushed at the insult, but still, I shrugged. "I have no desire to meet Étienne's wife, or her friends. I'll spend the weekend riding."

"That will not do."

"It is my choice." My voice was steady; inside I understood her words and felt the wound, the raw, festering humiliation, and then a blinding fury aimed at the whole world and society and its unfair rules, at Étienne, and Émilienne, and, yes—yes, at Boy. I stalked to the balustrade and whirling, leaned back against it, crossing my arms over my chest while picturing the dull brown wrens descending this weekend upon Royallieu, all looking for husbands. For someone like Boy Capel.

"Don't be foolish," Émilienne said in an exasperated tone. "You're Étienne's irregular, not a friend, not a child."

I had not slept with Étienne since Boy and I fell in love. I opened my mouth to protest, but her hand shot up.

"If you should insist on staying, you'll place him in a difficult position, and Boy, too." She pulled on the second glove she'd been carrying, smoothing each finger. "And, of course, if you stay, you will sleep on the third floor with the staff while the guests are here. You will eat meals with the staff in the kitchen."

"I will not."

"Those are the rules." Standing, she angled her hat with the tips of her fingers. "You'll not be seen out riding, either. In fact, you must not be seen at all." Now, her eyes riveted to mine. "Because if that happens, *chérie*, Étienne will be forced to ask you to leave." A second ticked by. "That is," she added, looking past me, "if you are so stupid as to stay."

A tear rolled down my cheek and angrily I swiped it away.

"It's just for a weekend."

"I have no place to go." I hated the catch in my voice.

"Boy says you may stay in his apartment on boulevard Malesherbes in Paris."

"Alone?"

She lifted one brow. "Of course. Boy stays here for the ball. To leave with you would cause a scandal." Seeing the expression on my face, she added in a softer tone, "He worried you wouldn't understand." A stone seemed to lodge in the pit of my stomach as I heard her words. Boy had confided in Émilienne. Here was yet another problem—when she told Étienne about us, I could lose my place at Royallieu, my home.

As if reading my mind, she said, "Have no fear, Coco. Secrets are my trade." With a glance at the gold-and-emerald watch on her arm, a recent gift from Étienne, Émilienne came to me, hooked her arm in mine, and began steering me toward the doorway. "Now, you've ten minutes to pack. I'll have someone come for your bags."

As our carriage rolled toward the gates of Royallieu, I saw Boy riding his horse away from the stables. He did not look our way.

Émilienne reached over and patted my arm. "Don't worry, you'll be together again soon. He is sorry things are this way. He loves you, he says. And you can trust Boy Capel."

I turned my eyes to the road ahead in silence. I should have known better, even then.

Chapter Ten

Paris
Summer 1940

A few days later, Coco stops at the concierge desk on her way from luncheon in the dining room. Géraud looks up from his radio. "Luftwaffe," he says, looking grim. "Mark my words, mademoiselle, they will be here soon."

"But our forces are fighting. They'll hold them off."

He shakes his head. "The Wehrmacht panzers are too much for us. They're smashing their way toward Paris, crushing our infantry. They're tearing up fields, flattening villages. Fighting is fierce, they say."

Coco lifts her brows. "How much time do we have?"

"Not long. The motorized artillery and infantry divisions are moving fast. And they know that Paris is open, unarmed." He lifts a finger. "Wait, one moment. Listen! Something is happening."

He motions to Coco and she comes around to the back of the desk. They are silent, heads together, waiting, listening to static.

Then from the box comes an oily voice. "Reich Minister

Doctor Joseph Goebbels speaking." His voice is higher than she'd expected, and with the static, difficult to hear. "I speak for Germany to citizens of France today; for Germany, guardian of the people." At these words, Géraud's fist softly pounds the desktop. "Parisians, for the sake of order you must stay in place! Remain in your homes and you are safe."

More static, then, "Again, once again! For the sake of order do not attempt to flee."

She'd been procrastinating on whether to leave Paris, or to stay. But the Reich minister's arrogance makes up her mind. Hurrying upstairs, Coco barks at Alyce. "We must go at once. Hurry up. We are leaving Paris."

When Alyce, staring, does not move, Coco snaps her fingers twice. "Quick, quick." The girl jumps. "*Now*, Alyce. There is no time to waste. You must pack immediately. We will return to La Pausa to sit this out, so pack the appropriate wardrobe. I must have two, no, three trunks. And my jewelry, other than the things in the hotel vault. The Germans won't disturb the Ritz. They'll want it for themselves. And bring your valise too."

"Yes, mademoiselle."

Remembering the crushing mob at the railway station, she adds, "Now, call downstairs and instruct Géraud that I will need a private compartment on the overnight train to Cannes. And we must have the car to get to the station. Tell him to have it sent around."

"The hotel telephones are not working, mademoiselle. They say the lines are down."

"Then go downstairs." Lifting a bottle of No. 5 from the dressing table she dabs a bit behind each ear. "Oh, and tell Géraud that someone must pick up our luggage in one half hour. Not a minute later. The Blue Train departs at eight."

Three times Alyce delivers Coco's demand to the concierge—pick up the luggage right away—but everyone else in the Ritz has the same idea. As the bellmen arrive at last, Coco glances at her watch. Half past six and the train leaves at eight.

The Place Vendôme is deserted as Coco's little blue Rolls speeds across the plaza and then down the rue de la Paix. The evening is clear, save for the smoke. Alyce sits in the back beside her. There's little traffic visible so far, and soon Coco begins to relax. Pedestrians hurry along the pavements. Trucks piled high with goods barrel past. On each side of the street shop owners dash to and fro, climbing ladders, banging their hammers, shuttering windows, slamming grills over doors.

The heat is stifling, intense. When they left the hotel, she'd insisted upon opening the car windows over Evan's objection. The city is not safe, he'd said. Now the smell of petrol fuel and smoke burn her nose. Smoke permeates the car and her white gloves are soon covered with soot. Evan must stop and roll up the windows after all.

On the front seat, beside Evan, sits a basket ordered from the hotel kitchen by Géraud, containing cold roast chicken, ham, a quarter round of brie, a loaf of crisp hot bread, petits fours, and a bottle of chilled white wine, in case the dining car is closed. "I'm told this is the last train south out of Paris, Mademoiselle Chanel," he'd warned as they were leaving. "Your private compartment is reserved. Departure at eight o'clock. You have only one hour and thirty minutes."

Thinking of this, she glances at her watch. Six forty-five— fifteen minutes have gone by and the street is still clear of traffic. Despite the earlier delays, they've plenty of time to make the train. She thinks of the sweet serenity of La Pausa and realizes she never should have left the coast. This time she won't return until things are settled here in Paris, one way or the other. If the Germans get through, at least they are civilized—if austere and boring—and she's never believed the strange stories circulating about them.

When they turn the corner onto the Avenue de l'Opéra, a crowd blocks the smoke-fogged street. They slow to a crawl as Evan struggles to maneuver the car through the mob, honking the horn, swerving one way then the other through the growing crush. A woman walking alongside the car stumbles when Evan jerks the wheel to avoid a bicycle. The basket she holds flips from her arms, spilling clothing into the street. Glaring at Evan, she shakes her fists, shouting as the car inches forward. Angry faces press against the windows as they pass, jeering, peering in, noses flat against the glass, some cursing.

"It's the Rolls making them angry, mademoiselle," Evan says, catching her eyes in the mirror. She nods, thinking of the workers' strike, how hard she'd worked to earn this automobile, and now this! She shudders as she thinks of the new France, the workers and communists and Jews stirring up trouble, the rabble in the streets of Paris so eager to tear down rather than to build.

Five more minutes pass while the car grinds slowly through the crowd, then ten and more. Beads of perspiration dampen Coco's forehead as she scans ahead for a glimpse of the station, looking again and again at her watch. Already seven fifteen; only forty-five minutes until the train departs. The last train from Paris.

Suddenly the car rolls to a stop.

"What is happening, Evan?" Peering through the windshield, Coco grasps the back of Evan's seat and pulls herself forward.

Alyce moans, throwing her face into her hands. "They say the Boche will rape the women before they kill us."

"Hush!" Coco snaps.

"The station is ahead, mademoiselle, but look!" Evan sweeps his arm over the scene ahead where thousands swarm—men, women, children, bicycles, baby carriages, carts—all blocking the street and pavements between the Rolls and the railway-station entrance. Ahead, guards stand behind a barricade, guns ready. She watches a man climbing up the station wall, heading toward the roof. When at last he scrambles over the gutters and reaches his destination, he stands high, legs apart, arms waving. A grumbling roar rolls through the crowd, feeling the thrill of his defiance.

She turns her head to Evan, frightened for the first time. Paris has transformed into a snarling beast. "What now?"

Alyce gasps and Coco jumps, turning to a bearded face pressed against the window just beside her. Wild round eyes glare back at her beneath thick gray brows as he pounds on the window. She slaps her hand against the glass and the face disappears. As she sits back, Alyce, still moaning, draws close to Coco. With her heart racing, Coco checks her watch again. Seven thirty already.

She leans forward. "I've changed my mind, Evan. We'll drive to Cannes instead of going by train …"

Quickly he interrupts. "I must stay in Paris, mademoiselle. I have a family to protect."

"Oh, I see."

"Besides, the roads are impossible once you leave the city, everyone's fleeing at once. It will be even worse when the petrol depots close."

She sits back, smoothing her skirt. He's correct about the petrol. "Well, all right. How will we get to the station then?"

"I'll get us there."

She gazes at the rowdy crowd just outside the windows. It won't help to complain or show her fear. "All right. And take care getting the car back to the hotel before you go home."

"Yes, mademoiselle."

"And see that it's kept safe."

He nods and falls silent.

She looks at the back of Evan's head, realizing that in all the years he's driven for her, she's never asked about his family. She had not known. She wonders if he has children. "You may take the petrol from the car, Evan, if you need it. That is, after you get back to the hotel."

"Thank you, mademoiselle." He shakes his head. "What will happen to France now, I wonder."

"Don't talk to me of France. I can think only of the train."

Beside her, Alyce whimpers.

Evan turns the steering wheel. "Hold on, ladies," he shouts as the car swerves with a sudden, sharp left turn. Coco closes her eyes and Alyce falls against her. When she opens her eyes again, they're rolling down a dark, narrow street hemmed in on either side by low cement-block buildings and walls streaked with grime. The windows are dark; garbage piles on the streets. The car bumps over the cobblestones and Alyce shifts closer. Coco gives her an irritable little shove, then, feeling the girl trembling, drops an arm around her shoulders. Gradually the noise of the raucous crowd behind them fades.

Ahead, Coco sees only darkness. "I think we're lost, Evan. Where are you going?"

"The hotel made arrangements in this case, mademoiselle. We're off around to the back of the station, to the freight depot there." She frowns. Over his shoulder Evan adds, "You'll be safe there. A guard is waiting."

Coco glances at her watch. "We've only fifteen minutes left before departure, Evan."

They turn onto an even darker, narrower street. Coco breathes slowly, holding on to Alyce as minutes seem to stretch to hours while the Rolls winds through the eerily deserted area. With no electric lights the streets are black; she can no longer even see her watch. It seems an eternity before the car slows.

"At last." She hears relief in his voice as Evan exclaims, turning the car into an open gate. The engine cuts off, and Evan speaks over his shoulder. "We are here, mademoiselle."

In the silence Coco looks about but can see nothing. Evan opens the door and comes around. With a sigh Coco slides out.

"Follow me, please," Evan says.

Coco snaps her fingers. "Come, Alyce, and stay close." Clutching her purse, she grips Evan's arm, stumbling blindly beside him while Alyce holds on to her skirt. She still cannot see a thing.

Just ahead, and close—too close—a loud mechanical sound startles. Abruptly Coco stops, even as Evan continues tugging her forward. "It's the warehouse door," he whispers. "Look, it's rising. Now, do you see him there?" She peers, squinting into the darkness. "There, the guard is waiting."

"Halt!" a voice booms.

As her eyes adjust, Coco makes out the form of a man just ahead. "You there, sir!" the guard calls. "Wait here while I take the ladies to the train. We haven't much time."

Before Evan can answer, Coco strides toward him. "Our trunks are in the car. Help my driver. There are three trunks, and a valise."

"No time for that," the guard snaps. "Departure is minutes away. Unless you wish to remain in Paris, we must go. Forget the bags."

Nothing could be worse than being left behind in Paris now. "Alyce and I will go with him, Evan. Take the car back to the hotel. Tell Géraud to put the small case, the jewels, in the vault, and store the rest in my rooms."

"Are the three of you deaf?" The guard moves off and, turning, Coco and Alyce follow, half running to keep up with him. In the station the train whistle blows, two short loud blasts.

"Two minutes, mademoiselle." The guard glances over his shoulder. His voice is strained and urgent. He will not be paid by the hotel if his charges don't make the train. "Hurry! Walk faster."

Only the tops of the train carriages are visible over the heads in the frantic crowd as they exit the warehouse and step onto the platform. Alyce clings to Coco's arm and Coco pulls her along while the guard charges people in their path, shoving them aside and clearing the way. Someone yanks at her skirt, and without a pause Coco twists around, ripping the cloth from the hands as she begins running. For the last time the whistle blows—the third and final warning to board. Clouds of steam rise from the underside of the train as they race for the nearest steps.

With a last great push, the guard spreads his bulk to clear the way while Coco and Alyce scramble up the steel steps. As the train jolts and lurches forward, Coco leans against the wall catching her breath, her purse still hanging from her arm—a miracle, that! Alyce trembles beside her as the train picks up speed.

"Mademoiselle, the picnic basket!" Alyce clings to the railing with both hands as the carriages sway.

Coco envisions the carefully prepared basket of food. Peering over her shoulder into the third-class carriage she gapes at passengers stuffed like sausages in the car. They crowd seats and perch on suitcases, boxes, and sprawl along the corridor floor, taking all the space in the car. It's clear she will enjoy no five-course meal in the fine-dining car tonight, and in an instant she recalls every detail of the basket so carefully packed by Géraud. Without it they will simply starve.

Chapter Eleven

Paris to the Pyrenees
Summer 1940

Coco drags Alyce through four carriages before she locates the first-class compartment reserved for her by the Hôtel Ritz. Pushing through the door with Alyce pressing behind her, she finds the compartment occupied. A man, a workman by his clothing, and his wife are ensconced in the window seats. They both turn to her, surprised. The woman holds a child, a boy not more than sixteen months, or at most two years. He sleeps with his head in his mother's lap, his short plump legs sprawling over the empty seat beside her. To her right, leaning against the corridor wall, an old man hunches in a corner. His suit is wrinkled, his white hair askew, his head is cocked to one side while he sleeps with his mouth hanging open.

"This is a private compartment," Coco says to the workman.

He shrugs and jerks his thumb toward the empty seats beside him. "Sit there, but don't wake the boy."

"You don't understand." Coco struggles to contain her anger. "I have reserved this room. I have paid for a private compartment. You must leave."

"Knock it off," the man says in a low growl. Even in the dim light, she sees his fierce expression. He'd have fought his way through the mob to claim these seats. "If you sit quiet, you can stay. Otherwise you're both out. And don't talk to me about your money or I might decide to charge you again for the seats." A hand on his knee curls into a fist.

"I beg your pardon?"

"Listen, I've friends on this train you don't want to meet, woman." The wife reaches over the child and taps his arm. Shaking her off, he turns back to the window.

"I will not allow you to speak to me this way." Coco lifts her chin. "Who do you think you are?"

With a weary laugh as the train gathers steam, he inspects her. His eyes travel from her shoes up to her small, black half-moon hat. Coco glares back at him, fingering the pearls around her neck, the long triple strands that she always wears. "The gods are with you today," he says at last. "I'm fagged, too tired to argue. If you will just shut up and sit down, you and your maid there, I will *allow* you to stay."

She is speechless. The workman goes silent, turning to the window again. Outside, where she knows they're passing fields, villages, and towns, everything is dark. As in Paris, again, no lights. Motioning Alyce to take the seat by the stranger, she sits in the corner. The elderly man across from her still sleeps. His feet splay in the aisle between them. But even in the uncomfortable position, sitting upright, her eyes soon close. Exhaustion and the clacking rhythm of wheels on the tracks finally lull Coco to sleep.

Hours later, a jolt, and then the screech of steel on steel as the train slows, wakes her. Alyce snores, her head on Coco's shoulder. As Coco moves, the little maid's head lolls back against the wall. Amazed at the ability of the young to sleep through anything, Coco rubs her eyes, drags her fingers down her cheeks, and looks about. The workman is the only other person awake in the compartment. His face pushes against the window as he peers outside, seemingly transfixed.

She drops her hands onto her lap. "What's going on?"

"Workers along the line up ahead," he mutters, glancing over his shoulder. "They've got torches. Don't see a sign of a town though. We're nowhere. Looks like something's wrong."

Coco squints at her watch. It is dark inside and out and she cannot read the time. "Where do you think we are?"

He shrugs. "How would I know?"

The brakes squeal again as the train rolls to a stop. The man heaves to his feet, and, stepping over his sleeping wife's legs, Alyce's, Coco's, and the old man's, heads for the corridor. The door wheezes as it opens. He disappears. Coco closes her eyes. She is hungry and thirsty and every muscle aches. Ten minutes pass before the man returns, his shoulders hiked, his brow creased.

She looks up. "Well?"

He works his way back to his seat. The wife is awake now. "The tracks after Orleans are destroyed," he says.

The wife cries out.

"Demolished. Bombed to hell. The Luftwaffe has visited." As he speaks, the train begins slowly moving. "We're on our way to Tours instead, and then, God willing and if the enemy allow, to Bordeaux."

Coco's plan for refuge on the peaceful coast shatters. La Pausa is in the opposite direction. Her pulse quickens, but she says nothing. She must stay calm in order to think, to reassemble her thoughts.

She hears planes flying overhead. In the distance she sees

occasional bursts of bright light and then hears the muffled sounds of explosions. Once, the bombs come close, rocking the train. Alyce, half awake, moans, moving closer, clinging to Coco's arm.

Coco double-taps her arm. "You are damp."

"It is the heat, mademoiselle. I sweat from the heat."

She clucks her tongue. "Ladies do not sweat, my dear. Ladies glow."

The train wheels click away the minutes, then hours, and Coco gathers her thoughts while they move farther and farther from La Pausa. The town of Tours is gone, the man said. But if the tracks are clear to Bordeaux—that city is within driving distance of André's house in the Pyrenees.

As the sun rises, the child wakes and begins to cry. "Hush," his father says, but his tone is surprisingly gentle.

"He is hungry," the wife responds. She turns to Coco. "We lost everything in the crowd getting to the train."

On station platforms they pass along the way, people sleep on concrete floors, on benches, crates, steps, in doorways, on porters' carts, atop mattresses and piles of clothing and their suitcases. The train slows as it nears Tours and the whistle blows, but they don't stop. The station's glass roof overhead is gone, shattered, and the platform is buried in glass and rubble and dazed humans, some with bloody bandages wound around their heads and limbs. They run alongside the carriages waving and shouting until the train gains speed and leaves them behind.

Coco lets out a sigh of relief. This must mean the tracks between Tours and Bordeaux are intact. If they make it to Bordeaux, she will find something to eat. And then with luck she will find someone with a car and petrol, willing to drive two passengers into the mountains to André's chalet.

Farther out, beyond the Tours station, Coco sees masses of immobile vehicles—trucks, automobiles, carts, bicycles, all dead on the roads and in yards and in gardens between the houses. Perhaps, as Evan warned, the petrol's gone. And again, near the tracks thousands of people mill about, or huddle on the ground. As the town of Tours disappears behind them, for miles, thousands of makeshift camps cover what's left of the farmers' fields.

Alyce turns to Coco. "Where will we sleep when we stop, mademoiselle?"

"At the home of my nephew, André Palasse and his wife, in the foothills of the Pyrenees, if we're lucky." She pauses for a beat. "André, the son of my dead sister, Julia-Berthe. Now hush." The house was a gift to André from Auntie Coco.

She is hungry and tired. But she can feel the grade under the tracks rising. They are approaching Bordeaux.

"How long will we stay?" Alyce asks a half hour later.

Her head will explode if she's forced to consider one more problem. "Do not ask so many questions."

"Yes, mademoiselle."

They reach the station at Bordeaux midmorning. Last stop, the porter calls. With no luggage, Coco hurries Alyce along, pushing through the other passengers toward the exits, hoping to find breakfast before the rest of the hoard descends.

She is pleased to see the streets are not yet crowded. Bordeaux is not yet in the state of panic they left behind in Paris, Orleans, and Tours. A café a few blocks from the station is open, offering cheese, stale bread, and hot tea. Coco pays—fifteen francs—and afterward they walk back toward the station. Coco, longing for the bath and clean clothes she'll find at André's chalet, searches for a taxi. At last, for a price of three hundred francs, a young man with the inclination of a thief agrees to take them there.

Hours later, outside a small town in the steep hills, the taxi winds up a long, pebbled drive and rattles to a stop. Coco, exhausted, pays the sullen driver, opens the door, and climbs out, with Alyce behind her. The moment Alyce closes the door, the driver takes off. For an instant Coco sways, standing there, looking about. They've arrived, they are safe! The high rocky cliffs in the distance glisten with snow even in June. The war has not yet arrived in these mountains. Here are tall green trees—no snarling traffic, no shoving crowds.

A few seconds breathing the cool fresh air revives her spirit. Beside her, Alyce stares at the two-storied old stone house. "At last," the girl breathes. Then the front door opens and a pretty young woman comes flying down the stairs, arms stretched wide, calling to her. Coco cannot remember seeing a finer sight.

"Catharina, *ma chérie!*"

"Auntie Coco!" André's wife reaches out, pulling her close. "What a wonderful surprise. Thank the Lord, I worried you'd stay in Paris."

Coco takes her hands as Catharina kisses her cheeks. "I thought we would never arrive. We booked the express for Cannes, but the tracks were bombed at Orleans, and then again the station at Tours and ..." She pauses, pressing her hand to her forehead. Catharina slips her arms around Coco's shoulders. "Oh, I am fine now. But what a horrible experience this has been. Imagine sitting up all night with strangers. And we have no trunks, no clothes."

"Come, you must rest at once." Catharina's voice is warm as they start up the steps with Alyce close behind.

"And where are the girls? And André? Is he home?"

"Gabby and Helen are off with friends. They'll be thrilled to see you!" Catharina takes a deep breath. "I must tell you, Auntie Coco ..." She pauses. "André is not here. He was mobilized several months ago." Coco stops, turning to her in silence, and Catharina blushes. "I'm so sorry," she says. "I should have written."

Yes. You should have written.

"Have you heard from him? Is he safe?"

Her eyes drop. "I think I'd have heard if not." Coco turns cold;

her thoughts scatter as Catharina goes on. "You know how your nephew is. I've received only two letters since he left. Come," they move again toward the door. Coco's heartbeat hammers and her throat swells. She cannot speak.

For months André's been gone! Her feet turn leaden as they walk.

"It's difficult for the men to send out letters from the front," Catharina says. "In my heart I'm certain that he is well." She nods. "That is ... my prayer."

Coco stammers. "Where is he stationed?"

"His regiment fought—is fighting—near Alsace-Lorraine on the Maginot Line." The corners of Coco's mouth tremble as André's wife looks at her. "Have you, by chance, heard reports of the fighting in that region?"

"No." Her words rush out. "No one in Paris knows what is happening." Sometime, somewhere, Coco remembers hearing the Maginot Line had fallen, that it was destroyed. But that cannot be right, and she will not say the words aloud, lest they come true because of her.

Coco pulls away from Catharina—this woman who knows nothing of her real pain. Her tone is bitter. "While André is off fighting for France, Paris sits waiting for the Germans. The government has invited their armies into our city. Catharina, can you believe this?" She's talking too fast, she realizes, but she'd expected to find André here and safe. "Yes, it is true! Our brave government fled to Tours, and then to Bordeaux. Yesterday I heard bombing near Paris before we left, but the city was in chaos and we were on the train all night and I've heard nothing since."

She puts her hand to her forehead to stop the room from moving around her. The world is at war and André is in the midst of the battles. Standing here, she feels so helpless. Her pulse races, beating in her chest, her throat.

Catharina's voice comes from a distance. "Are you well, Auntie Coco? Let me show you to your rooms."

"Yes, Catharina. I would like a bath and some sleep right now. See to Alyce, will you?"

"Of course. Let me take you up. I'll have my maid tend your bath, and then you can sleep."

She must be alone right now in this house steeped with André's spirit.

Chapter Twelve

Royallieu
1905

The château was filled with Étienne's friends on the evening that turned the course of my life forever. Everyone was there to celebrate Étienne's latest win at Longchamp's racecourse in Paris. It was a beautiful night. The guests were out on the terrace drinking champagne and watching the sun set over the hills of the Compiègne.

Inside, in the gloaming of the library, Boy and I lay together on a settee, his body warm and hard against mine. Four months earlier we'd first made love by the stream, and the days since were the happiest in my life. I'd never felt so loved. Boy filled me with joy. Even my body was different, more sensitive to his touch—my breasts plumper, my flesh soft and smooth as cream, my belly starting to swell.

Boy loved me, he swore each time we were together. We are interlocked souls in the spiritual world, he would say, we are one. Theosophy, he called this idea of unseen connections. I had been reading everything he gave me on the subject, studying hard, and I was finally beginning to understand his profound ideas. I trusted him completely. I believed in Boy Capel and everything he'd taught me. Boy was the first man I'd ever loved.

And the last.

That evening as we lay on the settee, with Boy propped on his elbow while bending over me and brushing hair back from my forehead, I heard footsteps coming down the hallway. Boy's shirt was open and his trousers lose and unbuttoned, as was my blouse. Feeling languid in a flushed, lovely haze, I wasn't quick enough to warn him or to move. When the door creaked open, we both jumped. Boy twisted around to see, and I pushed up behind him, peering over his shoulder.

Étienne stood in the doorway, arms dangling at his sides, staring.

In one smooth motion Boy sat up, swiveled, and swung his feet to the floor. My mind went blank. As Boy began buttoning his shirt, I scooted up and sat behind him. Without moving my eyes from Étienne, I pulled my blouse together, covering my breasts, a sight that Étienne had seen before. My hair was disheveled, hanging long and loose over my shoulders as though we'd been caught tumbling in the hay instead of a library. I looked a mess, I knew. It seemed an eternity had passed since Étienne opened that door. From outside I heard cicadas singing the sun down, as though everything was fine in the world. I could hear the horses snorting in the stables while they settled in for the night, and a dog barking in the distance. Now and then, explosions of shrill laughter came from the terrace.

Étienne's recovery was faster than ours. "Sorry to disturb you," he said, stepping into the room. "I was looking for my pipe." I followed his eyes to a table near the settee between the windows and the bookshelves. On top were his pipe, several small crystal glasses, and a bottle of port.

I said nothing, longing to disappear.

Boy slapped both hands on his knees. "Well come in, Étienne." His tone was too hearty.

Étienne crossed the room, picked up his pipe, turned back toward the door, and then, changing his mind, fell into a chair facing us. While I buttoned my blouse, he ducked his head, taking some time with the business of a pipe, tamping the bowl against the palm of his hand and bending to light it. Boy buckled his pants and tugged on his boots. Then he moved aside and I sat next to him. Étienne sank back in the chair and, gazing at the ceiling, took a long, deep draw of the pipe.

My first coherent thought was this: Étienne will now ask me to leave Royallieu, my only home. And I could not let that happen.

Plucking a piece of tobacco from his lip, Étienne finally looked at us. He reached for the bottle of port and poured two fingers into each of two glasses. Then he glanced at me, raising a brow, but I shook my head.

Étienne extended his hand and Boy rose to take the glass, returning to sit and landing a few feet from me this time. They drank in silence. The voices outside now seemed far away. The sun sank below the horizon and the room was filled with shadows. The only sound for a few minutes was the ticking of the grandfather clock in the corner.

The time had come, I realized.

Étienne broke the silence. "Well," he said. "Do you love her?"

Boy's voice beside me was steady, confident. "Yes."

Étienne's eyes shifted between the two of us for an instant. Then, tipping back his head, he downed the rest of the port. Lifting the glass in our direction, he looked at Boy and said, "All right, then, Capel. I give her to you."

The earth's firmament rocked beneath me. I looked at Boy. He merely nodded, as if the transaction was sealed.

I turned to Étienne in disbelief but saw no evidence of outrage in his face. Twisting my hands in the hem of my blouse, I fought down the rising fury. How dare they barter me like that?

Infuriated, I stood up, lifting a finger. "I beg your pardon, gentlemen," I said, looking from one to the other. "But I'm not a tasty treat to pass around your table."

Boy's eyes grew wide. "Coco, that's not what we meant."

Étienne's brows drew together. He looked bemused. "Of course not, *petite amie*," he said in his gentleman's tone—so steady, so polite. He dipped his chin, watching me. "I should have asked."

"Listen," Boy interjected. "I bear the blame, Étienne. I should have told you at once."

Étienne ignored him. With smoke drifting from a corner of his mouth, he said, "Coco, do you love him?"

"Of course I do," I said. I bent, picking up my shoes, avoiding his eyes to hide the anger building inside. When I straightened, arms dangling with a shoe in each hand, with my blouse hanging loose over my skirt, and my tousled hair and my lips swollen from Boy's kisses, all I could think was that Boy had not yet said one word of marriage, nor about taking me under his wing. He'd not given a thought to the consequences when Étienne found out about us. I glared at one, then the other. Neither man had ever been without the necessities of life—a roof, a bed, a meal.

That's when the idea came. My secret would save me.

"I do love Boy," I repeated. "And I love you too, Étienne, in a different way. But neither of you has a say in my future at the moment. Even if I wanted, I could not leave Royallieu right now." I paused, gathering my courage as these two fine fellows stared at me, waiting.

"I cannot leave Royallieu yet, because I am ... as they say, with child." And before either man could ask, I added, "And one of you is the father."

Boy choked.

Étienne set down the glass on the table beside him.

"When is it due?" Etienne finally asked.

I had seen a midwife in the nearby village. I tossed my head. "Five months, or thereabouts." I could almost see the calculations running in his head. The timing was ambiguous, with the date of conception around the time I'd left Étienne's bed for Boy's. I looked at Boy and saw the question in his eyes too. But I was in no frame of mind to tell either one the truth. I reminded myself how both had sent me off with Émilienne on the weekend of the ball.

I longed to marry Boy, but both pride and fear guided me now—he had to ask the question on his own. Boy had sworn he loved me, but I also knew a mistress could be left behind. What if I told him he was the father and he walked away? Papa had sworn he loved me too. And he'd left.

So, I had hedged my bets. Until Boy asked me to marry him, I knew I wasn't safe. I needed Étienne. He was a friend, but I was not above using him if I must. Without Boy, Royallieu was my only home. And this way, if neither man was certain, I guessed both would help.

This was harsh, I knew. Really, it wasn't my fault. I was just a girl and they were men.

The months sped by. Boy did not ask the question I longed to hear, but he treated me tenderly, pampering me. Étienne, too, took great interest in how I felt, imagined scenarios of whether the baby was a boy or girl and when would it appear in this world. Did I need a cushion to support my back when we sat at the table? Should I still be riding? Étienne assigned a maid to assure my comfort, and a driver for trips to see the midwife. For someone outside our little family of three, it would have been difficult to discern which of the two men was the father of the child.

For my part, I kept up the charade. I knew the baby was Boy's, but weeks passed and still no mention of marriage. At first, I felt desperate, frightened, angry, hurt. But I kept these feelings inside. I fought them until gradually I realized that this tedious self-pity was shading the joy I should be feeling as a mother. After all, I had two men I loved—in different ways—caring for me. And Royallieu was still my home, as Étienne had promised.

I convinced myself that the deadline I'd set for Boy to ask me to marry him was a false one. Boy's love was real, I told myself. I would be patient. I would remain calm. In time we would marry and create our family. I was certain of it. Our love was real.

At Royallieu, together with Émilienne, and my personal maid, we kept the secret. I was small. I loosened the jodhpurs, let my shirt hang out. I all but disappeared into the library for the last two months, working on a study Boy had set for me, I said.

When the water breaks, the midwife had warned, your time has come. My water had broken that morning, and yet there I was, hours later, still writhing on that bed, doubled over each time the waves of pain spiked through me, again and again and again. It was too much; I wanted nothing more than to die. I begged the Lord for grace, to let me start over from the beginning and live in a convent.

Boy stayed in the bedroom with me at first. Étienne had chosen to wait in the library. I'd refused to lie down in the bed—the pain was worse that way, all stretched out. But the midwife was growing irritable. Between the waves of pain I huddled against Boy, who sat behind me, leaning against the headboard with his strong arms and legs curled around me.

I remember when things changed. I'd heard the clock in the hallway strike two in the morning when suddenly a dagger ripped through me. I think I screamed—this one was worse, much worse.

"Mademoiselle!" the midwife cried, hurrying to my side. Ignoring Boy she clasped my shoulders, shaking me now as she leaned so close that I could smell her cabbage breath. She said the time had come, that I must lie down now to birth the baby. Behind me, Boy shifted, and I whimpered as he struggled to free his arms and legs, even while I clung to him.

"Come now," madame barked in an angry tone, holding on to my arms. "I insist, mademoiselle. Lie down at once. At once, or I will not answer for the baby's health! And the gentleman must leave."

"Do as she says, Coco." Boy was free now, and off the bed. As I reached for him, crying, the midwife pushed my shoulders down and pulled my legs from under me.

"Boy!" I turned my head, my eyes begging him to stay.

"Monsieur!" Arms akimbo, the midwife stepped between us. "You must go. You will bring bad luck."

Moving around her, Boy bent and kissed my forehead. Then, untangling himself from my arms, he escaped.

I don't remember much until after the baby came. I remember the midwife forcing my legs apart, pushing up my knees, and the pain, the pain, the hard, exquisite pain, and then Émilienne's voice murmuring in my ear, and her scent of soap and old roses. Sweet, beautiful Émilienne holding me while I wept, feeling a knife splitting my body in two, and after that, through a long, raw trail of pain I recall madame's voice urging me to push, to push—coddling, commanding—push, push!

It was the baby's wail, a strong, demanding cry that told me it was over. I must have fallen asleep then. When I awoke, there were Émilienne and Boy and Étienne, all three standing by the bed and smiling. The midwife stood beside them holding a tiny bundle of blue blankets in her arms.

"A boy?" I asked.

She nodded. I held out my arms and she gave him to me. His

eyes were closed as he slept, but he snuggled against me and a little shudder ran through him. Gently, I touched the tip of my son's nose, ran my finger over his soft red cheeks, kissed his forehead, and pulled him close. At that moment, a feeling swelled inside like nothing I'd ever felt before. *This child is mine.*

He was perfect. I held him in my arms, his delicate head nuzzling bare skin in the curve of my neck. I touched the fine wisps of hair and nuzzled the top of his head. He gave off a yeasty, powdery scent that transformed my dreams, replacing the old ones with new desires, a new kind of wanting. This child must have the best life. I would love and protect my boy. Looking down at him sleeping, I prayed joy for him, and peace and comfort. He would always be safe, he would always be healthy and happy and full of life.

And with his mother and two fathers, he would always be secure.

I named him André, because I knew no one by that name. Even when Boy and I married, André would be my secret—my nephew I would say, son of my poor dead sister, Julia-Berthe. That way my child would never be branded a bastard. He was my secret, and Étienne and Boy's.

Étienne said that he would find someone to vouch as the father, someone claiming he was the widower of Julia-Berthe. He could write a letter to that effect. That would do.

How was I to know this new consuming love, this sweet, sweet love I felt for my baby in that moment, was the beginning of the end for any chance of happiness, and not the other way around?

Part Two

Chapter Thirteen

Paris
Summer 1940

On June 14, 1940, Paris falls silent as the Germans arrive. From an alley off the Champs-Élysées, Alain, wearing workman's clothes and a billed cap pulled low over his forehead, watches triumphant Wehrmacht soldiers goose-stepping in lines of eight down the avenue behind their generals, followed by a barrage of monstrous ironclad tanks and canon. Citizens, drawn by curiosity or defiance, gather in small groups on the pavements and balconies along the route. Most are stone-faced, some quietly weep. Alain is surprised to see three ladies nearby clapping gloved hands while the soldiers pass.

Stores around the city are closed, windows boarded. It's almost impossible to believe what he sees before him—Paris, taken without a fight! The hot and heavy air still thick with smoke and ash closes in around him, almost smothering. Sweat trickles down his neck, dampening his shirt, itching. Alain ignores the discomfort, overcome with rage at the cowards running the city who fled when the enemy approached. His eyes fall on an old man standing erect at the curb, watching. An old soldier from the Great War—the war to end all wars they'd called it. The old man's head is high, but his arms hang limp at his sides. His eyes follow the field of gray-green Wehrmacht uniforms moving down the boulevard. The old man's proud face contorts with grief, tears streaming.

After they're gone Alain works his way back across the river to his rooms. He averts his eyes from the sight of soldiers already tearing the flags of France from buildings, monuments, the Louvre, the bridges over the Seine, raising the black, red, and white swastika instead. By the time he reaches the Pont Neuf, the Nazi flag flies even from the towers of Notre-Dame. The enemy's efficiency stuns him. They were well prepared for a quick occupation. On the Left Bank, fliers announcing a curfew are nailed everywhere—on doors, windows, posts, boards. Citizens must clear the streets by seven o'clock, German time. All clocks in Paris must be set ahead one hour in accordance with the invaders' watches.

By dusk Alain is in his rooms, slumped on the chair beside the window, elbows resting on the windowsill, his head in his hands. Minutes pass, then, straightening, he drags his hands down his face and looks out the window, turning all he's seen today over in his mind. He struggles to accept that the City of Light is now governed by the Reich. This is a day he will never forget.

Electricity in Paris has been cut off by order of the Reich. As darkness descends, a black Citroën trolls the street below. The Gestapo—everyone knows they prefer a Citroën. Alain eyes them with hatred; they'll be the ones soon rounding up Jews. His people. He watches the automobile until it is out of sight.

At midnight on this June 14, the deepest, largest bells of Notre-Dame—the ancient Emmanuel, weighing over thirteen tons—toll the city's sorrow in F-sharp. Alain listens as the mournful sound rings out over the city, loud enough even to be heard in the suburbs. Citizens will weep when they hear them tolling on this day. Slowly he heaves himself from the chair, wondering if he'll ever hear those bells again.

Like a somnolent waking from a trance, Paris slowly rises from the sick bed over the next few days, shuffles out into the gray dawn and takes full measure of the city's downfall. The curfew remains in place, although there is a rumor that the occupiers will extend it to nine o'clock if citizens remain calm. Food and wine are scarce. The Boche requisition every vehicle with an engine and wheels. That does not much matter since they've taken all the petrol too. Citizens are required to turn in their automobiles at once. Bicycles are now treasures.

A grocery market in Alain's neighborhood pulls up the shutters and opens doors. The shelves inside are almost empty, and prices have quadrupled. Francs are losing value against the reichsmark and grocers want to see the German mark, not the falling franc. Alain has some gold, brought along for such a situation, but he hikes halfway across Paris to purchase food with it. Gold would label him with suspicion in his neighborhood. Worse, change comes in francs. And the bread is already stale, the wine sour, meat and vegetables spoiling. Real coffee, unless you've funds to drink in cafés catering to the Germans—even if a Frenchman ventures in—is nonexistent.

Every second day since the Boche arrived in Paris, Alain strolls across the river to the offices of BancLeval. He's hoping Henri's Swiss citizenship will allow the banker to return soon to his office in Paris. While he waits, his American passport is hidden in the valise. Walking around without identity papers is a risk, but producing a passport bearing a known Jewish name is worse. He's in danger until he receives the new papers Leval will provide.

One ordinary afternoon, he pulls the cap low on his forehead for the usual trudge and makes his way down the building's dark stairway into the street. As almost always, the street is deserted. Alain assumes a neutral expression. Hands in his pockets, he strolls along whistling a tune. He is a block from his building when he hears a car turning behind him onto the street. Immediately he tenses. Only the Boche drive automobiles in Paris these days. Keeping his head down as the car moves close, he searches for any avenue of escape ahead—an alleyway between buildings, an open entrance to a building, stairs to a cellar.

The engine hums and the Citroën slows behind him. Pulling his hands from his pockets—*see, hands free, no weapon here*—Alain keeps to his pace. There! Ahead he spots an opening between two buildings. It's twenty, maybe thirty yards ahead. Still the car trails, engine purring. Eyes burn into his back.

The alley could be a dead end. Or it could be open, an escape. Should he take the chance and run? Or continue on and hope for the best? It they are Gestapo, they could be playing him right now, hawks with a mouse.

The Citroën accelerates, pulling up alongside him. Sweat rolls down his neck. Doing what any man would do, Alain glances at the car. From the window glacial eyes examine him. The eyes seal his decision. The Gestapo mean business. They will stop him soon—demand his papers and take him in when he gives his excuse. And if they discover he's a Jew—despite the ringing silence of news reporters and politicians in Paris and Manhattan, he's heard the stories filtering out of Germany, Poland, Austria. Every Jew has heard the stories.

With a brief nod, Alain shifts his eyes so he's looking ahead again. The alley is at most fifteen yards away. He'll take a chance; he has no choice. The good luck is there are only two in the car. He can take them if they come at him together—before they draw the guns.

He takes a long deep breath. Almost time. At the alley entrance, he'll wheel to his right. If it's a dead end, he'll stand and fight. Anything is better than capture. He focuses, preparing to run. Eight yards now, seven—he tenses, five yards, adrenaline racing.

The unexpected sound of the car accelerating startles and he sucks in his breath, almost stopping as the Citroën flies past him, engine whining. Without breaking stride, Alain watches the car, walking on, forcing one foot in front of the other as the Citroën disappears down the street. Where the pavement ends at the corner of a cross street, he stops. Glancing back over his shoulder, he wipes his forehead. With a shrug, Alain sticks his hands in his pockets and turns, walking on through the quiet, deserted area.

Five minutes later he rounds the corner onto boulevard Saint-Germain and stops dead. Lifting his cap, he stares, blinking in disbelief. Pavestones shimmer in the June heat, even under the shady chestnut trees. Soldiers in Wehrmacht uniforms swarm in every direction. Ahead at the river, more soldiers flow over the Pont Neuf, spilling onto the avenue and the river quay. They mill about on the pavements and streets and in the open-air cafés, which are now festooned with colorful balloons bobbing on their strings, pitiful offerings from conquered Paris.

These are not the grim soldiers he'd watched marching down the Champs-Élysées a few weeks ago, he realizes. A holiday spirit permeates this scene, creating a surreal mosaic. These conquerors stroll along eating ice cream, posing for pictures, singing, laughing, while a stone's throw away behind the shops and cafés, hungry Parisians hunker down, waiting, terrified of what may come. Five soldiers come toward him arm in arm, harmonizing while blocking the street ahead. Alain steps aside. This is the song they sing everywhere: "Horst-Wessel-Lied"—it seems to wind them up. When the soldiers have passed, Alain hurries on, head ducked, eyes narrow, alert for trouble.

A few weeks later, Henri returns to Paris. "It's good to see you again. Sorry for my delay. With the reichsmark climbing and the French franc in free-fall, Paris welcomes Swiss bankers." He pauses. "Although getting back to Zurich tomorrow won't be easy either."

The day is dark and gloomy, slightly chilled for the middle of July. Outside, rain beats against the windowpanes. They sit in matching blue leather chairs facing each other before an unlit fireplace. Henri shifts in his seat, resting his arms on the chair, regarding Alain. "So, you've kept safe I see. How is Paris?"

"The city's adjusting, so far. But worse is coming, I suspect. People are worn out. They're angry, frightened. Worse, they are hungry. The Boche confiscate everything but shoes and underwear." His expression is grim. "It's for the war effort, they say, but everyone knows it's all shipped out to the Fatherland. My guess is this is just the beginning."

Henri nods. "Hitler's initial reparations for Germany's costs incurred."

"Worse, word is food rations are next. They'll be set at starvation levels. Even people with money are worried." At the thought of food Alain's stomach rumbles.

"Oh!" Henri slaps his hands on the chair. "I should have thought—you must eat. One moment, Alain. I'll ask my secretary to bring something." He smiles, preparing to rise. "And a cup of real coffee; I brought it with me from Geneva."

Alain shakes his head. "Later, thanks. Let's finish our business first. Time is short." He holds Henri's eyes. "Has Pierre filled you in?"

Henri nods, gesturing toward a heavy mahogany paneled desk set before two long windows overlooking the street. "I've prepared the trust agreement and ancillary documents in accordance with his instructions. You will see that Pierre has designated a fellow named Félix Amiot as trustee. Amiot is a Swiss citizen, and he has already signed. All that's left is your execution of the documents on behalf of Pierre and his brother." He gazes at Alain. "Of course, I understand the trust agreement is confidential. I assure you, not even my secretary knows of its existence. No one knows but you, me, and the parties to the agreement."

"Fine. That's as Pierre would have it."

Henri hesitates, then cocks his head. "I presume you've brought along the instructions and powers of attorney authorizing you to sign for the Monsieurs Wertheimer?"

Reaching into his jacket, Alain hands over a leather folder containing the papers.

"Good then." Henri rises, heading toward his desk, and Alain follows. Rain pelts the glass panes behind the desk as Henri takes his seat. Alain settles in a chair facing him, watching in silence as Henri retrieves the papers from the folder and begins to read. Outside, lightning flashes, and then comes a long roll of thunder.

Henri looks up, seeming satisfied. "As you may know, Pierre has already transferred the money to Amiot's account in Geneva. Under the trust agreement, if necessary, during Nazi occupation, Amiot will use the funds as he sees fit to take full control of Société Mademoiselle, and other Wertheimer property in Europe, like the factory in Neuilly. He is Aryan, you understand." Alain nods. "And, he can be trusted. Félix Amiot will never reveal the existence of this agreement to anyone other than the signatories.

"After the war ends …" Henri pauses, looking off for an instant before turning his eyes back to Alain. "Then, well, we shall see. But Amiot has agreed to return ownership of the company to Pierre anytime upon his demand. This also is confidential."

"Yes. I understand."

"There are certainly risks involved. But given the German laws on Jews in other occupied territories …"

"Pierre has no choice."

Taking a deep breath, Henri sets the powers of attorney aside. "Good. Then all is in order. The trust agreement will be held in our Geneva vault." Sliding a pen and two stacks of papers across the desk to Alain, he says, "You may execute these. One set for Pierre and one for Monsieur Amiot."

Twenty minutes later, Alain puts down the pen. Henri reaches for the signed papers and taps them on the desktop, squaring the edges.

"On another matter," Alain says, feeling relaxed now. "Have you managed to secure that supply of oils Pierre needs for the perfumes—the rose, and, most important, the jasmine absolute?"

"Yes, rose was no problem. The jasmine supply, however, is limited." He spreads his hands. "Everyone's worried with the war on, and this close to the harvest season. I was able to obtain some from Grasse, and a smaller amount from the House of Besse, a family farm nearby. The product from Grasse will ship right away. The Besse oils will ship after the summer harvest, through Marseille."

"Good." Pierre will be pleased. "And my new papers?"

Reaching into the desk drawer, Henri pulls out a thick packet and slides it over to Alain. "You are now Peter Gnann, citizen of Switzerland and vice president of BancLeval. In here are your Swiss passport issued in Geneva, your identity card, and a few other things." As Alain picks up the package, Henri smiles, rubbing his hands together. "Now, how about that cup of coffee and something to eat."

"Wonderful. Thanks."

Alain sorts through the documents, while Henri rises and walks out to speak with his secretary. When he returns, Alain places the papers back in the packet, and the packet down on the desk before him.

"Greta's preparing coffee and cake," Henri says, sitting down again. He nods toward the papers. "Now, Alain, you'll get out through Spain. I don't know how much you've heard, but the new military administration has divided France into a northern zone which they occupy, including, as you know, Paris, and a so-called unoccupied free zone in the south. There's a demarcation line between the two zones where you'll be searched and questioned when you travel. A new southern-zone government was just formed in Vichy. However, be on your guard even after you cross the line—Vichy is a puppet, under tight German control—even if everyone pretends otherwise."

Nodding toward the packet of documents, he adds, "Inside you'll also find your *ausweis*, the German pass required to travel across the demarcation line. Also, your entry visa for Spain. After you cross the Spanish border, of course, you will use your US passport."

"Thanks." Alain slips the packet into an inner jacket pocket.

"Greta will provide a map of Geneva when you leave. Study it, Peter Gnann. The location of your residence there is circled. You'll recognize the area. I understand you know the city well, but, be prepared for questions. Be aware they could demand papers anywhere—at any railway station, random checks on the train, at the demarcation line, as well as at the border crossing. Study the map of your home in Switzerland—as usual, you'll likely be questioned."

"All right."

"We've made reservations for you on the morning train, if that's convenient?" Alain nods. "Yes, we thought you might be more than ready to leave."

"Correct." Alain's smile is wry. He's carried out several covert assignments for Pierre, but this one is probably the worst.

"You will take the train to the border crossing at Hendaye, five hundred miles. You will depart from the Gare d'Austerlitz in the morning. The train will stop at the demarcation line for inspection of your papers, then on to Hendaye. At the border you'll be searched twice before entering Spain. First, by the Wehrmacht, then the Spanish guards. After, from Hendaye you'll catch the train to Madrid. The American Embassy is expecting you there. They'll book your passage back to the United States."

Alain lifts his brows. "Are you certain the trains are running? I heard rail lines were destroyed by the Luftwaffe at Orleans and Tours during the fighting."

"They were." With a glance at the door, Henri lowers his voice. "But we are in luck, my friend. Line repairs are suddenly a priority for the Reich. From Paris to Hendaye, a track has already been repaired." He pauses, watching Alain. "What I'm about to tell you is strictly between us."

"Of course."

"Swiss intelligence tells us Hitler's train will soon travel from Berlin to Hendaye, where he will meet with Spain's General Franco. We don't yet know the date. So, it's good you're getting out of Paris before security intensifies."

"Yes."

Henri spreads his hands on the desktop. "We believe this meeting with Franco is an attempt to bully the dictator. Hitler is determined Spain will join the Axis powers."

"I never thought I would say this, but it will be a pleasure to leave Paris."

Henri sits back, clasping his hands before him. "Things can only get worse for France, you know, even in the south. Vichy officials are already groveling under the boot. What they call cooperation is no more than complete surrender to German rule." He shakes his head. "So stay alert. Don't let down your guard once, Alain. Not here in Paris, nor on the train, and not after you cross the demarcation line into the southern zone."

"I will take care. And, thanks, my friend." Just as Alain's stomach growls, the door opens and along with the secretary, the fragrance of real coffee and food enters the room.

Chapter Fourteen

Paris
Summer 1940

After languishing in the Pyrenees for what seems an eternity, in mid-July Coco accepts a ride with her attorney's parents, Clara and Aldebert de Chambrun, traveling from Bordeaux to the town of Vichy, where the new French administration sits. In Vichy she will obtain a travel pass permitting her return to Paris. It seems her attorney, René de Chambrun, now has high connections in the new government of southern France, which answers—indirectly, they say—to the Führer. His father-in-law, Pierre Laval, has just been named deputy prime minister of Vichy. And so the elderly couple is blessed with an automobile and petrol rations for the drive.

It is strange, but Coco is relieved to depart André's villa. Catharina has done her best to make Coco comfortable during the visit. And the girls, especially little Gabby—her favorite—are a pleasure. But constant worry over André prevented Coco from any thought of relaxing in the countryside. Perhaps in Vichy, miles away from the villa infused with fear for her son, she will feel calmer, more in control.

Vichy is a surprise, the town surreal. Once a sleepy spa from the belle epoque, a watering place for the old and rich, Vichy is swollen with people seemingly unaffected by the war. An armistice has been declared, and France is no more than a state of Germany. No one in Vichy seems concerned. Here, thoughts of war carry the weight of feathers. Here, ladies still wear colorful silks and ribbons, regardless of the fabric requisitions. Here, they sip champagne and gossip the hours away in outdoor cafés. In Vichy, the cafés and restaurants flourish, bandstands and parks are jumping, and music halls and gambling casinos house government business.

At the Hôtel du Parc, Coco is informed that every hotel in Vichy is full. However, exceptions will be made for Mademoiselle Chanel, and Monsieur and Madame Chambrun.

And it is here Coco learns the Reich has indeed commandeered the Hôtel Ritz in Paris, as she'd expected all along. A telephone call to Géraud at the Ritz, on a private line reserved for officers and diplomats, confirms that mademoiselle remains an approved resident of the Ritz, although she will now reside in a smaller suite on the third floor. Her own rooms have been requisitioned for a senior military officer of the Reich. However, Géraud assures Coco that she may retain her private table in the grand dining room, near the windows overlooking the Place Vendôme.

Coco longs for Paris—for the familiar sounds of the city, for the comforting surroundings of the Ritz and her Maison. She longs for the days before the war, when André managed her fabric mills, before the materials were taken by French forces for the damned parachutes and uniforms. Her patience is limited—she must find André, she must take control of the plant in Neuilly and production of No. 5, she must deal with Pierre's treachery. Every minute ticking by while she waits in Vichy is a minute lost.

Days pass, and then at last René's father-in-law remembers her request. She is given the *ausweis* necessary for her return to Paris.

Coco is not the only outsider invited to stay at the Ritz after the Germans move in. The beautiful film star known by only one name—Arletty—remains in residence. And also Daisy Fellowes, the Singer sewing machine heiress, despite the claim she's related to Winston Churchill by marriage. And Laura Mae St. James is here, too, although the wealthy American heiress was kicked up to the third floor like Coco, to make room for Reich Marshal Hermann Göring in the Imperial Suite. Laura Mae says her move was arranged so quickly she hadn't even time to remove her collection of emeralds from the safe. With the help of a friend, she only just managed to move the huge armoire over to hide it before she was evicted. She's praying Reich Marshal Göring does not find the secret safe.

Laura Mae says the hotel is busy installing a massive tub for Göring in the old suite, in which he will loll for hours sipping champagne. Only Laura Mae would pass along gossip like that about Hitler's second in command. Coco smiles at the thought—indeed, Göring is rotund.

Since she's returned, from time to time Coco catches bits and pieces of conversation among the hotel staff which are irritating—complaints of hunger in the city streets, empty store shelves, closed markets, and even if you've the luck to find a loaf of bread it's priced in reichsmarks, which no citizen owns. The franc is worth nothing!

But Coco does not believe these rumors. Proof otherwise is right before her eyes. The Ritz has electricity, lights, fans, and heat, and the workers who are complaining—the maids, butlers, porters, and waiters here—still have their jobs, do they not? Many, like Alyce, live in opulent staff quarters. Yes, the occupation is inconvenient, but life continues. Not much has changed within the walls of the Ritz, except the occupants. Breakfast, lunch, and dinner are served as always in the hotel dining room, although Coco prefers her breakfast in bed. The Ritz still hires the finest chefs in France; good wine is still served. Her new rooms are smaller, yes, and without a balcony, but just as comfortable. The truth is—after the initial terror, which emptied Paris in June, things are returning to normal.

If not for worries over André, and of course Pierre's latest trick, she'd be fairly content. German Ambassador Otto Abetz—a dear acquaintance for years—is attempting to ease her burdens a bit. The ambassador has saved her little blue Rolls from requisition—that's something, at least. And she's been issued generous petrol rations. Even with the occupiers in charge, she has only to ring the front desk and Evan, or whoever is on duty when he goes home, arrives with her car.

Besides, even if the staff rumors are true, what can one woman do? If in fact people are suffering in Paris, she can change nothing. Events are out of her control. Boy always cautioned her against worrying over things she cannot change. And truly, she has neither the time nor energy to focus on strangers right now—she must find André. His suffering is real. This she feels in every fiber of her being. This she understands.

You have grown hard over the years, Coco.

No. The Nazis are in charge. This is how I survive.

A recent meeting with her banker confirmed her suspicions—her Paris account balance is falling. No. 5 still sells in Paris and Germany, for those with reichsmarks. But no funds have been received from foreign sales in over a month. It is as she'd thought. Pierre has cut her out of the business. Worse, thanks to this war, her banker advises that access to money in her Swiss accounts is prohibited under the new German laws. So, as if worrying about her son's very existence is not enough, she must quickly deal with Pierre.

René de Chambrun remains absent, off on some mysterious diplomatic mission his secretary won't explain. Coco burns with impatience. To protect her perfume interests she must file a case in the courts immediately against Pierre. Every day the lawyer dawdles is another day which benefits Pierre. Pacing her rooms, Coco telephones René's office each day to no avail.

You are obsessed, just as you were with Boy Capel.

Quiet!

Chapter Fifteen

Paris
Summer 1940

With reichsmarks and francs in his pocket and the identity papers Henri has provided, Alain hurries back to his rooms from BancLeval. It's near the end of June, later than he'd planned, for certain. But tomorrow morning he will leave. He checks the lining of the valise, assuring the US passport and formula are hidden safe, and then smooths the lining so the cut remains invisible.

Glancing at his watch, he clicks on the wireless radio, keeping the volume low. Radios are now forbidden in Paris. The drums signaling the nightly BBC broadcast sound: *dit, dit, dit, dah*— three short beats and one long one, drawn out—as in the first four notes of Beethoven's Fifth Symphony. In Morse code the four beats are the letter *v*, for *victory*.

Alain sits on the floor beneath the window, listening. The bland BBC voice announces the arrival of ten pounds of potatoes at Marseille two nights ago, and then, that various nightingales are singing. Open code for the newborn French Resistance. The voice takes on a harder, more urgent tone after those first messages, reporting on the nightly bombing raids on London. Then Charles de Gaulle begins to speak, the general no one knew before this war. He's rallying the French, urging French soldiers and sailors evacuated from Dunkirk and now on British soil, to join him, to continue the fight for France.

He snaps off the wireless radio. The fight could take years, and meanwhile what will happen to the Jews? Not just those in France, but all of Europe. Lying on the mattress with one arm thrown over his eyes, Alain tells himself that he's not a traitor to his people for returning to the lights and luxury of New York.

With a heavy feeling of guilt, he thinks of how easy life is in America, even as Nazi evil rages through Europe. While Paris suffers, New York is a city of laughter, music, light. His apartment in the Plaza Hotel is warm in winter and cooled by the park breeze in summer. It's filled with bright sunlight from large windows overlooking Central Park during the day, and muted electric light at night—no need for blackout rules in Manhattan. Automobiles glide through streets with plenty of unrestricted petrol, sidewalk cafés and nightclubs are bustling, Broadway is hopping. Girls still smile and flirt with a guy, not having to wonder if he's Gestapo. Girls like Letty.

He thinks of Letty's bright blue eyes, her short, bobbed hair swinging when she dances, as if she has not one care in the world. As if she has never had a care in the world.

This afternoon he saw desperate men, even some women, digging through garbage cans, hunting for food. He'd had to look away. Why, restaurants in the Plaza and up and down the avenues at home are open at almost any time of day or night. There's no food shortage in New York.

Above all, New York welcomes any religion—Jews, Christian, Hindu, Muslim, Buddhist. Any religion is welcome in New York City.

One side of the Atlantic is alive, crackling with excitement and opportunity. Across the ocean, almost all of Europe is dark, struggling to live.

He should be looking forward to getting back to the city.

So, why is he feeling shame instead?

Twenty-four hours later, the station in Hendaye swarms with people, all moving toward the border crossing into Spain. The station, located in the foothills of the Pyrenees, in Basque country on the Atlantic coast, is dark, but bustling. As Alain steps from the Paris train with Peter Gnann's papers in his pockets, Wehrmacht soldiers on the platform eye him.

Ignoring the soldiers, he walks along the platform toward the station house where a crowd swells before a line of doors. Behind those doors are more guards—German, then Spanish, as Henri said—and beyond is Spain, and freedom. The combination of traveling with a neutral Swiss passport and in the first-class railway carriage has insulated Alain somewhat from the harassment other citizens endured during the trip. He's encountered only two casual inspections of his papers and bags so far, one in Paris before boarding, the other at the demarcation line. BancLeval carries weight in France, or so it seems.

Now, striding casually along the station platform, valise and suitcase in hand, Alain scans the area ahead. Regardless of his good luck so far, there will be questions and thorough searches of his bags by the German border guards. The train whistle sounds, the first signal echoing through the chilly station for return to Bordeaux, Tours, Paris.

Reaching the restless crowd, Alain steps aside as a grumbling old man shoves in front of him, followed by his wife, dragging a suitcase behind her. Ahead people haul trunks, suitcases, boxes, crates along with them as they shuffle slowly toward the checkpoint. These travelers do not wait quietly in lines, but maintain a constant flow of nervous energy, swarming for a door each time one opens, pushing and shoving into opening spaces, jabbing elbows, calling out to one another.

An hour later, Alain still waits, inching slowly forward each time another soul disappears behind the doors. At last one opens before him and he's motioned inside. A gray-green uniform pats him down, then nods, gesturing for him to step ahead. Another guard extends his hand, demanding papers.

His stomach tightens. This is it. Alain sets the suitcase and valise on the floor and hands over Peter Gnann's passport, identity card, visa, and travel permit. Someone grabs the luggage, swinging the bags up onto a long table a few feet away. Both bags are locked. The soldier turns to Alain, snapping his fingers. "Open them."

Alain unlocks the valise and suitcase and steps back. A voice behind him barks, "Turn around," and before he can move a baton slaps his thigh. Turning, his eyes flick from the guard with the baton, to an officer now flipping through his passport. A lieutenant, by his uniform. Alain waits, counting numbers in his mind to maintain a blank expression, while the lieutenant studies each page in silence. At last the man closes the passport, scans the visa, and looks up.

His light-blue eyes are suspicious and hard. "Your name."

"Peter Gnann."

"You are a citizen of Switzerland?"

"That is correct."

The lieutenant looks down again at the passport. "Residence?"

Alain gives the address.

"Occupation."

"Vice president, BancLeval, Geneva."

The officer fixes his eyes on Alain's. The guard with the baton stands beside him. "What is your business in Spain, Monsieur Gnann?"

"I'm on my way to Madrid, to our offices there."

"What is the exact nature of your business in Madrid, Monsieur Gnann?"

"Exchange currencies, at the moment, sir." He meets the officer's eyes without blinking. "It seems the reichsmark has overwhelmed the French franc. BancLeval is working to protect Spain's currency from the same fall."

The lieutenant snaps the passport shut. "Raise your arms."

Slowly Alain raises his arms, palms out. Over the officer's shoulder he can see the soldier lifting the lid on his suitcase. The man yanks out each item of clothing one by one, tossing each of them onto a growing pile.

The baton taps his thigh again. "Spread your legs."

The soldier at the table turns now to the valise containing the stolen formula and his real passport.

"I said, spread your legs!"

Alain shifts his eyes away from the table, looking straight ahead as he complies. The lieutenant stands aside while the guard slides his hands up and down Alain's legs, along the inside pant seams and then the outer; up over his hips and around his torso, feeling under his arms and around and under his shoulders.

The soldier at the table is opening the valise. From the corners of his eyes, Alain watches him pull out the raincoat and hat. And now he's pulling the valise open wider, bending to peer inside. Slipping his hand along the inside of the bag, the soldier seems to freeze—something has caught the man's attention. His heart thumps double-time.

"Take off the jacket."

Alain removes the jacket. The guard steps aside and the lieutenant takes the jacket. Alain fixes his gaze on a spot in the distance, away from the soldier at the table with the valise, but his pulse races and he works to maintain a casual, unconcerned expression while the lieutenant searches his jacket. The search is methodical and thorough and seems to take forever; first the outer pockets, then the lieutenant slides his hand and arm through each sleeve. Seconds stretch to minutes while he turns the jacket inside out, patting the lining. At last he slides his hand into the inner pocket.

His eyes meet Alain's.

"Lieutenant!"

Alain turns as the soldier inspecting the valise calls to the officer. He's found the documents under the lining, Alain realizes with a sinking feeling. He swings his eyes back to the lieutenant. The name in the passport will reveal he is a Jew.

Slowly the lieutenant pulls his hand from the jacket, handing it back to Alain. He stamps the passport and the visa, handing them both to Alain. "You may go, Monsieur Gnann." His tone is crisp. "Move on, Schmidt," he orders the soldier holding on to Alain's valise.

Alain stands motionless. After a slight hesitation, the soldier shrugs and follows his lieutenant and the guard, leaving the valise and suitcase open, and Alain's belongings strewn across the table and floor.

Alain's heartbeat slows as he gathers his thoughts. It worked. He eases out his breath. For a moment there he'd thought maybe the Boche were different from other border guards he'd encountered. But it seems not. The bribe worked—four gold coins, Louis d'or—more money than the lieutenant has ever hoped to own. He slips on the jacket and strolls to the table where the valise and suitcase wait. He tosses his clothing back into the suitcase, and the raincoat and hat into the valise, quickly feeling along the bottom of the valise for the passport and formula. They are there, safe.

Snapping the valise shut, Alain picks up the baggage and heads for the outer doors where the Spanish border guards wait. Those guards are not likely to give a damn about him now, not this time of night and with his documents stamped by the Wehrmacht. He whistles a tune in his mind, already seeing the lights of Manhattan. He wonders if Letty will be around when he arrives in New York.

He smiles, thinking of the look on Pierre's face when he hands over the invaluable formula for Chanel No. 5, and Henri's promise of the jasmine oil.

Chapter Sixteen

Paris
Summer 1940

This evening's soiree is hosted by Ambassador Otto Abetz and his French wife, Susanne. As always, Susanne and Otto's residence at the Hôtel de Beauharnais on rue de Lille buzzes with the zing of the old days—the glamour, the laughter, the impossible gossip, always lifting Coco's spirits. She is fond of the hosts, although Susanne is wearing one of Schiaparelli's designs tonight and not Chanel. It's unfortunate, because Schiap, the Italian, has no style.

Susanne asks if Coco had left Paris when everyone fled.

"Oh, la, la, indeed." Coco flutters her fingers as she replies. "And exile was terrible, darling. But now—" she spreads her hands, "I'm home, as if I'd never left."

Susanne smiles. "We're happy you've returned."

She and Otto turn around just then, greeting new arrivals, switching to German. Coco has never bothered much with the guttural language. Besides, she's found most officers are surprisingly fluent in French. One would think these men were specially trained for party assignment in Paris. She recognizes many of the German officers here tonight now residing in the Ritz. They pay their respects to mademoiselle in the dining room in the evenings and send their secretaries around to rue Cambon the next morning for complimentary bottles of No. 5 to send home.

As the new guests wander off with Susanne, the ambassador turns back to Coco. "Susanne says you were visiting your nephew in the Pyrenees?"

"Yes, it was pleasant enough. The mountain air is fresh. The temperature cool, and my hostess, my niece, so gracious. But I find the country dull. Too quiet! It's difficult to concentrate in all that silence." A waiter stops at her elbow. She lifts a cocktail from the silver tray. Should she ask about André now?

"Did you have a comfortable trip home?"

"The trains were efficient, but I was forced to return by way of Vichy in order to obtain a travel pass. Vichy was crowded and lively." She shrugs, watching him. There's something different about Otto tonight; an annoying touch of arrogance which wasn't there before the occupation. He is a ruling conqueror, she supposes.

She sips the drink, watching him over the glass. "Traveling is complicated now with France split in half. I obtained a pass through the good graces of the new deputy prime minister."

"Excellent," Otto says. "I am not yet acquainted with Pierre Laval. Now, your new prime minister, Marshal Pétain—there is a real soldier!" He kisses his fingertips with a flourish; his smile is triumphant. "The Führer has great confidence in Marshal Petain."

He seems almost giddy at the irony that Hitler has installed Marshal Henri Philippe Pétain as his Vichy puppet. Pétain, France's greatest hero in the First War, forced Germany to submit to a humiliating defeat in 1918. The revenge must be sweet. But she modulates her tone. "Yes. Well, I have known Henri Philippe for years. He is a fine man."

"The marshal understands the need to restore order in your country," Otto says. "What do you think of him, Coco?" There's something in his tone that causes her to hesitate: *Which side are you on?* he is asking.

Flattery, not truth, is best in this case. She answers sotto voce. "In my opinion, Otto, Marshal Pétain has neither your judgment, nor your stature. But, as you say, for a long time our problem in France has been the degeneration of order in society."

She shrugs. "Perhaps the old soldier will do the job."

The ambassador sips cognac, regarding her. "And this French problem includes your Jews, of course. Doesn't it?"

Another slight change of tone warns this is not a casual question. In fact, she realizes, this is a test.

There are Jews she likes very well, and others—fingering the pearls around her neck and thinking of the shopkeeper in Limoges years ago who gave Papa only ten francs for Maman's pearls—she despises.

"France has always had problems with certain types of Jews, Otto. There was the Paris Commune. And then, as you know, many of them joined the communist mobs during the strike several years ago." Her eyes shift to an arrangement of paintings on the wall behind the ambassador—Dutch old masters she's seen before at the Rothschild apartment. The Jewish family has fled to Switzerland, she's heard, to escape persecution.

Baroness Rothschild was a good client of the House of Chanel, and—Coco had thought—a good friend. They had idled away many an afternoon gossiping in her private apartment in the Maison. But once at Longchamp, in public and surrounded by her usual aristocratic entourage, the baroness had given Coco only the briefest of nods. Coco, a woman in trade. She's never forgotten the humiliation. Anger at the old slight rises.

Otto still waits. She cannot afford to alienate the ambassador. For all she knows, even at this moment, André may be imprisoned in Germany. And if so, she will not hesitate to ask for the ambassador's help. Her voice is light, airy as she modifies her answer. "To be honest, France has long had problems with the Jews, as a group. Tribalism disrupts the natural order of a nation." She shrugs. "As in Germany, and France. So it is all over Europe."

Otto nods. His eyes glint with approval, and then he looks past her. "Ah, here you are," he says, his tone once again jovial. Reaching out, he pulls an officer to Coco's side. SS, she realizes, seeing the black belted uniform glittering with silver buttons and eagles and lightning-bolt runes.

"Mademoiselle Chanel," the ambassador says. "Please allow me to present SS Colonel Horst von Eckert."

The officer clicks his heels in the high, shining black boots. "I am honored, Mademoiselle Chanel." With a slight bow he lifts his hard, square chin; his eyes meet hers.

Coco extends her hand. "I am pleased to meet you, Colonel Eckert."

He presses her hand to his lips. "I came tonight especially to meet you, the most interesting woman in Paris." His French is flawless.

The ambassador sips his cognac, watching them over the glass. "Mademoiselle Chanel was just admiring the art," he says, his tone turning slightly sinister again as his eyes flick to the Rothschild paintings. Otto is swollen with his new power. Her heart quickens; surely this is her imagination. He was always such good company before the occupation.

"And that is what I'm also doing," the officer says, eyes on Coco. "Permit me to say, mademoiselle, the stories are true. You are indeed a work of art."

"Well said." The ambassador lifts his glass.

"Thank you, Colonel Eckert."

"But I ask a favor. Please, call me Horst." Hard lines punctuate the corners of his mouth. His eyes do not smile.

"And I am Coco."

Rubbing his hands together, Horst glances toward the bar across the room. "Will you have a glass of champagne?"

Coco smiles. "Champagne would be lovely."

While Otto turns to greet another guest, Coco hands her glass to a waiter, allowing Horst to capture her arm. He leads her off in the general direction of the bar. As with any evening social gathering in Paris, the ladies glitter, even despite the war's disruption of the spring and summer fashion shows. German officers are spectacular in their dress uniforms, having come prepared for more than war. And, of course, civilian gentlemen are all white tie.

German manners are impeccable tonight. They are smooth— not as bad as many had feared. She's heard the stories of Nazi cruelty as their armies and planes pushed into Belgium, the lowlands, and France, but these officers make that difficult to believe.

On the other hand—she saw the blood and destruction at Tours. But that is the nature of war, she supposes. And France declared war on Germany, as well.

War is too big to contemplate; she will stick to seeding her survival. After all she is only one woman—and a fashion designer and perfumer at that. What can she do about war? Horst whispers something in her ear and, without really hearing, she smiles. She will enjoy this evening. She must conserve her energy to focus on finding André and then, when he is safe, battling Pierre.

Take things one step at a time, as Boy taught. To survive she must judge each person she comes across and each event as it occurs, only as each affects Coco Chanel.

She looks about and her spirits lift. Music comes from a

piano in the corner. Lights are turned low, people mill about, conversation is pleasant, the food and wine are France's finest. Here it is late in July, and nothing much has changed since the beginning of the occupation. People in this room seem content, friendly. Unlike rumors, these things are real.

Horst stops to speak to another officer while Coco waits. Outside Paris may be dark, but the ambiance of this gathering is pleasant. Coco's eyes rove to the bar seeking familiar faces. Ah, yes—there is Simone, and Maurice Chevalier too. Perhaps he'll sing tonight. Maurice catches her eye and waves. Just then a man beside him turns his head toward her, and Coco starts. Baron Hans von Dincklage has returned to Paris. And he's more handsome than she recalls.

Dincklage grins, spotting her. With a word to his friends, he comes toward her.

Her startle caught Horst's attention and he turns, following her eyes. "Someone you know?"

"Yes, an old friend." She gives him a sideways look. "Do you know Baron Hans von Dincklage? He was Special Attaché to your embassy last time I saw him in Paris. Perhaps you are acquainted?"

"We've met."

"I wonder where he's been. I've not seen him in years."

"Lovely Coco," Dincklage says, reaching for her hands. Horst stands aside as he leans in, kissing her cheeks. He smells of salt and sunshine on the Côte d'Azur, reminding her of old times. "I'd hoped to see you here," he says, stepping back. And, to Horst, "Greetings to you too, Colonel Eckert."

Horst nods. "Von Dincklage."

Coco rests a hand in the curve of her neck, inspecting her old friend. Spatz—Sparrow—to her and their set. "But where is your wife? Where is Catsy?" Before he can reply, she turns to Horst. "Hans and his wife have often stayed with me at La Pausa, my retreat on the coast near Cannes."

"Catsy's in Spain at the moment, I believe," Spatz says. After a brief pause, adding, "We are divorced." Before she can ask more, he smiles at Horst. "We Germans believe we've conquered this city, but in truth, Coco and Paris have conquered us."

"Mademoiselle Chanel ... Coco ... and I have just met. And you are correct; she's as charming as expected." Turning to Coco, Horst nods in the direction of the bar. "I shall return with champagne."

Spatz moves closer as the colonel disappears into the crowd. "Darling, it's wonderful to find you here. It's been too long." With a little laugh, he leans in. "I should have known you could not leave Paris. Now, I believe the last time we were together was at Cap d'Antibes. And you ruffled some royal feathers that night."

Coco lifts a brow, smiling. "Yes, that's right. We dined with David and Wallis as I recall." She taps his arm. "But it was your fault we deserted them, you know. You're the one that suggested a midnight swim during dinner."

"My idea! You were the one!"

"And everyone ended up in the sea in our evening clothes."

"Everyone but the Windsors." He takes her hand in his. "The duke took it well. But she was in a fury."

"Yes, Wallis is tight as a tick, though we made up. Anyway, my lovely beaded gown was ruined."

He shrugs. "Make a new one." Then, lifting her hand to his lips, he gives her a long look. "Those were good times. The parties you hosted. And the summer balls in Cannes."

"And that night in Monte Carlo at the New Year. Remember? Everyone was there—Wallis and David, you and Catsy, Picasso, Serge Lifar ..."

"Ah, yes, the dancer from Ballets Russes."

"And my friend, Misia Sert."

"I have not seen Misia in years!"

"She lost a fortune at gambling that evening. It was just after she married José-Maria, and"—she rests her hand on his arm—"when the sun came up we all left the casino, forgetting poor Pablo. Do you remember?" They laugh together, then Spatz turns sober.

"Let's get out of here, Coco." After a beat, "Unless you're otherwise engaged with Horst Eckert?"

She hesitates only a moment. "No, I've only just met the colonel." Spatz's hands are soft, not rough like a soldier's hands. A wave of nostalgia moves through her—so few old friends are still around.

An enigmatic smile crosses Spatz's face, as if he's had the same thought. Coco slips her arm through his. Well, why not? The colonel will have no trouble finding someone else to drink that glass of champagne. Spatz steers her toward the door. Downstairs, Coco's car is waiting.

"To the Ritz," Spatz says to Evan as they climb into the Rolls. Settling back, he turns to Coco. "I'm at the Lutetia for the night. But the Ritz bar is far more lively."

And the Ritz is more discreet, at least for Spatz. Unlike the Ritz, the Lutetia, as with several other grand hotels in Paris, is requisitioned not only for lodging, but also for German diplomatic and administrative headquarters.

Spatz is off to Berlin tomorrow, he explains while they wind their way to the hotel. But when he returns, he will find a permanent address in Paris.

"The Ritz is the place to be," Coco says. The Ritz is the moon to the circling stars of the German elite. She looks about as Evan pulls the car up to the hotel. All entrances are blocked by sandbags, and anyone entering or leaving must present papers to the guards. She does not mind the guards or the sandbags. Parisians still simmer with ill will, she's heard. And thinking of the riots during the communist workers' strike a few years ago, she feels safe here.

Besides, now most of the Nazi high command reside at the Ritz, so who would dare attack? Laura Mae says she's certain the Ritz was deliberately preserved by the Luftwaffe. Diplomats also live in the hotel, like Foreign Minister von Ribbentrop when he's in town—that pompous fool, Wallis's old flame.

After passing through the guard at the entrance to the Ritz, they enter the grand hallway. Géraud is not on duty at the concierge desk. "Shall we have a drink in the bar?" Coco's voice is husky, she realizes.

Spatz takes her arm, saying nothing, and Coco looks up at him. At six feet, he's much taller than her. He holds her eyes, then, with a little smile, instead of heading for the corridor to the hotel bar, he steers her toward the elevator, to the third floor, to her rooms.

Together later that night in the afterglow of lovemaking, Dincklage cradles Coco in his arms while they muse about old times in Paris before the war. Spatz confides that Reich Chancellor Hitler holds a special awe for this city. The Führer preserves Paris for his pleasure, he says. "Just look at the Luftwaffe strategy, darling—how the central arrondissements were spared—the monuments, the parks, the old buildings."

Just as she'd suspected.

How does he know this? Can it be that Spatz is in Hitler's inner circle? Vaguely she recalls some rumor that he was a spy. He did seem to be well acquainted with Nazi officers at the party tonight, despite his lack of uniform and medals. Slowly the idea dawns on her—perhaps Spatz could help her find André.

But it's too early to mention André yet. Cupping the back of her neck with his hand, he kisses her and she's glad he is here with her. He is warm and comfortable, this old friend. She'll never love any other man than Boy Capel. But long ago Étienne taught her the pleasures of make-believe in the bedroom.

The next morning, propped up against her pillows, Coco

watches him dress, preparing to leave. He's putting on his shoes. She will miss his companionship. It's nice to have a man around again. "Why not stay here instead of finding another place," she suddenly says. "You could stay with me. We're friends after all."

Holding one shoe, Spatz glances over his shoulder. "What an idea." His tone is amused. She merely looks at him. Then, he cocks his head. "Are you serious?"

"Why not? We'll come and go as we please. No commitments."

The idea seems to delight him. After a quick trip to Berlin, he'll return to her, he says. He's only got a few bags at the Lutetia. Most of his possessions remain in his villa at Sanary, on the Riviera. He sits on the side of the bed, and, leaning down, his lips meet hers—hungry, lingering. "I'll race back from Berlin, Coco, sooner than I'd planned, I hope."

Her new rooms in the hotel are smaller—the ceilings low under the mansard roof, and of course she's lost her balcony. She's had some furniture, screens, and paintings moved to the Maison, satisfying a strange urge for more space in less room, and less color, dim light. The walls are close around her, and she finds this comforting at the moment. Stunned by worry over André, the Hôtel Ritz becomes her sanctuary as she waits for news. Besides, the streets of Paris are strangely empty, drab, and silent, as if the entire city is stunned.

One afternoon, she has cocktails with Susanne Abetz, delicately confiding concern about her nephew, André. Susanne did try to console her, said she'd ask Otto if there was anything that he could do. But Coco's heard nothing yet from the ambassador or his wife. Days pass in a blur of routine. Breakfast in bed, lunch and dinner at her table in the dining room filled with officers of the Reich who, she's certain, could lift a phone and within minutes locate André. But she can't take the chance with these men. Not yet.

Eight days after he'd left for Berlin, Spatz returns and moves into her rooms. His presence pulls her from the lethargy. She's missed him while he was gone, she realizes. Although what she feels for him falls short of love, he is good company, full of gossip and purpose, coming and going in a way that seems to give the long days of waiting for news some structure. And he seems to know every officer residing in the Hôtel Ritz.

She will take a chance on him, she decides—she will ask Spatz to help find André. She doesn't really trust him, but on the other hand, where else can she turn? At breakfast the next morning, Coco confides in Spatz, telling him of her anxiety over her nephew. Her hand trembles on the coffee cup while she tells him of André—of her most beloved nephew who served on the Maginot Line before the occupation, and now he is missing. She tells him of her love for this boy, and of Catharina and the little girls waiting at home, not knowing if André is alive—or dead.

Dead. Ah, she almost cannot speak the word.

When she finishes, she sets the coffee cup down in the saucer with trembling hands, waiting. He's on the other side in this war. What if he turns cold, hates her for the boy she loves who fought as an enemy of Germany?

But, Spatz reaches across the table, covering her hands with his. She breathes a sigh of relief at the expression of sympathy she sees on his face.

"You should have told me sooner, Coco!" He pats her hand. "I will help. This afternoon I'll inquire at the Lutetia—the Abwehr is a good place to start."

When he leaves for the Hôtel Lutetia, Coco takes to her bed, overwhelmed. There is still hope! Even Pierre is forgotten while she waits for Spatz to return with news. Coco has a headache, she tells Alyce. She must stay in bed and sleep, and if the telephone rings and it's not Spatz on the other end, she must take messages. She wants to speak to no one—no one but Monsieur von Dincklage, that is.

She will sleep—until Spatz returns with news.

She's dozing when she hears the hall door open in the sitting room and Spatz calls out her name. Before she can rise and brush her hair or even add a swipe of lipstick, he enters the darkened room. "What's this?" he says, walking over to the bed. He switches on the lamp and sits down beside her. "Are you ill?"

Coco pushes up, back against the pillows, running her fingers through her curls. "Did you find out anything about André?"

Nothing definite, he says, and the energy which had lifted her from the soft mattress, dissolves. But his next words swing her back to hope. There is a chance her nephew may be a prisoner of war, he says, sitting on the edge of the bed beside her. Her heart skips a beat. He glances around, then lowers his voice. "Nothing is certain, but I've heard some talk."

She presses both hands to his chest while he goes on. He's heard there is a certain French soldier held prisoner at a certain stalag near Berlin, one who's provoked some interest.

Coco opens her mouth, but he shakes his head. "This news is not yet confirmed, *liebchen*," he warns.

Coco drops her hands into her lap. "I just cannot stand this waiting." She turns her eyes to the window. Outside, the light dims, as if the sun hides behind a cloud. "When will you hear?"

"Have patience, darling. If the information is correct, you should take some comfort in that. At least you will know he's alive and in good hands. French prisoners of war are well treated. He will work hard, but he'll be fed and clothed, and then, once we're certain it's true, we will take things from there."

A stone seems to have lodged in her chest. She watches his

expression, his eyes—she's analyzing. His expression: calm. Tone: measured, soothing. Surely he would not lie. She thinks perhaps he is holding something back. But his eyes are opaque; they tell her nothing more.

Still, terror rises to the surface. André's unit fought on the Maginot Line, a joke now to the Luftwaffe pilots who blew it apart from the sky. A cry bursts from her: "I must know if he's alive, Spatz, or I'll go crazy. Tell me, if you know only that much, just tell me."

"We'll find out." His voice is calm. She regards him, the stone twisting and turning in her chest. For some reason she is convinced he knows more than he's telling. Perhaps he's afraid to raise her hopes. She must be careful now, patient. He's all she has right now.

Days pass with no further word of André. She wrings her hands; berates herself for not having pressed to have her boy excused from mobilization. For not having realized in time that this could happen. Every morning Spatz goes off to the Hôtel Lutetia. Every evening he returns with nothing new on André. At night, with Spatz lost in sleep, Coco paces between the bedroom and the drawing room, smoking.

One afternoon Misia comes to visit. Radiant Misia from another era, the beautiful times. Today she wears her titian curls piled into a loose knot atop her head. With warm eyes dancing, her red lips curling, Misia takes one look at Coco's haunted face, her shadowed eyes, and prescribes medicine at once. Laudanum.

"You need to rest. It will help you sleep," she says.

Misia knows everyone—she always has an answer. What would she do without Misia?

Spatz insists the medicine is morphia. She waves him off. What does Spatz know of suffering? The medicine helps her sleep, and forget for a short time that André is missing, and, as through all his life, once again his mother has let him down.

Misia's medicine is blessed relief, like scratching a terrible itch.

Without it she cannot sleep. Without it she lies abed staring at the ceiling and wondering about André. Guilt slowly weighs her down.

She has never protected André as a mother should. From the beginning of her son's life she has been a bad mother. She was never there to help him when he needed her.

Chapter Seventeen

Royallieu
1905

They took him from me right away, and I could not stop them. My baby, my boy—Étienne and Boy agreed.

First, it was just the wet nurse. "You cannot nurse the child," Étienne insisted. "The nurse will care for him and she lives in a village nearby. What you ask is impossible—he cannot stay here. Royallieu is your home for as long as you choose, Coco. But how would I explain a baby's sudden appearance here? Word would spread. My wife would hear." He reached for André, but I held on tight, turning my face away.

"I will nurse him in my room." I gave Boy a sideways glance. His eyes glistened. Were those tears? But he shook his head.

Étienne frowned, crossing his arms over his chest. "And where would you keep the child?" He glanced about, then back at me, still frowning. "In this room? Will you hide André in the armoire, Coco?"

I closed my eyes.

Reaching out, he turned my chin so I was forced to look at him. Little André squirmed in my arms. Boy, too, shook his head. "I am sorry *petite amie*. But you cannot keep a baby hidden. For one thing, they're noisy. And they must be able to move around, to be free, to play, and learn—even at such a young age." Straightening, he looked down at me with sad eyes. "And if he *is* my son … it's out of the question! You cannot keep him cooped up in here. It would be cruel. Be reasonable, Coco!" Slapping his hand to his forehead he turned in a circle, then flung his arms into the air.

He walked over to Boy. "Tell her, will you?"

Boy sat down on the bed beside me. I waited for him to speak. *Please, please.* If we were connected through the spiritual world, as he'd always said, surely he would understand how much I needed him now. André needed a father. It was never a matter of money. Étienne and Boy would take care of that, regardless. But unmarried, I could not keep André with me, as I longed to do. Unmarried, the infant must remain a secret—to do otherwise would brand him as unwanted.

Boy knew all of this.

I closed my eyes. I had been so certain that when the baby arrived, Boy would claim him. We would marry, live in Paris, make a family. Together we could take our boy to play in the sand on the beaches in the south. We could take him to the Luxembourg Gardens in Paris, where the children sail their little wooden boats in the pond.

I cuddled the baby, watching him. *Claim us!* But I did not say the words aloud. *The child is yours, Boy Capel.* Because I wanted him to choose. And Boy was silent.

"Come, Coco," Étienne urged, holding out his hands. "Give him to me."

At last Boy spoke. "He is right." His whisper ripped through my soul.

I stared at him, tightening my grip on the baby. I'd known from the beginning there was no place for my son at Royallieu, and yet I had clung to the hope that Boy and I would marry. He seemed not to notice my pain—every word of his cut deeper. "Étienne is right, Coco. For the child's sake, you must give him to the nurse. He'll be happy there. He'll want for nothing."

My chest ached. My throat ached, my eyes blurred with tears. My boy. I bent over André, closing my eyes and touching my forehead to his. He seemed to understand; he snuggled close, his soft little hands knotted together under my chin.

What could I do? I could not give up my baby, and I could not keep him here.

Boy stroked my shoulder while I cradled André. His voice was kind. "The wet nurse is a good woman, Coco; she will love him. Madame Charbonnet lives on a small farm, with five little children. She grows fresh vegetables. The children will love him almost as a brother." He put a smile in his voice. "Why, they'll spoil him. He'll have plenty attention and playmates."

While I struggled with this thought, blinking tears away, he lifted his hand from my shoulder. "Come now … the cottage is not far. Only a short ride away. We'll visit him there often."

I looked into his eyes. "When?"

"As soon as you wish," Étienne interjected, and Boy folded his arms and nodded.

"As often as you want," he said. I lifted my head and looked from one to the other, searching their eyes. Then, reaching down, Étienne lifted André right from my arms. I'd let down my guard.

He might as well have ripped out my heart.

Boy held me while I wept, whispering over and over that he loved me.

At first Boy and I rode to the cottage to visit André every weekend. Madame Charbonnet's cottage was twelve miles from Royallieu, built on a scratchy patch of earth her husband called their farm. My baby seemed to melt in my arms when I held him. His tiny fingers would wrap around mine and hold on tight, as if perhaps he knew who I was. As if he loved me.

Always, always, the time would come when he grew hungry and then Madame Charbonnet would take my place and then we'd leave. I could not stand to watch him suckling at her breast. I taught myself not to look back when we rode off. I told myself this was best for André.

Étienne came up with the plan. He procured an affidavit from a man surnamed Palasse, one of my sister Julia's former lovers. He swore that they were married and André was his child. There was no birth certificate of record; only the affidavit. In time, the years would blur the dates of births and deaths and the past would be forgotten. No one would even think to question André's parentage. He would never bear the stain of bastard. And just like that, in the eyes of the world, my son became my nephew.

A spark of hope lived on within me. "Soon, when he no longer needs a wet nurse, I will take him back and present him as my nephew." I looked at Étienne. "Could he live with me then at Royallieu?"

Étienne's tone was vague. "Perhaps. When he's older."

But, at one year, when André was learning to walk, and then again when he was two, when I begged Étienne to allow my boy to come to Royallieu, still he refused. It was too soon, he said. Boy was no help either. We often talked of marrying one day, but he never asked the question. He never set a date or offered a home for André and me. He never introduced me to his family.

Émilienne laughed when I mentioned the family. "Darling," she drawled, "I've told you before, we cannot dream of darkening the family's door." We, she said, including me. I was of the demimonde, women who are mistresses, but never wives.

At the age of three, André left Madame Charbonnet's care to live with Father LeCure, a country priest near Normandy—a Jesuit. The child was now too old for Madame's crowded cottage, Boy said. The priest would prepare André for his future education. Like Boy, André would be educated in England. He would grow up an Englishman, Étienne and Boy agreed. I protested, but they stood together, a citadel, urging me to be practical. And Royallieu remained out of the question for André.

I met Father LeCure on the day he took André away from Madame Charbonnet. We met at the cottage. The priest was a kind, studious old man, fifty years or so, with gray streaks in his dark hair and an easy smile. He was well educated, although not polished or sophisticated like Boy and Étienne and their circle. I liked that he conversed with André in a way that I could not, casually asking all the right questions. He thought André unusually bright for his age—he said this to me, Auntie Coco. He would teach my nephew in English as well as French, with plenty of time left over for games and sports and fishing, things that young boys love.

Things that I, alone, could never provide.

Before the priest took André off, my boy ran back to Madame Charbonnet, clinging to her skirts and weeping. I stood alone, tears burning my eyes as she picked up my son, hugging him. I watched her kiss my son's soft pink cheeks and whisper in his ear. I watched him give her kisses that should have been mine. Then she carried my boy in her arms back to Father LeCure. As the automobile drove away, André's face was pressed to the window, his eyes fixed only on Madame Charbonnet. Not on me.

I told myself, one day, Boy and I would marry and things would change. We would adopt André in the courts and our family would be intact. I believed that someday soon this would happen—and why not! Already Boy loved André, I was certain. When he was still a babe, it was Boy who looked to his future. It was Boy who enrolled André at Beaumont, his old British boarding school, when he was six.

True enough, the knife's edge dulled over time. Days passed, weeks, months, then—in a flash it seemed—another two years were gone and I was still at Royallieu waiting for Boy Capel's arrival each weekend. And André was still growing up without me.

Chapter Eighteen

Paris
Summer 1940

At last, long last, René de Chambrun has returned to Paris. The secretary wrote Mademoiselle Chanel into his August calendar, and today is the day they meet to discuss Pierre Wertheimer's theft of No. 5.

On her way to the attorney's office, Coco exits the hotel elevator, passing the concierge as she heads for the door. Géraud, behind the desk, with Reich Marshal Hermann Göring standing before him, hands splayed on the desktop, seems to be inspecting a brilliant jewel on Herr Göring's finger. SS Colonel Horst Eckert stands beside the Reich marshal, waiting. Spotting Coco, he lifts a brow, and smiling, takes one step back and bows.

The Reich marshal looks up then, and, retrieving his hand, he turns to her. With a click of his heels and a slight bow he says, "Good morning, Mademoiselle Chanel."

Coco inclines her head and hurries on. Colonel Eckert also resides in the Hôtel Ritz, she's learned. He is friendly when they meet in elevators and the lobby, despite her desertion of him for Spatz at the ambassador's party. But Horst's close relationship with Reich Marshal Göring gives her pause. The American, Laura Mae, says Herr Göring is moody and volatile, and one must be careful around him. Worse, the man holds frightening power in the ranks of the Reich.

At the hotel entrance, outside beyond the security barriers on the Place Vendôme, the Rolls waits. Evan stands at the passenger door. He helps Coco onto the running board and into the back seat. When she's settled, they head for René's office on the Avenue des Champs-Élysées.

In the anteroom of René's office, to her surprise, Coco finds Arletty sitting quietly in a chair, paging through a magazine. The secretary—a new one Coco does not recognize—rises and greets her from the desk near the door to René's office. At this, Arletty looks up and, seeing Coco, breaks into the famous red-lipstick smile that lifts her high cheekbones and lights her face on the film and stage.

"I will let Monsieur de Chambrun know that you've arrived," the secretary says.

"Yes, please do."

Arletty drops the magazine into her lap. Her long, dark hair is pulled back this morning into a chic braid wound and tucked at the nape of her neck. Coco pushes her short unruly curls from her forehead, feeling envy. They exchange kisses. "René mentioned you were coming this morning. We're having lunch. Will you join us?"

Coco sits down beside her. "Not today." Glancing at her watch, she says, "I must return to the Maison as soon as business here is finished."

"The Maison! Have you opened again? Have you dresses to sell?"

"Only the boutique is open in the Maison. But we've perfume, jewelry, and all the accessories."

She pouts. "It's your fault I've nothing to wear, you know. I wish you'd not shut away your dresses. The war didn't slow down Jean Patou. I hear the German ladies are making him rich. I don't see why you cannot do the same."

"Fabrics," Coco murmurs. "And equipment. Impossible to obtain, even now. Everything goes to Germany I hear. Jean has made connections, I suppose."

"Still … by the way, have you heard Schiap has fled?"

"The Americans can have her." Coco pulls off her gloves. "I saw you at Otto's soiree last week, but then I blinked and you were gone. Who was the handsome officer accompanying you?"

Arletty smiles. "Hans Soehring is his name, and he's my flying colonel."

"Ah, Luftwaffe."

"Of course. We'd just returned from a respite in the country."

Across the room the door opens and René de Chambrun strolls out wearing his usual dark double-breasted suit, plain tie, and white shirt with a stiff, starched collar. A spray of lines around his eyes, and shadows underneath, betray an otherwise youthful authority. With a smile for Coco, he slides his hands into his pockets. "Darling, it is good to see you again. I understand you stopped in Vichy on your return from the mountains."

"Yes, where I also understand you've been sipping champagne for the past few months."

He shrugs. "Not quite, but we'll have some today," he says, with a glance at Arletty. "Will you join us for lunch?"

Coco stands. "No. No, thank you, I cannot. But we have some serious business to discuss before you head off."

"Let Coco have you now, René." Arletty waves them off, lifting the magazine again. "I shall wait."

"As you say." René smiles and takes Coco's arm. His office is spacious and bright, overlooking the avenue. Sunshine streams in through the row of long windows, illuminating even the most subtle colored threads in the woven carpet on the high-polished wood floor. A carved mahogany partner's desk sits to her left; the conference table, polished to a sheen, is to the right.

Following Coco to the long table, René pulls out a chair for her, and moves to the chair beside her, nearest the windows, with the sun behind him. Coco sets down her purse and gloves and regards him, still standing.

"May I offer a cup of tea? Or a sherry perhaps?"

"Sit down, René. You will not believe what happened. I'll let you know if there's a need for sherry or something stronger after we talk." Coco opens the purse, pulls out her cigarette case and extracts one. He's quick with his gold lighter, and she nods her thanks as she sits down and leans back. Lifting her eyes to the ceiling, she takes a long draw, emitting a smoky sigh. At last, she is here.

"Now tell me," René says, clasping his hands together before him on the table. "To what do I owe this visit?"

Smoke curls toward the high ceiling. Coco drops her chin and turns to her attorney. "Pierre Wertheimer brings me here once again, of course."

He lifts a brow and a corner of his mouth curls up. "I'd hoped with the two of you on different continents and war as a diversion, the feud would simmer for a while."

Of course, she understands his tone. He's represented her in court against Pierre so many times over the years that now he's bored. But this time is different.

"Pierre is a thief, René." His pleasant expression does not change. She reaches out and rests the cigarette on the edge of an ashtray, holding his eyes. "You will not believe what he has done this time."

She describes Alain Jobert's theft of the No. 5 formula from Neuilly. René's smile slowly fades and a deep line appears between his eyes. She explains that Pierre will produce No. 5 in America and, in the process, will cut her out of the profits. The war will be his excuse. This is clear, she states, from the fact that Pierre has already purchased supplies of Provence jasmine to be shipped to New York City for just that purpose.

René sits back when she's finished. "That is quite a story. Perhaps we both need something stronger than sherry."

She manages a brittle smile. "I must take control of the company, now, while he's gone."

"So we're going to court again."

Coco shakes her head. She's given this much thought while waiting for René's return to Paris. She's changed her mind—courts are too slow. She's losing time. Rules and regulations governing court procedures were already a burden before the war, and now the Germans, with their love for paper and records, have made things even worse.

"That's not good enough, René. We must act at once." Her voice turns strident. "Société Mademoiselle is a French company. You must write a letter to management at Neuilly instructing that, as Pierre has abandoned the business, I am immediately taking charge. Schedule a meeting of the directors of my company right away and advise that I will attend, as will you."

He gazes at her, unblinking. "This plan is somewhat familiar, Coco."

Her eyes flash. She must have revenues from her perfumes immediately—her bank account daily diminishes. Still, no one can know that she's in need of funds. Not even René. She is Coco Chanel, the most formidable woman in Paris.

"Things are different now." Planting one hand on the table, she leans forward, holding his eyes. "Pierre has gone too far this time. He is a traitor to me and to our country. While he's living comfortably in America, loyal French citizens suffer. That must count for something in our new government." She picks up the cigarette and takes a puff, watching him through the smoke. "You should know since your father-in-law is Vichy deputy prime minister."

René frowns. "That is one point of view." He looks off, thinking; then back at her. "It's possible, I suppose."

"I am right, I know I am." She lifts her chin. "Write the letter, René. Demand an accounting of Neuilly's inventory for No. 5 and my other perfumes too. I want a detailed accounting of the plant's current stock—perfume, ingredients, materials, absolutes—particularly the jasmine absolute."

"You are no longer a member of the governing directors, Coco. Pierre had you removed after your last battle in court."

"He is using my name to sell my perfume in America, René. Circumstances have changed." Coco stifles a sigh of impatience. "Contact the board and schedule a meeting. Prepare an agenda. Use whatever tools you have on hand. Given Pierre's actions, I want a vote soon confirming my authority to act as the new executive director of Société Mademoiselle."

Really, life should not be this difficult for a woman. Men have such power. If Boy Capel were here right now, he'd take care of this in a snap. Things would be different.

Chapter Nineteen

Paris
Summer 1940

It's been over a week since her meeting with René and Coco has heard nothing yet. She's conquered the urge to annoy the attorney by telephoning while he's investigating solutions, but if he does not call very soon, she will surprise him with another visit regardless of his schedule.

After breakfast, with Alyce's help, Coco dresses for a meeting with Director Prudone and her accountant. House of Chanel sales of perfume, scarves, and jewelry locally remain brisk, thanks to the influx of German soldiers wanting presents to send home. But, without revenues from outside France or Germany—particularly sales of No. 5—or access to her accounts in Geneva, that limited income won't pay ongoing expenses.

Perhaps she should reconsider couture. Really, she's waited too long. Fabrics, any instruments made of steel, anything like scissors and pins and needles, are impossible to find. Even if she reopened her mill, the fabrics would be instantly requisitioned by

THE QUEEN OF PARIS

the Germans. The few designers left in Paris must have stocked up on necessities before the occupation.

Alyce bustles about while Coco pins her hat on her head. A quick glance in the mirror pleases her. She's wearing one of her favorite skirted suits today, a light-gray fitted to her slim figure, a crisp white blouse—open at the collar—the usual pearls, and white stockings with midsize pumps. Alyce hands her a pair of gloves and her purse, and with the bag hanging from her arm, Coco heads for the door. Just as she reaches it, the telephone rings. She waits while Alyce answers in the bedroom.

The young maid appears in the doorway. "Monsieur Chambrun wishes to speak with you, mademoiselle."

Coco drops her purse on the table and picks up the telephone in the living room as she points Alyce to a pack of cigarettes near the windows. "Good morning, René. I hope you have news."

"Prepare yourself, Coco. It is not good."

Her heart beats faster. "All right, then. Just tell me." Alyce brings over a cigarette and lighter. Coco, shaking, pinches the Gitanes between her lips and leans forward while Alyce lights it.

"Pierre has Neuilly management locked in a choke hold," René says. "They refuse to provide the information we've demanded."

As the maid disappears back into the bedroom, Coco leans against the wall, taking a long draw and listening.

"Monsieur Baudin is adamant he'll cede no control with respect to the company or production of No. 5 or any other of your perfumes without Pierre's express consent. Georges Baudin says he takes his orders from Pierre and the company board. I take it Baudin is receiving instructions directly from New York."

"So Monsieur Baudin is complicit in the theft."

"He does not see it that way, of course," René replies. "Pierre owns the majority shares and is the executive officer of the company—these are Baudin's words. He is only the local manager, he says; merely an employee. And as such, claims he's legally bound to the existing protocol set by Pierre; unless of course, the board of directors instruct otherwise."

Coco grips the receiver. "Well then, convene the board, René! I care nothing for the protocol. My instructions are to *override* whatever orders Pierre has given, whatever protocol Baudin thinks exists—to save the company. Pierre is in New York. I am here. I must take control at once."

A deep sigh comes from the other end of the telephone. "I remind you again, Coco. You are no longer a member of the board of directors. You have no right to demand a meeting. Furthermore, you are a minor shareholder and I doubt the directors would back you over Pierre on this." As she splutters, he goes on. "Yes, yes, I understand what you want, darling. And as I told you years ago when you first arrived in my office, my time is yours. What I'm attempting to explain …"

"I don't need explanations. I want action."

"… is that according to Monsieur Baudin, Pierre has already begun construction of a manufacturing plant for No. 5 in Hoboken, New Jersey. That plant will now replace Neuilly as the production center for your perfumes."

With the cigarette frozen to her lips, Coco closes her eyes, picturing the endless gray landscape of factories and smoke hanging over New Jersey across the river from Manhattan. She'd been struck by the thick dark haze on her last visit to America. What René says is simply not possible. Slowly shaking her head, her voice rises, climbing the scales. "You must be wrong, René. Pierre Wertheimer would never attempt to produce my exquisite perfumes in such a place. They belong to France! The fragrances must absorb the air of France! They are mine!"

At the crescendo of this tirade, Alyce hurries in from the bedroom, takes one look, and wheels about, fleeing. Pressing her hand to her forehead, Coco paces the length of the telephone cord and back again. "There is some mistake. Georges has misunderstood. Pierre would not produce my perfume in …"

"New Jersey." René's tone is flat.

"Then he really is cutting me out of the business. If Pierre already goes this far, without Chanel to protest, he could even begin degrading the formula by cutting costs, using inferior materials."

"Coco, he's not likely to do that."

"There's no telling what he'll substitute for the jasmine if the war cuts him off from the supply in Provence next year." Gasping for breath, she pulls off one earring. "He will ruin my name, René." Tears form in the corners of her eyes. "Why, he could even sell my No. 5 in drug stores!"

René heaves a sigh.

"I will not allow this catastrophe to occur. We must find a way to stop him. No. 5 is mine. Mine! It is a *French* treasure. Manufacturing must remain at Neuilly." She wheels about, pacing.

"I'm sorry, but I see no solution to this without the directors behind you."

Worthless lawyers. Balling her hand into a fist, Coco presses it over her heart. "You do not understand, René. My name, my very survival is now at stake." Gripping the receiver, thoughts of her dwindling account and every ongoing expense which she must pay fly furiously through her mind. She must take control. She takes a deep, shuddering breath. "Are you prepared to fight with me, Monsieur Chambrun? If not, I will find someone else to take up the flag, someone with courage."

"I am yours to command, mademoiselle," René says. She can almost see him rolling his eyes. "Again, I shall enter the brawl with you, if in the end you decide that is the only choice."

"Good. Yes." She squeezes her eyes shut for an instant. "I suppose we must go to court after all. Prepare the papers. I will sue for my rights. Obtain a writ against the company immediately, René, prohibiting distribution of No. 5 and all Chanel perfumes anywhere in the world by the company or Pierre until my position is clarified under the laws of France."

"The laws of Germany govern occupied France today."

She flips a hand. "Never mind, never mind all that. Then we shall fight Pierre in a German court. Perhaps that's even better." For a moment she hesitates, struggling to recall something she heard not long ago about these new German laws.

"Go ahead and do it, René. Petition the court. Demand an audit—balance sheets, profits and losses, the books—I no longer trust my partner. Records for ten years past must be reviewed. Demand copies of minutes of the board, if they even exist, concerning the theft of my formula and transferring the business to America. Everything! I want all company reports on the theft as well."

He sighs. "I will see what I can do."

"You do that." Slamming down the phone, Coco leans back against the wall, gazing out the window into the Place Vendôme, at the bronze obelisk in the center, a tall plated column holding the statute of Napoleon on top. Now reinstated, erect and shining, it was once a sign of privilege and contempt, torn down in riots during the Paris Commune years ago. Tightening her mouth, she straightens, rubs the cigarette out in an ashtray, and retrieves the purse. She is late for her engagement. As she reaches the door, she stops. Something's knotted in the back of her mind, and she pulls on the thread, struggling to free the thought.

Taking over Société Mademoiselle is a drastic measure. She'll have to utilize Pierre's factory to produce the perfume without his consent too. On the other hand, Pierre has left her with no other choice. She shakes off the reticence. This is a matter of her survival. And this idea is a path to almost certain victory against Pierre.

She'll do it. At least now she has a plan.

You must not, Coco. Boy would agree this is not right.

I haven't time for Boy's philosophical musings. Besides, Boy certainly thought that all is fair in love and war.

She's made up her mind. She will begin at once—while Spatz is out of town.

Chapter Twenty

Paris
Summer 1940

At dusk that evening, the sun touches the horizon, sending waves of mauve and tangerine light rippling over Paris. Lamps around the Place Vendôme already glow as Coco prepares for dinner with special care. Alyce has laid out the dress she will wear. Tonight, she dines at her table downstairs with Colonel Horst von Eckert. She issued the invitation earlier and immediately he sent word he'd be delighted.

Horst is a man hardened by war and vulgar philosophy, a man who vibrates with tension. He is a man who clicks his heels and rarely smiles. But most importantly, he is a man with power and influence which seems to far exceed his rank. She's noticed even the highest Reich officials in Paris, diplomats and military officers alike, show the colonel unusual respect. Even Herr Göring greets Horst Eckert with warmth.

Standing before the mirror in her chemise, she studies her reflection. Dark eyes inspect for imperfections. She's tried something new tonight with her thick curls, twisting one side up and anchoring it high with a diamond comet clip. This is a more delicate, feminine look. She is small, petite, yet Colette once wrote in a magazine article that Mademoiselle Chanel resembles a little black bull. She's never gotten over that. Colette has always been too blunt. Perhaps she's envious of Coco.

Besides, Colette has not weathered the years so well. Years ago, Colette was a plump little pudding with vivid coloring—pale skin, bright pink cheeks, natural bowed red lips. She was much prettier back then. Coco hasn't seen her lately—perhaps she's in hiding. Life cannot be easy for a woman married to a Jew, although Coco loves Colette's husband, Maurice. Maurice is a witty, brilliant little man—a true intellectual. And although he is Jewish, and the Germans are hard on those of that heritage, he is also French. His citizenship will protect him, she is certain.

Coco picks up the bottle of No. 5 on her dressing table, touching some behind her ears, in the hollow of her neck and between her breasts. She pulls on silk stockings, and then lifting the dress from the bed, slips it on. Turning before the mirror, she admires the design, one of her best—the fabric, a long shimmer of silver-green mist barely skimming her breasts and hips, touching just above her silver sandals. A one-inch lace inset at the waist emphasizes her slender curves. She lifts ropes of pearls and emeralds from the dressing table, looping them around her neck one at a time.

Then she steps back, smiling. Mademoiselle Chanel is ready for Horst Eckert. The SS officer desires her, she is certain. He does not often smile, but his eyes pierce hers when they meet in hallways or the dining room downstairs. With a swift turn from the mirror, she paces to the window and back, fingers pressing against her lips. This plan must work. René de Chambrun is useless. With one last look at her reflection, she lifts her silver beaded purse from the dressing table and hurries to the door.

It is in the beginning of a romance that a woman holds the most power in a relationship. And if anyone understands the fleeting nature of a man's desire, it is Coco. After tonight, Horst will help her take back what is hers.

They sit at Coco's usual table in an intimate spot near the windows overlooking the Place Vendôme, in her corner of the hotel dining room. Outside, streetlamps glow through the darkness. It is ten o'clock and already the dining room is crowded. The waiter has brought champagne and Horst examines the label while the waiter stands very still, hands folded. A nervous muscular tick at the outer edge of the man's right eye reveals tension.

Looking about the glittering room, Coco spots Arletty at a table near the center. This evening the beautiful actress is surrounded by not one but three handsome officers. Her Colonel Soehring, like Spatz, frequently travels. As if she feels Coco's eyes on her, Arletty looks up and waves.

Beside her Horst grunts and gives the bottle back to the waiter. Coco sits in silence, hands in her lap while the waiter takes the bottle from Horst, murmuring, "Very good, sir," and pops the cork. Horst nods, and the waiter pours both glasses. After he is gone, Horst lifts his to Coco and takes a sip. The SS colonel sits with his back straight, watching her unsmiling as she picks up her glass.

A light orchestra in a far corner strikes up nostalgic tunes from the Fatherland. The tempo is subdued, as required by the Reich's new regulations. The New Order requires moderation and discipline in all aspects of life. Coco leans forward, watching Horst under lowered lids as she sips her champagne. "The uniforms in here tonight are quite colorful, Colonel. Together your officers present a fine picture." But as she works to spark a conversation with questions about his home—Berlin—the war, his family, his travels, he answers in a bored tone while his eyes wander past her over the room.

She falls silent again, as Horst's attention is suddenly caught by someone. Without thinking she turns her head to see the porcine figure of Reich Marshal Hermann Göring, Laura Mae St. James's great nemesis. He catches her eye—his own glaring back in return, narrow half-moon slits above flushed pudgy cheeks. The Reich marshal presides over a table with two companions. Coco recognizes them at once. They are all alike, these young and glittering ladies of the demimonde.

A chill runs through her as the general seems to inspect her. Then, clutching the white napkin in his lap, he pushes back his chair and struggles to his feet. He dabs the napkin at one corner of his mouth and bows to Coco. He is a repulsive figure. Coco dips her chin in response. A waiter rushes up to push in his chair when the Reich marshal sits again.

Horst leans in. "Are you acquainted with Reich Marshal Göring?"

"I've only met him once."

"Well." He gives her a reflective look, turning his wine glass in circles. "It seems you have caught his attention tonight. An honor, as you must be aware. He is the Führer's favorite."

"Yes, I've heard."

"He is a man who, ah, appreciates fine things."

Herr Göring's lust for fine things is frightening. Only yesterday Laura Mae confided that the general had taken a liking to her favorite diamond brooch. She's refused to sell, so far, she said. But she'll likely be forced to set a price soon, as she's been advised Göring will just take it otherwise.

She had better pray he never finds the safe in his suite, either, Coco thinks. If so, Laura Mae will lose her emeralds too. Colette said before the government fled Paris, the Louvre and the Jeu de Paume Impressionist Museum hid away their best art, anticipating Herr Göring's arrival.

Horst leans closer. "Herr Göring is a collector of perfumes, have you noticed?"

Startled, she looks at him. "Are you saying he wears ladies' perfume?"

"Yes, often. He is, by the way, a great admirer of your fragrance, the one you call No. 5." The waiter appears at his elbow and Horst looks at Coco. "I understand the chef has prepared a special dish tonight in honor of Reich Marshal Göring. Shall we have the same?"

"Yes, of course." She touches the diamond clasp in her hair, distracted by the thought of Göring's greed.

The waiter bustles off, but a new voice intrudes.

"Excuse me, Mademoiselle Chanel." Coco and Horst turn to find the maître d'hôtel gaping down at them.

Horst's brows draw together. "Can't you see we're in the middle of conversation?"

The man turns pale. "Yes, please excuse my interruption, Colonel Eckert. But it is most important. Reich Marshal Göring sends a message to Mademoiselle Chanel." His throat convulses as he swallows. Bending to Coco, he lowers his voice. "The Reich Marshal sends his regards, mademoiselle. And also a personal request."

Coco's eyes flick from the maître d'hôtel to Horst and her stomach tightens. "Yes?" Sliding her hands from the table, she clasps them together in her lap.

"The Reich Marshal wishes to have twenty bottles of your best perfume, Mademoiselle Chanel. The perfume which bears your name. It is No. 5, he says."

With relief she brushes a loose curl back from her forehead. "Please tell General Göring that I am flattered by his request. I shall have the perfume brought to his suite first thing in the morning."

Perspiration beads on the man's brow. "Pardon, mademoiselle. But the Reich Marshal says he requires the perfume this evening."

"What?" Her eyes dart to Göring's table. He is engrossed with his companions.

The maître d'hôtel pulls out a folded pocket handkerchief and pats the perspiration gleaming on his forehead. "The Reich marshal sends his apologies for interrupting your meal, but asked me to inform you the matter is urgent. The perfume is required this evening." He straightens, dipping his chin in an apologetic way. "Now." He blinks and glances at Coco. "That is the Reich marshal's word, Mademoiselle Chanel."

She presses her lips together. The muscles in her shoulders, neck, even at the corners of her mouth, stiffen as she replies. "Please tell the Reich marshal that the Maison is already closed and locked for the night."

"Mademoiselle." Horst's tone carries a warning note. He folds his crisp white napkin and places it on the table.

The maître d' clears his throat. "The Reich Marshal asked me to say that he is certain Mademoiselle will have a key," he adds.

Planting one elbow on the table, Coco leans toward Horst, hissing, "Surely he does not mean now, right this moment! I will not allow myself to be pushed around this way."

Horst narrows his eyes at her. "Do not mistake this for a request, mademoiselle. He means exactly what you heard. Reich Marshal Göring snaps his finger and even officers jump." He moves close and the maître d'hôtel steps back. Coco bends to hear his words. "My advice is use this to your advantage. Do not attempt to fight the inevitable. This way, your cooperation will be appreciated."

Sitting back, she looks at him, breathless with fury. "I am to go to my Maison at this time of night to gather bottles of perfume?"

"Yes." His voice is firm. "I will accompany you, and we'll

have someone come along to carry the collection." He stands, slipping his hand under her elbow and pressing. "Smile. Rise. Your shop is right across the street; am I not correct?"

She stands, her thoughts still muddled. "Yes, the Maison, the House of Chanel, is on rue Cambon."

Turning, Horst instructs the maître d'hôtel. "Convey this to the Reich Marshal immediately. Mademoiselle is pleased to grant his wish. The perfume will be placed in the Imperial Suite within the hour. Oh, and see that our meal is hot when we return."

"Yes, Colonel."

Horst takes her arm. "Swallow your anger, mademoiselle. Turn to the Reich marshal with a big bright smile as we leave."

Sometime after midnight, after arranging the delivery of No. 5 to Göring's suite and dining, Coco and Horst retire to his rooms. Entering the residence, Horst goes directly to the terrace, wanting his cigar. She watches as he opens the long glass doors, walks to the balcony railings, and stands there, looking out over the Place Vendôme, just as she'd used to do—before the Germans came, when she had a terrace. For a moment, she stands watching him. The August moon is full and bright this evening. Horst Eckert is tall, with broad shoulders, and, bending now over his cupped hands to light the cigar, he resembles Atlas holding the world on his shoulders. A strong, handsome man.

Coco glides into the bedroom. Shedding her gown, she tosses it over the back of a chair. Wearing only a pale silk chemise and the ropes of pearls and emeralds, she kicks off the silver shoes. She sits on the edge of the bed to roll down the stockings. These she places on the chair with the dress. Then, walking to the mirror, with a twist of her fingers she pulls the diamond clip from her hair. Loose strands of short dark curls fall around her face as she shakes her head.

At last she stands back, studying herself. The chemise, cut on the bias, emphasizes her small round breasts. Turning, she looks over her shoulder, admiring the silk clinging to the curve of her back and her boyish hips. Now is the time to ask her favor.

Horst still stands at the railing, his feet apart, puffing on his cigar. As she walks onto the balcony, moving toward him, he turns. His eyes run over her. Smiling, she stands beside him, hands resting lightly on the rail. Seconds pass. The air is warm. The city tonight is quiet—she will never get used to this silence in Paris. Except for the sentries below, the plaza is deserted. Horst moves to a wrought iron chair near a small round table. She turns around and leans back, bracing her elbows on the railing, regarding him.

"Come here, *liebchen*," he says, patting his thighs. She smiles, lowers her eyes. Pushing the cigar to the corner of his mouth, clenching it between his teeth, his voice softens. He spreads his arms. "Come to me."

Coco moves toward him. Just so, the bargaining begins. Settling onto his thighs, as his arm curves round her hips, she pulls up her knees, curling into a ball on his lap. He groans. Horst plucks the cigar from his lips, tossing it over the balcony railing. The tip is a small golden flare arcing through the darkness. He wraps both arms around her, pulling her close. Arching her neck, Coco flicks the tip of her tongue over the soft flesh under his earlobe.

"Ah ..." She feels his shudder. "What game is this, little tiger?"

With his knuckles Horst tips up her chin, looking into her eyes. "You want to play, I see." His voice is a growl. "But you want something too, yes?" She does not answer. He taps the tip of her nose with his finger and for the first time this evening, he smiles. She is surprised to see his eyes crinkle at the corners.

"Come, tell me what you want. Everyone wants something

from Herr Eckert these days. But I warn you there will be a price."

Brushing a finger across his lips, she says, "It is a small thing, Horst. A little point of law I need to understand. Perhaps you can explain."

"Law! What do I know of the law?" One hand caresses her hip, slides up and up and stops just under her breast, raising gooseflesh. Spreading his fingers he cups the breast, squeezing. Coco holds his eyes as slowly she slides her hand around the back of his neck.

"I am not a lawyer, mademoiselle. I fight with my body, my muscles, not with words." His voice is low and husky. His hands are hard with a soldier's calluses, but warm.

"Ah, yes," she sighs. "But this is only a question. And since I am French, not German, I ask your help with German rules." Dropping her eyes, she snuggles closer. "If anyone knows the answer it is you."

He squeezes her breast again. This time it hurts.

"Am I correct, Horst, that German law prohibits Jews from owning property in France? Not even a business?"

He grows still. When at last he speaks, he sounds surprised. "Yes, of course. Owning property is a privilege, not a right. In the New Order, property ownership, even permission to work, is reserved only for those of Aryan blood. Those who are pure." She looks up and he frowns. "But why do you ask?"

She must answer with care. From below, faint strains of music come from the dining room as the orchestra starts up again. Automobile headlights pierce the darkness, briefly illuminating the balcony as the car stops at the hotel entrance. Horst stiffens at the intrusion of noise and light, and then the engine cuts off. Car doors slam. A woman's high brittle voice joins the music. A few seconds later, a man's deep voice comes, teasing, and the guards laugh. Then silence and darkness descends again.

Coco touches his chin. Horst turns his eyes back to her.

Settling in his arms, she tells him about Pierre, about how when she was young and stupid she let the wealthy investor barge his way into her business; how this was a man at the top of the perfume industry, with factories and distribution systems and money, and how he offered to help and the next thing she knew he owned the rights to her perfumes. As she speaks, she waves the underside of her wrist, letting the scent drift to him.

"And this man, he left you with nothing?" He gives her an indignant look, shaded with disbelief. "I don't understand. You are Mademoiselle Chanel! How can this be?" He lifts one brow, waiting.

"I own ten percent of the perfume company. He and his brother own ninety percent."

"Ach—the bastard."

"Understand, Horst, I was just a girl back then, just starting out, and Pierre Wertheimer was well known. He offered money and a factory, and customers." She lowers her voice to a whisper. "What could I do?"

As he shifts slightly, she feels him tense. "Wertheimer, did you say?" Before she can answer, his hands tighten on her waist. "A Jew?"

She reaches up to touch the side of his face, but he grabs her wrist, repeating the question. "Yes," she says. If only she were softer, if she could weep on command, like Arletty does in her films. Still, she blinks as if tears are on the way.

Horst's lips tighten; his eyes are hard as he stares down at her. She falls still. He does not understand. She must make him understand that she'd had no choice.

Shaken, her next words rush out. "Pierre is a Jew, but he's so wealthy, and no one thought anything of it. Oh, there were rumors of their pride, and the Dreyfus trials of course, but really, I did not think of those things. I was too young. I only knew Pierre would expand the business."

Horst is silent. She begins to relax. He seems to be listening;

surely he will understand the circumstances. She throws up her hands. "Can you believe such a thing? Now my partner has fled to America, stealing my No. 5 formula, my most precious fragrance."

She drops her hands into her lap, looking at him from underneath her lashes. "This while I am in Paris and cut off from my business by the war. And with my stolen formula, Pierre will produce and sell the perfume in America—he will sell it everywhere!—using my name as he steals my profits." She touches a corner of her eye, as if wiping away a tear. "I thought perhaps Germany's law could stop him."

Horst's voice is hard, flat, when he replies. "Under the law any person caught associating with a Jew is also suspect. Anyone! Don't you know that, Coco?" He shifts back, holding her at arm's length. Suddenly, she's afraid.

Astonished, she lifts her chin. "You cannot blame me for my business partner's theft!"

"You are a fool." Closing his eyes, Horst pinches the bridge of his nose. "But stupidity is no excuse. This is a clear question of morals and judgment."

She folds her arms across her chest. "No. 5 is mine. It belongs to me, and to France."

Horst looks at her. "No, mademoiselle. France is now a state of the Fatherland. You and your perfume and everything in France are property of the Reich. Herr Göring only required twenty bottles of your perfume tonight, but if he desires,"—he snaps his fingers—"he will take your entire stock like that!"

His face swims before her while she listens. Göring's demand tonight was humiliating enough, and now this. If only Boy were here to advise her. A strange helplessness comes over Coco. Boy was her rock, her anchor. Now her anchor in the world is No. 5—it is her legend, her security, her entire identity. How arrogant this man has become; how confident and arrogant and cruel. She is Chanel—she will not put up with such disrespect.

She stands, moving away from him, taking three short steps back to the railing and then she wheels about, glaring—feet apart, hands on her hips. "I, too, am Aryan, like you. My blood is pure." Horst's eyes narrow.

A little flattery mixed in might help. She lowers her eyes for a moment before looking up at him again. "I thought you were strong and brave, that you would help, that your power could stop Pierre." Sorrowfully, she shakes her head. "It seems I have misjudged."

His hands hit the arms of the chair; his eyes flash. "You guard a dangerous secret, *liebchen*." Standing, he takes her arm, he leads her through the terrace doors, through the drawing room, and into his bedroom. There, he sits on the side of the bed, unbuttoning his jacket.

Her mind clears as she realizes she still holds a powerful bargaining chip. She will do anything to beat Pierre. Coco slips off the straps of her chemise, one at a time, letting it slide to the floor, the silk pooling around her bare feet. Horst sits before her, saying nothing, watching as she comes to him.

As she reaches him, the SS colonel pulls her down onto the bed. His voice is harsh. "You want my help with your partner. But do not forget, little one. For a favor from the Reich, you will pay a price."

Of course. She understands. There is always a price. She almost smiles, a sad smile—she learned that lesson long ago.

Chapter Twenty-One

Paris
1909–1914

Yes, for everything there is a price.

The price of loving Boy was the misery of waiting for his commitment to me, and to André. The price of living at Royallieu and holding on to Boy—my anchor, my rock—was burying my pride. And the price of securing André's future, and mine, was losing my child.

Four years passed while André grew into a boy without his mother at his side. At Royallieu, with nothing more to do than miss André and wait for Boy, I shriveled inside. A woman must have a purpose in life. At Royallieu, each day was like the last. I was bored. If Boy and I were married, I told myself, I would have a child to raise, a family to care for, a home of my own.

I owned nothing of worth. I was dependent upon Étienne and Boy for shelter, food, clothing. Despite Étienne's protection and our long, deep friendship, slowly I came to realize that I was merely a guest at Royallieu, as Émilienne had first warned years ago. I could be displaced on a whim by Étienne's wife. I needed security. I needed a reason to wake up every morning. I wanted more.

Little did I know how my life was about to change, that my life's purpose would find me soon enough on one ordinary—yet extraordinary—day, on a Sunday afternoon at Longchamp racetrack.

Boy was there, and Étienne and Émilienne and others in our party from Royallieu. The weather was hot and humid. Before we left Royallieu, on a whim I tied a black grosgrain ribbon around the rim of a straw boater, a lighter, cooler hat than fashionable ladies wore. The hat was comfortable, and the brim provided a little shade. Émilienne took one look when we climbed into the carriage and said she must have one too.

How was I to guess what happened next? Every lady in the steamy bath at Longchamp's that afternoon suddenly craved my little round hat, even those who'd barely acknowledged me before. They tried it on, loved the comfort and simplicity, such a contrast to the wide brimmed chapeaus then in fashion, weighed down with fruits and flowers and too many ribbons and bows. Before we left that day, I found I'd promised hats to several of Émilienne's friends.

It was a shrewd move, if I may so compliment myself—Émilienne and her fashionable friends wore my hats everywhere in Paris, and women flocked to me when she gave my name. I set a price for the little boaters at triple the cost of bare goods I'd purchased at Galeries Lafayette to make them up. And I found myself in the business of selling hats. To begin, I made only hats to wear in the daytime and evening based on my simple concept of the boater. And, as if touched by fairy dust—I was suddenly earning money.

My own money earned with my own two hands.

The power of selling something I had made with my own hands roared through me, carrying a whorl of dreams. I had created something others wanted to buy! Already I could see the future; my hats bobbing along on the streets of Paris, London,

Brussels, and yes, on the Côte d'Azur—everywhere, if I worked hard enough, fast enough. With each hat I realized I must move faster on the next, before the ladies fell in love with another style! And I found there was a name for this business of selling hats.

I was a milliner. I was in the trade.

A good milliner, I realized, must establish herself in Paris. The thought of leaving behind the security Royallieu offered was frightening, but I yearned for the chance to go further, to establish my place in the world. Moving to Paris would be a risk without first developing a plan. I could not risk losing the only home I'd ever had. I needed Étienne's blessing. And his money, at least to get started.

Étienne merely laughed at the idea of moving to Paris to sell hats; Boy—my Boy, disagreed. Boy believed in my dream, said I had talent. And style. Finally, after weeks of begging, Étienne gave in. He and Boy invested funds, and Étienne offered the use of his *garçonnière* in Paris on boulevard Malesherbes, not far from Boy's apartment. I could make and sell my hats in one room on the ground floor of the small apartment, and sleep in another behind the shop.

I must admit, the day I left Royallieu for Paris, I felt a sudden rush of fear. Étienne—kind, generous Étienne—read my thoughts. He understood. If my hobby failed, he promised, Royallieu awaited.

And so, from Étienne's *garçonnière* I made my hats and, with Émilienne's help, word soon spread. Business exploded. I fashioned hats to suit the customer now—a cocky flip of a larger brim, an unusual touch of color, a feather or two—but still the simple shape and style. It wasn't long before I needed more space, employees, a better location.

Boy—Boy Capel, my love—leased a shop for me at 21 Rue Cambon in the 1st arrondissement, the most elegant district in

Paris, and right across from the Hôtel Ritz. What a thrill to see "Chanel Modes" painted above the door and my hats on every woman's head. But it was the windy beach of Deauville in the first summer of the Great War that led me further, to sportswear. Fine fabric was scarce. Jersey was the only cloth available, even for fashionable ladies. So, I experimented, using the loose jersey for beachwear—for soft, practical designs which clung to a woman's curves in and out of the water. Ladies loved them—and the old men still left in the beach town loved looking.

Then came jackets and skirts and blouses from the same easy cloth. Even in Paris, I used jersey back then, subtle colors and styles, toned down for the war. And to my surprise, clothing sales soon surpassed sales of my hats! My designs were classic, simple, without frills and corsets, clothing never before imagined for stylish ladies. Demand increased, so that even despite the war, and with Boy's help, I expanded the business, opened two new boutiques. One in Deauville; another in Biarritz a year later.

My life, now, was work. Years flew by working day and night on my hats and sportswear, designing day dresses, too, until at last, at last the war was over, and I found myself designing dresses in the finest fabrics, lovely new creations lighting each woman's beauty with my needle and scissors, using embroidery and skill and the drape of the fabric, tossing out corsets and padding and excess ribbons and lace. My dresses were comfortable to wear, made to order, each design unique to the woman's body and desires.

I was designing couture.

During all this time, André grew into a strong young boy. He was still with Father LeCure. I gained some comfort from the knowledge that my boy was secure and happy. I told myself it was not my fault André was not with me. I told myself I was just a girl who had no other choice. And I was busy.

In the end, I lost my boy.

To this day I bear the guilt of abandoning my son to others who could never love him as I would—only as a mother.

One day, after the war, Boy came for me, wearing a mysterious smile. I had no idea what he was up to. "There's something I want to show you," he said. I protested that I was busy, but he insisted. "I'll bring you back soon," he promised.

He took me to a building on Avenue Gabriel. Up a lift we went, into a hallway, and there we stopped before a large mahogany door. He pulled a key from his pocket and unlocked the door and handed the key to me.

I raised my brows. He nodded. I pushed the door open and stepped into a spacious room with high ceilings, lovely dark wood floors, and windows overlooking a beautiful vista, rows of chestnut trees down the avenue on one side of the building and rue du Faubourg Saint-Honoré on the other. The room was lit with sunshine. The mahogany shone on doors and window frames, the floors, on cornices and mantels, the wood polished to a soft, golden hue. Stunned, I looked about, recognizing some of Boy's family heirlooms—gilded mirrors, objets d'art made of porcelain and silver, antique tables, a silver tea set—and small framed photographs of our times together. Even his beloved Coromandel screens were there. His books filled the bookcases. His art hung on the walls.

Turning, I stared at him. "Is this for us?"

He grinned. "Yes. Who else?"

"Together?"

"Well, of course." He laughed.

I flung myself at him. He lifted me off the floor, covering

my neck with kisses, and spun around. We landed on the settee, breathless. Then I fell back against him, speechless. *Was this a dream?*

But Boy's Coromandel screens told me this was real. The rich colored panels framed in lacquered wood were his most prized possessions. Delicate Chinese figures, swirling landscapes, strange animals, flying birds, all inlaid with jade, porcelain, and iridescent pearl that told whimsical old stories. In the wash of sunshine, the screens were translucent. And they meant this was his home, and mine.

"Let's bring André here," I said, turning my eyes to him.

He smiled, twisting a curl of my hair around his finger. "Sure. We'll have him for a visit soon."

I was silent. I'd meant for the child to come to live. Unaware, Boy untangled me from his arms and legs and rose. "I've some business in London, Coco. The timing's bad, I know, but I must leave this afternoon. I still have to pack."

He'd just returned from business in Spain.

Deflated, I lay still, sprawling on the settee. "Come, Coco." Standing over me, he stretched out his hand. "I want to show you the rest of the place."

I took his hand and jumped up, smiling again. I would not allow myself to become a jealous burden. I would not allow myself to think of Boy in London without me, a city seething with pallid young women of old family names hunting for husbands, men like Boy. I told myself he loved only me, that our spiritual connection was my protection. As we walked through the rooms, I told myself no matter what, no other woman could ever replace me. I was different from the women he'd had before me. Our souls were joined before we met in this life, and for eternity, Boy once said. I treasured those words.

As we entered the bedroom where his empty bag lay open on the bed, I couldn't help asking a question.

"What did you do with the apartment on Malesherbes?"

"Oh, I kept it." His tone was light and breezy. A wave of fear and suspicion rushed from my head to my toes, tingling, a warning. I sat down on the edge of the bed, forcing back the dark thoughts as I watched him folding shirts, laying them carefully into his bag. Then he turned to me, placing his hands on my shoulders.

"I will always love you, Coco," he said. "Don't you understand? Why, I'd rather cut off a leg than live without you."

That would have to be enough, I knew, at least for now. I thrust away thoughts of marriage, and of bringing André to live in Paris. I pushed aside the deadly suspicion and jealousy I'd felt. I would have to trust him.

Yes, the price of Boy's love was high. Still, I held on to his love and trusted him, as I'd not trusted any person since Papa left me behind years ago.

Chapter Twenty-Two

Paris
Summer 1940

One warm afternoon near the end of August, Spatz surprises her with his arrival. Coco finds him lounging on the long beige sofa in her apartment in the Maison. She'd not expected him to return from his business in Berlin so soon. But she's elated at his presence—perhaps he brings news of André. He'd promised to find out what has happened to her nephew. Why else would he come back early?

But Coco does not want to seem too eager. She must be subtle and wait for him to speak. He must not feel she's using him—Spatz is proud. He'll fly right out the door if she presses him too hard. Besides, she does not fully trust him, and, truth is—he's sharp, and if she's not careful, he'll suspect there's more to this story than she's telling. She will not hand Hans von Dincklage the power that would come from knowing the truth, that André is her son, and the depth of her despair. The truth is a weakness, which he could use as a weapon somehow.

She sits at the opposite end of the sofa, facing him, her legs stretched between them, ankles crossed, with one hand in her lap and the other arm resting on the sofa back. He has been here for forty-five minutes already and she's growing impatient, feeling on edge. He's certainly taking his time getting around to the subject as he rattles on about his trip. Still Coco says nothing. He knows something, she's certain—it's almost as if he's toying with her emotions. What if the news is bad? The earlier elation is rapidly dissolving.

It seems—he's saying—this time around in Berlin the Führer personally received Dincklage. He says this casually, as if such a meeting were not unusual. Over the last few months, Coco has pondered Spatz's mysterious place in the hierarchy of the Reich. She never really believed the rumors years ago that he was a Nazi spy. Why, he is so pleasant, so easygoing that she's never given those stories much thought.

Now, as he speaks of meeting with Adolf Hitler so casually, as if this is routine, she wonders. Perhaps the real man is a hawk, not the sparrow. Only someone high in the Nazi elite is allowed to move this easily between Paris and Berlin these days. And only someone important and trusted could meet the Führer face-to-face.

His casual bonhomie has put her off guard. She's been naive. She's always known he's German through and through. Perhaps those stories were right. If he meets personally with Hitler, then he's more complicated than she's thought.

Coco sits quietly pretending to listen, while a miasma sinks through the room with each passing moment. Spatz knows something. He knows she's eager for news about André. Why is he stalling? Suddenly the scent of No. 5, long ago absorbed into the heavy tapestries and fabrics of the salon, seems almost suffocating. Sounds from the street below, usually muffled, seem heightened somehow.

And then he stops talking and she looks up. For an instant

his eyes seem to strip away her inner secrets. Then he blinks, and his expression transforms, softens. He is her old friend again. Perhaps her suspicions are wrong.

"My little Coco," and his voice is low, turning intimate. "You have made a terrible mistake." As he hesitates, the room turns cold. With a shiver, she folds her arms together, waiting. "It seems your friend Colonel von Eckert has stirred up a nest of trouble."

She frowns, confused at the turn in the conversation. What could Horst Eckert possibly have to do with André? Spatz reaches to the low table before the sofa, plucking a cigarette from the onyx box. He gives Coco a questioning glance and she nods—his words are sinking in. He pulls out another, lights it, and hands it over.

"What are you saying, Spatz?" Her voice, at least, is steady. She takes a long draw on the Gitanes.

"I'm talking about the troubles you confided to Colonel von Eckert." He grimaces. "You told him of your business problems and Pierre Wertheimer and Société Mademoiselle." Coco lifts her brows. How can he possibly know all this?

"You were especially foolish to tell him of your partnership with a Jew." Smoke drifts from his mouth with each word. "For one thing, he is Göring's man."

Aghast, she cannot speak. Spatz is well aware of her dislike for the Reich marshal.

He pinches the cigarette from his mouth, studying it. "For another, he is SS."

Of course she's known that, but as he speaks the words her skin pricks. Does he know everything that happened that night?

From his end of the sofa he gives her a look of pity. She tenses—no one pities Chanel. But his next words crush her pride. "Listen, darling, the SS are a rough crowd." After a tick, he adds, "And worse, according to my source, von Eckert took your request regarding the Nuremberg Laws straight to the Reich marshal."

"The Nuremberg Laws?"

"The Jewish laws, darling. You expressed your desire to control the company, Société Mademoiselle. You want to use German law to Aryanize the company, to seize it from Pierre."

Coco was an idiot not to realize a blunt tool like Horst Eckert would bungle her request. She must not let Spatz see how he is frightening her. She sinks down into the sofa, dropping her head back over the rounded arm cushion, blowing smoke, watching it slip stream toward the ceiling. "I only asked a favor of the colonel—a small favor."

Spatz says nothing.

Lifting her head, she regards him with impatience. "Well? What else have you heard?"

"The Reich marshal's greed is infinite, Coco. Thanks to your friend, the colonel, Göring is now also aware your business partner is a Jew. He has suddenly developed an interest in the idea of seizing not only Société Mademoiselle, but all rights to the perfumes the company produces. Worse, he's taken a particular interest in No. 5, which he agrees is a French treasure, and thus German property. It's said he believes such a valuable property will be diminished in the hands of a Jew—or, perhaps, even someone associated with that Jew."

"What!"

He nods. "In fact, I hear he's considering not only confiscation of the company and No. 5, but also moving the entire business to the Ruhr Valley, in Germany."

She sits up straight.

"This would be a significant coup for the Reich, you must understand. The propaganda value attached to owning No. 5 is enormous, benefiting not one but two Reich officials. Göring, as father of the idea, and Goebbels, minister of propaganda."

As his words sink in, a deep shudder runs through her.

What has she done! Pulling her legs to her chest, she wraps her arms around them. Something in his tone tells her there is more to come.

His eyes roam past her. "You should have known not to trust von Eckert, Coco. Nothing is confidential with the SS." After a slight pause, he shifts his gaze back to her. "Not that your request for help with Pierre was out of the question, you understand."

She studies the tip of her cigarette. Her hand shakes. "You're right. I thought Horst would merely look into the law."

Dincklage lets out a laugh. "That's just what he did, darling. Below the Führer, Herr Göring and Doctor Goebbels are the law."

An image of Göring's bloated face rises in her mind, his sharp little eyes piercing her from across the dining room, like a lizard poised to catch a fly. Bending to one side, she stabs the cigarette into an ashtray, drops her feet to the floor, and rubs her arms. Suddenly she feels cold.

"I will not allow this, Spatz!" She curls her hands into fists as she speaks. "I am a French citizen, and the company and perfume are rightfully mine." Pressing her lips together, she shakes her head. "No. No! *I simply will not allow Göring anywhere near No. 5!*" Coco declares, her voice rising.

Dincklage's tone turns sharp. "Lower your voice!" She gives him a hard look. "It's ironic, really," he goes on. "The very laws you planned to use to your advantage can also work against you." He points his cigarette in her direction. "Listen to me! Count yourself lucky your name has value, Mademoiselle Chanel. If Göring and Eckert had their way right now, you would be under arrest."

She gasps. What is happening? Fighting back the raging anger and fear, she forces herself to remain calm. She takes a long deep breath, turning her eyes to him. "Tell me, Spatz. What should I do?"

"We must turn this around, darling, and quickly." He rubs out the cigarette and looks at her. "I know of only one person in the Reich with the power to slow down Göring on this matter. But you'll have to work for his help."

Of course—as Horst had said, she must pay. Nothing is free in life. "What do you want in return?"

"Not me. Someone much higher up than me. I've spoken with him about your business partner's scheme, and also your desire to find your nephew. He has a particular concern too, one in which you may also be of help to the Reich, Coco. If you're willing to assist Germany in this matter, he may be willing to help you solve your problems with Göring and Pierre."

She does not hesitate. "What must I do?"

"You will go to Spain. You will use your name, your connections, and your prestige to influence a certain outcome, which will be explained if you agree to the bargain. You will write reports; provide information."

Incredulous, she stares. "Are you asking me to spy for Germany?"

He shrugs. "Call it what you will. I am the messenger." His eyes hold hers. "I bring this message only because I care for you, Coco. I do not want to see you lose all that you've created."

Her thoughts spin. How have things come to this? She merely asked Horst Eckert for a small favor. And suddenly she's facing threats from Hermann Göring, and demands—ultimatums!—to spy for the Reich.

She knits her fingers together in her lap. "Would this matter in Spain harm France?"

"What does that matter?" His tone is brisk. "France is already defeated."

"But you are suggesting I betray my country?" When he says nothing, Coco stands, looking down at him; this new Hans Dincklage is a stranger. She moves to the Coromandel screen placed behind him, tracing the figure of a tapestry bird with her finger. She is caught between two powers of the Reich—one known, Göring, and one unknown, Spatz's mysterious stranger who, he says, could save her. What would Boy advise? Even as the question enters her mind, she knows. Boy would be shocked at even the thought of betraying her country.

"I cannot do what you've asked," she says, blinking back tears. No. 5 is hers—her only hope, her only real security. But France! France is her country, her home from birth. She rests a hand on his shoulder. He is offering her a way to defeat Göring's greed, she knows. This price truly is too high. "There must be another way."

He sighs, patting her hand. "You're caught in a vise, Coco. You're associated in business with a Jew. If you refuse this offer of assistance, you can be certain nothing will stop the Reich marshal from seizing the company and perfume. You have given him the easy weapon—the business is owned by a Jew. He will take the company, and with it your name, and perhaps your freedom."

What has she done! Coco presses her hand over her eyes. If Göring succeeds, her name, her Maison, will be linked in history with Adolf Hitler and the Reich. She storms through the sitting room into the hallway, and there she stops, spinning around. Spatz, elbows on his knees, watches her, his expression full of pity.

An icy feeling settles deep in her bones as she paces to the doorway and back, over and over again, rubbing warmth into her arms as she walks. Spatz waits in silence.

Returning to the sitting room, he gives her an expectant look.

"What happens if I agree? You say the Reich will assist in my case against Pierre?"

"Yes, that's how it works."

With a sudden wave of despair, she closes her eyes. Spatz reaches up, curling his hands around her hips.

"I cannot think," she says. "I must have time to think."

"Don't wait too long, darling. Hermann Göring is not a man to cross." Sitting back, he watches her. "Neither is the man who sent this message." After a beat, he adds, "I am sorry I'm the messenger."

Turning her back on him, Coco stalks to the front door, slamming it behind her. She marches down the hallway, past the atelier where her little hands did their work and on to the spiral stairs. She walks through the salon and across rue Cambon to the Hôtel Ritz, down the corridor to the elevator, and on to her rooms where she can order her thoughts. Here she can ponder the despicable offer in peace.

Chapter Twenty-Three

Paris
Summer 1940

After warning her against further delay, Spatz is off again. Between worrying about André and this new development, Coco cannot sleep without her medicine. The morphia haze is a blessing on this hot August night. During the day her thoughts are erratic, swinging back and forth from one problem to the other. Time is passing, and time is her enemy. She must make a decision. Otherwise, Pierre will win, or Göring will confiscate the company and, along with it, her No. 5.

But to spy for Germany? Her head aches when she thinks of it.

On the fourth day, sitting in the back of the Rolls, returning from a desolate visit to her accountant, Coco gazes through the windows. According to her accountant, the balance in her bank account is diminishing more quickly than she'd thought—due not only to the lack of perfume revenues owed by Pierre, but also by the precipitous drop in the franc. Almost worse, because of the war, he says it is still impossible to obtain money from her vault and investments in Geneva.

Worst of all, André remains missing. Spatz claims to be searching, yet so far he's found nothing. Leaning against the car door, she presses her forehead against the cool glass window. Really, it's all too much. She digs into her purse and pulls out the card stating that she's a Catholic. Closing her eyes, she rubs it between her thumb and fingers. If the medicine were in her purse, she'd take it this moment, right here in the back of the car, to blunt the worries. André, Pierre, Göring, Horst Eckert. The problems won't leave her in peace. And now she's faced with the message delivered by Spatz from some mysterious power in Berlin, a bargain which would make her a traitor to France.

"Mademoiselle?"

Evan's voice rouses her. The car rolls to a stop. Confused, Coco looks about. "What's happened? Where are we?"

"Near the Jewish quarter, mademoiselle—the Marais." He waves his hand toward a line of cars ahead. "They've blocked the street."

"Who? What? What is blocking traffic?" A rowdy crowd is gathering on the pavement near the car. What has happened to the renowned German order and efficiency? Sliding forward, she glares over her chauffeur's shoulder at the scene ahead.

Two men in uniforms are hauling a young woman in the direction of several trucks. It's the vehicles that block the traffic. These are French police, she realizes, not German soldiers. As the policemen step down off the curb into the street, the woman fights, twisting and turning, screaming for help while they drag her between them. A small boy runs behind, crying, reaching for the woman's skirt.

"It's something official, mademoiselle."

Evan's tone is grim. Her eyes dart between the woman and the policemen and the boy.

They watch as the policemen shove the woman into the last truck. An old man wearing a butcher's apron hurries from a shop nearby, calling out. Making his way through the growing crowd to the child, he grips the little boy's shoulder. The child still wails as the butcher turns him about, stooping down and pulling the boy into his arms.

"What's happening here?" Coco blurts, reaching for the door handle.

"No! Don't open the door, mademoiselle!" Startled, she freezes. Evan's eyes meet hers in the rearview mirror. "The crowd is not safe. Please stay where you are." His voice is sharp. Coco lifts her hand away, surprised at his urgent tone. Ahead, the trucks begin moving forward, one by one, and the boy turns, calling out for Maman and fighting the old man's grip. Horrified, Coco stares as the butcher lifts the screaming child, his little arms flailing, his thin legs still beating, beating in the air.

"Maman!" The thin panicked voice pierces the barriers she's built over the years. She shuts her eyes, remembering the sheer terror she'd felt as she'd watched Papa leaving that night at the abbey. It had taken a year or more before she'd faced the truth— that she would never see Papa again.

When she opens her eyes, two policemen approach the line of cars. Rolling down the window, she thrusts her gloved hand through the window, beckoning. The closest man looks at her, back at his companion, and then again to Coco. "Yes, you," Coco says, resting her hand on the windowsill. "Come here."

With a surprised look, he walks to the Rolls, stopping several feet away.

"Come closer. I have a question."

He steps forward, bending, touching the bill of his cap. "Yes, madame?"

"Tell me what is going on here. Why are we stopped?" The words flow before she thinks. "And why did you take that woman away?"

"It's nothing, madame," the man says. "We're under orders. The Germans are taking a census. Counting, that is all."

Over his shoulder she watches the grocer lead the weeping child into the store. "Counting what? Counting whom?"

"Only Jews, madame. Those in the Marais." He jerks his head toward an area behind a line of shops, toward the Pletzl, as she's heard some call it—in Yiddish, the little place. The cars ahead begin grinding forward.

Moving to the front window, the man ducks his head and says through the glass to Evan, "I'll have to ask you to move along, sir."

"Right away."

As he strides off, Coco calls after him, "But why are you counting them?"

He does not answer. Perplexed, she sits back.

Stop the car and go into the store to check on the child, Coco. It's not my business. Let the Jews take care of their own.

Back at the Ritz, Dincklage looks up from a book when she opens the door to her rooms. She stops, startled. Spatz has returned from Berlin. She'd expected him next week. And as always on his returns, hope flutters in her chest. Perhaps he brings news.

"André?" Her voice catches on his name.

He puts down the book, rising. "Not yet." Walking to her, he gathers Coco in his arms, kissing her cheeks. She rests her head on his chest for an instant, suddenly fatigued, drained from the scene she'd just witnessed. At last Spatz holds her out at arm's length, inspecting her. "Are you all right?"

In that split second, Spatz seems almost like an enemy. Why is it taking him so long to find information on André? Freeing herself from his grip, she walks into the bedroom, where she removes her hat. When she returns to the sitting room, Spatz is once again planted in his chair.

She looks about. "Where is Alyce?"

"I gave her the afternoon off."

Coco frowns. One would think this was his place. Still in turmoil from the afternoon's events, she stalks to the low table between their chairs, picking up the pack of Gitanes. "When did you begin paying my maid's salary?" She digs a cigarette from the almost empty pack.

"I told her to leave so we could talk in private," he says, and her heart starts beating double time again. She touches the pulse in her throat, then her fingers slide to the pearls and cling there, waiting. "In Berlin I spoke with Admiral Canaris."

"Canaris, Canaris … Is this someone I've met?" Her tone is sharp and tense, she realizes. But she's impatient. Lighting the cigarette, she sinks into the chair facing him, splaying her hands over the chair arms.

"Admiral Wilhelm Canaris is chief of the Abwehr, our military intelligence. He's the person I mentioned before, the one who can hold off Göring, if you're willing to take his offer."

"*Mon Dieu*, Spatz!" She shakes her head.

He lifts a brow. "Don't worry, darling. He already knew the story. Colonel Eckert has been busy." He steeples his hands together, resting his chin on the tips of his fingers. "You must make a decision about Spain before it's too late. Before Reich Marshal Göring acts. Admiral Canaris wants to meet with you."

"Am I correct that he is willing to help not only with Herr Göring, but also with Pierre?" Coco clamps the cigarette between her lips.

"It's possible." He tips his head to one side. "The admiral understands your problem with Pierre. He mentioned someone who could be helpful in resolving the matter, assuming you two reach a satisfactory agreement. He has in mind Louis de Vaufreland, a Frenchman. Do you know him?"

"The marquis?"

"So he says. He's an attorney, I believe. Living in Paris."

"And?"

"Vaufreland is well acquainted with certain officials, both Vichy and German; those tasked with implementing the Jewish laws in France. If Admiral Canaris gives the word, Vaufreland is the man to expedite your claim against Pierre." He pauses for a moment. "Again, assuming you come to terms with the admiral."

She smokes, looking off, affecting an unconcerned expression. If she agrees, one of her problems may be solved. Société Mademoiselle, and No. 5, its most valuable asset, would likely be hers. Turning her eyes to Spatz, she leans forward, resting her elbows on her knees, cigarette in hand. "So, tell me again. What exactly does Canaris want from me in exchange for his help? In simple terms, is he really asking me to spy?"

"Yes, in a manner of speaking."

"Spatz, I must hear details."

"I am authorized to say only this much." He picks up a cigarette, lights it, and sits back. "Your name carries weight in certain quarters. You have powerful friends in both England and Spain; people who could be helpful to the Reich."

Her lips part; her eyes widen. "He wants me spy on my friends?"

"Some will benefit."

Coco looks at him. She is not past using friends. She's done it before. Still, as part of a bargain, this has a dirty feel.

"Admiral Canaris is the one man who can help you with Göring, Coco." His tone turns wry. "But the admiral wants a favor for a favor. Not a bad deal on your part. It's only a matter of sharing information, and of communication."

The admiral requires she spy for the Reich. She looks at Spatz without speaking. She is French through and through. Regardless of the details, this bargain with the country occupying France is treason, no matter how he chooses to describe the mission to Spain. Still, while the thought of spying for Germany is overwhelming, so too is the thought of losing No. 5 to Hermann Göring. And, as between the two, Göring is worse than Pierre.

Damn Pierre. He started all this. He's made her life a misery. She rubs out the cigarette in an ashtray. Well, this is life. She's already made her decision on the admiral's proposal. Reluctantly she rises, moving behind her chair. Facing Spatz, she lifts her chin.

"Tell the admiral I cannot do what he asks." Her throat catches, realizing what she's giving up.

Spatz holds her eyes, his expression unreadable.

"I will not do this, Spatz." She lifts one hand. "I won't betray my country, even for No. 5."

He sits up straight, dropping both hands to his thighs. His lips tighten into a thin straight line. "Think carefully, Coco," he says. His voice holds an ominous note.

"Oh, but I have."

"Then think again." Pausing, he looks directly at her. "If you refuse to cooperate for your own benefit, then do this for André."

She grips the chair. "What did you say?"

"I speak of your son, André Palasse."

Her son? Is that what Spatz just said? Seconds pass as she wills the room to stop spinning around her. Wills herself to hold steady, to hold on to his eyes, wills herself to breathe.

"What has any of this to do with my nephew?"

"He is your son, Coco. We know."

Her mouth goes dry. She cannot take this in. Her fingers dig into the upholstery of the chair, knowing that if she lets go, she will fall. Outside, a police siren blares across the Place Vendôme, screaming the warning—they know, they know. Somehow they know about André. After all these years pretending, protecting her son's secret, they've found out. After suffering such heartache and telling so many lies—they know. And they will tell.

She can barely speak the words. "Is he alive?"

"Yes," Spatz says, and the answer sends her spinning again, this time with relief. André is alive. "At the moment he is a prisoner of war, interred in a work camp, a stalag near Berlin." His usually vibrant voice is flat, emotionless.

An initial flare of joy suddenly turns to terror. "Is he well? Where was he captured? Did you speak with him?" She wants answers right now, before she faints. "When will he be released?" Spatz will help. He must!

"He was taken at the Maginot Line. Early June, I believe."

That long. She goes very still. *Madonna, Saint Theresa, Little Flower, pray for me.* While she was comfortably ensconced in André's house, her son was prisoner in a work camp in Germany. Catharina's cook served up fine meals for André's mother in André's house while he was in that prison, in that camp. A terrible thought strikes her. Her voice comes out a hoarse whisper, "Have you known all along?"

He's quick to deny. "Of course not." He takes a deep breath, watching her. "I heard the news of André from Admiral Canaris for the first time during our visit in Berlin yesterday. Since the admiral manages security in France, he has your file as a resident of the Hôtel Ritz. You speak of your nephew—ah, your son—often. It was not difficult to put things together. Every nonmilitary resident of the Hôtel Ritz is fully investigated." He pauses and adds, "Our security services are talented, Coco; good at unearthing secrets."

He pauses, and then adds, "But also at keeping them."

She clasps her hands together, pressing them over her lips as she takes in his words. It is unbearable to hear him speak of André as her son; she's held the secret in for so long, protecting him from the mark of the unwanted, of the illegitimate, a boy without a father's surname. She squeezes her eyes shut. Is it really possible she's listening to someone speak of André as her son, other than the three people who've known from the beginning—Boy and Étienne and Émilienne?

"He is ill, Coco."

Spatz's voice comes from far away. She chokes back tears as her eyes blur. She hears him rising from his chair just as she loses the battle and the tears spill over. As he comes close she steps back, holding up her hands between them. "Stay where you are, Hans von Dincklage. Don't come near until you've told me everything I want to hear."

His brows draw together, but he nods and steps back. "He has contracted a tubercular infection."

André's lungs were always weak, even as a baby. When he was a child and she'd worry aloud, Boy would insist that he was just pale—that all Englishmen are pale. Besides, a woman will never understand how a British boarding school turns a boy into a man. Trembling at the memories, Coco rounds the chair and slowly sits and Spatz follows.

"The doctors say he does not have long to live, Coco." His voice is gentle now. "Not without hospitalization and medical care."

She catches her breath at these words. Hands fly to her chest. "But with hospital care?"

"His chances of recovery are fairly good in hospital."

The room is dim, full of shadows. The sun is going down. She holds his eyes. "How much time does he have?"

"I don't know."

"If I do what is asked, they must free André."

He nods once. "Yes."

They've already talked of this, she realizes. This is the admiral's leverage in the bargain. She pushes back. "They must free him first, before I go off to Spain."

Spatz's face contorts. "I'm sorry, Coco. That is not possible."

"I demand this."

He shakes his head. "I cannot change the message. And you are in no position to make demands."

"Then I won't cooperate."

"Please, Coco. Think. André will die." He gazes down at his hands. "If I had the power, things would be otherwise."

"So, I'm a beggar now?"

Spatz shakes his head. "Of course not, darling. But understand," he holds out both hands to her, palms up. She does not move, and he drops his hands. "You're caught between two powerful men, Göring and Admiral Canaris." His face turns grim. "You really have no choice—Canaris is not SS. We must act fast."

"And what if I'm no good at this thing and fail to deliver in Spain?"

A moment of silence passes. "Then André loses."

She drops her face into her hands again. *Oh God, Lord Jesus Christ—please, please, please, please, please, forgive my sins. Punish me, but not my son.*

But when she answers, her voice is firm. Of course she will go to Spain. She will do whatever it takes to save André's life. "I must see Canaris right away." Looking up, curling her hands into fists. "Do you hear, Spatz? I must see him immediately." The words drive through her and Coco collapses, weeping.

Spatz takes her hands, pulling her from the chair. She swings her head from side to side—but there is no one else to help or even care. As Spatz lifts her into his arms and carries Coco to her bed, she fully understands—he is one of them. But she needs him now. She must lean on him, because no one else is here to help.

Boy ... Boy, where are you?

Spatz lowers her onto the bed and places a soft pillow under her head.

"I need my medicine." Her voice is a whisper. Seconds later, he brings the morphine.

Coco closes her eyes, moaning as the medicine takes effect. Already her mind is a haze.

She is a bad mother. She lost her boy when he was young. She must find him now. She must save him. That is the only thing that matters.

Chapter Twenty-Four

Paris
1910

André was five and a half years old and still living with Father LeCure, Boy's Jesuit friend, when the child came to me for his first visit to Paris. He was to enter Beaumont in the fall. We'd seen him now and again since he'd left the wet nurse, when time permitted. Not often; not enough. I was so busy in those years and Boy was too, and time just flew and the years passed.

Boy's car delivered him to our door. As André stepped forward, he gave a little bow, saying, "Good morning, Aunt," and shook hands with Boy. I saw a solemn child with a broad forehead and haunting eyes inspecting me. His skin was pale, his features delicate. His fine brown hair was parted on one side. He wore short pants and knee socks, a crisp white shirt with a tie, and a navy jacket. I bent and kissed his cheeks, then took his hand. My insides were in turmoil. I don't know what I'd been expecting, this child was almost a schoolboy. He was no longer the toddler I'd dandled on my knee.

I hardly knew him.

For the first two days André said very little. He spoke when addressed, was very polite, almost formal, minding his manners. I often caught him watching us with those big dark eyes which never seemed to blink.

Boy gave him a small wooden sailboat painted blue and white. We took him to the Luxembourg Gardens and I sat on the edge of the fountain while Boy showed him how to sail the boat with the other children. All just as I'd once dreamed. We took him to Punch and Judy shows and to ride the carousel near the Louvre and to museums and on long walks for ice cream.

One afternoon, we walked with André along the quay of the Seine, looking at real boats. It was a chilly gray afternoon with the sun hidden behind clouds. The river current was swift, the water brown and churning. Streaming ribbons of foam like white lace trailed in the wake of the boats. André walked between us, holding our hands. Sometimes we would swing him up, and when he laughed it was a sweet, twinkling sound, one I'd never heard from him before. My boy was beginning to relax with us, to have fun, I thought.

Anyone around would have seen a family.

As we strolled along the quay that afternoon a coal barge slowly moved upriver, making its way toward us. We stopped, watching it glide through the water. Boy hiked André up onto his shoulders.

"Look, son." Boy pointed to the barge. "That is one of ours."

André shouted, "One of ours!"

My heart skipped a beat. *Son?*

Had I heard that right? Boy's tone was so casual. I'd never actually admitted to Boy that he was André's father, not Étienne. I'd left it open between them. Pride, I suppose, since he did not probe. But now I realized all along he'd known. And yet, not once—not once had he spoken of marriage. The revelation was too much. Something snapped inside.

"That is *your* barge and coal, Boy Capel."

André looked at me over Boy's head. Boy shot me a careless smile. "I meant to say, when we're married." His tone was offhand as he swung André back down and set him on his feet. My heart burned, yet at the same time, leaped. I fell silent.

Boy bent, brushing dust from André's pants. He smoothed the part in our son's hair, as a father might. In that moment I knew that someday, at the right time, André would forge the bond between us. Boy and I would marry. Meanwhile, I would convince him that André belonged with us. He should stay with us—we could hire nannies to help. Surely Boy would come around.

But a few days later Boy arranged for his chauffeur to pick up André on the next morning. Time to return to Father LeCure, Boy said when I protested. "He'll be off to school in two months." Cupping the back of my head in his hand, he gave me a quick kiss.

I argued. "England will be cold and damp. He'll be alone. He's still too young."

"It will be good for him. He'll meet the right people there, form valuable friendships for life." He shook his head. "A woman could never understand."

I sank down onto the settee. If only my business was established. If only my finances were secure, I could make the decision without Boy's help. This taught me a lesson I have never forgotten. Work is freedom. Work is security, and independence.

The next morning, André marched into the drawing room carrying his little suitcase, already packed. My heart squeezed in my chest. I knelt, telling him goodbye, looking deep into his eyes, wanting him to feel my love. But his eyes flicked away. He watched the door as I kissed his cheeks, and I felt him flinch. So I pulled up his collar, brushed a stray lock from his forehead, and then stood.

I stood there, letting him go.

Chapter Twenty-Five

Paris
Fall 1940

Coco has thought of nothing but André's plight over the last two days, and now the meeting with Admiral Canaris is set for nine thirty this morning. She does not know how she'll make it through. As the blue Rolls glides across rue de Rivoli to rue du Boc, heading toward the Pont Royal and boulevard Raspail on the other side of the river, she sits on the driver's side in the back, gazing through the window. Spatz sits beside her, keeping up a running monologue of instructions on how she must act in the presence of Admiral Canaris, about how she must charm him. Not many French citizens receive this honor, he says.

She turns her eyes to him at this last comment, but he seems serious. "Straighten up, Coco. Whatever's stirring inside you must keep hidden in this meeting. You must convince the admiral that he can trust you with this mission." She shoots him a glare. He frowns, adding, "This is no time for emotional indulgence."

He is right, of course. She will hide her anger and this

desperate feeling because the clock is ticking away on André's life. How many weeks can her son survive in that camp? How many days, hours? Since hearing the news she's barely eaten or slept. Her reflection in the mirror this morning sent a shock through her. She is a ghost of her former self.

As they cross the River Seine, thankfully Spatz falls silent.

"We have arrived, mademoiselle," Evan says, pulling up to the entrance of the hotel off a wide, busy confluence of streets. The Hôtel Lutetia houses not only Hitler's top spy, but the entire Paris Abwehr staff and many officers—the entire hotel was requisitioned. Dincklage seems to think this is a secret. Nothing the Nazis do in Paris is a secret.

Two bellboys in their brass-buttoned, cherry-red tunics approach the car. As Coco steps out she squints her eyes, ignoring the sandbags and guards as the familiar belle epoque hotel, with its balconies and arches, rises before her in an amber mist. While Dincklage talks to the guards and leads her forward, for the first time in days she almost smiles, remembering an evening two years ago, before the damned war came to France.

They are in the Lutetia bar—Coco, Picasso, Misia, and Daisy Fellowes, wearing her sparkling smoking jacket—with nothing on their minds but the gay evening. There is cold Taittinger from the hotel's cellar, on Pablo's room account, of course. There is the piano man, and laughter, singing, dancing. And such surprise when at last they noticed the morning sun slanting through the windows.

But this is September 1940, the terrible present.

They ascend the steps under the canopy while more bellboys hold open the entrance doors. She clings to Spatz's arm, suddenly overwhelmed with fatigue born of terror and fury at this blackmail. Moving into the lobby she's almost dizzied by the magnificent frenzy of black and white floor tiles, the tall gleaming mahogany counter just ahead, the marble columns, the swagged red-velvet curtains, fragrant roses, glittering chandeliers—a familiar scene from the earlier days, from another life.

She must have faltered; Spatz takes her arm.

A junior officer in dress uniform arrives before them, clicks his heels, and salutes. "Heil Hitler."

Spatz waves him off. "We've an appointment with the admiral," Spatz says, his tone imperious. "I know the way."

Without saying anything, the officer falls in with them. No one speaks in the elevator. Only the sound of their footsteps breaks the silence when they step out into the long hallway. Coco sets her jaw. The place has a sinister feel. Near the end of the corridor, Spatz stops before a pair of large wooden doors. Two men wearing gray suits stand at attention. As they salute Dincklage, the junior officer returns to the elevator.

Dincklage turns to her. "They must search you first, Coco."

She takes a step back, arms crossed. "I will not allow these strangers to touch me."

He lifts one brow, smiling. "It's protocol, just a pat down. Come now, this won't take long."

Before she can utter another word Dincklage steps aside and the expressionless guards herd her into a small room across from the suite. She is to hand over the purse. She is to remove her jacket. One of the men takes the jacket and slides his hand down through each sleeve, pats the pockets, runs his fingers along the seams, then hangs it over the back of a chair.

He turns again to her, while the other guard takes her pocketbook to a table, opens the purse, and begins removing items one by one.

"My apologies, mademoiselle," the first man says, the one who checked her jacket. "Now I must ask you to raise both arms above your head. Please. Like this." His French is adequate, but still he illustrates.

She complies, watching the man searching the purse. Two hands slip under her arms and slide down her torso, skimming her breasts, down to her waist. She will not allow them the satisfaction of enjoying her discomfort. The hands move around her waist, a finger slips under the waistband in front, in back. The hands move down, over her hips, down the outer edges of her thighs. She takes in quiet shallow breaths, holding still until he's done.

She is returned to Spatz. Smiling, he slips his hand under her elbow and guides her through the doors across the hall. They walk through a large bright room with several closed doors. Turning left, they enter a smaller room. A pretty young woman with straight blond hair cut sharp to the length of her chin looks up. When she greets them by name, Coco realizes she is French.

"Please have a seat," she says, rising. Her suit is smart, a copy, probably Galeries Lafayette. "I will let Admiral Canaris know you've arrived." Seconds later she returns, asking them to follow her.

Coco grips her purse. Everything she says in this meeting must be prudent, careful, as she's practiced when she's alone. Every choice she makes today will have its effect. There can be no unplanned words or actions for Coco Chanel from now until her son is free and under a doctor's care.

As they enter the office, she glances about. In contrast to the elaborate decor of the Lutetia entrance, Canaris's office is serene. The colors are soft and soothing—the blue-gray walls are bare except for a formal portrait of Adolf Hitler. A sweep of gray carpet contrasts three oversized burgundy leather chairs arranged around a low round table. The admiral's desk is clear of all but a single sheet of paper upon which he's writing, a brass pen holder nearby, and a model ship on one corner. He looks up as they enter. "Good, you've arrived." Carefully he places the fountain pen back into the holder, and removes the round gold-rimmed spectacles, setting them on the desk.

"I am honored to meet you, Mademoiselle Chanel." Pushing up from the chair, the admiral comes around the desk to face her, and gives a slight, almost imperceptible bow.

As if she's here by choice. Coco inclines her head and smiles. "The honor is mine, Admiral."

With a nod to Dincklage, he extends his hand toward the leather chairs. "Please," he says. His voice is low, but firm. "We will sit here. Tea, coffee?"

"Tea, thank you."

Canaris nods to the secretary standing near the door, and the three take their seats. Coco studies him while they settle.

The head of military intelligence is a slight man, slim and short. Fine gray hair parted on one side sweeps over his ears. His uniform is loose, almost disheveled. Despite that, the high forehead and combed gray brows, the sculpted features and strong broad chin give him a commanding appearance.

The admiral's eyes lock on Coco's as he takes the chair facing her—the hard, direct look of a man confident of his place in the world. His eyes seem to penetrate right through her. "I understand, mademoiselle, that you are well acquainted with the Duke of Westminster."

He's wasting no time. She folds her hands in her lap. "Yes, we are old friends."

Canaris nods. "And Prime Minister Churchill?"

"Yes. We first met some years ago at Eaton Hall, the Duke of Westminster's home in Scotland. He loved fly fishing on the grounds." She holds the smile and waits. He names a few more of Bendor's friends, frequent guests on the *Flying Cloud* and weekends at Eaton Hall, and she nods. She knows everyone, adds a few idle tidbits, stories from those days.

The room falls silent when the door opens and the secretary returns balancing a large tray, on top of which is a shining copper tea service. She sets it down on the low table and straightens, looking at Canaris. "That will be all, mademoiselle." She nods and leaves, closing the door behind her.

Leaning forward, Canaris pours tea into each cup. "Cream? Lemon?" He glances at Coco.

"Lemon, please."

He places a slice of lemon on the saucer and hands the teacup to Coco. She wills her hands to remain steady as she takes it. Dincklage reaches for his own, as does the admiral.

"I understand from Baron von Dincklage that you have a problem with your business partner, Mademoiselle Chanel," Canaris says, sitting back, cradling the cup in his hands and watching her. "I understand your partner is Pierre Wertheimer, the owner of a conglomerate of fragrance companies." He sips the tea. "And, of course, he is the majority owner of the company you formed together."

"Société Mademoiselle." She holds the cup and saucer on her knees. "Yes, but, Admiral Canaris, my first concern ..."

"No need to explain." He waves off her words. "Hans has briefed me on your problem with Monsieur Wertheimer, and your son's condition as well." Suddenly he fixes his eyes on hers. "First, it is you I'm concerned about for the moment."

Coco leans forward, placing the cup and saucer down on the table. "André is very ill, Admiral Canaris. He needs medical care right away."

Canaris turns to Dincklage.

"Mademoiselle Chanel is here to offer her assistance," Spatz says. "She is willing to travel to Madrid."

He turns to Coco. "We agree that grounds for mutual benefit exist?"

"That is correct, Admiral." Coco's heart leaps to her throat. She slips a glance at her watch. Minutes pass—precious minutes of André's life. "As you must know, my son's condition is urgent."

Again, he turns to Spatz. "Mademoiselle Chanel has your complete trust, of course."

"Yes, Admiral."

Canaris gazes at the blank wall behind her, expressionless.

Then, setting his teacup down on the table, he rests his arms on the chair. He turns his eyes to Coco wearing a thin smile, a warning, like faded green light shining from behind a thunder cloud, illuminating a coming storm. "A room will be booked under your name at the Hôtel Ritz, Madrid. You should feel right at home. You will be accompanied on this trip, mademoiselle. A companion to whom you will report to each and every day. I believe you are acquainted with him. Monsieur de Vaufreland?"

"Yes."

"To all appearances, the purpose of your trip is to promote sales of your perfume throughout Spain. You will say the market for perfume in France is weak, particularly in areas outside Paris. Since Spain is neutral, you're testing the prospects for expanding business there. You will promote your business in Madrid, take what usual actions a proprietor takes when surveying such possibilities."

"All right."

"We expect you to open doors for us. You will contact the British Embassy and your acquaintances in the city, particularly those who have the ear of your friend, the British prime minister. In addition, you will socialize with the upper crust and Spanish nobility." He studies her for a moment.

She nods, praying he has not overestimated her social connections. She is not royal. And although she has dined out on her friendship with Churchill for years, the truth is, he was mostly Westminster's friend. But for André, she smiles back at him and says, "Of course."

"In addition, we want you to become acquainted with those

around General Franco." He neither moves nor blinks as he speaks. "You must immerse yourself in the social life of Madrid to accomplish our goals."

She works to hide her growing impatience. "And in return?"

"I've not quite finished, mademoiselle." Coco feels the flush rising. "What I have just described is what others will see and hear." He pauses. Reaches for his cup and sips the tea.

"From our perspective, your mission for the Reich has two goals. First, Germany seeks an alliance with Spain. Germany desires that Spain join forces with the Fatherland. You will identify for us those in Spain with political or social influence who are sympathetic to our cause; who might be counted upon to convince General Franco to align with Germany in the war." After a pause, he adds, "And, of course, you will identify for us those who are not."

Leaning back, he crosses his arms. "Do you have questions so far?"

"You only want the names?"

"Names of everyone you meet or speak to who might be of assistance to us, or enemies. We want details of the conversations, with dates and times. Report on concerns expressed, personal or otherwise. What attracts them, what they like and dislike, their passions. Anything that strikes you as unusual, or which you think could possibly assist our analysis."

He glances toward Spatz. "Hans will provide more precise instructions. In general, report anything you come across which could be useful concerning Franco's future relationship with the Führer, or Germany."

She nods. "I understand."

Spatz looks at her. "You will write the information down, Coco. The paper on which it is written must be given to your contact each evening. You will keep no copies. We'll go over this again later."

Coco turns back to the admiral. What does she get in return?

"Second. In social situations—dinners, parties, teas, any social gathering—you will consistently and publicly support the concept, the possibility, of a truce and alliance between Great Britain and Germany." She starts at this. Rumors are flying that the Führer intends to invade England, and yet the admiral's exploring a truce?

"Talk it up, as they say. Your name and reputation give your opinion weight, mademoiselle. The purpose is to get your words to the ears of your friend, Winston Churchill. Report every detail of every conversation on the subject of a possible truce between England and Germany, a negotiated end to the war." The admiral watches her.

"When you speak of truce, are you negotiating for peace?" That is not so bad after all; that should not be treason to France. Her voice trills up the scale of hope.

He gives her a mild look. "You will be testing reactions and reporting back. And, yes, for peace. But, a separate peace."

"What do you mean by 'separate'?"

"This must be clear in your mind. This is what you must fully understand: a truce would not include Russia. Fighting between Great Britain and Germany will cease. Germany will band together with the British against Russian aggression in Europe, together, as allies."

"But what of France?"

He frowns. "France is a state of Germany and will remain so, as will the other occupied territories."

Here it is—the betrayal; the treason. She is forced to promote peace for England and Germany, but not for France. After the truce, Germany will keep its boot on the neck of the French.

"I'm surprised this idea shocks you, mademoiselle." With a glance at Spatz, Canaris adds, "I've been given to understand your life has changed very little under German occupation."

As Boy said, every choice has an effect, leaves an eternal mark. Choose your highest value, and then give it everything you've got.

André.

Her smile comes on command. "That is correct, Admiral Canaris. And I will do as you ask."

He folds his hands together, fingertips touching his lips. "Good. Good. As you say. And your assistance will be rewarded, mademoiselle." He turns to Spatz. "You will speak with Schellenberg, and if necessary, Heydrich, on this matter before Mademoiselle Chanel leaves. As soon as possible."

"Immediately."

"I'll want a full report."

Coco's heart beats wildly. "And my son? May I see my son before I leave?"

"I'm afraid that's impossible."

"When will he receive help?" She wrings her hands in her lap. "Really, the medical issue is urgent. André must see a physician at once."

"Coco." The warning in Dincklage's voice halts the rush of words. She looks from Spatz to the admiral.

The admiral's voice is surprisingly kind. "On your return, if all goes well, your son will be released and brought immediately to Paris, to a hospital of your choice."

She cannot help herself. "I must know he's safe before I go."

"I understand a mother's love." His face is grave. "I will have a doctor visit your son. Rations will be increased. We'll try to keep him as warm and comfortable as possible, given the situation. But he remains a prisoner of war until then."

The door opens. The secretary steps in. "Your next meeting begins in five minutes, Admiral."

Canaris looks up, lifts his hand. "Yes. Thank you." Turning to Coco, he grimaces. "I regret my time is not my own, Mademoiselle

Chanel. I would have liked to talk longer with you this morning."

Dincklage rises with the admiral, and Coco, feeling weak, follows suit. "Hans," he says, "see that Mademoiselle Chanel reads and signs everything before she leaves."

"Yes, sir."

Canaris walks with her to the door and Spatz follows. "By the way, mademoiselle, we will have someone look into the matter of your company—your business problem, when you return from Spain." As he opens the door and steps aside, he adds, smiling, "After all, we cannot have production of your wonderful perfume removed to America."

When she leaves the Hôtel Lutetia one hour later, after signing many documents, Coco Chanel is Abwehr Agent F-7124. Code name: Westminster.

Chapter Twenty-Six

Paris
Fall 1940

That evening Spatz calls downstairs for cocktails—a martini for him, a sidecar for her. Then he disappears into the bedroom for a change of clothes. Coco, sitting in her chair beside the window, puckers her lips. The September leaves are turning. A day has passed since the meeting with Admiral Canaris, and she thought she'd be packing for Madrid by now. Yet Spatz says these things take time. The schedule is out of his hands. She must wait. He's acting as if this is any other evening and nothing has changed.

When the doorbell rings, she sits unmoved. Spatz opens the door and takes the drinks from the waiter, carrying them to the table between the chairs. He hands over her drink and, holding on to his martini, sits down across from her.

Ignoring Spatz, Coco sips the cocktail and looks off. She thinks of nothing but André. Not even the possibility of losing No. 5, nor of Pierre, or Göring. André has tuberculosis! She stares at the straight sturdy column in Place Vendôme feeling fragile. It's as if she's made of shattered glass, as if the bits and pieces of her formerly ordered life have been rearranged in a pattern she does not understand.

Take care, Coco. Boy taught that fate is the consequence of choices.

"How soon, Spatz?" A moment ago she'd felt overheated. Now she is cold. "I cannot stand this waiting."

He nods. "Not long. But you must have patience. We're traveling to Berlin next week to see Herr Walter Schellenberg."

"What!" She starts, sits up straight, and sets the glass down on the table. "Why?"

"Schellenberg is head of all SS counterespionage, not only in Germany, but for all of Europe, including France. His power mirrors that of Admiral Canaris in foreign military intelligence—the Abwehr." He raises the martini to his lips, watching her over the glass. "Schellenberg insists upon meeting you before approving the Abwehr agreement to free André."

Coco opens her mouth, but nothing comes out. She'd thought the agreement was complete.

Spatz lifts a brow. "Schellenberg wants to look you over."

Rising, she stands looking down at him. "I thought everything was agreed. You told me everything was agreed after this meeting. I have been cleared by the admiral, isn't that so?"

"Sit down. This is protocol. The trip is just a bow to the SS and Walter Schellenberg—Heydrich and Himmler's man." He gives her a sympathetic look. "Schellenberg is friendly with Canaris, but he trusts no one, not even the admiral. Most likely he'll go along with the admiral. Why, they even exercise their horses together every morning when the admiral's in Berlin."

Coco says nothing. Spatz leans back, clasping his hands over his stomach. "Walter Schellenberg is a fine fellow, Coco. Hitler appointed him deputy director of this division of the Gestapo last June. You'll appreciate his style. You'd never know he's SS from his mild manner. He has charm. He's smart, yet subtle."

"I don't care about his charm, or brain, or personality. I only care about getting my son out of that prison camp."

"All right. We leave on Sunday afternoon by train for Berlin. Our meeting is set for ten o'clock next Monday, September ninth." He gives an airy flip of his hand. "But don't mark that on your social calendar."

"And what then, after that?"

"We'll see. Admiral Canaris will let me know. I'm certain things will move quickly after we see Schellenberg. Now, dinner at eight downstairs?"

"No." The last light of the sun slants through the windows, glazing crystal facets of a glass bowl she keeps on the low table. Her thoughts are dark, but she fixes her eyes on that light.

He frowns. "Your habit is cocktails in the dining room, then dinner. We've not followed that routine for several days. No sense in letting the Reich marshal know you're worried. You should dine downstairs tonight as usual."

"I think not." She cannot stand the sight of Göring. She turns her eyes to Spatz. "I will not appease that man. Do you know I saw him wearing lavender pants in the hotel yesterday, and carrying around a gold baton."

Spatz lets out a laugh and, after a moment, she laughs too.

"Laura Mae says Herr Göring sometimes wears silk kimonos when he's not in uniform."

Spatz quirks an eyebrow. "I wonder if she knows firsthand."

"Terrible thought." She clucks her tongue. "I will tell you one thing. Göring will not have No. 5. My perfume will remain at Neuilly, or I'll visit Adolf Hitler myself to plead my case once I return from Spain. Göring won't get his pudgy hands on my perfume."

Dincklage's smile dies. "Lower your voice," he snaps. He leans forward, takes Coco's glass, and places it on the table. Then he gathers her hands in his.

"Understand this, Coco. The Reich marshal is not a man to take lightly. Admiral Canaris seems agreeable to assisting you in the matter of Pierre Wertheimer once your mission in Spain is successfully completed. But with your business partner a Jew, you remain vulnerable. Göring could still complicate matters."

Her face turns pale.

He nods. "And so. We will go downstairs to dinner together. And you will acknowledge the Reich marshal with your best smile."

She pulls her hands from his.

"Until the mission to Spain is complete and André is free, you are trapped. Afterward we will deal with your business problem." He gives her a hard look. "Is this clear?"

He is right. She can almost hear Boy's voice. *Take a step at a time, after considering all possible consequences.* She will complete the mission first and free André. Then she will take on Pierre, and if necessary, Reich Marshal Göring.

If only Boy were here—he would find their son. He would know what to do.

But the truth is she was a fool to have ever trusted Boy Capel. A fool. Even when she'd heard the talk, even when he was absent for weeks at a time, even when he would not answer her questions—she'd still believed. She'd trusted him.

She'd thought their love and son would bind the three of them together, forever.

Part Three

Chapter Twenty-Seven

Paris

1918–1919

Betrayal is a wound that cuts deep, but does not let you die. It was 1918, the year I learned this lesson well: trust no one.

Boy spent the years of the Great War contracting coal for France and acting as liaison between war ministers Lloyd George in England and Georges Clemenceau in France. He was always away. He was a man who loved his work. We both loved our work.

I suppose that is why his long absences did not signal an alarm. For one thing, I was busy too. Chanel Modes bloomed; the House of Chanel rapidly expanded to 31 Rue Cambon, and we'd opened the new shops on the coast in Deauville and down south in Biarritz. And through all this time, I believed that Boy was mine and I was his. We were forever lovers, partners in life. And we had André.

It was in Paris I first heard the talk—Boy's name bantered about, linked with other women. Misia warned me outright, in her own acerbic way. She was delighted to tell. And of course, then came Colette. Several times I'd hear his name spoken as I walked into a room, and then, people turned their eyes to me and conversation stopped.

I steeled my mind against the false rumors. They envy our love, I told myself. Boy was my life. He was mine. He was André's father. No other woman could come between us, I was certain. And in Paris, flirtations do not count.

Still, sometimes, alone at night and despite every conscious effort, suspicion and jealousy seeped in. I fought to control my thoughts—to banish the doubt. I fought to exercise control over my mind, as Boy had taught. Bad thoughts can quickly spark rash actions, bringing unintended consequences.

Then, on a chilly evening in October, Boy walked through the door of our apartment with his suitcase in one hand and a look on his face that, at last, I could not ignore. He'd been in London. I stood immobile as he placed the suitcase on the floor, closing the door behind him in silence. Then he turned to me, taking a deep breath.

"Ah, wonderful," I said, working up a smile, through some instinct, not wanting him to speak. "You've come in time for cocktails." I moved toward him, reaching for his coat as usual. But instead of shrugging off the coat, he stepped back and jammed his hands into the pockets. I stopped, struck by the pain I saw in his eyes; the pain now etched in his face. Outside the bells of Notre-Dame tolled six o'clock, joined by the louder, closer bells of La Madeleine. Funeral tolls; I counted them as I stood before him, waiting—one through six. The room almost seemed to turn upside down in that instant. Reaching to one side, I clutched a nearby chair.

"So, it's true?" I whispered.

He knew what I meant. "Yes."

That one word seared my soul, my heart. I knotted my hands together, staring at him. I would not fall; I would not allow myself to faint.

Boy looked at me through his long lashes and I saw terrible pity in his eyes as disembodied words drifted between us. "Lady Diana Lister. We're marrying, Coco. An English girl, and widowed."

The church bells ended, vibrating through the silence. He held out his hand. I shook my head—no, no. The hand is not real. You are not real. Lady Diana Lister is not real. None of this is real.

I should have known the day would come. He loved my strength, the fact I'd earned my wealth and place in the world, but that can't compete with another English rose, and the right surname.

I watched him remove his coat as if this were a pantomime on a stage. As if my world were not ending, he folded the coat and hung it over a chair. I thought of the day of Étienne's ball at Royallieu, when he'd forced me to leave so as not to humiliate Étienne's wife—and Boy too? This last thought almost felled me to my knees. Was I forced to leave Royallieu with Émilienne that day to save Boy humiliation too?

I'd never thought of that before. I thought of the day André was born, when Boy should have offered marriage and a home, security. And as the truth sunk in, and while he shifted to an almost casual, conversational tone as if now everything would be fine since he'd confessed, I realized the full extent of Boy Capel's deceit.

"Her former husband was half-brother to your old friend, Westminster," he was saying. He lifted a brow. "Perhaps you know her?" His eyes were clear, his expression almost relieved—now the worst was over.

For a moment, I hated him.

Oblivious, Boy came toward me, arms outstretched. "Now, now, darling." He smiled. "This changes nothing between us." Taking my shoulders, he tugged me close to him. "She's a lovely girl, Diana Lister. But she's not my little Coco."

I shifted away, pulled back my hand, and slapped his face—hard. Boy flinched and stepped away, his eyes wide, his expression cold. And then he turned toward the door, moving away from me, and I knew that he was leaving me forever.

I could not lose him. I could not bear to let him go.

I collapsed. Sinking to the floor, I dropped my face into my hands, racked with sobs. Boy knelt beside me, gathered me into his arms, whispering something, words I could not hear. Sometime later, he swept me up and carried me to the settee. There I sank against him, my head tucked under his chin, my fingers clawing his chest while he held me and I cried. I wept for hours, it seemed.

Later—when the sun was gone, the room was dark—he cradled me in his lap, just as I'd always wanted to cradle André. Boy stroked my hair—my Boy Capel—whispering how he loved me; how nothing should change between us. "We'll keep this place," he said. He twirled a finger in my curls while he talked, a habit I loved. He loved my dark silk curls, he'd always said. "I'll come to you here often, darling." Bending down, he kissed me. "You are my only love."

But how could I live on in this place without Boy? My eyes roamed over the room I'd thought was our home together. Already, everything had lost its luster. He would take all the best things—the Coromandel screens, the family silver service, the things he valued. He would take the best for his wife and leave the rest for Coco.

I shuddered. He tightened his grip.

"One more thing, Coco," he said after a while. I felt his breath on my ear. "There is one more thing to tell."

Drained, I dropped my chin, bracing.

"Diana is having a baby. Mine." I closed my eyes. This is the end of my life, I thought.

"In April."

April! He'd known for some time. I wept again and he sat very still, holding me and whispering his love; but with no mention of his son. No mention of André.

He will earn his thirty pieces of silver, I swore to myself later that night, even as I clung to him in bed. But I knew despite his betrayal that I could never stop loving Boy Capel.

He knew this too.

Boy moved out, taking the things I'd expected that he would take—the things he valued. At the beginning of the New Year, 1919, I could no longer live in the apartment without him. I rented a lovely villa in Saint-Cloud, an elegant suburb a few miles north of Paris, and immersed myself in work. I was a known couturier now, already on the way to great success. I told myself, Boy may be married to Diana Lister, but he was still mine.

The irony was I saw Boy more than ever before. That did not stop the birth of the child in April; Diana Lister's girl. I told myself I did not care. Boy loved me, and André was our son—Boy's only son. André was our secret bond.

Christmas was almost upon us when the last blow struck. It happened two days before that holy day, in the year 1919.

I was sound asleep in Saint-Cloud when the bell downstairs shook me from my dreams. I lay abed listening as Girard's slippers flapped along the upper hallway and down the front stairs to the door. Lying between the soft silken sheets with my eyes half closed, mind still dull, I heard my butler open the door. And then I heard two voices.

I rose from the warm soft bed and hurried to the bedroom door. Wearing only white silk pajamas trimmed in white satin— it's strange the things you remember later—I walked into the hallway and looked down over the balcony into the entrance hallway. Two faces peered up at me, one from under a bowler hat.

I frowned, confused. The visitor standing by Girard was Léon de Laborde, an old friend from the weekend crowd at Royallieu.

He lifted his hand. "Coco. Please, come down."

With my mind fogged from sleep, I stood there stupidly, brushing my fingers through my hair. "What time is it, Léon? Why are you here at this hour?" And then something caught in my throat and my hand flew to my chest. Étienne.

Léon's face crumpled. He motioned for me to come.

By the time I made it to the top of the stairs, I was trembling. Étienne, my oldest friend; so kind. So good. He'd taken me from poverty to refuge and a new life at Royallieu. I stumbled, grabbing the railing just in time. Étienne!

Léon took my arm, guided me into the salon to the left of the grand stairway. He sat beside me on a settee near the fireplace, close—too close—and wrapped his arm around my shoulders. I sat up straight, hands in my lap, like a schoolgirl transfixed by a bolt of lightning. I did not want to hear the words, Étienne was gone.

Girard, behind us in the doorway, asked if we'd like tea.

"No," I said, looking at him, confused. Surprised to hear another voice.

Léon held up two fingers. "Whiskey." Girard nodded and disappeared.

I closed my eyes, hanging on, waiting for the terrible news. Léon was so close to Étienne—I would be brave for Léon now.

And then, with his arm curved around my shoulder, a hand gripping my arm, his face close to mine, I heard him speak the words that turned my life again. Boy Capel was dead.

It was an automobile accident just before Christmas on a high winding road near Cap d'Antibes overlooking the Azur sea. A tire burst on a curve. Boy always drove too fast, like he rode his horses. Such a random thing to end his life, and mine—the car had spun, hit a tree, and burned.

Léon drove me down to the coast and I stood by the burned-out car on that once-lovely country road, staring, touching the twisted metal in disbelief. I refused to move. I stayed for hours in the place where Boy had died, struggling to understand that he was gone. I prayed for a sign that somehow he was still with me. Perhaps his spirit lingered in that very spot.

Hours later, Léon took me to some other place, a house far from Boy's spirit. It was a sad house, I remember. We walked through a large salon where people wept—no one I knew—and off into another room where I sat alone with my grief.

I did not attend Boy's funeral. I would not share my deadening sorrow.

Boy's death was, for me, the end of love. The end of happiness. At night I often woke with racking sobs, shuddering cries for Boy, animal sounds I did not recognize as my own. Utter despair drove me from one church to another seeking comfort, seeking hope that someday I would be with Boy again. From La Madeleine to Notre-Dame to Saint-Sulpice to Sacré-Cœur I prayed on my knees, bargained with God, made offerings, lit candles, swore, wrung my hands.

Mother Madonna. Saint Theresa, Little Flower. Pray for me.

In his will Boy remembered me with forty thousand francs, the same amount he left another mistress. A woman in Italy he'd kept a secret. But even that deep cut was not the greatest wound. He'd left nothing for André. Boy Capel's fortune went to his new wife and his daughter, and the new baby Diana Lister already carried in her womb, a second child.

I had not even known.

I'd thought he loved me with all my heart and soul. Only me.

In the end, I understood. He loved, but not enough for my son and me. A great void slowly took Boy's place in my heart and walls grew around me. The man I'd loved and trusted had betrayed my heart, my soul, my mind. His kisses were lies. For me, 1919 was the year love died. I resolved that I would trust no one to take care of me, but me. I would depend upon no one but myself. I would look only to my work, my talent, and my creations for security. Including, a few years later, No. 5.

I swore the only obligation I would acknowledge in life was this: I vowed always to protect André.

Chapter Twenty-Eight

Berlin
Fall 1940

As Coco and Dincklage disembark the train at Anhalter Bahnhof in Berlin a week after meeting with Admiral Canaris, the wind whipping across the station platform is bitter. Coco tugs the wool cloche over her ears and pulls her coat around, tightening the loose belt. This early cold must be a warning of a bad winter to come.

She's brought no luggage because she does not want to stay overnight. Spatz promised after the meeting with Herr Schellenberg they'd have plenty of time to catch the afternoon train back to Paris.

As they hurry along the platform, she tilts back her head, admiring the swooping iron-and-glass arched roof. "Each time I visit Berlin I'm amazed at the opulence of this railway station, given the natural austerity of your people. It's a wonder, Gothic, yet light and airy." She glances at Spatz from the corner of her eye. "Your county is made up of many such contrasts, don't you agree?"

Spatz grunts, guiding her toward the terminal. "Remember

my warning, Coco. Be careful what you say in Berlin." She nods, shivering in the damp cold, walking faster.

There are six railway platforms under the glass roof. To her left is the train they just disembarked. To the right, another seems to be overflowing with people, reminding her of the crowds in railway stations in early June, when she'd fled Paris before the German invasion. Here, in carriage after carriage, faces press against the window, men and women of every age, and children, too, all packed together, their eyes wide as they peer out. Coco's skin prickles—they look frightened. Something is wrong, she senses it. Boy believed these instinctive feelings flow from other planes of existence, from a former life, and that they are real.

And that when we feel this way, we should pay attention.

She slows her pace, turning to Spatz, gesturing to the train. "Those passengers, Spatz. Who are they? Why are the carriages so crowded? Where are they going?"

He shrugs. "It's nothing. They're just uncomfortable. With the war we've reduced civilian trains. Fewer trains, less passengers. They are lucky to have tickets." He starts to walk faster. "Come, we must hurry or we'll be late."

At the end of the platform, before they reach the main terminal entrance, Spatz veers off to the right. "No need going through the guards," he says. "We'll go through the royal waiting room and out that way."

She gives him a sly look. "Are you accepting royal prerogatives these days?"

"Not until I'm crowned."

With a Hitler salute to the guard, Spatz leads her through the private reception room and out the entrance, past waiting taxis and rows of racked bicycles, out onto the busy plaza.

"There's our car," he says, lifting his arm. A large black Mercedes pulls up and stops before them. "We should have planned to stay the night." He nods toward the Hotel Excelsior across the plaza. "There's still time. Sure you won't change your mind? The city is lively in the evening, even during the blackouts. I'll show you my favorite places."

She shakes her head as the driver comes around to help them into the car. "Let's just get this over with."

As the car pulls away from the station, Spatz instructs the driver to take them to SS Headquarters. "The entrance on Prinz-Albrecht-Strasse," he says.

Coco lowers her voice, turning to him. "Please, Spatz. You must somehow convince Herr Schellenberg to give his approval quickly. I must leave immediately for Madrid. The longer the trip is delayed, the more André suffers."

The car pulls up before a stone building several stories high, situated in a small and lovely, but deserted, park. Enormous Swastika flags fly at either side of the stairs. At the top step Spatz stops before two large, heavy doors. The guard, wearing the familiar belted black uniform, seems to know him. They salute, and she's taken aback when Spatz issues a brisk command in German.

The guard's eyes stray to Coco. He straightens and clicks his heels. "Yes, Herr Dincklage."

The entrance hall is a hive of black uniforms and expressionless faces hurrying back and forth, moving in all directions. An officer walks quickly toward them, his runes, silver buttons, and eagles shining.

After the formalities, the guard says something to Spatz Coco cannot hear. They appear to disagree. But Spatz takes Coco's arm in an offhand manner, guiding her forward and leaving the officer behind. The man's boots click on the polished floor as he hurries after, and then marches alongside without another word. As they enter a long, wide hallway, Coco lifts her eyes to German letters carved into an archway above.

Spatz bends to whisper. "It says: My Honor Is My Loyalty. This is the SS pledge."

Coco asks no questions. Spatz has warned that every word spoken inside the building is captured by microphones and analyzed.

They take an elevator up to another floor, then walk another long hallway, this one stark, lit with acid light. Spatz stops before a door and—here again—the officer following them moves on.

"Here we are, Deputy Director Schellenberg's office. I have made it clear a personal search is unnecessary this time. We are not in enemy territory." He makes a sweeping gesture. "Please—before me, Coco."

Inside, she takes a comfortable chair against the wall while Spatz speaks with a pretty girl sitting at a heavy, ornate oak desk. A picture of the Führer hangs behind her, and a few large maps are pinned on the walls, but nothing more. A swastika flag stands beside a closed door near the girl's desk. The concrete floors are bare. Metal cabinets are pushed back against the walls.

In addition to the girl, two other secretaries work at a long metal table off to the side of the room. Occasionally they glance at Coco while clacking away at typewriters. Piles of paper lay beside the machines.

Last night Spatz prepared her again for this meeting, reminding her that it is merely protocol, and adding, "And it doesn't hurt that our proposed spy is the famous Mademoiselle Chanel."

With that in mind, she'd added an extra swipe of red lipstick before leaving the train this morning. She'd chosen her wardrobe carefully for the visit too—a light wool suit in cream beige, of her own design. Creamy beige is her favorite color. It is calm and soothing and sets off her dark hair and olive skin—and the red lipstick. She also wears her usual crisp white blouse and pearls, off-white stockings, and beige-and-brown two-toned low-heeled shoes, with white gloves and a small plain hat.

And, of course, a good spritz of No. 5.

The wait seems interminable. The overhead lights are hot. The seats are hard. Coco pulls a handkerchief from her purse, dabbing her forehead, her upper lip. There are no windows in this room and the air is stale.

Glancing at her watch, she realizes that twenty minutes have already passed since they arrived. At last a buzzer sounds at the secretary's desk, and she rises. She escorts Coco and Spatz through the door with the flag, into a spacious, luxuriously carpeted room. At the other end, behind an enormous walnut desk, sits the man she presumes is Walter Schellenberg. With a brief glance, he lifts a hand and continues writing.

In silence the secretary directs them to a pair of leather armchairs before the desk. Coco rests her purse in her lap and looks about. Schellenberg's desk is clear except for the writing materials. The windows behind him are covered with wire mesh. On the trip from Paris, Spatz told her the wires were sensors containing a system of photoelectric cells which alert guards if anyone approaches. Schellenberg's office is impenetrable, from inside and out.

The window mesh reminds her of the narrow bars over the small abbey cell in which she slept with her sisters at Aubazine. The dim gray haze filtering through the windows is the same cold light.

They wait while the secretary departs and Schellenberg continues writing, seeming absorbed in the work. He appears quite ordinary, Coco muses, for a man with such power. To her right is a fine crafted cupboard containing books; it is an elegant antique piece. To her left, beside his desk, is a round table holding a mass of telephones, recorders, winding cords, a pistol, and other mechanical things. Her eyes pause on the pistol.

At last Schellenberg sets down the pen and looks up. His face transforms, as if he's just removed a mask. His eyes light and he rises, drawing Coco in with his smile. Without thinking, she smiles back.

"Mademoiselle Chanel," he says, with a little bow. But instead of coming around to properly greet her, he sits down again. "How kind of you to come."

Catching herself—Spatz warned her of his charm—she merely inclines her head. She does not want to like this man. She must be on guard. For men like Walter Schellenberg, charm is a weapon.

Schellenberg turns his attention to Spatz. "I hear that you and Mademoiselle Chanel have had a friendly talk with the admiral." He speaks fluent French with them, with a slight accent she recognizes from the Alsace-Lorraine region.

"Yes. As you know, Mademoiselle Chanel has agreed to assist with our Spanish concern. She is willing to travel to Madrid on our behalf." Spatz spreads his hands. "Here we are, and our time is yours."

"Of course." Schellenberg swings his eyes to Coco. "As I understand, you've been briefed by Admiral Canaris. I'm certain he made clear that our first priority in Spain is forming an alliance with General Franco. In Madrid you will socialize with those supporting General Franco, and in particular General Serrano Suñer, and those around him." He pauses. "You must remember the name, Serrano Suñer."

She nods.

"At all times you will listen carefully to what you hear on the idea of Spain joining us against Russia. You will bring it up in subtle ways, when possible."

And then he adds, emphasizing each word, "We especially want to know Serrano Suñer's opinion on this matter. We expect to receive detailed and timely reports each day you are in Madrid, mademoiselle."

She nods again. She does not trust this man.

"As to the second part of the mission," he picks up the pen, tapping it against the desk. "That is to say, laying the groundwork for consideration of a truce between Germany and Great Britain— we expect you to make your opinions clear. You will use your name and influence to promote the benefits of such a truce to Europe, to the world. Our primary targets here are those connected with the British Embassy. In particular we are interested in those who associate with your friend, Prime Minister Churchill." Again he pauses, asking if she understands.

"Yes, I understand."

"Good. So then." He slaps his hands on the desk before him. "I understand you have concerns over the impact of a German-British truce upon your country?"

She stiffens at the thought that France will remain under the German boot. *A French State, indeed.* But she's made the decision, she is here. And she will keep her part of the bargain.

Coco chooses her words carefully, holding his eyes. "It is true I am somewhat concerned about France's position under this truce. But I assure you, that will not affect my ability to carry out this mission."

He almost smiles, but his eyes are cold. "And I assure you, mademoiselle, that the German people hold the French close in our hearts. In the New Order, my personal goal is to preserve the great history and beauty of your country." He touches his heart. "Myself, I was born in Saarbrücken, in Alsace."

An area now subjugated under German rule.

His eyes pin hers. "Our countries are one, our people are one. We understand each other. Both Germany and France, as a state, will benefit from closer economic cooperation. United in purpose, our countries will stand strong."

"Yes, I agree." She polishes the top of her purse with a gloved hand, suddenly nervous. She must take care with each word. "As I've often said, we in Europe are family. Germany and France are cousins. What benefits Germany, also benefits France."

"Good. That is good." Folding his hands together, as in prayer, he adopts a contemplative look. "Then we are in agreement."

"We are."

He pauses. He wants more from her, she knows.

He watches her. Seconds pass. *Encourage him. Give him something, fast.*

She touches her pearls, wrapping one strand around the tip of her finger. "Believe me, I do understand your point, Herr Schellenberg. The occupation has restored order in France. Paris was anarchy before. Communist mobs and decadence brought us down in the first place." She catches her breath. She will say it: "France has got what she deserved."

Schellenberg sets down the pen, spinning it around until it stops, pointing in her direction.

She will grovel if she must. "You may count on me. Together our countries will lead the way to the new Europe." And then, she manages another smile.

He leans back, seeming satisfied at last. "My point exactly," he says. "And then, of course, there is the matter of your son, André Palasse."

At last, André! "Yes. My son." Leaning forward, bracing her hands on her knees, she looks him in the eye and does what she has never done before. She begs. "Please, Herr Schellenberg, you must help my boy. He is close to death, I hear. He requires medical care immediately." Her breathing turns shallow, her voice turns hoarse. "Please, I will do my part, but I beg you to release André to a hospital now."

His tone is amiable when he replies, but firm. "I am sorry, mademoiselle. Your son is a prisoner of war. My power does not extend to granting a prisoner's release; at least not without something in hand to show in return." He regards her under heavy, lowered lids. "As a businesswoman you are aware, a bargain usually requires compromise on both sides."

Slowly she releases the thin thread of hope she's clung to from the moment she learned they were traveling to Berlin. She asked the favor, even though Spatz warned that it is Schellenberg's superior, Heinrich Himmler, who commands the work camps, and therefore, André's care. And Himmler, in turn, reports to Reinhard Heydrich, chief of Reich security, whom Hitler refers to as "the man with the iron heart."

These men have only reluctantly agreed to André's release from prison, Spatz says, conditioned upon Schellenberg's approval. And they have done so only at Admiral Canaris's request and his assurance that when the mission is complete Mademoiselle Chanel will have successfully provided services of value to the Reich.

It is this last vague condition that so terrifies Coco.

She lifts her chin, holding Schellenberg's eyes. "I will do my best," she says. "You will have your reports."

Smiling, Deputy Director Walter Schellenberg stands. Beside her, Spatz touches her arm and together they rise. Schellenberg saunters around the desk and slaps his hand on Spatz's shoulder as they walk toward the door through which she will escape. There are only five more steps to that door.

In the station waiting for the train returning to Paris, Coco begins to relax. The interview is over. Coco pulls a platinum cigarette case from her purse, a recent gift from Spatz, and extracts two Gitanes. One for her and one for Spatz. He takes them and lights one, handing it back to her. As he cups his own and flicks the lighter, the platform door opens and a guard looks in. He tips his hat to Dincklage and closes it again.

"Almost time to go," Spatz says. He crosses his legs and leans back, exhaling smoke. "Did you notice the gold signet ring Schellenberg wears? He never takes it off."

"The one with the large blue stone?" Coco wrinkles her nose. "Too big. And gauche."

He smiles. His tone is irreverent now. "But useful, my pet. He keeps a cyanide capsule underneath. Never goes without it."

Smoking, she gives him a sideways look. "Shall I take one along to Madrid?"

His frown makes her laugh, a small release from the afternoon anxiety. His eyes dart to the only other people in the royal waiting room—two severely chic ladies sitting near the door to the platforms. A loud announcement comes over the speaker in German. The women across the room gather their packages and handbags.

Coco drops the cigarette on the stone floor and rubs it out with the toe of her shoe. "How did I do in the meeting?"

Spatz stands, waiting. "You did well. Which is luck, darling, because Walter Schellenberg's desk hides two machine guns underneath. They were pointed right at our hearts, and the door behind." Motioning toward the platforms, he says, "Come along. This is our train."

She picks up her purse and starts toward the door. "Is the man paranoid?"

"No. He's just a charming killer." But Spatz does not smile. At the door, he opens it and stands aside. "And about the machine guns,"—he gives her a look—"that was just a joke."

Chapter Twenty-Nine

Madrid
Fall 1940

Each turn of the train wheels carries Coco closer to Madrid. Coco's assigned companion, her minder, Baron Louis de Vaufreland, travels with her in a separate compartment. She stares out the window, smoking, seeing nothing as the train rolls on. At last she's doing something, working for André's freedom. Her mind is set—there is nothing she won't do in Spain to save her son.

Nothing.

The car, waiting for them at the station, now pulls up to the entrance of the Hotel Ritz Madrid on the Plaza de la Lealtad. A doorman appears at once, greeting her with a smile. Tense from the trip and the enormity of her mission, Coco stands, waiting for Louis to exit the car. Here in Spain, they've agreed, they shall be presented as old friends on a first name basis. He's all right, she supposes. A diminutive man, spry, a bit plump, and somewhat affected in manner.

Coco glances about, shading her eyes from the glaring light.

The late September sunshine washes Madrid in gold, it seems. In fluent Spanish Louis is haggling with the bellhops as they remove luggage from the trunk. She moves toward the entrance, gliding down a shaded path through a forest of orange trees and pomegranate, boughs of yellow roses, beds of yellow daffodils, and masses of fragrant red carnations. Doormen open the doors to the lobby as she arrives. There she stops again, waiting for Vaufreland.

"You speak Spanish well," she says, when he catches up. "I know only a few words." She laughs, flutters her hands. "Polite phrases, how to order drinks. Barely enough to carry on a conversation."

He takes her arm. "I am half Spanish, mademoiselle, nephew of the Duchess of Almazán. I hope to introduce you while we're here." With a nod to the doormen, as they enter the hotel, he executes a few spry samba steps. Coco looks at him, surprised. Spain has brought him to life—he's less intense, less morose, as if he's been freed from prison. This, together with the warm sunshine, the revelation of his connection to the duchess, and the light, airy lobby, all combine to lift her mood.

"Are you close? With the duchess, I mean."

"Yes, of course. I'm her favorite relative." He leads her through the enormous vaulted lobby toward a decorative arrangement of chairs. They pass long mirrors, one after the other, and Coco catches a glimpse of her image, a woman looking younger than her age, slim, resembling a well-dressed schoolgirl.

Louis places her into a chair covered in plush velvet stripes of russet and gold. Then he lifts a finger, "I shall be back in an instant, mademoiselle."

"Coco," she reminds him as he hurries off. Crossing her legs and beginning to relax, her eyes roam over the lobby, bright with sunlight, glazing the marble floors and columns. She looks past a large bouquet of red carnations on a table nearby, infusing the air with fragrance, to the far end of the lobby where a group of stylish guests wander down a grand staircase—whimsical architecture from turn-of-the-century belle epoque.

Louis soon returns carrying two large brass keys and trailed by bellhops. His room is on the third floor, he says. Coco's suite is on the fourth. Together they ride the elevator. As Louis steps out, he turns and announces that he will see her on the terrace at two o'clock.

She purses her lips. His tone is very close to a command.

Coco is quiet while the lift ascends. On orders of Admiral Canaris, Spatz has instructed her to provide Louis de Vaufreland with a written report each day she's here. She must give details of every engagement—names, dates and times, place, specifics on all conversations, specifics on all gossip, no matter how trivial it appears.

She'd complained that she would have time for nothing but writing out the reports.

Each daily report will be delivered by Vaufreland on the following morning into the diplomatic bag at the French embassy. Each report shall be delivered and read at the Hôtel Lutetia in Paris, and a copy sent to Walter Schellenberg's office in Berlin.

"Not a day must pass without a report," Spatz said.

The unspoken words: for André's sake, and your own.

The elevator shudders to a stop, the bell rings, and the operator slides back the doors. "This is your floor, mademoiselle."

Her trunks are open and spread across the suite when Coco walks in. A wide archway separates the sitting room from the bedroom. A maid wearing a starched black-and-white uniform is unpacking.

"Welcome to Hotel Ritz, Madrid, Mademoiselle Chanel," the girl says as she pulls a blouse from the trunk.

With a glance at the maid, Coco nods, then turning, looks around. The walls in the sitting room are covered with pale-green silk the color of the sea near La Pausa. The light wood floors are polished to a high shine; sofas and chairs are covered in cream-colored linen and bordered with green-and-white striped braiding.

Small marble tables placed strategically throughout the room hold vases of lilies, roses, and daffodils; some are adorned with small sculptures. Across the room, double glass doors open to the terrace. This is a serene, pleasant room.

She crosses to the terrace, where sheer silk curtains in the same pale green as the walls are pulled back, framing the tall doors. Coco opens the doors wide, walking out onto the balcony. From a terrace below comes tinkling laugher, soft music, and the scent of fragrant flowers. She leans on the parapet, gazing out over the gardens and the Prado Museum just beyond, with the full glory of Madrid before her.

For the meeting with Louis on the terrace downstairs, Coco chooses a short, pale-yellow linen afternoon dress and braided gold sandals. No purse; no gloves. But she wears a brimmed straw hat with a black ribbon to shade her from the sun.

Despite the canopy of trees over the stone-paved terrace, green-and-white striped umbrellas also shade every table. The place is crowded for the time of day when the Spanish usually rest. And each table is occupied. Aware of eyes turning her way, she looks for Louis. He sits at a table near the fountain, deep in conversation with a stranger. Coco crosses the terrace, and as she approaches, she lifts her hand, recognizing the stranger with delight.

"Sam Hoare!" It has been years since they met. The tall, distinguished gentleman with the high forehead, fine nose, and sharp features—an unmistakable Brit—was a regular guest at Westminster's weekend Eaton parties. Even in this heat he wears a light linen jacket and a tie, along with a sensible straw hat.

"Ah, Coco." Rising, Sam reaches out, taking her hands in his. "Good to see you again, my dear." He leans in, kissing her cheeks. "Imagine my surprise when Louis mentioned you were in Madrid."

Louis has risen also, and as he greets her, he pulls out a chair. Sam hovers until she's settled, then returns to his seat. "It's been too long. I believe the last time we were together was on the *Flying Cloud*."

"Yes, too long." That, of course, is Bendor's fault. She wonders if Sam realizes Westminster dropped her for someone else—she hopes not.

"Louis and I encountered each other quite by accident in the lobby," Sam explains. "I've known this fellow for years. His auntie, the duchess, and I are old friends." He gives Coco a fond look. "And you, my dear, are lovely as ever."

Turning to Louis, Sam lets out a chuckle. "We used to fish together at Westminster's Eaton Hall in Scotland. You may not be aware that Mademoiselle Chanel is an expert fly fisher. Neither Churchill nor I ever won a bet off her."

Coco laughs. "You were both easy prey."

Louis pretends surprise at this. But of course the Germans know everything about her past—that is why she's here. The waiter appears at her side and she orders Earl Grey, lemon. No milk.

"Sam is Ambassador Hoare, now," Louis says.

He nods. "We've only just arrived, a few months ago."

"And Lady Maud is with you?"

"I cannot do without her." He sips what appears to be a gin and tonic. "She'll be thrilled to learn you are in town."

Not too thrilled, Coco understands. Wives were never invited to Bendor's weekend parties at Eaton Hall. Still, that was years ago. "Please tell her I'll call."

Sam lowers his voice, bending toward her. "Splendid. Between us, Maud is frantic with worry. We were forced to leave the family in London. The children are in the country, but with everyone else in town and the bombing every night, the constant raids, the destruction, well, I think a friend will help."

"I look forward to seeing her again." Louis is watching her.

Touching the brim of her hat, Coco murmurs. "The war must end soon. There must be some way. I am sick of war."

The ambassador nods, but says nothing.

Coco smiles. "Oh, now this glorious Spanish sun is delightful." The waiter brings the tea tray. "How I've longed for sunshine, and flowers." Spreading her hands, palms up, she looks about. "Imagine! Paris is gray at this very moment, already turning cold. And here we are in such lovely fall weather."

"Is that why you've come?"

"That, and a bit of business." Avoiding Louis's eyes, she sits back while the waiter places the tray on the table, on which are a cup, saucer, spoon, and a small plate of bright-yellow lemons, quartered, with an accompanying porcelain tea pot. When he's gone, she pours the tea and looks again at Sam. "I'm considering opening a new boutique in Madrid."

"Wonderful. Maud will be your first client." He removes his hat, fanning his face. She squeezes the quarter-moon lemon into the tea. Sam Hoare's gone partially bald, she notes as he replaces the hat.

"I suppose I must get going." He sounds resigned. "But, listen here, we're hosting cocktails at our home this evening." He glances at Louis. "You must come if you're free."

"I'd be delighted," Coco says.

Louis smiles. "We will be delighted."

Ah, the minder at work. She must remain focused on the purpose of this mission night and day. Not only because of André, but Spatz has said when she returns to Paris, Louis de Vaufreland is the man with connections to assist in her claim for control of Société Mademoiselle and No. 5.

"Good, then." Rising, Sam Hoare tips his hat. "With that promise, I shall be off."

Coco and Louis watch the British ambassador stroll toward the wrought iron gate from the terrace to the street. A bevy of pretty young girls wearing colorful summer dresses and no hats and gloves greet him as they enter the terrace, fluttering past—a kaleidoscope of butterflies. They are followed by a handsome young man in a white linen suit. Spotting Sam, he whips off his hat, his blond hair gleaming in the sun. The ambassador stops, says something to him, and walks on. The young man then quickly follows the girls to a nearby table.

"They're from the British Embassy," Louis says, his eyes on the girls. "Staff, secretaries, stenographers. The fellow with them is Tom Burns, press attaché to the British Embassy." After a brief pause, he adds, "Or so they say. Pay attention to Burns."

His tone has changed. He's back to business. Coco sips her tea in silence, letting her eyes roam over the terrace.

"Burns is more than a press secretary, we're certain. He's a source to develop—knows everyone in Madrid. He's sure to be there this evening, Coco, so your work begins right away."

"With Burns?"

He nods. "Just get to know him this evening. An Embassy party is a good start. And you must stay sharp. Everyone knows Mademoiselle Chanel resides at the Paris Ritz along with the Reich's high command. That will mean only one thing to the guests this evening."

That she is a collaborator? She gives him a sharp look and places the teacup down a bit too hard.

"I only meant that to be persuasive you must be subtle. Before you raise the idea of a truce, you must establish your heart is French in truth, but that you are also pragmatic. Your opinion must be clear—while France is indeed defeated, life with Germany also brings a certain sense of order. Do not forget—you must communicate that you believe, even with France subjugated to Germany, a separate truce between Britain and Germany is the only way old Europe will survive."

Here is a German bourgeois bore masquerading as a

Frenchman and lecturing her on love of country. She presses her lips together, but says nothing.

"Are you listening?"

"Shall I write down my script for your approval?"

His eyes turn hard. "We are here for several weeks, Coco. Make the most of the time. This is your assignment. And this evening you begin."

Laughter comes from the butterfly table. Pressing her hands hard against the edge of the table, she rises. "I shall go for a walk in the gardens near the Prado now. I will meet you at seven o'clock in the hotel lobby."

A line forms between his eyes. "I'll join you."

She's misjudged him. He's not the gay young man he'd seemed when they first arrived. And he does not yet trust her. "No." She gives him a cold look. "I prefer to be alone at the moment." She feels his eyes on her as she walks toward the terrace gate.

Coco wanders through the large garden separating the hotel from the Prado, through a winding maze of flowers and more of the red blooming pomegranate trees. She drifts between hedges of lantana and delicate wax flowers, rose bushes bursting with velvety pink and red blooms, beds of ubiquitous carnations and Spanish bluebells, yellow gerbera, delphinium, calla lilies as tall as she's ever seen. Carnations are the flower of love in Spain, Louis told her.

The combination of the fragrant bouquet and the warm sun slowly calms her. The roses, the top note in the garden, bring memories. She takes a seat on a bench under a shade tree, recalling the day with Boy that she'd first sensed something wrong between them, like the smell of a fruit on the cusp of rot. It started when she'd simply complained to Boy that he no longer sent her flowers.

They were living on Avenue Gabriel at the time. On the very next morning, a huge bouquet of red roses arrived at the front door. She'd buried her nose in the flowers, ecstatic. The maid carefully arranged them in a crystal vase and set them on a table in the center of the drawing room.

One hour later, a second bouquet of roses arrived—and then, every hour after, on the hour, more and more roses delivered by the same young boy until she'd become annoyed. By noon annoyance sparked to anger. By midafternoon, the cloying scent drove her mad. She left the apartment and instructed her maid to toss the roses out. To rid the apartment of every flower.

"It was to teach you the true meaning of love and happiness," Boy claimed that night when he found her weeping. "Roses die. Love is eternal," he'd said. "True love is spiritual. It does not require such physical proof as flowers."

Not long after, he married Diana Lister.

She leans against the hard back of the bench, closing her eyes and lifting her face to the sun. Surprisingly, the memory doesn't hurt as it used to do. Boy was always teaching, as if she were a child. She will always love him, she supposes. She is resigned to that fact.

And, she realizes the worst sting of the whole affair with Boy is gone. She has other, more important things to consider now; other, more important matters requiring her energy and attention. Revived, with new resolve, she shifts her thoughts to the evening ahead and the mission she must accomplish.

Control your thoughts and you direct your fate.

Half an hour later, taking a deep breath, Coco stands, heading back through the flower beds to the hotel. It does not matter whether she likes or dislikes Louis de Vaufreland, nor anyone else for that matter. She will complete this mission for Germany to free her son. And then she will use Louis Vaufreland as a weapon, waging total war against Pierre.

Chapter Thirty

Madrid
Fall 1940

She's been in Madrid for over a week, and Louis says her reports are banal litanies of no consequence, and meanwhile André lies in that prison. She's heard the weather in Germany, even in October, is terrible, cold and wet, and she's growing desperate for something to give to Canaris and Schellenberg.

She keeps busy every minute of every day, accepting invitations from people she'd never otherwise have considered. She has traipsed all over the city pretending to search for locations for a new Chanel boutique. She has reported details of breakfasts, lunches, afternoon teas, cocktails, and dinners. She has reported on the lives of British aristocrats and Spanish royalists and nurtured friendships with whirlwinds of gossip, like Piedita, the Marquesa de Belvís de las Navas, an acquaintance from the past who knows everyone in Madrid.

And to no avail, according to Louis. But how does one talk of war in a city already beaten down by its own civil war—everyone's sick of the subject—or with others wealthy enough to have escaped from German territories to Spain only to forget the war?

And she has yet to meet General Serrano Suñer, Schellenberg's particular concern. Well, Piedita brags of connections with General Franco. She has prospects, Coco thinks.

Louis de Vaufreland, as usual, disagrees.

This afternoon, Coco waits in the hotel lobby for Gloria von Fürstenberg, recently divorced from a German aristocrat sympathetic to Hitler's cause, with whom she will have tea. Fresh from Berlin, Gloria has the latest news. Gloria is a connoisseur of great couture, so Coco wears her favorite dress, loose and short, made of white lawn and garnished with intricate tucks. She's sewn a white camellia, also made of lawn, to the collar. And, of course, she wears her pearls.

Coco glances at her watch. It's five thirty. Gloria is late—and as if conjured by the thought, Gloria strides through the lobby toward her, a wild mass of dark hair flowing around her head. With that figure, one would never know the woman birthed a son just one year ago. She wears Chanel today, the loose silk pants and embroidered white jacket. The embroidery from Coco's Maison was sewn with royal Russian hands, but with Germany and Russia at each other's throats, she won't mention that today.

Gloria opens her arms and flashes for Coco the wide smile for which photographers swoon. Coco rises. "At least you're wearing one of mine this afternoon," she says as they exchange kisses. Yesterday, to Coco's annoyance, Gloria had worn Schiaparelli.

"But of course." Gloria posing, fingers a diamond earring. "And I also wear your perfume. No. 5, can you tell? It's my favorite."

"Mine too." Coco takes her arm, turning toward the terrace. "Shall we have our tea outside?"

"Heavens no, we go to the embassy this afternoon. Come, my car is waiting."

Coco pauses. "Which embassy?"

Gloria laughs, pulling her along. "The embassy tearoom on the Paseo de la Castellana, darling. It's the only place to be, especially in this heat." Her eyes sparkle. "Have you not been there yet?"

"I have not."

"Well, then, I shall introduce you to the place. We'll have cakes and tarts and aperitifs, and in that small café you will find everyone who counts for anything in Madrid—British, American, Spanish, German, French, all together in one little room despite men's wars." She gives Coco a sideways look. "It is—how do you say?—spicy."

The concierge holds the door as they pass through. Bellboys line the walkway. At the entrance curb Gloria's shining black Mercedes waits with the motor humming.

"To the embassy," Gloria says, then, turning her eyes to Coco, she gives a throaty laugh. "You will hear the latest gossip here, darling. People sit at tables ranked by loyalties, of course. I must avoid the British table, for obvious reasons."

Coco straightens her collar, looking ahead. "But why? I attended your last wedding in the heart of London, at Kensington."

"Yes, I know. But some old memories must be forgotten. Friendships come and go according to wars. And considering my dear late husband's estate,"—she flashes a wicked smile—"my heart is with Germany, at least for the moment."

Coco pulls a folded fan from her purse. The heat is intense. "How are the children? Are they here with you?"

"No, they're in Lausanne. We left the house in Paris before Franz-Egon was born, and now I'm alone, I don't know when I'll go back. Germany has been good to me, but I do miss Paris." She sighs. "Or, who knows, perhaps I'll stay in Madrid."

Coco sniffs and wrinkles her nose. "Do you notice the odor here in the center city?"

Gloria flicks her hand. "So much damage from their civil war;

such ruin in a lovely place. I've argued over this with General Franco many times. It's the heat. Workers here do everything backwards. They clean the suburbs first and by the time their carts arrive where we reside, the sun is high and the rot has set in."

The car slows before a shop looking much like a bakery. Large square show windows on either side of the door boast a luscious display of pastries. As they enter, Coco glances about. The room is small and crowded. But sunshine slants through the windows and the place simply shimmers with style. The men wear tropical-colored formfitting suits. Most of the women wear gauzy bare-shouldered dresses. A mixture of Spanish, English, German, French, and Italian flows from every direction, everyone talking at once. Waiters in white shirts and dark jackets with red sashes tied around their waists remind Coco of Picasso's latest fad. Carrying tarts, candied fruits, cream-filled pastries, cocktails, and champagne on trays held high overhead, they dodge and weave between the tables.

A smiling dark-haired woman greets them just inside the door. Her English holds the hint of an Irish brogue. Gloria introduces her to Coco as the owner of the lively tearoom. While she and Coco converse, Gloria scans the room, then waves to someone. Turning to Coco, she interrupts the conversation, linking her arm through Coco's.

"Excuse me, Margaret. But, Coco, see over there, darling? Do you see that man looking our way?" Coco stands on her tiptoes, peering through the crowd. "Well, if you don't know him you must make his acquaintance. He is a fine man—Baron von Stohrer, Germany's ambassador to Spain." She pulls Coco forward. "Come with me."

The ambassador stands as they approach the table, gesturing for everyone to make room for two more guests. He greets Gloria profusely, and taking Coco's hand, he turns to an elegant gentleman beside him who now rises from his chair. "Serrano! You are already acquainted with Gloria, Countess von Fürstenberg, but allow me to present you to Mademoiselle Chanel."

Coco tenses. At last Schellenberg's general has appeared. As the ambassador makes the full introduction to Spain's minister of the interior and, as Louis has also advised, Franco's brother-in-law, Coco turns to him with her most charming smile.

The general, a slight man, holds himself with aristocratic bearing as he rises to greet Coco. The man Schellenberg has ordered her to cultivate is handsome in a rough way, and imposing with his smooth, broad forehead and streaked silver temples and trim mustache. As he takes her hand, greeting her, his intense hawklike eyes radiate an aura of power and confidence.

"Mademoiselle Chanel," he says at once. "I have heard good things of you from your friend, Wallis, the Duchess of Windsor. She and the duke charmed all of Madrid on their visit last July, as you are probably aware."

His words startle her. "Why, no, I have not spoken with Wallis since early summer. I'm sorry that I missed them. Did they return to their villa in Cap d'Antibes?"

"At that time they were on their way to Lisbon." A waiter slides chairs on the other side of the table, and the general escorts both women to their places.

"Lisbon. I wonder why?" But he has already turned away, moving back to his seat across the table.

Coco lowers her eyes, studying Serrano Suñer under half-closed lids. Perhaps this outing will be profitable after all. A waiter hands her a menu. Gloria leans toward her. "The ambassador has asked us to join him and General Suñer and a few others for dinner later at Horcher's, if you're free."

"That will be delightful." Coco sets the menu aside. Things are looking up. A waiter appears at her elbow. Vermouth is what she needs, ordering a white Noilly Prat. When she turns back to the table, Suñer's eyes meet hers. With a long slow smile, he lifts his glass.

Perhaps now her work really begins.

At nine o'clock, after three hours of cocktails and small talk, the ambassador sweeps Coco and Gloria, followed by General Suñer, out through the embassy door. They crowd together just outside. The sky is streaked with silvery stardust; the new moon is just a sliver in the sky. "Where is your huge topless automobile?" Gloria asks the ambassador, as an ordinary Mercedes pulls up.

The ambassador smiles, opening the passenger door even before the driver can come around. "That car belongs now to El Caudillo, my friend—General Francisco Franco." He shrugs, moving aside for Gloria and Coco. "He admired the car, so I had it delivered to him as a gift from the Reich." Serrano Suñer follows Coco into the back seat. Ambassador von Stohrer sits in front.

"Franco loves the automobile." Serrano turns to Coco. "It is a rare model, a Mercedes-Benz W31 type G4. The Führer, Joseph Goebbels, and Benito Mussolini all have one like it." Leaning forward, he slaps his hand on the ambassador's shoulder. "And now, thanks to you, my brother Francisco has one also."

This will go in her report tonight—General Serrano Suñer's appreciation for the wonderful gift from Germany's ambassador to his brother-in-law, Franco. The admiral and Schellenberg should be pleased. The general's good will must bode well for the Reich.

Restaurant Horcher is situated in the El Retiro Park, not far from the Ritz. Inside, General Suñer requests a private room with a table for six. Two more in the party will arrive shortly, he says.

Wives, perhaps? Coco does not ask.

After profuse greetings from the maître d', General Suñer leads them through the opulent dining rooms, one after another. Conversations stop and heads turn as they pass. While the embassy tearoom radiated light, here the heavy wood paneling, lush carpets, thick fabrics, and tapestries seem to absorb it. Silver candelabras gleam, candles flicker, elaborate wall sconces glow, but still the rooms they pass through are dim, heavy with the fragrance of spicy dishes and perfumes.

In contrast to General Suñer's party, these diners wear evening dress; the waiters, tails. "We should have changed for dinner," Coco whispers.

Gloria arches her brows. "Don't worry, darling. We are with Serrano. The general writes his own rules."

They are shown into an intimate room. A round table is set for six. A mural of colorful painted flowers covers the four walls above carved walnut wainscoting, giving the space the ambiance of a small garden. Moments after they've arrived, the two last guests appear. Coco is delighted to find Piedita joining them, with a handsome young man on her arm. He is, in fact, a significantly younger man.

Slinging his arm over this young man's shoulder, Serrano Suñer introduces him to Coco. "This scalawag is Pedro Gamero del Castillo—my spiritual brother." With a grin, the general nudges the fellow's chin with his knuckles. "Pedro is the youngest minister in Spain's government."

His presence is something more for the report.

Serrano Suñer then arranges the seating at the table with Piedita to his left and Coco to his right. She would love to engage Serrano, but immediately he's taken with Piedita's flirting. Pedro is seated on Coco's other side, and to his right is Gloria, who is engaged in conversation with the German ambassador.

Pedro turns to Coco. "I understand you've just arrived in Madrid. Is this your first time dining here?"

"Yes. Although I've dined at Horcher's in Berlin."

He grins. "Then, you have a treat ahead. The food here is excellent, as good as in Berlin. Did you know that Reich Marshal Göring is so fond of Horcher that he recently issued personal orders exempting the restaurant's key employees in Berlin from military draft?"

Göring. With a polite smile she ducks her head, smoothing the napkin on her lap. Even here she's plagued with the Reich marshal. A waiter stands behind her, pouring wine.

"I made the acquaintance of some friends of yours in Lisbon not long ago, mademoiselle."

"Ah, the Duke and Duchess of Windsor? General Suñer mentioned they'd visited Madrid recently on their way to Lisbon." She sips the wine, watching him over the rim of the glass. This man is Serrano Suñer's spiritual brother. She will listen and report.

"Yes. They were in Lisbon for several weeks, then on to the Bahama Islands."

"What?" She frowns, setting down the glass. "Are you certain? No, that cannot be right. Why, Wallis would shrivel up and die on those islands."

"It's true."

"But this is exile. Why did they go?"

He shakes his head. "General Franco admires the royal couple. We attempted to convince them to stay here in Spain, since Spain is neutral in the war in Europe." Pedro leans close. "Between us, I visited them in Lisbon with a formal offer of sanctuary before they sailed."

Intrigued, she lowers her voice. "My word! Why should they need sanctuary?"

He takes a long drink from his wine glass, then glances around. "The duke was afraid of Winston Churchill. And, in my humble opinion, Churchill is afraid of the duke."

Coco draws back, clucking her tongue. "Nonsense. Winston and David were always close."

Straightening, Pedro shrugs. "No longer, mademoiselle. I have it from good friends at Cambridge who know."

"Ah." She will have to give this conversation more thought. Her voice turns light. "And have you spent much time in England?"

"Oh, yes, mademoiselle. I taught at Cambridge, before entering the diplomatic service to serve my country."

"Cambridge, such a lovely place. All lovely spots should be exempt from war." She catches his eye, smiling. "I do wish this war would end. Europe suffers."

He turns to her, his eyes narrowed. "Spain is no part of Europe," he hisses. "We have no part in this war, we've just finished with our own. Thanks to God the Pyrenees separate Spain from the rest of Europe; the mountains are our barriers, our protection. Spain is independent, Mademoiselle Chanel—ruled by El Caudillo and the Vatican, and no one else." Then, lifting his eyes, he signals the waiter for more wine.

"You're Catholic?"

"Devout, as is Serrano." His eyes dart past her to the general, still engaged with Piedita. "Franco does what he can to rebuild our country. But for the past few years the church has been the only source of hope for our poor." He places his hand over his heart and his eyes burn as he speaks.

"This is my most pressing concern, mademoiselle—our working poor, the sad leftovers from our civil war. We have our own problems to solve. Food for our poor is first." As the waiter approaches, he falls silent.

"Misery is the terrible price of war."

"Yes, but our war is over now. It is time for Spain to think of putting food on the table. I speak for the children, and the old, and our young men with no future." His voice is low, intense.

"You cannot understand until you see this. Entire villages outside our cities starving, families without a loaf of bread." His fist hits the table. "This must be Spain's first priority."

Before she can reply, General Serrano breaks in. "What is this!" His tone is hearty. "Such a serious conversation on this beautiful evening, Pedro?"

Pedro Gamero's face transforms. "You're correct, as always, General. We shall restore harmony." Smiling, Pedro scans the table. "Who will order first?" He grins. "I must have a bite of everything. We will start with the smoked eel and spiced radish sauce." Turning to Coco, "The eel is succulent. You will think you are in heaven."

"And roast sea bass with tomato compote," Piedita calls out.

The voices around her fade while Coco composes this night's report. Pedro Gamero has indeed added a little spice to the cooking pot this evening. Something new to consider—Serrano Suñer's spiritual brother is vehemently against Spain entering Europe's war. How much influence will he have?

And while everyone orders the feast, she feels Pedro's eyes on her, this self-proclaimed friend of the Windsors; this man who has the ear of Serrano Suñer and thinks not of war, nor of power, nor guns. Nor of an alliance. This man who thinks only of food for the poor in Spain.

Who would have guessed!

Chapter Thirty-One

Madrid
Fall 1940

Coco sits on the terrace of the Madrid Ritz sipping tea and watching small brown birds scavenge an empty table nearby. A waiter saunters over, flapping a napkin across the tabletop, and the birds scatter. The lunch crowd has dissipated and it's too early for cocktails, so the terrace is quiet, at the moment. Sunlight flicks between the canopy of trees, and the air is pleasantly cool this afternoon, unlike Paris which is already wet and cold.

"Good afternoon, Coco."

She lifts her eyes to see Tom Burns from the British Embassy standing there. She'd not seen him cross the terrace. When they'd first met at Ambassador Hoare's party the night she arrived in Madrid, almost three weeks ago, she had hoped he would be a friendly source, given her own past relationship with Winston Churchill. But she'd never managed to engage the man in any meaningful conversation.

His presence at her side this afternoon is a surprise. "Where is your harem?" Coco says over the rim of her cup.

"Oh, they're around." Removing his straw hat, he waves it toward a chair across from her. "May I?" Before she can answer, he sits. "Since today is Friday, I suppose they'll be here soon. Though I can't stay."

The waiter moves toward him, but Tom shakes his head. Then, leaning back, he crosses his legs. "Well, mademoiselle, are you having a pleasant vacation?"

"I'm here on business too."

"That's too bad." A smile lifts his cheeks as he cocks his head to one side, regarding her. "I stopped by hoping I'd find you here."

She lifts her brows. He's suddenly too direct.

"I hear your social schedule is full; you're busy day and night." He winks. "The embassy girls give me the scoop. All I hear from them is 'Mademoiselle this, Mademoiselle that.'"

"Good. I will have some bottles of No. 5 delivered to them." She glances at her watch. Almost four o'clock. People begin drifting out onto the terrace. Umbrellas go up over tables as they're gradually occupied by the Friday-afternoon crowd.

"You're very generous. It will cause a commotion." He laughs, then uncrosses his legs and moves the chair closer. "Now, I have come with a special request." He hesitates.

She waits in silence.

"We, the British Embassy I should say, publish a weekly newspaper which is circulated here in Madrid, a small one with all the goings-on about town. I was wondering, have you anything interesting for our rag? A good story from Mademoiselle Chanel would increase our circulation."

Coco sips the tea, studying him. He's a minor bureaucrat after all. She's been wasting time attempting to cultivate him at the British soirees. Still, she has a role to play. So she hides her annoyance, smiling as she sets down the cup. "You're a brash young man, Tom Burns."

He grins. "That I am."

"You may write that I love Madrid, and am considering opening a new boutique here, particularly for my perfume, No. 5. That way you'll save me the expense of advertising."

Or perhaps she should tell the world of Pierre's theft—that should stir things up.

He nods. "Wonderful." He picks up his hat. "May I have our reporter call to set a meeting?"

"Yes, I suppose."

"Thank you. His name is Ralph Crumson." His eyes roam over the idle groups around them. Then, turning back to her, he gives her a probing look. "Tell me." His tone is casual. "How are things in Paris?"

She chooses her words carefully. "Life is tolerable there," she says, cupping her hands around the teacup. "Of course, France is defeated, but we do what we can to survive."

He merely nods.

"I must say, however, that Germany efficiency has brought, perhaps, a certain sense of order to my country." She lifts a shoulder, just a little shrug. "Wars do cause such deprivation. But the occupation is not unbearable, and in the end, France, like all of Europe, just asks for peace."

Fingering her pearls, Coco looks at him, this shallow bon vivant, and wills him to take her message back to his ambassador, even if he does not understand. Her voice turns light, teasing, and she smiles. "Perhaps you should arrange a truce between Germany and Great Britain, Tom Burns."

He cocks his brows. "Then, what arrangements shall we make for France?"

She gives him a hard look. Perhaps she's misjudged. Who is Tom Burns, after all? He's asked the right question and he's given her the opening, and now she must say what she's come to Madrid to say. And she must be clear. This conversation will be sent to Whitehall, she is suddenly certain.

"France understands the value of any truce, Monsieur Burns. For Europe to survive, her people must join as one. Russia is the real enemy of Europe. If borders must be erased for Europe to survive, if that is what it takes to arrange a truce between England and Germany which would end this war, then the truce must be arranged." She clasps her hands in her lap. "At least, that is my opinion."

The words took all her strength. She sits back, aware that Tom Burns studies her. She holds her expression blank, inscrutable— she hopes. Something in his eyes makes her want to weep. Before she can say another word, with a nod and tip of his hat, he's up and striding toward the gate.

Her eyes follow the British press attaché. Coco Chanel has shocked him. At the terrace gate, with Piedita coming in and Tom Burns departing, they stop and speak for an instant. Then Burns hurries off, and Piedita, spotting Coco, comes toward her.

With no time to consider what she's said to Tom Burns, and his abrupt departure, Coco manages a smile. Today Piedita is wearing another of her flowery afternoon dresses and a floppy brimmed straw hat. Coco stops a grimace.

"*Aiiiee*, Coco, I am sorry to be so late!"

Coco brushes a curl back from her forehead and sips her tea. She must compose herself—not much gets past Piedita. "No matter." Her tone is bright. "I'm enjoying the sunshine." She lifts her face for the kisses, and then Piedita falls into the chair abandoned by Tom Burns.

"Our driver is old and traffic was a mess." Whipping off the hat, Piedita smacks it down on the table and fluffs her hair. "I cannot stay long, I have an appointment." She leans forward. "Tom Burns is charming, don't you agree? Everyone loves him, you know. Max and I ran into him at the casino last night, surrounded by beautiful ladies as always. All the British ladies are in love with him."

"I cannot imagine why."

Piedita taps her forehead with two fingers. "Max says he's smarter than he looks."

"I will have to take his word for that. The British are sometimes opaque." She feels the flush rising to her cheeks as she recalls the look of contempt Tom Burns wore as he'd listened to her rehearsed opinion. She'd seen it in his eyes; he'd thought her acceptance of a separate peace between England and Germany, leaving France subservient, was treason.

Don't worry about that young man's opinion. He knows nothing of what a mother will do for her child.

And time is running. Louis still complains that her reports impress neither the admiral nor Canaris. She must pull herself together. And she must remain on guard with Piedita, a woman who moves from hive to hive gathering information.

"Tom Burns is no fool," Piedita says, lowering her voice. "He may be a Brit, but he supported Franco during Spain's civil war, so he's trusted here. He has deep connections in the Franco regime, even drinks with the Falange. Max thinks he could be British Secret Service, but you know men—they'll find intrigue everywhere." Piedita looks about for a waiter, and spotting one, waves him over.

"Monsieur Burns supported Franco?"

"Yes." Piedita arches her brows, glancing back at Coco. "I hear he was also involved in that recent mix-up with the Duke of Windsor in Portugal."

"*Voila!*" Coco produces a bit of laughter, throwing up her hands. "Here it is again, this talk about the Windsors. One month they are in Madrid, the next in Lisbon. Now I hear they're off to the Bahama Islands. And yet, I,"—she presses a hand over her heart—"I, who love them, know nothing of all this. Are they truly exiled? I have not seen my friends since before the occupation, and now I am worried."

The waiter approaches and Piedita turns to him, ordering a champagne cocktail.

Coco picks up the teacup. "The duke and duchess are dear friends, Piedita. Tell me what you've heard. Ease my mind." She sips the tea, regarding the marquesa. "I am certain Wallis and David had no desire to leave Europe."

Piedita pulls a colorful fan from her straw bag and flips it open. "My dear, Madrid papers were full of the news when they were here." She fans her face, looking about. "They were frightened. The newsmen say Prime Minister Churchill was planning to drag the Windsors back to London, to imprison them—or worse." She lifts a brow. "Everyone was worried—most of all the duke and duchess."

Coco remembers Pedro Gamero's story. "But that is impossible, Piedita! Winston is quite fond of David." She purses her lips, then shakes her head. "No. Winston Churchill would never do such a thing."

Piedita turns her eyes to Coco. Her smile is sly. "Don't be so certain, darling. The war has changed the prime minister, it seems." She lowers her voice. "It's obvious the Duke and Duchess of Windsor are sympathetic to the Führer's cause. Everyone knows. I hear this is, ah, to say the least, embarrassing to the royal family and Whitehall."

Just then the waiter returns with Piedita's cocktail. Coco lights a cigarette. She regards her friend through a haze of smoke. "Still, chérie—such threats to the former king of England? Come now. You must give up all the gossip. What's behind this story?"

With a long sigh Piedita snaps the fan closed. Sliding her hands to the nape of her neck, she lifts her heavy mane of hair and lets it fall. "Glory, the sun is hot today." Coco waits in silence while Piedita reaches forward, and lifting the cool champagne glass, with half-closed eyes, presses it to her cheek. Seconds pass, and after another sip of the champagne, she places the glass down on the table and looks at Coco. "Max says I talk too much."

"Don't be foolish. I'm concerned for my friends."

Piedita gazes at her, smiling. "We mustn't talk about the Windsor matter any longer. It's dangerous." Gathering her hair again, she twists it up, tucking it up under her hat. "Besides, I'm really not the one to ask for details."

"Then who?"

Piedita leans on her elbows. "Listen, darling, if you want the whole story you must talk to Nicolás Franco, El Caudillo's younger brother. He is also Spain's ambassador to Portugal—resides in Lisbon. Pedro Gamero can introduce you, they're friends." She lifts a finger. "Dangerous friends, however. Both are Falange."

Drawing back she sits up straight. "Just don't mention my name, will you? But I can tell you this—give Nicolás enough to drink and he'll spill anything you want to know. It's a wonder he's still alive." Then, curving her lips into a smile, she finishes off the cocktail. "You remember Pedro from Horcher, I am certain."

"Yes, of course." The devout Cambridge professor who believes Spain has no part to play in the war in Europe. She dropped that information into one of her reports, but Louis was unimpressed. Pedro Gamero is young and idealistic, Louis says. He may be close to Serrano Suñer, but he's not among General Franco's circle of advisors. And even if he were, Louis says, it's unlikely he could influence the tough Spanish dictator on foreign affairs.

Something tells her whatever happened to land Wallis and David on that rocky group of islands on the other side of the ocean could be important. If Piedita thinks Franco's younger brother Nicolás knows something, then she must find a way to meet him.

"Good then." Piedita's voice rouses Coco. "I must go." Adjusting her hat, Piedita's tone takes a sunny turn. She smiles. "First some news. Have you heard that General Franco has just appointed our friend Serrano Suñer as Spain's new foreign minister? He holds much power now, my dear. Serrano is a fine man."

Piedita glances at her watch and rises. She picks up her straw bag, looking down at Coco. "Oh, by the way—Herr Himmler is visiting Madrid soon. Did you know?"

Coco stares wide-eyed at Piedita as a cold chill cuts through her. Herr Himmler, Walter Schellenberg's superior, coming here to Madrid? What does that mean for her own mission here?

Piedita does not seem to notice. "No? Well, my dear, that is what delayed my arrival this afternoon. Workmen are swarming over the Castellana, hanging swastikas along the route from the airport to greet him. Max says Herr Himmler will be granted the honors of a visiting head of state."

She can hardly take in Piedita's words. Swastikas flying over the Castellana! Has Spain already agreed to fight with Germany in the war? If so, her mission here is finished, she is useless. Perhaps that explains Louis's complaints about her reports. She is no longer of value to the Reich. Coco struggles for calm.

Somehow she manages a smile as Piedita departs. While the marquesa floats toward the terrace gate, Coco gazes off. What will happen to André now? There must be something more that she can do to make this mission count. She will not allow the time and effort she's put into this trip to go to waste, even if an alliance between Germany and Spain is already assured. She will not return to Paris defeated.

Besides, some instinct tells her the Windsor gossip could be important. Everyone who's mentioned the royal couple was evasive. There is something there for Schellenberg and Canaris to feed on, she is certain. She curls her fists at the thought. Yes, she feels this is right.

Intuition demands she cast one last net. She must meet Nicolás Franco. And, as bait, Coco uses the woman's first resort.

She will throw a party.

Invitations to Coco's dinner party in the Goya Restaurant at the Hotel Ritz Madrid are hand delivered to each guest. Coco prevailed upon Pedro Gamero to assure Nicolás Franco's appearance. Louis is annoyed when she tells him of her dinner plans. And Louis is not invited. He is not acquainted with her new friends in General Suñer's circle—his presence could chill the conversation. Besides, she cannot be her best with a minder watching every move. She must shine.

Louis, of course, does not see things that way. He is angry. "Serrano Suñer, Gloria von Fürstenberg, Pedro Gamero, Elsa Bruckmann …" He looks up. "Why is my name not on this list? We work as a team, Coco. You should have consulted me first." They are in her hotel suite, Louis pacing.

"The table seats only six." He gives her a hard look. She sits, smoking, unmoved. He is a curious man, so eager to please, yet always on edge.

"And Nicolás Franco, General Franco's brother, is a guest?"

She nods.

"But he is Spain's ambassador to Portugal. He resides in Lisbon. What is the point?"

"This is my party, Louis." She watches as a red flush rises to his cheeks. "I am searching for a particular connection. This is important."

Tossing the list onto a table, he stalks to a chair. "This is a complete waste of time."

"It is my decision." Coco blows a stream of smoke in his direction. "Do not forget that I am the one responsible for the reports."

His mouth curls down and slowly he shakes his head. "Then you'd better make this fast, Coco. Because given Himmler's visit, events appear to be moving in Germany's favor without our assistance. Unless something of interest is reported soon, our mission will be deemed irrelevant. No doubt we'll be pulled back to Paris within the week."

"Perhaps," she says. "But first I will host my party." Suddenly Coco realizes that Louis fears failure as much as she. And given the company they're in, he is right to worry.

Chapter Thirty-Two

Madrid
Fall 1940

Ten o'clock in the evening and most guests have arrived for cocktails before dinner. Coco is pleased; the private dining room of the Ritz's palatial Restaurant Goya is lovely. Candles in fluted glass sconces cast a soft glow on the pale, yellow walls, flattering light for the ladies. The oblong dining table and surrounding rose tapestry chairs are placed off to one side. The table, set with crisp white linens and masses of bright, colorful flowers, shining candelabra, delicate porcelain, crystal goblets, and silverware, is set for six.

The remainder of the room is large enough for her guests to circulate, with small antique settees angled together in corners for conversation. Music drifts in from the main dining room, guitar and piano, softly muted by the closed doors. Waiters circulate among guests offering champagne, Spanish wines and cocktails, and fine caviar and tuna tartar on silver trays. Everyone except Gloria and Nicolás Franco has arrived.

Coco took the tiniest bit of her medicine this evening, and so, for the moment, her clock has slowed. She is relaxed. She has reviewed the menu for the last time with the hotel chef, and has also conferred with the sommelier, assuring that each course of the meal will be paired with only the finest Spanish wines. She's chosen a simple silver tissue gown to wear tonight, cut on the bias; shapely, but loose and comfortable. With her curls caught up on one side with the diamond clip, ropes of creamy pearls around her neck, and dark-red lipstick highlighting her tanned skin and dark hair, she knows she looks her best.

The door opens and with relief she turns to see a small but well-built man entering the room. Her most important guest—the reason for the party. Nicolás Franco stands eye to eye with Coco, his bald head gleaming while Pedro makes the introduction. He clings to her hand a moment too long greeting her. And she smells alcohol on his breath. She's asked around; Franco's brother is fond of the ladies and fond of drink.

He is delighted to meet her at last, he says. As she's extracting her hand, he adds, "I have heard wonderful things about you from your friend, Wallis, the Duchess of Windsor."

"Oh, yes. I understand they were in Lisbon recently."

He inclines his head. "They were guests at my villa near Cascais. It's a lovely place on the coast, outside the city."

"Oh? I hadn't known." She fingers her pearls. "I cannot understand why they would choose to leave Lisbon in favor of those islands so far away."

His eyes narrow. "They did not choose to go. The British prime minister commissioned the duke to the Bahamas. They were reluctant to leave, mademoiselle." A waiter arrives and Nicolás lifts a drink from the tray.

Before he can say more, the door opens and Gloria sweeps in, seeming breathless. "Have you heard the news from the arena, from

Las Ventas?" Everyone turns to her. "Tom Burns was arrested a few hours ago. I was there!"

Serrano Suñer nods. "It's like the Brits to cause such a commotion over nothing."

"Who arrested him?"

Nicolás swings around. "Burns, again?"

"Nicolás! I did not see you." Gloria crushes him in an embrace.

Holding his drink up above his shoulder, Nicolás laughs.

"But tell us what happened at Las Ventas!"

Gloria releases Nicolás and lifts a drink from a passing waiter's tray. "As you all must know," she pauses for a sip, "Herr Himmler arrived in Madrid today." With a glance at Nicolás, "Your brother arranged such a spectacle for him—Himmler came gliding down the Paseo in General Franco's new open-air Mercedes surrounded by Moorish guards. It was a sight."

"But what did Burns do to get arrested?"

"Gloria takes too long to tell a story!" Pedro interjects. "Herr Himmler was seated in the presidential box, and as the matadors made their way to him, the band struck up 'Deutschland Uber Alles.'" He spreads his hands. "That is Germany's national anthem as you know, but Burns refused to stand and sing."

"Well, he is British, after all."

"But that is impolite, with Himmler present as an honored guest. He could have at least stood."

"The Gestapo thought so too." Pedro shrugs. "They dragged him from the arena. Had him on the ground when we came along. I vouched for Burns, so finally they let him go."

Gloria pouts. "Ah, Pedro, you've ruined my story."

Coco, spotting the headwaiter standing near the table, hands clasped and waiting, slips away from the crowd.

"Shall you be seated now, Mademoiselle Chanel?" the man says when she reaches him.

She walks slowly around the table, inspecting the place cards. Nicolás Franco seated to her left; Pedro Gamero to her right, as she'd instructed. She nods. "We are ready."

Elsa Bruckmann is laughing, adding tidbits to the gossip when Coco rejoins the group. "And if that is not enough bad luck, the bullring turned to mud in the downpour."

Serrano Suñer chews on his cigar, listening with a detached smile.

"Ladies and gentlemen, shall we be seated?" Coco says.

Dinner, with an endless parade of waiters with trays of delectable dishes, lasts for hours. Course after course comes—duck liver stuffed with confit and figs, grilled sea hake loin from the Mediterranean sprinkled with Iberian vinaigrette and green-pepper nectar, risotto with truffles. With each course the sommelier pours the perfect wine into each glass. As Coco has instructed, the sommelier pours Nicolás Franco's glass to the brim on every round.

When at last the table is clear, except for thick hot coffee for the ladies and brandy for the gentlemen, Serrano pats his stomach, declaring he's sated. Everyone agrees. On Coco's right, Pedro leans close to Elsa with his arm draped over her shoulder, whispering into her ear.

It is time. She turns to Nicolás. He gazes past her toward Pedro, his eyelids drooping. "She's an enchanting woman," he says, his words slightly slurred. "Have you known her long?"

Coco follows his eyes, "Who, Elsa Bruckmann?"

He blinks and waves his hand before his eyes. "No, no. I was thinking again of your friend, Wallis, ah … the Duchess of Windsor."

He's in his cups. She switched to tea in her wineglass hours ago.

"Yes, we've been friends for years." She draws her brows together, turning to him. "But I am distressed they fled Europe. Why they've a house in Paris and a lovely villa at Cap d'Antibes."

She spreads her hands. "It's a mystery why they agreed to leave the continent."

"It is no mystery, senora ... mademoiselle. They were driven from Lisbon." His lids half close; his tone turns almost surly.

She leans toward him, resting her hand on his arm. Nicolás lifts sleepy eyes to her. "Explain please, Nicolás. Why do you insist they were driven away?"

At that moment Pedro rises and assists Elsa Bruckmann, pulling back her chair as she stands—the couple catching everyone's attention. Coco must attend to her departing guests. Coats and hats are collected, and the hostess tenses as each one departs, until at last only Nicolás Franco is left. She turns to him now, still seated, his head nodding, eyes closed.

Coco rests a hand on his shoulder, bending to whisper in his ear. "Shall we continue our conversation downstairs in the bar?" Her voice is low and husky.

His head snaps back and he blinks up at her. Then a slow smile crosses his face. "Why certainly, mademoiselle. I would enjoy a nightcap, and even more, your company."

They sit close together on a banquette in a corner of the King Bar, just off the lobby of the hotel. Low light and dark paneled walls emanate warmth, inviting secrets. Nicolás sips a cognac; Coco a martini. She asks for a cigarette and Nicolás pulls from his jacket a box of Craven A's and an engraved gold lighter. She holds the cigarette between her lips, leaning forward for a light, but Nicolás's hand wavers so that she must take his hand and guide it to the flame. After, she leans back, looking off as she inhales.

Nicolás lights one too. Slumping, he cradles his cognac glass while he smokes. In a corner of the room a piano and guitar play and a young woman sings. The music is sensual, melancholy. Only a few tables in the bar are occupied tonight.

"She sings of life during our war," Nicolás murmurs. "We had no music in Spain during those years."

"Another reason to hate war. Life without music is unimaginable."

He shrugs. "Everyone was busy struggling just to live." The song ends. A couple seated near the piano applaud, call for more. The musicians break into a passionate bolero; the singer flings her head back, building the percussion with tapping heels. Slowly her arms snake high overhead while she clicks the castanets, hands fluttering, wrists crossing and back arching as she turns and turns, one long fluid line from her swaying hips through her long graceful neck to the tips of her fingers. Beside Coco, Nicolás falls silent.

Coco bites her lip. Time is wasting. Struggling to hide her impatience, she slides closer to Nicolás, speaking softly in his ear. "Tell me why you said earlier that the Duke and Duchess of Windsor were driven from Lisbon. I find the story difficult to believe."

"It is as I say." With his eyes still riveted to the dancer, his words are clipped. "They received an ultimatum."

"An ultimatum from whom?" Her pulse quickens, but her tone is casual. This could be important. As the bolero builds, the dancer swirls, glancing at the small audience over her shoulders with a seductive smile, turning, turning. From across the room she seems to catch Nicolás's eyes. Coco gives him a sideways look—the cognac glass is frozen at his lips.

This she will not accept. Coco trails a finger down his arm and Nicolás starts, tearing his eyes from the dancer toward her. "An ultimatum, you say?" A low chuckle rolls from the back of her throat as she speaks. "I don't believe you. Who could dare threaten the former king of England?"

"Winston Churchill dares." His eyes shift from Coco to the empty cognac glass in his hand and he signals the waiter for another. Nicolás lolls back against the banquette cushion, his fingers now drumming the beat of the music on the table. His tone is insistent, impatient. "I tell you, the prime minister hates them both."

Coco draws back, shaken. What he says is just impossible! Even after the abdication, Churchill and the Duke of Windsor remained close. "You must be mistaken, Nicolás. Why should Churchill hate David?"

He rolls his head to one side, pinning her eyes. "It's simple, mademoiselle. David—your David—abdicates the British throne in 1936. One year later he and his new wife accept Hitler's invitation to visit Berlin. They are treated as if he's still on the throne." His brows draw together. "And this at a time when already Germany prepares for war."

"But …"

He continues, as if she's not spoken. "Not only do your friends travel to Germany, but Hitler provides them a royal welcome in Berlin in the manner usually reserved for sovereigns." He shrugs. "A complete humiliation. So why should you be surprised to hear the Windsors are disliked at Whitehall? Their Nazi sympathies are clear. Churchill and the royal family see them as a threat."

Piedita had hinted at this.

For a long time Nicolás is silent. The waiter arrives with a new cognac. Nicolás cups the glass bowl and rests it on his stomach. Coco waits—this little man's ego will not allow her to push too far with her disbelief.

Coco takes a long draw on her cigarette, rubs it out in an ashtray, and taps the box of Craven A's on the table until another one slides out. She must remain calm; Nicolás must have more to say. She clamps the cigarette between her lips.

Nicolás watches as she lights this one herself. "Churchill and the royal family's threats a few months ago were well known in Spain and Portugal. Speculation was everywhere, even in the headlines of our newspapers—the duke and duchess would not live a week if they returned to London." He glances over at her. "It was that bad."

When she says nothing, he dips his chin and lifts the glass to his lips. "I got to know them well in the short time they stayed at my villa. Of course, they did not know what to do, which way to turn. For a while they did consider returning to their home at Cap d'Antibes."

"They'd have been comfortable there. The south of France, as you know, is not occupied."

"Yes. But Wallis was certain Churchill could reach them there, even in France."

Her mind spins at this intrigue.

"The threat was real." Nicolás pushes out his bottom lip, watching her. "British eyes were on them day and night in Lisbon. We spoke together of this many times, David and Wallis and I. At Germany's urging, my brother finally offered them sanctuary in Spain. They'd have been safe in Spain. And Germany agreed to honor the sanctuary if they accepted. Still they dithered—just unable to make the decision."

How strange that Germany and Spain were involved in this together. So strange that she's beginning to believe the story is true. "If this is correct, I cannot imagine the state of Wallis's mind."

"She is made of steel. David was more frightened than she." A glance tells her that Nicolás is falling asleep. His lids are heavy. He balances his glass at an angle which will soon cause it to drop. She's got to keep him talking.

She turns her shoulders, so she's facing him, his eyes level on her cleavage. She tips his chin up with one finger. "I suspect you had some plan in place to solve the problem, yes?" She places a light kiss on his forehead. "An intelligent man like you."

He lifts his eyes to hers as she draws back. "Yes, of course. I worked with a German, a man named Schellenberg. He came from Berlin."

Coco drops her hand, swallowing the gasp before it escapes.

Nicolás doesn't seem to notice. "The plan was his. We met in the casino in Lisbon."

Schellenberg, involved with the Windsors and Nicolás Franco? Impossible.

"And then?"

He stares into the cognac, swirling the liquid. A deep amber sheen clings to the inner curve of his glass, like the penumbra of a falling shadow. She watches, waiting.

"Schellenberg planned to smuggle them across the border into Spain where they'd be safe. My brother—El Caudillo—even sent someone to help; a Spanish angel to the rescue." He flips his hand in the air with a little laugh. "An angel of the Falange arrived in Lisbon." He gives her a look. "His name is Angel Alcazar. Have you come across him in Madrid?"

The Falange, Franco's political party, is a rough crowd. Before she can answer, he shakes his head. "No, you wouldn't have." Tipping back his head, he takes a long drink.

"Angel was once a famous bullfighter," he says, looking off. "Retired now, but still revered in Spain and Portugal. He was to slip the duke and duchess over the border at night along with Schellenberg's men. The Germans were to protect them. The arrangements were made by Herr Himmler on his visit a few weeks ago."

His words run together; Coco strains to hear.

"Still the duke could not decide. Finally, Schellenberg had enough. He was determined to get them into Spain, into neutral territory, voluntarily or not. He set the night to smuggle them across the border, regardless—one way or another."

Her eyes grow wide. "You mean he planned to kidnap them?"

He grins. "If necessary."

"The plan obviously failed. What happened?"

Nicolás shrugs. "Well, they would have come on their own if given more time, I think. And they would have been safe from Churchill here in Spain. I gave the duke my word. The Falange could have protected them. And Germany wanted this."

"Why does Germany care?"

"Can't you guess?"

"Tell me."

"Hostages," he snaps. "Hitler's plan was to hold the Duke of Windsor hostage, of course." He looks at her; she shakes her head, confused. "Whether a truce is reached between Germany and England, or Germany invades England—either way, Hitler knew he'd hold the power of the throne through the Windsors."

Coco slaps her hand to her chest. Nicolás chuckles.

"Yes. This is true. The Führer was convinced that the Windsors, waiting in Spain, were his royal flush. Think of it!" He's still smiling. "A former king ready to take the throne when the royal family are … removed."

She stares at him. Of course. With the Windsors on the throne in England, Hitler would have held all the cards. Coco stares at this strange little man, understanding at last.

"The plan would have worked without Tom Burns and Pedro Gamero."

Heaving forward, he sets the empty cognac glass on the table. She shifts, impatient while he lights another cigarette. When he leans back, smoke seeps from a corner of his mouth. "Your great friend Pedro Gamero double-crossed us, including Schellenberg."

Resting her elbow on the banquette, she purses her lips. "I'm barely acquainted with Pedro Gamero. Whatever happened?"

"Schellenberg trusted Pedro—let him in on the plot, so he could smooth the way for the Windsors in Spain." He removes the cigarette from his mouth, holding it between his thumb and finger. "Pedro double-crossed him. Met with Tom Burns and offered him a deal—money and supplies from England to rebuild Spain, and food for Pedro Gamero's hungry flock. In exchange he warned the British of what you call Schellenberg's 'kidnap plot.'"

"I thought Burns was just a press attaché at the British Embassy."

"That is what we are supposed to think." He frowns. "And, of course, Burns agreed to the deal. The Brit's worst fear right now is an alliance between Spain and Germany. Food from England for Spain's poor would make that almost impossible. So, Pedro gave him Schellenberg's plan. Burns relayed details to the British Embassy. And by the next morning, the duke's old friend from London, Walter Monckton, arrived at the villa. Just in time to nail the Windsor coffin shut."

Monckton. David's lawyer during his abdication from the throne when he married Wallis. The one person the Duke of Windsor trusts most in the world. David would listen to Monckton.

"Monckton came to my villa. I heard the conversation from another room. He was quite persuasive. Warned the duke of court martial unless he left at once for the Bahamas."

She nods. This makes sense. Vanity is the Duke of Windsor's greatest weakness. The humiliation of court martial would have been too much for his pride.

"And so they left for the Bahamas?"

He nods. "Immediately; that same day."

"Does Schellenberg know he was double-crossed?"

"Yes, but he'll kill anyone who claims he failed. He will convince Himmler that Spain stalled, allowing the Windsors to flee with Churchill's help." He speaks with his eyes almost closed. "But if Hitler learns the truth, Schellenberg's a dead man."

He lets out a bitter laugh. "Schellenberg dared to threaten me, as if I answer to Germany! Even me, El Caudillo's younger brother!" He gives her a sideways look, a sly smile. "You're in an exclusive club now, mademoiselle. Not many people know what really happened." His eyes close on the last words.

She is silent, contemplating what she's heard. Schellenberg's mistake was trusting Pedro. She'd learned firsthand that night at Horcher's—Pedro's only interest now is rebuilding Spain and feeding its poor. Secretly, long ago Pedro had rejected any idea of assisting Germany in the war. Food—not war—is Pedro's crusade, and it seems he's convinced General Serrano Suñer, Spain's new foreign minister, of the same. Because Pedro could never have made such a bargain with Tom Burns and England without the general's approval.

So, General Suñer has agreed to this trade too—food for Spain's poor in exchange for the Windsors being whisked away to the islands, safely out of Hitler's hands.

She smiles. Schellenberg thinks he has covered up his failure. He failed because he trusted Pedro with his plans, and Pedro used the information instead to barter a deal with England, ending any hope of Spain joining the Axis powers. The Führer does not condone mistakes—but Schellenberg will ensure Hitler never learns the real reason for the failed alliance.

The waiter is now cleaning off nearby tables. She catches him stealing a glance at Nicolás and her. Carefully Coco slides away from Nicolás, picking up her purse. She must get out of here. She has a report to write. She will make use of Schellenberg's secret humiliation.

Chapter Thirty-Three

Madrid
Fall 1940

In the sitting room of her suite in Madrid, Coco stands at the windows to the balcony, looking out over the gardens and the Prado. On the other side of the room, Louis de Vaufreland sits on the sofa reading her report. She'd written down everything about the Windsor kidnap plot after returning from the bar last night, before she forgot the details. The sun was coming up by the time she fell into bed. And now, only hours later, she waits while Louis reads, praying the information from Nicolás is interesting enough to free André.

"This is amazing," Louis says at last, looking up. She crosses the room, lowers herself into a chair beside him. The information exposed in those papers is lethal. Any failure to fulfill a mission set by Adolf Hitler would be deadly if the Führer found out. Schellenberg would kill to keep his secret. But this is her last chance, and worth the risk.

Louis taps the papers against his thigh. "You've mined some surprising information." His eyes catch hers—we're in this together they say, for the first time on this mission.

Not so fast, Louis.

"This is risky, Coco. Your report places Walter Schellenberg in a bad light. Makes him look like a—what do the Americans say—a patsy? He was duped."

"Worse, he failed to get the Windsors to Spain." Girding herself, she pulls her skirt down over her legs. "I will not change the report."

His face flushes. "Do you realize what you're saying? It's almost November—Hitler and Franco are scheduled to meet soon to discuss the possible alliance. When the Führer reads this and learns that his vision has been destroyed by a secret agreement between England and Spain, and it's Schellenberg's fault ..." He slaps his hand to his head.

"Yes. I know."

"Well then? Don't you understand we cannot send this report? Schellenberg will have us killed. And with Hitler's habit of spreading blame, Admiral Canaris will be forced to go along with him. Because if Hitler learns the truth, Hitler will have them both peeled raw."

And André dies. She takes a deep breath. "That's true only if Schellenberg believes Hitler will learn of his failure."

"Why won't he?" He shakes the pages at her. "It's all right here."

"Pay attention, Louis." Coco clucks her tongue against her teeth. "Hitler need never know the Windsors' move to Bermuda was anything more than happenstance. Schellenberg and Canaris can burn the report so far as we're concerned. The two are friends; they'll come to some mutual agreement. And you may assure both men that I will say nothing of the facts, unless they force my hand." Coco lights a cigarette. "That is, so long as they free André."

"Blackmail."

"Yes." She cocks her head. "Look at it this way. Why should they care about André? They have the power to free him and bury the report, with no one the wiser. No one has to know it was Schellenberg's fault the Windsor hostage plan failed."

"What if General Franco mentions it to the Führer when they meet?"

She shakes her head. "He won't talk. Hitler is too volatile. Franco will find a less provoking reason for refusing an alliance. Serrano Suñer will see to that."

Louis leans back against the cushion and closes his eyes.

Her voice is firm. "If you're thinking of tearing up the report, do not. I have already sent a copy to someone I trust in Geneva, with instructions to place it unopened in my bank vault there." She has not, but how will he ever know?

His eyes fly open at these words.

"My attorney has been instructed to open the envelope and release the contents to an international news service if I am harmed."

Twisting toward Coco, he grips the sides of her armchair. "Are you insane?"

"I think what I've said is clear. Now," she purses her lips, watching him, "I have completed my assignment in Spain. This report and my silence are payment in full on my side of the bargain. I will keep silent on the Windsor kidnap story, and Walter Schellenberg and Admiral Canaris will remain blameless, so long as André is freed at once."

He shakes his head. "They could kill us both."

"The copy in Switzerland is our security."

He drops his head into his hands.

"There is one more thing." Without looking up he shakes his head from side to side. "Do not forget—my silence protects you, too, Louis. When we return to Paris, I fully expect to have your assistance in my fight for my business—the company and my perfumes, particularly, No. 5."

Minutes pass. Louis straightens, blowing out his lips. He stands, smooths the report, and folds it in half. She says nothing. He slips the papers into his inside jacket pocket.

"We'll leave on the next train to Paris, Louis."

"That's in two days." He nods and walks slowly to the door.

When he's gone, Coco stubs out the cigarette, leans back, and closes her eyes. Her limbs feel heavy; she's exhausted. Louis could be right—either Schellenberg or Canaris could decide not to trust her silence. But this is a gamble she's willing to take. Nothing else will save André.

She sits alone in the silent room as the clock ticks.

Listen, Boy Capel, wherever you are! Watch and see what I can do for our son on my own.

Since boarding the train, Louis has said nothing more about the report, although she knows by now it's been delivered to both Canaris and Schellenberg. And he's also said nothing about André.

Despite her earlier bravado, Coco is tense. She weighs the odds of either Schellenberg or Canaris coming to a conclusion that she's better dead, notwithstanding her promise to keep quiet. On one hand there is this: she has connections too. She is Chanel. But on the other hand, she is blackmailing powerful men.

She closes her eyes, pressing her fingers against her temples. All this weighing, analyzing, worrying gives her headaches. She's tried to sleep, but not even the sway of the rocking train crossing the foothills soothes her. Thoughts of Schellenberg and Canaris and André whirl through her mind.

Coco glances at her watch. It's only two o'clock in the morning; hours until arrival in Paris. Will she be met by the Gestapo? Eyes still closed, she prays—*Madonna, St. Theresa, Little Flower, pray for me. Pray for my boy.*

When the conductor knocks on her compartment door in the morning, announcing arrival in Paris in one hour and fifteen minutes, she rises gratefully. She's taken no medicine so as to keep her mind sharp, and as a consequence has not slept much at all. She pulls on a skirt and sweater and goes in search of Louis de Vaufreland. He is not in his room. She finds him in the dining car, eating a soft-boiled egg.

Her stomach turns. How can he think of food at a time like this?

Louis looks up as she walks in. He dabs his mouth with his napkin, places it on the table and stands. "You are just in time for breakfast. I believe we arrive in Paris in about an hour." Turning, he waves the waiter over.

"Just a cup of tea," she tells the man. He pulls out a chair across from Louis and she sits down. Louis returns to his breakfast. Minutes pass, then the words burst from her, like bullets propelled from a firearm. "I must know. Is André alive?"

He lifts his eyes. "Yes." His tone is mild, but a quiet smile appears.

"He is alive?"

He nods. "As I said." Her throat grows tight and her eyes fill with tears, but she fights them back. "Canaris and Schellenberg acted quickly. He is in the American Hospital in Neuilly, Coco."

She watches his eyes, his expression, while conflicting emotions swell inside—a flash of hope, swallowed by fear—is he lying to buy time? It is all too much. A tear rolls down her cheek, then another. She weeps for the first time since Boy Capel died. Louis hands over a handkerchief.

"Canaris received the report. I was notified before we left that André was being transferred by ambulance." She wipes away the tears, struggling to catch each word. "He is being treated. You may see him as soon as we arrive."

She holds his eyes, twisting the handkerchief in her hands. "The American Hospital, you say?"

"Yes." He returns to his breakfast. "It's the best, don't you agree?"

She can only nod. She knows the hospital well. Aldebert de Chambrun, René's father, is the director of this hospital, located in the suburb of Neuilly. Everyone knows the American Hospital has the best equipment and doctors in Paris.

Louis spreads a layer of jam on his toast. "We will go straight there when we arrive in Paris, if you like." He smiles.

Coco nods again. Louis is not her friend, she understands. But she warms to this kindness.

"Yes, I would like that." Her voice is hoarse when she speaks. Can this horror with André really be over? She turns her head, overwhelmed by the sudden release of terror. Through the window she stares unseeing at the blurred hills and trees, at horses feeding in a meadow, a farmhouse in the distance. Madrid and Nicolás Franco and Pedro Gamero and Tom Burns are far away.

Each second the train moves closer to Paris and André. They will go straight to the American Hospital when they arrive, Louis just said.

She will hold André in her arms, and later, when he is well, they will make plans for the future. She cannot ever reveal what she's done for her boy. But perhaps someday she will find the courage to tell André the truth—that she is his mother.

"Thank you, Louis," she whispers. "I would like that very much."

Chapter Thirty-Four

Paris
Fall 1940

Upon arrival in Paris and then during a rambling taxi ride to the American Hospital in Neuilly, Coco slowly revives. Even without a night's sleep, the prospect of seeing André renews her strength. She's always sensed a cool distance in André's feelings toward his auntie Coco. But now, she'll take care of him—show him her love. She imagines the look—the smile—on André's face when he sees her.

At the hospital, Coco marches up the steps with Louis de Vaufreland trailing behind. A woman in a white nurse's uniform mans a desk in the spacious lobby. She picks up her spectacles, slipping them on as Coco comes her way.

"André Palasse," the woman murmurs, flipping a page. She scans a list. "No visitors, mademoiselle. Monsieur Palasse is in quarantine. Shall I ring the floor nurse for you?"

Coco waves her hand. "No, no. You misunderstand. I am his closest relative. I must see him. What floor, what number is his room?"

The woman peers at Coco over the rim of her glasses. "Monsieur Palasse is in the phthisis ward. I am sorry, but no visitors are allowed."

Coco clucks her tongue. "Tell me where this ward is, madame. This instant. Or I shall call for the hospital administrator at once."

The woman's lips draw into a thin tight line. With a frown, she looks at the list again. "The ward is on the next floor, but you will not be allowed to enter." She points across the lobby. "The elevators are there. Follow the signs when you get off."

With a pointed look at Coco, the nurse picks up the telephone receiver.

A nurse wearing a white aproned uniform and brimmed white cap waits for them when they step from the elevator. Her arms are crossed over her chest. "The phthisis ward is closed to visitors," she says, speaking only to Louis.

Coco touches her arm and the woman turns to her. "I am Gabrielle Chanel, nurse." The woman sucks in her breath. "The director of this hospital, Aldebert de Chambrun, is a family friend." At least he is her attorney's father—that should count for something. "My nephew, André Palasse, is a patient in this hospital. He is a former prisoner of war. I have not seen him since he was captured— he is here and it is imperative I see him at once."

The nurse steps back.

"Now," Coco adds.

"I understand, mademoiselle." The American's French suffers from her accent. Still, Coco sees a flicker of sympathy in the big blue eyes peeking from under long brown bangs. "Your nephew has contracted a tubercular infection. It is highly contagious, as you may know. That is why no visitors are allowed."

Sensing defeat, Coco's hand flies to her throat. "I must see my nephew. Just allow me to visit him for an instant. How is he, nurse?" Her eyes drop to the label on the uniform. "Nurse

Ambert. Does he eat?" Suddenly, she is breathless. Louis rests his hand on her shoulder. "Where is the doctor? I must speak to André's physician."

The nurse's expression softens. "I am sorry," she murmurs, taking Coco's arm. She leads Coco to a chair, one in a line against the wall. Louis, following, sits down beside her. Coco is vaguely aware the nurse is speaking to her as if she is a child, but she cannot work up the energy to object.

"Please wait here, Mademoiselle Chanel." Nurse Ambert's voice is gentle. "I'll find Monsieur Palasse's doctor and he can speak with you."

Coco fixes her eyes on the nurse's back. At a closed door, she pulls a large brass key from a pocket, unlocks it, and steps into a hallway, shutting the door behind her. Coco stares ahead. An elevator bell rings on a lower floor and Coco flinches. The sleepless night is taking its toll.

She straightens at the sound of the lock clicking again in the door. Glancing about she sees that Louis has gone—she must have fallen asleep. Coco smooths her hair, her skirt, as Nurse Ambert approaches, followed by a young man in a stark white coat. His face is thin, with a furrowed forehead and prominent cheekbones. The nurse steps aside, and the doctor comes toward her. He does not smile.

She rubs her arms, feeling cold as she looks up. The rims of the doctor's eyes are swollen and red.

"Mademoiselle Chanel?" He extends his hand and she takes it, holding on. "I am Doctor Raymond Wood. Your nephew, André Palasse, is under my care."

"Yes. Thank you. How is he, Doctor?"

He takes a seat on the chair vacated by Louis, freeing his hand in the process. "Your nephew is very ill, mademoiselle. He only just arrived. Imagine what he's been through in the prison camp fighting this infection. We are doing all we can for him."

For a moment despair renders her mute. Coco ducks her head, gulping for air. With racking sobs, she drops her head into her hands. The doctor rests his hand on her arm, a firm touch, assuring her boy will receive the best care now.

Still she cries through the tears. "Please! Let me see André, just for one minute."

A hand reaches from behind, touching her shoulder. She turns to see Louis holding out a cup of coffee. "It's black, as you like it, Coco."

She shakes her head, brushing tears from her cheeks. "I cannot, not now."

A clock somewhere in the hallway ticks through the silence. Beside her, the doctor heaves a sigh. Then he stands. "Nurse," he calls. "Bring a mask."

Coco lifts her head. The nurse disappears through the heavy door to the ward. This time she hears no lock.

"Only for a minute, Mademoiselle Chanel," the doctor says. She nods even before he finishes the sentence. "I cannot let you into the patient's room, you understand. We maintain tight control of temperature levels and humidity in these rooms. And in addition, there's the problem of contagion." Patting her hand as she stands up, he adds, "You can see him through the window in the door."

"Oh, yes, oh, thank you, Doctor. Thank you." How she loves the Americans. She has always loved America.

"He will be asleep. He's not aware of his surroundings yet, you understand." He turns to Louis. "Monsieur, you must wait out here."

"Yes, of course," Louis says.

Together Coco and the doctor walk toward the heavy door separating her from André. "You must prepare yourself for this, mademoiselle," the doctor says as they enter a long hallway. Gray walls extend on both sides before her. Tiled floors are black and white. Overhead lights are dim. As they walk the length of the hallway, almost to the end, they pass a row of steel doors on the left, also painted gray and blending into the walls. Each door has a small glass window at eye level. Each window is covered with steel mesh.

"Your nephew has been through a difficult time." The doctor stops before a door.

She stands looking at it. "Will he be all right?"

"It will take time. God willing, we will get him there."

Slowly she moves toward the window. Standing on tiptoe Coco peers through the glass at André.

His room is so small, no larger than her closet at the Hôtel Ritz. There is one window to the outside world on the opposite side of the room. Near his bed, near the far wall, stands a shining steel cylinder, a machine of sorts, about half the height of a man. A table near the narrow bed holds a large bowl and several folded towels.

As the doctor warned, André sleeps. He lies on his back in a light-blue gown, with a white blanket covering him to his chest. The blanket is tucked close around him. Even from the distance her son's face looks drawn and pale. She watches his chest rise and fall. Yes, he is alive.

"He is at peace," Doctor Wood says.

Coco grips the bottom ledge of the window, eyes fixed on André. And squeezing her eyes shut, she prays directly to the Lord while struggling to hear her son breathe.

A hand touches her arm. A voice says, "We must go."

Her fingers slip from the small ledge and slowly she steps back. Then, turning away from the door, she lifts her chin and looks at Doctor Wood. "How long must he stay here?"

"If all goes well, several months. But when he leaves, he'll require more rest in a contained environment. In a sanatorium, perhaps."

"Oh." Her hand slips to her chest, covering her heart. "So long?"

"We must go," he says, taking her arm. "It is difficult, I know. We can only wait."

"May I come again?"

"Yes. Ask for me."

Her fingers grip her purse. "Will you tell him I was here? Tell him that his aunt Coco loves him."

He smiles at last. "Yes, mademoiselle. That is the best medicine of all."

Chapter Thirty-Five

Paris
Winter 1941

January is the bleakest month of the year, Coco reflects. Flowers are long gone, trees are bare, and spring seems far away. This winter is the coldest ever in Paris, they say. The wet cold is stubborn, wrapping the city in gloom.

André's been in the hospital for over three months, yet seems to make little progress. Coco gazes out the window while Evan drives—she has an appointment this morning with René de Chambrun to discuss her claim against Pierre. But all she can think of this moment is her son. André is awake most days now, but Doctor Wood says he will not eat. Her boy is so thin and frail.

A wave of sorrow washes through her. Her son has changed. When she was finally allowed into his room for that first visit, André had turned his head to the wall. He'd answered her questions with a yes or a no, or merely a shake of his head. Doctor Wood says she must have patience, that this is not unusual behavior, given what he has endured. The hospital is his entire world right now—patients often withdraw this way.

She wonders if André has any idea how he got from the prison camp to a hospital in Paris—wonders if he will ever realize how much she loves him.

Or if he will ever think to thank his auntie Coco.

She opens her eyes, already knowing the answer.

Still, he is alive. Admiral Canaris and Walter Schellenberg have kept to the bargain. The report was buried, so far as she can tell.

Hitler and Franco met in Hendaye, on the French-Spanish border, one week after she left Madrid. Spatz told her the news. Foreign Minister Serrano Suñer accompanied General Franco to the conference. "Franco dodged and twisted, agreeing only that Spain would fight with Germany when the time was right. He gave Hitler one reason after the other for his refusal." He shook his head. "Hitler was furious afterward, saying he'd rather have his teeth pulled than bargain again with Franco."

She'd pretended surprise. Spatz seemed befuddled. "Given Himmler's successful visit to Madrid a few weeks earlier, everyone had merely assumed Spain would approve the alliance."

Coco had hidden a smile when he told her the news. The blackmail report was a hardy weapon. Spatz has no idea.

A sudden swerve of the car dissolves the memory. "Pardon, mademoiselle," Evan says. "The street was blocked. We'll take another route."

Coco gazes through the window, shaking her head. "Bicycles, bicycles," she mutters, catching his eyes in the rearview mirror. "Everywhere on the streets these days I see them. Oh, now, look there!" She leans forward as they pass it—a young man peddling, a pretty girl perched on the handlebars, skirts flying up over her knees in the icy headwind.

Coco shivers at the sight. Snow covers Paris. Even with the car windows rolled up and wrapped in furs she feels the cold.

"The girl must be freezing." She sits back. "But that's the young for you."

Evan slows for a bicycle taxi now—an old man wearing only a sweater and a wool hat and gloves is hunched over the handlebars, straining to pull a three-wheeled carriage with two hefty passengers. The men, German officers, look warm in their overcoats, scarves, fur hats, with blankets piled over their legs.

She frowns and turns her eyes to the street ahead. Things have always been this way. No one ever said that life is fair.

Evan turns the car onto a narrow side street, heading toward the Champs-Élysées to René's office. A few blocks down he slows the automobile, peering ahead. From the entrance to an alley, a disheveled group of men drag two huge rubbish bins out onto the pavement. One bin tumbles and the men scramble, digging into the spilled garbage. Evan slows, then drives around them and speeds up. Coco turns, watching through the rear window. "They're fighting over garbage."

"The Boche have reduced rations again," Evan says. She looks up, surprised. He's never used that term for the Germans before, at least with her. "Rations aren't enough to keep a man's family alive."

When they reach René's office, Evan parks the Rolls on the avenue and opens her door. As she steps out she is suddenly struck by the gray gloom of the deserted street, so unlike the busy Champs-Élysées before the occupation. The Nazis are proud of the New Order they're imposing on Europe and she's not questioned this before—after all, look what happened during the workers' strike. Regulations and limitations do preserve order, but on the other hand Paris today is almost as austere as Berlin.

Taking Evan's arm, she makes her way over the icy pavement toward the entrance of the building. At last she will go after Pierre. Almost nine months since the formula for No. 5 was stolen—long enough to birth a baby.

Louis de Vaufreland has agreed to smooth her way to obtain control of Société Mademoiselle and her perfume, using the Jewish laws in France. Her decision to make the claim against Pierre under this law is set in concrete, even though she'd never before given much thought to Pierre's heritage—before the war. She lifts her chin as they enter the building. Pierre brought this upon himself. These laws are the only tools she has available and the time has come for justice.

René shows her into his office as soon as she arrives. Louis stands as she enters, greeting her with pleasure. Coco conscripts her lawyer's usual chair at the head of the conference table. Today, with her back to the window, the others can be the ones to squint into the sunshine. Today is the day she's taking charge. René takes a seat two chairs down on her right. Louis is seated on her other side.

"Now then," she says, clasping her hands and planting them on the table before her. She looks from one man to the other. "What have you to report on the progress of my complaint regarding Pierre Wertheimer?"

Louis leans forward and stubs out his cigarette. "We were just discussing it before you arrived. I have an appointment to see Doctor Kurt Blanke next week. Blanke is chief deputy of the Paris office charged with elimination of Jewish influence in France. His responsibility includes laws governing seizure and transfer of Jewish property in occupied France."

"Good. When shall I meet this gentleman?"

He shrugs. "I know him well. I will urge a formal hearing as soon as possible."

René studies his hands, then looks up. "Louis will handle this claim for you, Coco. You may not have yet heard, but my father-in-law is embroiled in an unhappy political situation. At the moment, it's best I stay out of this."

She nods. She has heard the gossip. René's father-in-law, Pierre Laval, former deputy Vichy prime minister, was recently fired by Marshal Pétain. Now it's said the old marshal regrets his action and wants him back, and René is caught in the middle. She has enough problems without Vichy politics to consider.

"I understand. But have you verified that Pierre is really building a plant in America for my perfume, my No. 5?"

"Unfortunately, yes. In fact, it's near completion. They'll be in production soon."

Louis breaks in. "We will file a claim immediately under the Nuremberg Laws, seeking an order transferring ownership of Société Mademoiselle and its assets to you, an Aryan owner, including the plant at Neuilly, and all rights to the stolen No. 5 formula. Since your partner is a Jew, I don't foresee a problem. My hope is we'll obtain the necessary orders in our first hearing before Doctor Blanke."

Coco's eyes flash. "Pierre is in America. He will ignore the orders."

René leans forward. "As you have previously noted, Société Mademoiselle is a French company operating under French and German laws, as is the factory in Neuilly. Once you obtain an order rendered under this law, it should have global effect under international law. Any company doing business with Société Mademoiselle—vendors, perfumers, flower growers, retailers—will be exposed to sanctions under international law if it violates the French court's order."

"Add to that, Pierre is using my name to sell the perfumes."

Louis's voice drops as he looks at Coco. "Yes. Do not underestimate the impact of his vulnerability when the facts are known. Pierre started this fight. He has many other businesses to protect. With the court orders behind you, Coco, you will stand up and denounce him. You will tell the world the truth."

The meeting with René and Louis was exhilarating and Coco's mood is significantly improved. René's plan will work. A few hours later, at midafternoon, she sits alone at a small table on the indoor terrace of Café de la Paix in the Place de l'Opéra waiting for Colette to appear. Colette called, asking for this meeting.

She'd detected a hint of desperation in Colette's voice on the telephone this morning. Something about Maurice, she'd said. Colette is passionate about her husband. Indeed, the man is brilliant, an introspective writer, a constant seeker of truth. Coco smiles, thinking of the couple as she last saw them—Colette, plump as a ripe peach, and cynical, explosive. Maurice—gentle, kind, quiet. He is a small, lean man, almost frail, and dapper, always wearing a suit with a pocket handkerchief, vest, and tie. He is sixteen years younger than Colette, and the man adores her. Perhaps because of his wife's complicated past and many scandals, Maurice's steady love explains his hold on Colette.

Really, of the couple, Coco prefers Maurice, regardless of what others may think or say. She loves him even though he is a Jew. Maurice is a true intellectual—his intelligence fascinates her, much like Boy's ideas had. Colette, too, is brilliant and a friend, but she's just as prickly as a dry shrub.

Though Colette has been her friend for years, they've had their ups and downs. Years ago, Colette published several articles praising couture houses in Paris, and in one she'd referred to Coco as that "little black bull." When Coco confronted her, Colette claimed she'd meant only to pay tribute to Mademoiselle Chanel's strong will. *Hah!* Coco tamps down the anger threatening to rise once again at this thought.

Still, she has set the insult aside for the sake of their friendship, for the most part. Some things are better left alone.

With a sigh, Coco lights a cigarette and sets the case down beside her, letting her eyes roam over the forest of uniforms occupying many of the tables in the room. Before the Germans came, the Café de la Paix was a pleasant pause in any day for Parisians. Now, the Wehrmacht and Luftwaffe seem to have taken over here too. One small table in the back is even surrounded by Gestapo.

She picks up the cup of tea she's ordered without waiting for Colette. The high command at the Ritz are courteous gentlemen. These lower ranked soldiers are different. They seem to crackle with tension. Electricity is in the air. The few civilians at other tables talk quietly together, their heads ducked, shoulders hunched, as if at any moment terror could strike. Oh, how things have changed.

Coco glances at her watch. Colette, as usual, is late. Truly the woman is perverse. Leaning on one elbow, cigarette clamped between two fingers, she flips pages of the *Grinigoire*, a newspaper she lifted from an empty table on the way in. Her eyes stop on a page promoting a serial chapter from Colette's latest novel.

Look at this! Smiling, Coco flattens the page, reading. This is the story everyone's talking about. Fiction based on facts they say, with Colette skewering her old rival the Countess Isabelle de Comminges. They say Colette carves the young beauty to the bone in this book. She remembers the gossip years ago, when the countess swiped Colette's first husband, and how quickly word had spread.

She smiles—Colette's revenge here must be sweet.

A cool voice interrupts. "Good afternoon, Coco." She looks up as Colette slips into a chair.

"Ah, good. You've come." She watches as Colette yanks off an unfortunate hat and a mass of dark curls spring free. She shrugs off a worn brown coat and hangs it over the back of the chair. Her friend has gained a little weight, Coco notes. It strikes her that they've not seen each other in a while, perhaps a year or so.

"Where have you been hiding?" Coco asks.

Colette gives her a look. "Why, in our little rooms under the stairs at the Palais-Royal." Her tone is sharp. "Where else?" She nods at the open magazine on the table. "I see you're reading the first excerpt from my last novel. They're serializing it."

"Yes." Coco cocks her head. "I must say, Colette, I was a bit surprised to find you in this publication, given their rabid views." The right-wing *Gringoire* is favored reading among Reich officials at the hotel.

Colette shrugs and lowers her voice. "Maurice is no longer allowed to work, as you must know, so it's up to me now. He scribbles in his notebooks. But do you know of a publishing house in Europe today which publishes a Jew's work?" She yanks off her gloves. "If so, please let me know."

"I did not know. I am sorry for that."

Coco leans across the table, speaking barely above a whisper. "The new German laws—are you certain they apply to Maurice? Surely exceptions are made for ordinary people." She straightens, lifting the teacup. "Besides, he is French."

Colette's laugh is harsh. "How would you know anything about a Jew's life today?" Retrieving a coin purse from the bag, she regards Coco from under her lids. "Unfortunately, *chérie*, Maurice receives no special treatment. And at the moment, we are in retreat." With a wry smile, "Laying low, so to speak."

"Besides, nothing Maurice writes would pass the censors. Did you know that now all writing is submitted to censors before publication is approved? And even after that, every story or book or paper must also be licensed."

"Terrible!" Again, the German obsession with order.

Colette looks up, her eyes narrowed. "But why should you care?"

Taken aback, Coco regards her friend. "I am quite fond of your husband, Colette. If you ever get sick of him, let me know."

Colette cocks her head. "And what would you do with a Jew at the Hôtel Ritz, hide him in a closet?" With a little laugh, she turns her head, searching for a waiter. "Don't pretend with me, Coco. You live with Maurice's persecutors in that hotel."

"What are you saying, Colette? Maurice is Maurice! I care nothing for the fact he's a Jew. I have many Jewish friends. I have nothing against them." Stung, she studies the teacup, moving the saucer one way, then the other. When she looks up, Colette glitters back at her, knife edge slivers of light in her eyes.

Boy once warned her against speaking her mind in public on morals. Her thoughts on the subject of right and wrong are too complex to generalize. With a sigh, Coco lights another cigarette. Why did she come here anyway? Really, she's fonder of Colette when they're apart. The woman thinks nothing of crossing social boundaries. She inhales, letting the hot smoke glide down her throat and fill her lungs.

A waiter arrives and Colette orders a Bonal aperitif, an herbal liqueur. "The quinine's good for my nerves," she says as he goes off.

Coco then turns to Colette. "You telephoned. Why did you want to meet?" Colette fiddles with the coins. "We've been friends long enough, Colette. Out with it."

"All right then." She rests her elbows on the table and clasps her hands. "It's about Maurice," she says. Her voice trembles now. "I'm afraid for him, Coco. I'm afraid and so I've come to ask a favor."

"Of course, of course. Anything."

The waiter sets Colette's drink on the table. Handing him the coins, she turns back to Coco. "I would like an introduction to your friend, Susanne Abetz."

Startled, Coco studies her friend. "You wish to cultivate the German ambassador's wife? My dear, if all you've said is true, won't that put Maurice in danger?"

"Listen!" Colette's knuckles turn white. "Maurice does not

know what I'm asking. But I have a plan to keep him safe." She blinks, brushing away a tear. Coco pulls a handkerchief from her purse, handing it over.

"Safe from what, *chérie?*"

"Every night we wait for them to come, the Boches." Her voice breaks. "Did you know that every Jew in France must register now? Not just foreigners, Coco. French Jews too."

An image rises of the woman dragged to the lorry in the Marais months ago, and the weeping child left behind. Coco pushes the thought away, swallows a sip of tea. "They say they're just counting. It's a simple census of some kind."

"Doesn't it seem strange to you that they registered,"— Colette's voice turns hard—"or as you say, counted, only Jews?"

"I did not know."

"No, you wouldn't." Holding Coco's eyes, she shakes her head. "You don't understand, Coco, because you do not want to know."

For a second, anger flares. But she thinks of Maurice and she thinks of her friend Colette and she bites her tongue.

"They are hunting us, Coco. And I must be ready when they come." Colette drops her hands into her lap. "I have come to beg your help."

Coco straightens. "Don't be foolish, Colette. And do not beg, it's not necessary." With a little smile, she adds, "Before you get off your knees, tell me, why Susanne Abetz?"

Colette rolls her eyes. At last, she smiles.

"Madame Abetz sent a note some time ago, admiring one of my stories. It was such a friendly letter. I thought, perhaps, if you were to introduce us, we could have cocktails or tea together. Then, if ever Maurice is arrested, perhaps Madame Abetz would put in a word for him with her husband. I hear the ambassador adores his wife." With a glance around, she lowers her voice. "If she asks, he could free Maurice in an instant."

Here is something she can manage. Colette is right. Otto Abetz loves his wife. He will do anything for Susanne. A feeling of pity for Maurice and Colette swells, but she masks the emotion. Colette will never stand for pity. The woman may be France's greatest writer at the moment, but she's scrabbled her way through hard times just as Coco. Pity, especially coming from her, would humiliate Colette.

So her reply is measured. "You may be right. This is a good idea, *chérie*. I will certainly help. It never hurts to plan ahead." As she speaks, Colette's face transforms—muscles soften around her eyes and she exhales.

"I'll introduce my two friends. Women must solve our problems together."

"Oh, wonderful!" Colette's voice turns bright. "But keep this to yourself."

"Of course." Coco signals the waiter for her bill. "Now, I must go—I've just come from a frightful meeting and have things to do. But I will arrange a luncheon for the three of us right here, in the private room. The oysters are wonderful. Will that suit? Next Tuesday perhaps? Check your calendar and let me know if you are free on Tuesday."

"Thank you, Coco. Oysters! Why, I cannot recall the last time I had one." Her voice takes on a hint of irony as she adds, "And Tuesday will be fine. I am free on that day."

Handing coins to the waiter, Coco rises. She leans down to Colette, kissing each cheek. "Now give Maurice my love," she whispers. "You know, it's strange, but I never really thought of Maurice as a Jew."

Chapter Thirty-Six

Paris
Spring 1941

Coco paces the floor in the office of Dr. Kurt Blanke in the Hôtel Majestic, the Reich's administrative headquarters in Paris. "I have filed my complaint; let us get on with this. Pierre Wertheimer and his brother, Paul, are in America and I am here. Under your laws ..."

"Yours also, mademoiselle."

"... this should be simple. The Wertheimers are not permitted to own property in this country, or anywhere else in Europe for that matter. Société Mademoiselle's perfumes are mine. I created them, they carry my name. I am Aryan and thus the logical person to take full ownership of the company. This is for the good of France as well as Germany. It is my duty to save this treasure for France. This is my right."

"Mademoiselle Chanel, as I have tried to explain ..."

"But no." She lifts her hand. "What you say is impossible!" Kurt Blanke sits at his desk. Louis de Vaufreland, who arranged the meeting, is seated across from him while Coco paces the room. She glares at the pale, fleshy face of the man administering the Jewish property laws in France. He gazes back at her, impassive.

"This should be a clear case, Dr. Blanke. You say there's a question of current ownership? That Pierre may no longer own the company?" She throws up her hands. "That is absurd. Ninety percent of the shares are held by Pierre and his brother. The other ten percent are mine. I have not consented to any change in ownership."

Blanke sighs, his hands clasped on the desk. He looks up at Coco. "I repeat, Mademoiselle Chanel: Pierre Wertheimer's attorney in New York has wired a response to the filing of your claim. He asserts the Wertheimer shares were sold prior to the war, before the family left France. According to him, the shares were transferred to the new owner by his banker in Paris, Monsieur Henri Leval. And, he further asserts the new owner is Aryan. If he is correct, the Jewish laws do not apply."

As Coco opens her mouth, he lifts a hand. "So, first, we must determine the facts. Unfortunately, Monsieur Leval refuses to divulge the name of the new owner or discuss the details of the transaction." With another sigh, "Both, he says, are confidential."

"Then you must arrest the banker at once. He is lying."

"He is also a Swiss national."

"So what? This is fraud."

Louis interrupts. "Mademoiselle Chanel is right. Fraud is the likely case, Dr. Blanke." Blanke turns his eyes to him with a piercing look. Louis crosses his leg, nervously drumming his fingers on his knee. "I am certain we'll find the share certificates are falsely backdated when we examine them. We will find that a sham trust agreement exists, and that the same agreement requires the new owner to transfer the company shares back to Pierre sometime in the future, immediately upon demand. It's clear that Wertheimer anticipated the new restrictions."

Dr. Blanke does not blink. "So what do you suggest?"

"As you are aware, Admiral Canaris has evinced a personal concern on Mademoiselle's behalf in this matter. Commence a hearing to determine the facts. Summon the banker, put him under oath, and require him to name the purchaser. Demand the paperwork for the so-called transaction of sale. Let's hold the transaction up to the light. We must see everything—the agreements, the share certificates—everything."

Blanke slams the heel of his hand down on a bell. "All right," he says. "That is what we'll do." Coco slumps in relief. Admiral Canaris's name had a good effect. A woman rushes into the office, glasses atop her head, notebook and pen in hand.

He motions to her and hands her a file. "Call our clerk. Schedule a hearing on this matter no later than April first." He consults his calendar. "That is a Tuesday. Call immediately and verify the date, time, and hearing room we are to use. We'll need a stenographer, of course."

When the secretary is gone, Kurt Blanke looks at Louis. "My secretary will contact you this afternoon with the information. See that your own schedule is clear." His eyes turn to Coco. "And yours, mademoiselle."

Spatz invited himself to the hearing this morning. He offered to drive, although Coco would have preferred Evan. He's taken a wrong turn and they're driving all about, and she'll be late. She shifts closer to the passenger-seat door, eying him. Spatz drives like a madman today; he's speeding down the Champs-Élysées in the wrong direction, seeking a way to turn around.

A rusted old bus pulls out in front of them, and he slams on the breaks. "*Merde!*" he shouts, as burning wood and charcoal fumes swamp them from the Gazogene box atop the bus. He weaves around it.

Coco clamps her lips tight, hanging onto the edge of the seat. She breathes a sign of relief when they turn onto a side street and find a slow-moving black Citroën just ahead, forcing Baron Hans von Dincklage to slow the automobile to a crawl. The occupants' black uniforms are easily recognizable. Spatz slaps the steering wheel, then, giving up, rests his elbow on the window ledge, trailing the car.

Coco turns her eyes to him. "Have you seen the banker's documents yet?"

"No." With a glance at Coco, "Don't worry, darling. This is only a matter of procedure. No Jew will own Société Mademoiselle at the end of this investigation."

She looks away.

"To put it another way," she says, watching the car ahead, "Chanel will own the company at the end of this investigation?"

He does not answer. She studies him from the corners of her eyes. He frowns, peering over the wheel at the slow black car. He knows something. "Who else will be at this meeting, Spatz?"

His eyes dart to her. For a split second she sees him hesitate. "Your friend Colonel Eckert will attend."

"What!" Her head whips around and she stares. "What business is this of his?" She pounds her fist on her thigh. "No. I will not allow Horst Eckert to sit in on my hearing."

"You have no choice. He's Reich Marshal Göring's man, as you recall. Apparently, Göring's interest in your business and perfume has not waned. He's notified Kurt Blanke that Colonel Eckert will attend the proceedings."

She fixes her eyes ahead. "I thought we'd got rid of Göring after Madrid."

"The Reich Marshal does not answer to the Abwehr, nor to Walter Schellenberg's office." A beat goes by. "You might as well hear the worst, darling. Propaganda Minister Joseph Goebbels has officially professed an interest in having No. 5 produced in Germany. It would be a huge propaganda victory for him."

Leaning against the window, she rests her forehead on the glass. Her life is slipping out of control. Pierre still thieves from America and the Germans threaten her rights on this side of the Atlantic. It is all too much.

She turns on Spatz. "Listen, I will not keep silent if your Fatherland seizes my property. They will need my name to sell No. 5, but I will denounce them to the world in that case, just as I will do if Pierre ignores an order in my favor."

"You won't denounce anyone in the Reich, unless Germany loses the war."

Coco turns her head toward him. "I will appeal to Admiral Canaris. I will shout the truth from the Eiffel Tower. Germany has no right to my perfumes."

He gives her a quick glance of alarm. "Calm down, Coco. The admiral is interested in this matter on your behalf, but he's no match for the power of Göring and Goebbels combined. Be careful what you say."

She sets her jaw. "Turn the car around this moment, Spatz. I will not attend this circus. We will find someone else to hear my claim, someone who's not afraid of Reich Marshal Göring."

"No such person exists except the Führer." His tone turns conciliatory. "In the hearing, let us concentrate on the problem of Pierre Wertheimer. Later, if Göring remains interested in No. 5, it will be to his advantage to have your full cooperation, Mademoiselle Chanel. And Goebbels's too. They will need your endorsement to carry off the propaganda. You will have a chip with which to bargain then."

Spatz reaches over to pat her knee. "Let us solve one problem at a time."

She is caught in a vise of the greed and ambition of two powerful men, Pierre Wertheimer and Reich Marshal Hermann Göring.

Breathe, Coco. Breathe in, breathe out—slowly, slowly. Take each breath one at a time before worrying about the next. No random decisions—like Boy always said.

Coco and Spatz enter a smoke-filled room in which six people wait, positioned around a rectangular table. Thanks to Spatz, they are late. She almost cannot breathe for the smoky haze, but after that ride, she's desperate for a cigarette.

Kurt Blanke does not look up as she enters; he's talking to Colonel Eckert, who sits at his right hand. Horst Eckert watches her, nodding while he listens. And he does not stand to greet her, as any gentleman would. Louis rises and pulls out a chair and she sits. Spatz sits down beside her.

Pulling away from Eckert, Doctor Kurt Blanke greets Coco with a nod. A severe-looking woman sitting on Horst Eckert's other side ignores her entrance, sitting straight-backed and holding a pen at ready.

Two seats down from the stenographer, across the table, Coco spots a familiar face—Pierre's banker, Henri Leval. Red-cheeked and stocky, he pushes up from the chair, expressionless as he greets her, the very picture of a Swiss banker. He introduces the man sitting beside him as his attorney.

The room is silent while she settles and lights a cigarette. Then, Kurt Blanke clears his throat and everyone turns to him.

"As the parties are all present now, we shall begin the hearing." Pulling a bundle of papers from a folder before him, he selects one and gazes around the table. "Fräulein Schneider shall record our conversations. And, be warned, everything you say in this room is under oath."

With a glance at Fräulein Schneider, "Have you a record of the participants? Yes? All right, then, as a point of order, let us begin."

Lifting the page, Kurt Blanke reads aloud. "Mademoiselle Gabrielle Chanel, an unmarried Aryan woman and citizen of France, brings this charge against Pierre Wertheimer and his brother Paul, both Jews. Mademoiselle Chanel charges that, contrary to laws of France prohibiting Jewish ownership of property, the majority of shares in the company registered under the laws of France as Société Mademoiselle are in fact owned by men of Jewish descent, Pierre and Paul Wertheimer. Mademoiselle Chanel further alleges that currently the company is entirely managed from the United States by Pierre Wertheimer. The Wertheimer brothers, having fled France, currently reside in the United States of America."

The words ring in her head. Why, oh why, has Pierre brought her to this? She thinks of that sunshiny day at the Deauville racetrack when she and Pierre first met—how interested he was in her idea of marketing No. 5 as a perfume which turns every girl into a woman. At the time, his desire to invest had seemed a dream come true. She'd thought they were friends.

What else can she do? Soon, she'll run short of funds. For Pierre, Société Mademoiselle and No. 5 merely add to his fortune; it is one company among many in his conglomerate. But for Coco, the company and No. 5 are her life. They are her only security since closing her couture, her guarantee against returning to poverty.

No. 5 is her survival.

A band on the street strikes up—the usual syncopated music—lots of brass and drum. As Kurt Blanke drones on, she looks through the window. She will not allow guilt to bring her down. She will not allow emotions to interfere. This terrible consequence is on Pierre's shoulders.

She was forced into this fight. This is not her fault.

When Kurt Blanke comes to the end of his speech, he turns, frowning at the stenographer. The woman jumps from her chair and hurries to the half-open window, slamming it shut. This, of course, only muffles the noise.

As Fräulein Schneider returns to her seat, Coco leans back, cupping her elbow in her hand, smoking. Kurt Blanke's cold eyes peer down the table. "Have you anything to add to what I've said, Mademoiselle Chanel?"

She swivels toward Louis. "Do I?"

"Nothing," Louis says.

Blanke now turns hostile eyes to the banker, tapping his pen on the tabletop—once, twice. "Here we are then. Herr Leval, have you brought the share transfer certificates with you?"

"Yes, Herr Blanke. I have them here." Henri Leval turns to his attorney, who digs the papers from the briefcase on the table. Sealed certificates, Coco sees, as the lawyer hands them to his client. Except for the continuing din outside, the room is silent while Leval carries the certificates to Blanke at the end of the table. Outside it seems a crowd has gathered—they're singing now along with the band.

Blanke examines each certificate before handing them to Horst Eckert. Likewise, the SS colonel examines each certificate, setting them aside. At last he lifts the small bundle, looking at Louis. "Monsieur de Vaufreland?" Louis pushes back his chair, strides around the table and takes the certificates from Horst. He flips through them quickly and hands them back, returning to his place.

As Louis sits down again, Kurt Blanke looks down the table. "This is the first time we have seen these documents." He glares at Leval. "They appear to be share transfer certificates, representing the transfer of ninety percent of outstanding shares of the company, Société Mademoiselle, to another party. Each is dated as of September 5, 1939. The signatures indicate the seller in the transfer is Pierre Wertheimer, individually, and on behalf of his brother Paul Wertheimer, by virtue of a power of attorney given to one Alain Jobert. The signature of the transferee—a purchaser of the shares— is that of one Félix Amiot, purportedly a citizen of France."

Coco fixes her eyes on Kurt Blanke. "Who is this person, Félix Amiot?"

Louis elbows her.

"We do not yet know, Mademoiselle Chanel." Blanke's tone is mild. "But we shall find out. And, for the record, Fräulein Schneider, the complainant, Mademoiselle Chanel, also owns ten percent of the company." He dips his chin. "A minor interest, yet the primary product produced by the business does bear her name, after all."

Louis nudges her again with his foot under the table. Perhaps things are looking up.

Blanke turns to the banker. "Herr Leval. Are you acquainted with this Félix Amiot?"

"Yes. He is a businessman."

Blanke gazes around the table. "Is any person in this room other than Herr Leval acquainted with Monsieur Amiot?"

Horst is still, his face a mask.

"This is an outrage." Coco's voice is fierce as she moves to rise. Louis lays his hand on her arm, restraining her. "Pierre Wertheimer has no right to sell the company without my consent."

The inquisitor's eyes dart to her. "Is this correct, Mademoiselle Chanel? Do you have legal proof, something in writing to that effect? If so, please offer it into evidence now."

"What do you mean?" Coco turns toward Louis. "What proof does he want?" René de Chambrun keeps all such records;

every record of her interest in the company. And every record of the various court proceedings between the partners over the years. And she knows the file by heart. And she is certain no such written agreement exists.

Louis, having studied the same file and knowing the history, cuts in. "Mademoiselle Chanel was a young girl when Pierre and Paul Wertheimer invested in her business. The Wertheimers, experienced businessmen, used their own lawyers to draw up the agreements. Mademoiselle Chanel was alone and poor. At the time she was not yet represented by Monsieur René de Chambrun; she had no help." He spreads his hands. "Pierre Wertheimer made certain no such limitation on some future sale and transfer of their shares exists in writing."

Kurt Blanke frowns. Horst Eckert smiles.

Louis clasps his hands before him on the table, his eyes on Blanke. "We believe these certificates are falsified, Doctor Blanke. A sham, and backdated. The share transfer must be ruled null and void under German law." After a slight pause, "Regardless, Mademoiselle Chanel also claims moral law requires this court to order ownership of the company and its assets transferred into her name." He ticks off each point as he goes on.

"First, the Wertheimers are Jews, prohibited under German law from owning property in France. And Mademoiselle Chanel is Aryan. Second: the most profitable product sold by the company at issue bears the claimant's name—Chanel No. 5. Third: Although Mademoiselle Chanel receives—or did prior to a few months ago—only ten percent of company net revenues from sales of her perfume, Société Mademoiselle depends entirely upon her legendary status throughout the world for those sales. This situation is reprehensible. And now, Pierre Wertheimer has the nerve to claim that he has handed Mademoiselle Chanel's name, her identity, and legend over to a stranger, without which, the company has no value!"

Sitting back, he adjusts his jacket collar. "These facts alone show the transaction before us is unjust, a blatant attempt at theft."

Blanke observes Leval. His voice when he speaks holds a touch of malice. "Are you also a Jew, Herr Leval?" Outside the band plays a song which attracts Colonel Eckert's attention. Horst glances toward the window with a little smile. Coco pities the woman in his heart. She must be miserable.

The sheen rising on Leval's forehead gleams under the overhead lights. "No," he says. "I am not Jewish, Herr Blanke. And, as I have said, I am a citizen of Switzerland."

"Yes, of course." Blanke leans forward. "But we have several problems to solve. How are we to authenticate the signatures and the dates on the certificates which you claim belong to Herr Félix Amiot? How are we to determine whether they are valid?"

"I will swear to it."

"This proceeding requires the Wertheimers to swear to that fact, not their banker. Therefore, they must return to France for that purpose."

Leval coughs. "I do not believe that will happen, Herr Blanke."

He lifts his brows. "We are dealing with a French company worth a fortune. Is it your contention that we should merely accept your word on the validity of the signatures and dates on the certificates?"

"Again, I will swear on oath."

"I assume that you were paid for this paperwork you've performed for the Wertheimers. If so, you have an interest in the outcome. You are not an objective witness." He speaks, holding the banker's eyes. "Were you paid for this work?"

Leval flushes. "Yes, Herr Blanke."

Louis picks up his pen, holding it high in the air. Kurt Blanke turns to him. "Yes?"

"We are certain a separate trust agreement invalidating the purchase exists," Louis says.

Blanke's reptilian eyes swing to Leval. "Does such an agreement exist, Herr Leval? Remember, you are under oath."

"Not to my knowledge."

"My client will sign an affidavit to that effect," says Leval's lawyer.

"Quiet."

"But I ..."

"I said, quiet!" Kurt Blanke slams his hand on the table, leveling his eyes at the banker. "Herr Leval. Are you acquainted with Félix Amiot?"

"Yes. He is an aviation engineer."

This is too much. Coco pushes back her chair and stands, hands braced against the edge of the table as she turns to face Kurt Blanke. "Nonsense! What do you suppose an aviation engineer knows about running a perfume company? Nothing, I tell you! He knows nothing of the creative work involved, nothing of the product, or the customers, or the business." Flinging her hand toward Leval, "This is a travesty." Her voice breaks.

"Resume your seat at once, mademoiselle."

Coco blinks, holding on to the table. Spatz touches her arm. "Coco," he says in a soft tone, almost whispering. Her eyes roam over the faces around the table. Slowly she lowers herself into the chair.

For a moment the room is silent. Even the band outside has stopped the noise. Seated now, Coco lifts her chin, brushing a lock of hair back from her face, tucking it behind an ear.

Kurt Blanke turns back to his query. "Monsieur Leval, in regard to your claim that the company shares and assets have already been transferred to this Félix Amiot, is the man of Jewish descent?"

Leval shakes his head. "I do not know. I don't think so."

"Then we will find out." Placing his hands on the table before him, Blanke turns to his right. "Colonel Eckert, please have your men locate Monsieur Amiot immediately and bring him in for questioning." He fingers the pen on the table, rolling it one way and then the other, seeming deep in thought.

At last, he glances at his watch. "Unfortunately, it is growing late. But Monsieur Leval, we must ask for more of your time. We must get the facts straight."

The banker's eyes widen.

Leval's lawyer scrapes back the chair, shooting up. "Herr Blanke, my client is a citizen of Switzerland. I protest!"

Blanke turns, regarding the lawyer. "Your client will remain with us, and you shall leave." Coco watches Henri Leval's Adam's apple convulse as he swallows. His lawyer does not move.

"You will leave now," Blanke adds, his tone sinister. The man hesitates, then slams the briefcase shut. He rests his hand for a moment on the banker's shoulder. As he picks up the briefcase and turns, Leval's eyes follow the lawyer until the door closes.

"Good." Blanke leans across Horst Eckert, saying something to the stenographer, who is writing. She nods. "Now that order is restored we shall continue." He points a finger at Henri Leval. "Please consider your answer to these next questions carefully before responding."

Beside him, the stenographer waits, pen poised.

"Again, you are under oath."

Leval closes his eyes for a moment, then nods.

As he speaks, Blanke emphasizes each word. "Herr Leval, are you aware of the existence of an agreement of trust or of any other agreement existing between Pierre Wertheimer or his brother, and this person Félix Amiot, which could, now or in the future, invalidate the alleged purchase and transfer of the company?"

Leval's voice trembles, but his reply is quick. "No, Herr Blanke. So far as I know, no such agreement exists."

"Isn't it true the share transfers you've provided today are forged and backdated?"

"No." Leval shakes his head. "No!"

"Isn't it true that Pierre Wertheimer and his brother harbor a hope that the war will end one day, not in Germany's favor, and that if and when that occurs they will once again claim ownership of Société Mademoiselle and the Chanel perfumes? That Félix Amiot is a straw man—that he has been paid merely to hold the shares for the period of this war, to protect the Wertheimer interests from seizure under our laws?"

"I cannot know what is in another man's mind, but I am aware of no such agreement. Monsieur Amiot paid the purchase price at the time of the transaction, Herr Blanke."

"And have you proof of the payment?"

Leval's face goes pale. "No—that is, in a Swiss bank such information is confidential."

"How inconvenient for your client that you are unable to confirm payment by Monsieur Amiot prior to the Fatherland taking possession of France. It would be best for all concerned if you speak up right now."

"I cannot say."

Blanke lowers his voice so that Coco must strain to hear. "Then, without such proof of the validity of the sale, we can go no further today." Heaving a heavy sigh, he adds, "We shall locate Monsieur Amiot. And, absent more information,"—he points his fountain pen at Henri Leval—"it appears you will be our guest for a while."

Henri Leval pushes back his chair and stands, arms hanging at his sides. "I am a Swiss citizen. I am neutral in the war. My citizenship and profession demand ..."

"No one in this room cares what they demand. Sit down."

Leval hesitates, and then takes his seat again.

Kurt Blanke's eyes roam over the remaining occupants in the room. Beside her, Louis starts to speak, but Blanke lifts his hand. The stenographer begins writing. "This proceeding is now postponed. We will meet again, once I have had the chance to examine every aspect of the case."

He glances at Louis de Vaufreland, then Coco, then Spatz: "You will now leave. Colonel Eckert and I will speak alone with Herr Leval."

Across the table, Henri Leval's hands tremble. Horst says something to Kurt Blanke, stands, and leaves the room.

Louis walks out with Spatz and Coco. He will telephone when he hears from Doctor Blanke, he says. Coco protests—surely there's more he can do. Nothing, for the moment, he says.

She purses her lips. "Then stick to this Kurt Blanke like a shadow." With a kiss on her cheeks, he helps her into the car.

Both Coco and Spatz are silent on the ride back to the Hôtel Ritz. As they reach the entrance and stop, Spatz waves off the eager doorman, turning to Coco. "In my experience, darling, something strange is going on."

She leans her head against the car seat, closing her eyes.

"The entire process concerns me," he goes on. His voice sounds hollow, an echo in a long, deep well. "This is taking too long—something's fishy. Someone's been paid." He grips the steering wheel with both hands. "Why else would Blanke delay with more questions? And why bother finding this Félix Amiot? Blanke has the power to seize the company at once."

Turning her head, Coco regards him under half-closed lids. His questions unnerve her—he has made promises—he promised that Admiral Canaris wields power and would support her case.

Oblivious to Coco's consternation, Spatz shakes his head. "Confiscations don't require such detail. Never, not once, have I seen a Reich official give a fig about the rights of a Jew, particularly now he's already fled to America."

Coco should have known that nothing involving Pierre would be simple. Spatz opens his door and comes around to her, tossing his car keys to the doorman. With a salute to the guards, Spatz leads her into the grand entrance hall. Instead of heading for the elevator, he steers her toward the stairs and the passageway toward the bar at the rue Cambon entrance.

"Mademoiselle!"

They stop and turn as Géraud hurries toward them from the concierge desk holding up a small blue envelope. At once she recognizes the notepaper. It is Colette's. "This was left for you earlier."

Thanking Géraud, she continues down the hall with Spatz. He's attempting to console her, taking her for drinks, but that won't help. The afternoon proceeding was a blow.

"Perhaps I'm wrong," he says, seeming to sense her growing depression. "In the end, Coco, I am certain you will prevail. I'll speak with Admiral Canaris. I hope that Kurt Blanke is merely going through the motions to appease Göring's man, Horst Eckert." Throwing his arm around her shoulders, he pulls her close, smiling. "Meanwhile, a very dry martini will fix those blues."

She'd had her own medicine in mind. She sits where he takes her, a table in a dark corner. While he orders, she scans the letter from Colette. She has neither seen nor spoken with Colette since their luncheon with Susanne Abetz at Café de la Paix. When she comes to the end of the letter, her eyes return to the last two paragraphs and she reads them again.

"In case you have not yet heard," Colette writes, "the gendarmes—yes, our own Paris policemen—have rounded up all foreign Jews, at least four thousand. Perhaps more. Would you like to know something, Coco? No? I will say it anyway. The police knew where to find each and every Jew because they were registered in that abomination you prefer to think of as a census. That is why they were, as you say, counting.

"So now they are all gone, every foreign Jew, and no one knows where they've been sent. They were arrested for the crime of being foreign Jews and have simply disappeared. Maurice says they will come for French Jews next." She's signed the letter with a flourish.

The waiter comes with the drinks, followed by Spatz. Coco folds the letter in half and slips it into her skirt pocket while the waiter sets a martini on the table before her. She stares at the glass, hands folded and limp in her lap. What does Colette expect from her? This is not her fault.

Spatz turns to someone at the next table, chatting, laughing. Slowly she rises. The letter burns in her pocket. She will take it upstairs and destroy it. She will tear it to shreds and burn it. And then she will take her medicine and then she will fall asleep.

Chapter Thirty-Seven

Paris
Fall 1941

Coco's claim against Pierre is stalled. She's waited for months—through spring, summer, and here it is November and Kurt Blanke still seems incapable of making a decision. Spatz is no help at all since Admiral Canaris's most important battleship, the *Bismarck*, was sunk by the British last June. He spent the entire summer going back and forth to Tripoli, scurrying behind General Rommel instead of pushing Kurt Blanke. And now he's brooding because of Hitler's siege at Leningrad, and what he calls, when in his cups, the foolhardy odds of fighting this war on two fronts. Invading the Soviet Union does not seem a good idea to Coco either, given the winter weather.

This has not been a good year for the Führer, all in all.

Henri Leval was released from custody not long after the hearing, protected by his Swiss citizenship. But Félix Amiot, the stranger who thinks he owns her property, was located and remains under arrest. Even after all these months he hangs on, still denying his purchase of the company was a sham. Like Pierre, he is a stubborn man.

Worse, Spatz thinks Göring may have formed some sort of kinship with Félix Amiot. Coco cannot bear to think of her bad luck. Word is that Göring's Luftwaffe, having failed to overwhelm Britain's RAF and now faced with Russia, is in growing disfavor with the Führer. Perhaps the Reich marshal has decided his air force needs Félix Amiot. Spatz is worried Göring may attempt to trade Félix Amiot's freedom in exchange for the man's aviation expertise and her perfume. And who's to stop him?

The weather doesn't help. They're saying this will be the coldest winter on record in Paris. Of course, they said that last year. But this time it's true—each day is colder and grayer than the last. Day by day the frozen city runs down like an old clock. Snow swept to street curbs piles higher and higher, turning brown. And all the singing young blond men have disappeared, sent off to the Eastern Front in Russia. Poor young soldiers in the handsome gray-green uniforms, smooth-cheeked boys, really, and now they're fighting on the arctic tundra where the deep cold freezes the marrow of their bones. Doesn't history tell Adolf Hitler anything? Look what happened to Napoleon.

But still, newspapers celebrate the Führer's victories. Newsmen in Paris are not stupid—mentioning even the possibility of German mistake or failure is now treason, punishable by death.

The streets of Paris are also devoid of French men, too, they seem to have simply disappeared. Laura Mae says they're grabbed right off the streets, swept off to Germany in dragnets. She says in Germany they're slaves in mines and armament factories. Arletty says they go as volunteers, that Germany offers good jobs and pay. Her colonel told her so. Arletty's colonel swears the slavery rumor is not true.

While Coco waits on Kurt Blanke's decision, everything in Paris changes from day to day. Spatz inhales his scotch. André is sullen and she does not understand why. It's been over a year since he entered the hospital. On top of everything else, the old bonhomie is missing in the Hôtel Ritz. Géraud is somewhat curt, always in a rush. The staff, who used to laugh and gossip, are surly.

This war seems endless. What is next? Africa? Asia? America? The war of 1918 was supposed to be the last great war.

On a cold, bleak morning Coco rouses herself to visit André again. She fights off the feeling of lethargy, which has recently taken hold. They sit silently together in the hospital's garden courtyard—André in his wheelchair, bundled in an oversized wool coat, with a muffler around his neck and his legs covered with blankets printed with Property of the American Hospital. Coco perches beside him on an iron bench. Her boy is quiet, a stiff-backed martyr enduring her questions, as if she's the Spanish inquisition.

She steals a look at her brooding son from the corner of her eye. His skin remains sallow; eyes dull, fixed in the distance. She supposes he's longing to return to his room. She turns, asking if he is warm.

He coughs, covering his mouth with a clenched fist. "Yes, quite."

Silence again descends, broken only by his coughing. Two young nurses come into the courtyard, heads bent together, chattering. One of the girls glances their way and smiles, lifting her hand. Through a cloud of gloom, Coco waves back.

"Do you know them, André?" He does not respond. "They seem like nice young ladies." She watches them walking off into the garden, through the trees toward another wing of the hospital.

She wonders if her son's spirits will ever return to normal.

He was never an easygoing child—he often wore a haunted look when he was young. But then, like her, he'd never had a real home when he was growing up, moving from Madame Charbonnet to Father LeCure to Beaumont. He was never part of a family. He must have wondered why. On those visits to Paris when Boy was alive, did he ever suspect the truth?

Nonsense. She'd have sensed it if he had ever believed she was his mother. There would have been some sign of a special connection. One thing is certain, though Coco has felt the strength of her maternal bond, André has never felt a bond with her. He'd even married Catharina when he was only twenty-one without letting her know.

She closes her eyes for an instant. The wedding snub had hurt. But she'd kept that to herself, and as a gift she'd bought the couple the lovely château in the Pyrenees, where Gabby was born. And later, the house in Normandy, where Helen was born. And after that the one in Montfort-l'Amaury.

No one could say she has not taken good care of André. Even after schooling at Beaumont and the usual military service required in those days, she'd given him a job—named him director in charge of her fabric mills, Tissus Chanel. He'd done all right with that for fifteen years, before mobilization. But he's never had Boy Capel's ambition—or her own.

Looking back, she muses that André has always seemed a bit morose. He was polite, but reserved, somewhat distant. Not so withdrawn, as now. The war has changed him.

But he does love his girls, Gabby and Helen. She smiles, thinking of them. Despite his sullen mood, he still loves them, she is certain. Before the war he spent time with them, as a father should—as no father had done with him. And he was proud of them, always taking photographs when they were young. Before the war.

She turns to him. "Doctor Wood says you'll be released soon.

Catharina and the girls will be excited to have you home. We must make plans. The château will be so good for you, all that fresh mountain air will help you heal."

He remains silent.

With a sigh, Coco snaps open her purse. If only there were something she could say or do to make him care. She reaches into her purse and pulls out a pack of Gitanes and a lighter, longing for the smoke.

André turns, his eyes dropping to the cigarettes. "Not here, Aunt."

Of course, she's becoming forgetful. She drops the cigarettes and lighter in her lap, in the slack of her skirt, and looks about. Regardless of his feelings toward her, she must make plans for her son's future. She cannot leave André's future up to fate. He will need constant care for several years after he's released, the doctor says. Coco looks at her son. "Have you spoken with Catharina of your plans for going home yet?"

His eyes flick to her and away. "No."

"Well, we must make arrangements, you know." Her voice fills with false cheer. "You should telephone her this evening, André. With the right care, you can continue recovering at home."

He says nothing. She waits. But he does not seem to hear.

She slips the cigarettes and lighter back into her purse. "Now." She will try again. "Catharina must come here soon, for instructions on your proper care. When you are discharged, my chauffeur, Evan, will drive you to the château."

His hands curl around the arms of the wheelchair.

"Your wife must accompany you on the trip. It's a long way. You must take things slowly at first."

He does not look at her. When he speaks, his tone is flat. "I will make my own plans, Aunt. And I prefer not to see Catharina just yet."

What is this? Something's wrong between André and his wife, she realizes. She should have thought of this before. Although she's certain they've exchanged letters, Catharina has only come once to visit him, and that, almost a month after his arrival from the prison.

André coughs, and for the first time this afternoon, he turns to look directly at her. "Doctor Wood recommends a sanatorium in Zurich. He says he can arrange this with the authorities, so long as the transfer is on his order."

"You don't wish to go home?"

He shakes his head.

"But what will Catharina think? And the girls?" A lump rises in her throat. "André, Zurich is so far away. And with the war, I—we, won't be able to visit you." She stares at him. His eyes show no emotion.

A thought strikes. She straightens. Her lips tremble, but she smiles. "I have an idea. Why don't you stay with me in Paris—you can live in my apartment in the Maison. You've always loved those rooms. The Maison is not so busy these days. It will be quiet, and quite comfortable. And I will hire help." She is his mother, she will care for her son.

His voice jolts her from the dream. "No, thank you, Aunt. I will go to Switzerland."

She frowns. "But I would love this, André. You must stay here in Paris. I will continue at the Ritz, and you may have the Maison apartment to yourself. It is spacious, lovely."

His expression is blank, his voice cold. "I prefer the sanatorium in Zurich. The doctor says he can arrange my transfer. And I will go alone."

Drawing back, she regards her son. To him, she is an intruder. An aching pain grips Coco as she recognizes the full truth. Perhaps he does not love her. To him, she is not his family. Averting her eyes, she turns away, looking off. "I see. Well, yes, if that's what you really want." When he does not reply, she wraps her arms around her midsection, thinking of the day André was born. The day they took him from her.

I should have fought harder for him. But then, Étienne and Boy made the decision. And I let them.

A small brown bird flits past just then, landing on the branch of a silvery tree. The trees are bare, the days cold. His mother must have built a nest for him, where he will stay warm until the spring. She glances at André and tears well in her throat and she swallows them. She never built a nest for André. She never showed him a mother's love. She never gave anything up to keep him with her. To André, she's only a wealthy aunt. Whatever traumas he's endured through the war have at last severed him from her. Once he cared for her, a little—she's certain. And perhaps he will again. But she will never receive from him the love a son feels for his mother.

Lifting her chin, Coco takes a long breath, and turning to André, manages a smile. "The sanatorium in Zurich it is, then. I will inform Doctor Wood and let him make the arrangements."

André nods.

It is past time to leave. She glances about for a nurse, but the courtyard is empty. Standing, she brushes off her skirt and looks down at her boy. "Shall we go inside?"

"Yes," he says. And her heart cracks in two. Because, for the first time this afternoon, he smiles.

In the car she is silent while Evan drives. They've almost reached the Place Vendôme when she changes her mind about returning to the hotel.

"I want to walk in the Tuileries Gardens for a while," she says to Evan. She longs to be alone.

"Yes, mademoiselle."

A few minutes later, Coco leans forward, tapping his shoulder. "Drop me off over there," pointing ahead. "On the corner, near Le Meurice." The Meurice is another German requisition, but for years before the occupation, Misia lived on the top floor. Misia threw wonderful parties at the Meurice before the war. She smiles, thinking of the view from Misia's windows over the tops of the trees in the Tuileries, and over the Seine.

Evan slows the car at the corner after driving around the usual barricades. "This area of the gardens is not safe these days," he says over his shoulder. "There've been several robberies here."

She clucks her tongue. "The trees are bare now; it's not a forest this time of year. There's no place for a thief to hide. Stop here, Evan." She feels his eyes watching her in the mirror as he pulls the Rolls over to the curb on rue de Rivoli.

"You will find the park very different these days, mademoiselle." He opens the door and comes around to help her from the car. "I will wait here."

"There's no need." She slides out, waving him off. "Go back to the hotel. It's not far—I will enjoy the walk. And you may have the evening off." Holding on to the strap of her purse, she crosses the street toward the park.

"I will wait."

Surprised, she stops and turns, giving him a look.

He pretends not to notice as he glances at his watch. "It is four o'clock, mademoiselle. Soon it will be dark." His tone is placid. "I will wait."

Before she can say another word, Evan slides his hands into his pockets and leans back against the car, gazing off toward the Seine and on to the horizon, as if she's not standing right before him. For an instant Coco hesitates, then, with a little smile, she turns and enters the park through an opening in the yew hedge.

But the smile disappears as she strolls along the pathway. On her right, the fall flowers usually blooming before the Jeu de Paume, even in November, have disappeared into the weeds of an overgrown garden bed. The curators of the impressionist museum hid the fine paintings days before the Germans arrived, Colette says. Now Wehrmacht guards stand at the doors. According to Colette, the Germans now use the museum for storing their stolen art.

Farther to her right, past the Jeu de Paume, rolls of barbed wire barricade the Place de la Concorde, which is mostly used by the Wehrmacht as a parade ground now. The rose garden overlooking it is bare. A feeling of gloom swamps her again. Reaching the alley centrale, she turns left toward the round basin where children used to sail their boats. Gone are the children and their boats, gone the two-wheeled flower-painted ice-cream cart, the little puppet theaters, the laughter, the lovers necking on the benches. Farther on, the carousel is closed, the Louvre is dark.

Red and brown leaves carpet the path as she walks on, the damp leaves clinging to her shoes. In the gloaming, Coco gazes at the deserted pathway, the empty benches, the bare dirt under the trees where tended grass used to grow. She stops, looks about, over the entire unkempt garden, and it comes to her that perhaps this is the beginning of the end of the world as she has ever known it.

Coco sinks onto a bench near the path, letting the purse slip from her shoulder. She'd thought to sit in the garden and restore her soul. But these winter gardens offer no consolation—no color, no beauty. Paris is colorless now, no longer the beautiful city of light.

And soon André will be off to Switzerland without a backward look. A void opens up inside, a hollow. A damp breeze blowing from the river makes her shiver. She pulls the coat tight around, then hugs herself.

"Boy," she whispers, "we have lost him. We have truly lost our son."

She had loved Papa and he'd left and never returned. She waited for him until the day she left the abbey. She'd loved Boy Capel, had adored and trusted Boy, but he betrayed her too. And Pierre? Even through their earlier battles, she'd thought him a friend. But no longer.

Worst of all is André. He has no place for her in his heart. And it's too late.

Slowly the realization grows—she is alone. She is utterly alone.

Chapter Thirty-Eight

Paris
Winter 1941

On the third day of December, Coco rests near the window of her sitting room looking out over the Place Vendôme. Deep snow covers the ground. It is four thirty in the afternoon, but the day is dismal. Lights in the apartment are turned off. André left for the sanatorium in Zurich two weeks ago. He and Catharina are separated. He is free, but seems no longer to care about anyone, including his aunt Coco.

The sound of a key turning in the door rouses her. She's been sitting in this chair for hours, she realizes as Spatz walks in. In silence she watches him toss his hat and gloves onto the table near the door. He snaps on the overhead light, then picks up the telephone receiver and orders a bottle of Glenfiddich single malt whisky from the bar, and, with a glance at her, two glasses.

Scotch this early in the afternoon. Foreboding rises—she massages the back of her neck, waiting. Spatz never drinks scotch this time of day. Something has happened. Perhaps he brings news of her case.

"Where is Alyce?" he says, shrugging off his coat, coming toward her. She can smell the whisky on his breath as he comes close.

"Off on an errand. Why? What do you need?"

He throws up his hands. "The girl is never around. I want her to fetch those drinks. The bar will take too long to bring them up." He drops into the chair facing her. A small table sits between them. "Why do we pay the woman if she's not willing to work?"

"We?" Her tone is sharp, she realizes. But she does not care. Bad enough to mourn André. She's also balanced on the edge of a high cliff, holding tight while she waits for news from Louis or Kurt Blanke. It's been months. "Alyce is mine," she snaps, gesturing toward the door. "If anyone goes, it's you."

Spatz gives her a quizzical look. Then, his mouth tightens. "Well, perhaps that's what I will do. As a matter of fact, tomorrow I'm off to Berlin."

Coco leans her head back against the cushion. Any second she will hear the bad news—Kurt Blanke has ruled against her. She is ruined. Who now owns No. 5—Pierre, or Reich Marshal Göring? Minutes pass in a silence she is terrified to break.

A knock comes at the door. "At last," Spatz murmurs, strolling over to let the waiter in. He enters bearing a silver tray on which are placed two cut-crystal glasses, the whisky, and a pair of folded white linen napkins. Spatz waves his hand in Coco's direction and disappears into the bedroom. Coco, annoyed, watches the man set the tray down on the table between the chairs.

When the waiter has gone, she reaches for the whisky bottle and pours one inch of scotch into a glass, neat. Puckering her lips, she drinks it back. Spatz is in such a mood this evening. Something has clearly gone wrong.

Returning from the bedroom, Spatz sits across from her, reaches for the bottle on the table, and fills the glass halfway. She watches and waits as he tosses back his head and drinks. When he reaches for the bottle again, she regards him. New lines etch his face—the furrows between his brows have deepened overnight.

"What's gone wrong?" she finally says.

He gazes into the glass. "Everything, everything."

She must know. "Is this about my case?"

"Could not be worse." A chill slices through her. She leans forward, struggling to hear—already he's slurring his words. Listing to one side, Spatz lifts his glass, as if in a toast. "We cannot continue fighting war on all fronts without reliable allies." He sips the scotch, gazing out over the Place Vendôme. Then, squeezing his eyes shut, he rubs a spot between his brows. "The Japanese are always trouble!"

She looks at him, amazed. "The Japanese?" What do the Japanese have to do with her claim against Pierre?

Spatz rests the glass on the arm of his chair, curling his fist around it. "Sorry, darling. But it seems our Führer has picked a terrible time to fall into a rage. Our forces are stalled on the Eastern Front with losses no one can mention." His face is grim. "Thousands of our fine soldiers cut off in the snow and ice in Russia, starving. Freezing."

His tone is bitter. "It seems some fool sent our men off to Russia months ago with only summer uniforms. Only now does Hitler realize. He is rabid." He swirls the glass, gazing into the amber liquid. When he looks up, his eyes dart from her to the window and back again. "And what do you think is the Führer's solution?"

"I cannot imagine."

He lifts the glass and drinks again. "Our Führer's brilliant solution is to order every citizen in Berlin to give up their coats for the men in Russia." A sharp laugh escapes. "That is, if anyone is left alive up there to receive them."

But he has said these things before; something more is on his mind. These complaints are nothing new.

He sees her watching him. "I cannot say more. Don't ask."

Leaning forward, gripping both her knees, she inspects the sparrow. "Tell me, Spatz. About my case. Has Doctor Blanke come to his decision?"

"Not now. Things are worse." He fairly reeks of alcohol. "I can say no more!"

It's not like Spatz to obsess over the state of war. He leans back, closing his eyes, and she watches him. He knows something. There is something terrible on his mind and she must know. She cannot stand this waiting any longer. If Kurt Blanke has issued an order in her case, she must know at once, good or bad. She's lost André. Now she must know if she has also lost No. 5.

Rising, Coco goes to Spatz. She lifts the drink from his hand, placing the glass on the table. Then, reaching down, she takes his hands, pulling him. "Come with me, darling. You must rest. You're tense and tired."

Stumbling, he follows her into the bedroom. He slumps on the side of the bed while she unties his shoes and removes them. Then, making a smile, she stands and steps back and his eyes follow her. The smile is the one she's practiced for photographers many times before the mirror.

Slowly, she kicks off her shoes. He does not move a muscle. She unhooks her skirt, letting it slip to the floor. She unbuttons the blouse, tossing it off, and stands before him in only her black silk chemise and the loops of pearls. He tilts his head, focusing now as he watches her. She starts toward him, then suddenly stops, lifting one finger. "Wait, there is one more thing."

Swaying over to the dressing table, she feels his eyes on her. She picks up the plain amber bottle and pulls off the top. Turning, Coco watches her lover while she crosses herself with No. 5.

Half an hour later, Coco lies in the half-light, gazing at the ceiling. Spatz sprawls on his side, one arm curled around her as he drifts, eyes half closed, sated with lovemaking and whisky. A shaft of light from the sitting room slants through the doorway, a sliver of light cutting the room in half.

She runs a hand over his chest, feeling a new, almost imperceptible layer of fat beneath his sun-tanned flesh. Still, she cannot forget that the real Spatz must be hard and a little cruel to have survived so long in the Reich. She's heard the stories. She must be careful. Nestling closer, she whispers in his ear. "About my case. What did you mean earlier, darling, when you said things are worse?"

He turns his face to her, a dazed, puzzled look in his eyes.

She runs her finger up and down his arm, nibbling his earlobe, and repeats the question.

He grabs her breast, mumbling something in German.

She cannot understand. "What did you say?" She tickles his ear with her tongue.

"We got the news this morning." He speaks in French now. "Schellenberg," he adds … and the name trails off.

She swallows, suddenly frightened. Holding tight. "What news?"

"It came from his man in Japan. The fleet sailed at dawn two days ago. General Tojo has betrayed us; the Japs are attacking." Rolling onto his back, he flops his arm over his eyes. "America will enter the war." He rolls again, with his back to her. "I leave for Berlin in the morning. Now everything will change."

Three days later, Coco enters the hotel, heading for the elevator. She stops as Géraud calls to her from the concierge desk. "Mademoiselle, I've mail for you. Shall I hold it for your maid?"

"Oh. Well, no. I suppose I will take it up."

"Yes, all right then. One moment, please." And he turns back to a room where mail is sorted for delivery to residents.

Coco stands waiting. She gazes about. It's only the sixth of December and already the Ritz is decorated for Christmas. This is a season which never fails to send her into a melancholy state. At least, ever since Boy died two days before Christmas Day.

The hotel doors open and a gust of cold wind blows down the long hallway. The weather is fierce outside today. Coco shivers. She's just returned from a walk, driven to the extreme by sheer boredom. She can only sit in her rooms for so long. The days when she was busy creating, working with her hands, inspired, completely involved with her work and building the House of Chanel—those days are gone. Sometimes she wonders if perhaps they were only lovely dreams.

Géraud returns, hands over her letters, and turns to the concierge desk to greet a couple who've come in from the cold.

Upstairs, Coco drops the letters and her purse on the table beside the door. She will look at the mail later. She calls for Alyce, and with a mild feeling of disappointment, realizes the maid is not here. Spatz is off again, and she has yet to hear any news about her case. She is alone, and with nothing else to occupy her mind but her floundering case against Pierre, she wanders aimless into the bedroom while removing her coat, gloves, hat, tossing them onto the foot of the bed. The claim should have been adjudicated long ago.

Louis says Félix Amiot remains under arrest, still hanging onto his story that he is the true owner of her company, and no one seems to care. With Reich Marshal Göring still somehow involved, Spatz refuses to ask the admiral to interfere. She's complained to her attorneys so often that both René and Louis are slow to return her calls.

Coco falls on the bed, settling onto her back, and crooks her arm over her forehead, closing her eyes. She is tired—it seems lately that she does nothing but sleep.

Hours later she wakes in darkness. For an instant she's confused. Coco sits up straight in the bed, looking around. She is rested, but she slowly realizes she's slept the afternoon away. This won't do. She is Chanel—she will not allow herself to simply give up. Getting out of the bed, she stretches her arms overhead, feeling refreshed, filled with a rush of strange new energy, like a premonition of sorts.

"Alyce?"

Still no answer. The girl needs some discipline, she thinks, turning to contemplate the armoire across the room which is filled with her evening dresses. She will dress for dinner and go downstairs. Again she will show everyone that she's the most famous woman in the world. She will dine downstairs, alone or not. She is a woman who does not accept defeat.

She dresses carefully even though she's dining alone this evening. The spacious dining room will glitter with officers and diplomats with beautiful young women on their arms, so when she walks in alone she must look her best. She sits on the bedside pulling up her stockings. The Reich marshal will be dining downstairs as usual, with Colonel Eckert hanging on, of course. And, as always, with the certainty of a compass needle pointing north, at some moment in the evening the Reich marshal will turn and stare at Coco. And she will feel his greed as a tangible thing, his lust for No. 5.

This evening she will send back a brittle smile that says, *You shall not have it.*

But the usually lively dining room is less than a third full when she arrives. She stops just inside the door, looking about, surprised. It's as if the ringmaster has stopped the circus. The orchestra is missing. Only a few men are present tonight in uniform. Reich Marshal Göring is missing, as is Horst Eckert—that's a pleasant turn of events. Arletty waves to her from across the room. She's with her officer at the usual table.

The maître d'hôtel accompanies Coco to her table. The high arched windows are iced over tonight. Lamplight from the plaza dissolves into craquelure on the frosty glass.

"Where is everyone?" she asks as the maître d' seats her.

He bends, speaking low into her ear. "I do not know, Mademoiselle Chanel. Something about the Japanese—don't know what that means! Several hours ago Reich Marshal Göring and half his staff rushed out into their cars. They were in such a hurry Géraud cleared the elevators and grand entrance hall."

She turns her head, regarding him. "Do you mean they have checked out of the hotel?"

He straightens, with a look of alarm. "No, mademoiselle. The Ritz is requisitioned. And, they took no baggage." She nods, and he disappears. Despite the room being half empty tonight, the kitchen is slow. Dinner is long and dull.

The hotel is deserted as she passes through after dining, except for the guards at the entrance doors onto Place Vendôme. Géraud is not on duty; a new man stands behind the concierge desk tonight, so there will be no useful gossip. Exiting the elevator on the third floor, Coco heads down the hallway to her apartment, feeling the emptiness of the rooms she passes; sensing a sinister vibration in the air. No laughter comes from the other sides of the doors; no voices, no movement, no music.

She enters the apartment, glances at the mail she dropped on the table earlier, and steers on into the bedroom. In the dark bedroom, Coco stands before the long windows looking out over the Place Vendôme. Slowly, she undresses.

Pulling out a drawer, she reaches in for the envelope containing the hypodermic and her medicine, her morphia. The medicine will get her through the night. She slips on a silky gown and brushes her hair. And then, taking the needle and medicine with her, she goes to the bed and sits on the edge. She fills the needle and stabs it into the top of her thigh, remembering the time Misia did the same in the midst of a marketplace, jamming the needle right through her skirt. Coco was horrified then. Now she understands.

Already drowsy, she slumps onto the bed, dreaming of the years before this war, before Pierre's double-cross, the days when she was the queen of Paris—Coco Chanel, beautiful, gay, wealthy.

A feeling of bliss fills her as the room blurs. Luminous colors rise and spin, and suddenly there is Misia! Ah, Misia has come! Smiling, Coco lifts her arm, pointing at cruel and beautiful Misia with her famous pouting lips and rosy cheeks from Renoir's paint box. Now Misia is a red, red rose, her petals slowly fading into pink, and from the center of the rose out pops Jean Cocteau, and he's holding out his hands, and Coco takes one hand and Misia takes the other and they all dance together as they used to do—Misia and Coco and Cocteau—while colors whirl and curl around them and Rubinstein plays his Spanish love songs.

And here comes dear Picasso and he's glowing colors, tangerine, now amber, even as he perches high atop Misia's grand piano, and look at this!—Pablo's painting laurels on Rubinstein's bald and fuzzy head. She laughs, clapping her hands.

In a flash of golden light Igor comes, Stravinsky, her old lover, and he takes a bow and holding on to Coco's hand they fly together through the air, up and up and up through the flower confetti, and Dimitri's great white horse is in the feathers now.

Coco moans, her eyes fluttering as Serge Lifar springs up from the stage and now he's spinning, spinning, pirouetting through a rainbow vortex, pulling in Coco, Misia, Picasso, Rubinstein, Cocteau, Paris, all of Coco's world—everyone she loves flows through the universe in a silver ectoplasmic stream.

Everyone she loves is here but Boy Capel and André.

Chapter Thirty-Nine

New York
Winter 1941

Sunday, the seventh of December, and Manhattan is quiet as Alain Jobert leaves his apartment. He strolls through the Plaza lobby, and the doorman tips his hat. "Morning, Mister Jobert," he says, with a glance toward the curb. "No car today? The wind's blustering out there."

"Not today, John Henry. I'm going to walk." He tightens the scarf around his neck and heads south down Fifth Avenue. The bracing air feels fine. He's looking forward to a quiet Sunday afternoon in the office with no interruptions. The Hoboken plant is on line and everyone's awaiting results. If all goes well, Pierre hopes to deliver No. 5, and of course the other Chanel perfumes, to retailers in time for the Christmas rush. Getting ahead of his desk work will help when the headwinds hit.

The sidewalks are swept. Gritty snow, having absorbed the fumes and detritus of the city, piles at the curbs. But across the street in Central Park, snow on the low stone walls and trees remains pristine, glittering white. At the Grand Army Plaza, carriages wait, their horses snorting restlessly in the brisk cold, harnesses wrapped with red ribbons and bells. A flash of sunshine on the statue of General Sherman catches his eye. Sherman sits astride his horse, with Victory pointing the way. It is Victory, Alain thinks of—defeat for the dirty Boche. Freeing France from the occupation. He is a citizen of two countries. He loves both, and one is at war.

The whispers he's heard about what's happening in France are horrifying. He wonders if it's possible the stories are true—entire Jewish families shipped to Germany; crammed together into trains, even cattle cars. What happens to them then? No one really seems to know. Prisons? Work camps? He jams his hands in his pockets, suddenly feeling cold to the marrow of his bones. What happens to children in a country where they're not considered human beings?

He should be fighting the Boche in France right now, not strolling down Fifth Avenue.

Blindly he passes the gaily decorated storefronts, Rockefeller Center, and the tall Christmas tree. The display windows at Saks are almost hidden by swarms of wide-eyed children and parents. Parishioners pour from St. Patrick's Cathedral as the bells toll. But Alain sees none of this. The thought he's been turning over slowly crystallizes. A few more steps and the decision he's avoided for months is made.

As soon as the Hoboken plant is at full capacity, he'll be off. Tomorrow he'll tell Pierre he's leaving. He's mentioned this to him before—this desire to join the resistance fighters in France.

Turning onto West Forty-Sixth to avoid the crush around Grand Central, he heads toward Seventh Avenue and Lenthal's offices. Suddenly a door to his right flies open and a man stumbles out onto the sidewalk, colliding with Alain. The man staggers back, waving a bottle of whisky, and Alain's arm shoots out, steadying him. Behind the drunk, the barroom door slams shut.

The guy plants his feet wide apart, brushing off his sleeve while regarding Alain. His bright-red face is contorted; then he squints, holding the bottle high. "To hell with 'em all," he shouts. "You go listen, buddy; but I refuse!" And lifting the bottle to his mouth, he stalks off.

Alain turns to the door, peering through a barred glass window at eye level. The glass is thick with grime and it's difficult to make out what's going on, although he does see that a large group of men are crowded together on the far side of the room. Curious, he pushes the door open and enters. Despite the crowd, the room is strangely subdued, silent except for the sound of a staccato voice, the sound of a radio announcer speaking. The group of men are huddled before a bar, intent and listening.

A lone drinker, holding down a table near the door, looks up at Alain. He shoves his hat to the back of his head. "Listen. You ask me," he says, "it's about time."

"What's going on?"

The guy shrugs and turns his eyes back to the bottled beer in his hands.

Alain moves to the crowd, squeezing in at the back. Through spaces between shoulders he spots a large wooden radio resting on the bar. The voice inside comes and goes, fading under the sizzle of electric static. He taps a shoulder in front of him. "Say, what's this all about?"

With a glance the fellow snorts. "It's the damned Japs. They've hit us. It sounds bad; but hard to make out all the announcer's saying."

"Hit us! You mean they've attacked?"

"Wait a second." The man leans closer, cupping his ear with his hand. After a minute he relays to Alain, "They're saying we're to hold on for more news. It's John Charles Daly in the box. Says sit tight—

he's trying to make sense of what the reporters out there are saying."

"Out where?"

"Somewhere on the west coast, I think."

And then the static clears. A blunt, familiar voice bursts from the radio. "Ladies and gentlemen, this is CBS Radio News. We interrupt our broadcast of *The World Today* for a special news bulletin." Alain sucks in his breath, his pulse racing—and when Daly speaks again, his voice shakes with fury and emotion. Before he even finishes the announcement, Alain understands. On this day the world is changing.

"At 7:55 a.m. Hawaii time today, the Japanese attacked Pearl Harbor, Hawaii, by air."

The barroom erupts. Alain works his way toward the radio, still straining to hear. More static comes and then voices shout through space and time, blazing out over the radio waves. From thousands and thousands of miles away, he hears the terrible cries—"Look! Up there, look at that! They're back, they're circling, damn, they're a flock of vultures, why there's hundreds of planes up there! Would you look at that? Get down! Would you look at that!"

Alain curls his hands into fists as the voices are lost in chaos, a volley of rapid-fire artillery and screams, and then comes a deafening series of blasts one after the other, explosions which drown out John Charles Daly's voice altogether.

It is Sunday, December 7. America is at war.

On the next afternoon, Pierre Wertheimer sits before the radio in the offices of Lenthal in Manhattan, listening to the president of the United States addressing Congress. Alain stands before a window looking down on the intersection of West Thirty-

Seventh and Seventh Avenue in the garment district. Below, the wind whips racks of clothing as the push-boys race down the sidewalks and streets, dodging trucks and automobiles. A winter storm is on the way. A gust of wind rips a woman's hat from her head and she goes running after. Newspaper pages scuttle down the sidewalk before the wind.

President Roosevelt's voice on the radio is strong and measured. "Yesterday morning, December 7, the United States of America was suddenly and deliberately attacked by naval and air forces of the Empire of Japan." He pauses. "The United States was at peace with that nation ... the attack was deliberately planned many days or even weeks ago."

In fact, as of last Sunday, Alain knows, the Japanese ambassador and his American wife were still in Washington for ongoing negotiations on Japan's assets frozen in banks in the United States. Washington negotiating with an Axis power has always struck Alain as strange. But over the last summer, with the Japanese threatening Indo-China, Roosevelt took the step, freezing their accounts. Japan's diplomats have been here ever since.

Because of his business experience in Japan, at the president's request, Pierre has participated in some of the negotiations. The Japanese diplomats were always unfathomable, Pierre confided to Alain after a meeting just a few days ago.

The *New York Times* had the full story this morning. Japan's sneak attack claimed the lives of more than 2,400 American souls and wounded 1,200 more—most from the USS *Arizona*. The assault almost destroyed the Pacific Fleet at Pearl Harbor. The United States lost about two hundred planes. And this morning's report makes things even worse. Within the last twenty-four hours, the Japanese government has also launched surprise attacks against Malaya, Hong Kong, Guam, the Philippine Islands, Wake Island, and Midway Island.

When the broadcast is over, Alain takes a seat across the desk, facing Pierre. "This will hurt Germany in the fight against Russia," Pierre says. "They desperately need Japan's help on that front, but that hope's lost now. Japan's chosen the Pacific."

"Well, I'm signing up." Alain looks off. He will never forget this day. As Roosevelt said, this is a dark time which will live in infamy.

Pierre nods; puffs on his pipe. "Before you do anything though, I've a proposal for you to consider."

Alain lifts a brow. "I'm listening."

"I want you to talk to Bill Donovan. He's a lawyer in the city."

"Wild Bill Donovan—from the Great War?"

"Yes. General William Donovan. He fought with the Fighting Irish back then. The man has FDR's greatest respect. Everyone's really. Holds the Medal of Honor, Purple Heart. More honors than you can count."

"What's he planning?"

Pierre leans back, pulls the pipe from his mouth, and jabs it at Alain. "Donovan's setting up a new intelligence operation with the president's backing. He's coordinating with the Brits on covert work in Europe. He's looking for recruits, good people familiar with the occupied territories." A corner of his mouth quirks up as he regards Alain. "For France, in particular. He's recruiting former natives familiar with local customs and fluent in French. He'd like to meet you."

"That sounds interesting." Alain slides down in the chair, stretches his legs, and clasps his hands over his stomach. "How do I find him?"

"It's dangerous work."

He waves this off. "How do I find General Donovan."

"He's on East Sixty-Second. They call it the Room." Pierre reaches for a notepad, scribbling a name and address.

"Thanks." Alain takes the paper, folding it in half and sticking it into his pocket.

"By the way," Pierre says. "I heard from Henri Leval last week. Félix Amiot has been released in Paris, none the worse for his stay as a guest of the Gestapo."

Alain lifts his eyes to Pierre.

"At last we've prevailed against Coco's claim. They never located our trust agreement. Henri's got it in his safe, in the bank's Geneva office. Félix will control the company until we can take it back again."

"Coco will explode."

Pierre chuckles. "Keep your head down if you end up in Paris." His smile fades, and he turns, gazing through the window.

Despite Coco's outrageous behavior—attempting to Aryanize Société Mademoiselle—Pierre still holds a soft spot for the woman, Alain realizes. When they first met at Longchamp long ago, Pierre saw Coco as a naive young woman wearing that small round hat. That first impression seems to have stuck with him. Through all their battles in court, Pierre always forgives. She almost seems to amuse him. Alain just stops himself from shaking his head—Coco was never naive. She sees the world only from her own cut-glass perspective. She went into business with Pierre, despite his Jewish heritage, only because it served her purpose at the time, fed her ambition.

He's always wondered how Pierre could be so blind to Coco's open contempt for Jews, and others who don't meet her standards. Perhaps his confidence allows him not to care what a woman who designs dresses and creates perfumes thinks about the larger issues in the world. He admires her determination, her fight to survive, clawing her way to success.

Alain closes his eyes for a moment, remembering Paris as he'd left it—stunned, shamed, ravaged—and worse to come, he's certain. But the rot had set in years ago for ordinary Jews, the ones boxed into the Marais, the ones who are caricatured, vilified around society tables like Coco's for nothing more than heritage.

Curling his hands into fists, he opens his eyes, regarding Pierre. Pierre has ignored this dark side of his friend for many years now. She's only one woman, he'd probably say. But one plus one is two. Two plus two is four. Soon you have a crowd, like the mobs cheering Hitler in Berlin. And now? Now comes the hate—and the carnage—and it's out in the light for all to see.

Pierre heaves a sigh, leaning forward, pressing the buzzer on his desk. When Nina arrives, he instructs the secretary to call his lawyers, to obtain the transcripts of the hearing in Paris concerning Société Mademoiselle, and Coco Chanel. "I want to review them," he says.

Even now, Pierre is having second thoughts. Alain rubs the back of his neck, thinking of that visit to Henri Leval on his last day in Paris two years ago. And the millions Henri Leval received from Pierre, to be held in trust in Switzerland for Félix Amiot. A sinister thought slithers through his mind. Amiot must have used the money to obtain his release.

"Who'd Amiot bribe?"

Pierre hesitates. "I don't know for sure. Most likely, Göring is his man. If so, Kurt Blanke had no choice but to rule for us, with Göring on his back. Although, I'm certain Blanke benefited too."

"What makes you think Göring got the money?"

Pierre hesitates. He taps the pipe bowl against the desk—once, twice. When he looks up, his expression is grim. "Félix and Göring have a mutual interest now—aviation. Quite a coincidence, but it seems the Luftwaffe needs Félix Amiot's expertise."

Staring at Pierre, Alain's stomach turns. Göring—Adolf Hitler's right-hand man—one of the worst. When he'd signed the papers two years ago in Leval's office in Paris, he should have known. He should have thought this through. He'd known Coco would fight Pierre's plan to move production of No. 5 to the United States. He'd known she would go to any length to take revenge, including going back to court. The one thing he'd missed was the possibility that Coco would mercilessly attempt to use the Jewish laws against Pierre to win.

He should have realized this could happen, but back then in Paris, Alain had concentrated only on getting out of France.

"Did you know?"

"That some of the money would end up in German hands?"

He nods.

Puffing on the pipe, Pierre leans back in the chair. "It never occurred to me that Coco would be the one to force it. The money was to pay Félix for taking on the risk, protecting the business over there." He fixes his eyes on the desk. "It was his to use as necessary, Alain."

From the other side of the office door a telephone rings. Pierre's secretary answers. The stenographer's typewriter clacks away, and then the clatter stops and the two women laugh. Alain takes his jacket from the chair and turns to the door.

It is time to make amends with his conscience. He will meet with Bill Donovan, but regardless of the outcome, he's off to fight with the French Resistance. Already he's waited too long.

Chapter Forty

Paris
Winter 1941

On the same day in Paris, Monday, December 8, Coco's mind reels as she puts down the telephone. Louis de Vaufreland has called. As in a trance, she walks to the chair near the window and sinks into the cushions. Kurt Blanke has ruled for Félix Amiot in her case against Pierre, ending all hope. Kurt Blanke has ruled that the company shares were legally transferred to Félix Amiot prior to Germany's occupation of France, and since Amiot is Aryan the Jewish laws do not apply. Amiot is the true owner of Société Mademoiselle. And No. 5.

So it is ordered.

She did not believe Louis at first—made him repeat the entire story over again, and yet nothing changed. How is this possible? How is it possible she's lost the case! Louis admits the evidence was clear the share transfers were a sham, that Amiot's claim to ownership of Société Mademoiselle is false. Yet, still, she has lost.

Grim and terrible thoughts claw through her mind. Amiot

and Pierre are hand in hand, she is certain. In America, Pierre will continue as before. He has the formula for No. 5 and the plant in Hoboken, New Jersey. Pierre will go on producing No. 5, free to use her name any way he pleases while cutting her out of revenues. Her name will be on bottles of perfumes and signs in corner pharmacies. He'll economize with ingredients she has not approved. He's finally rid of her demands and lawsuits.

The hope she's nurtured for justice in the past few years has just been crushed.

She grips the arms of the chair, forcing back a scream.

It's bad enough to lose her name, but without perfume revenues, the balance in her Paris account is dangerously low. Her accountant insists the lack of revenues flowing into her account is due to the occupation—the same reason he gives for her frozen funds in Geneva. But he does not know Pierre. Besides, the occupation could last forever. And Pierre could find a way to get her share of No. 5 sales to Paris if he wished.

Will she be forced to move from the Hôtel Ritz? Tears escape; angrily she brushes them away. She will not accept defeat.

The thought of Pierre winning this final battle is too much to bear. And where is Spatz—still in Berlin? Rising, Coco goes into the bedroom, every step heavy as she drags her feet. She will have her medicine early tonight. She will go to sleep, because she does not really want to think.

The telephone wakes her. Coco, startled from sleep, sits up. Morning light shimmers through the windows, but the apartment is quiet. Alyce is not in the rooms, she realizes. Clearing her throat, she reaches for the phone. Her voice is groggy as she answers.

"Coco!" Colette's voice is shrill over the wire. "They have taken him, my Maurice!" She weeps into the telephone—her voice is thick, difficult to understand.

Coco sits up straighter, gripping the telephone receiver. "Who has taken him, Colette? Speak up, please. I cannot hear you."

"The Gestapo took him." Between gasps she repeats, "The Gestapo!" The bells of La Madeleine are tolling now—Coco hears them from her rooms, and from the other end of the telephone near the Palais-Royal. "Last night," Colette sobs. "They came at midnight just as we've always feared. They said—oh, Coco—they said Maurice is a hostage."

Coco's heart skips a beat. Why take Maurice? Such a kind and gentle man; so brilliant, yet he is fragile.

All this time, Colette's fear was real.

"One moment," Coco says, steadying her voice. "Stay calm and talk to me. Did they say where they were taking him? Colette, Colette! Stop weeping or I cannot help."

A series of sniffles come through the line. "I am sorry for this, Coco, but I don't know where he's gone! I don't know!" Coco waits through a long, shuddering sigh, leaning a shoulder against the wall and winding the telephone wire around her finger.

"It's something about the Resistance, they said. The Resistance or some others have cut a telephone line, they said. Reprisals, they said. But I tell you, Coco, I cannot think right now. I begged to go with him and they pushed me away. They dragged my poor Maurice between them down the stairs." Her sobbing voice runs up the scale.

The entrance door opens and closes, and seconds later Alyce appears in the bedroom holding a linen towel. Coco gestures to the maid to keep quiet as Colette goes on. "I waited as long as I could before calling Susanne Abetz at the ambassador's residence, but they say she's not available, and so I thought … perhaps if you telephone?"

"But of course, of course, *chérie*! There is some mistake here,

Colette. The idea of Maurice with the Resistance is laughable! Hang up the telephone and I will call Susanne."

Returning the receiver to the cradle, she looks up, frowning. It's too early in the morning for telephone calls to the ambassador's residence, but she will do this for Colette. She snaps at Alyce, "Fetch a cup of tea from downstairs right away. With lemon. And it must be hot."

"Yes, mademoiselle." Alyce drops the towel over the back of a chair and hurries toward the door.

With a long breath, Coco picks up the telephone. She speaks with the hotel operator. She speaks with the municipal operator. She speaks with the first butler in the Abetz residence. She speaks with madame's assistant. And then, at last she is asked to wait, Madame Abetz will take the call shortly.

Coco lights a cigarette. As she looks out over the Place Vendôme the smoke soothes. Susanne is the ambassador's wife, and she will know what to do. Maurice is a French citizen after all. He has rights.

By the time Susanne greets her on the line, Coco is certain Maurice's abduction is some terrible mistake. "Coco here, Susanne. Yes, hello, hello. Our friend Colette has called to say … Yes, our Colette, our great novelist. You remember; we had lunch together not long ago." Gazing at the ceiling, she listens.

"Yes, but Susanne, she is quite upset. Maurice, her husband, has just been arrested … Yes, of course I am certain; Gestapo, she thinks." After a pause, "This must be a mistake. I cannot imagine why they'd want to take Maurice."

In the hum of silence, Coco thinks perhaps the call has been disconnected. She feels the first flutter of fear. When Susanne speaks, her voice is hesitant. "Every Jew in Paris is registered, Coco. If Monsieur Goudeket has been taken, it is because he is a Jew. If the Resistance has struck or hostages are needed for some other reason, they'll have selected the most prominent ones in the city."

Is it possible to register every Jew in Paris? She'd not really believed Colette.

"There must be something you can do, Susanne."

"I don't think …"

"Please. Maurice is harmless."

By the end of the call, Susanne has promised to speak with her husband, the ambassador. After, she will call Colette direct, she says.

As Coco places the telephone receiver into the holder, Alyce bursts through the door carrying the tea tray. Coco presses her hand over her forehead as the maid places the tray over her lap. Spatz is still in Berlin. If only he were here, he would certainly know what else to do.

A half an hour later Coco rises from the bed, sending Alyce on an errand. She must have privacy, time to compose herself after those phone calls. Wandering into the sitting room, Coco flips through the mail she'd left unopened and ignored on the telephone table days ago. She'd forgotten. She sifts the envelopes, tossing them aside one after the other.

With a sigh, Coco gazes at the growing stack of bills. Polite notices from creditors. Each notice is a threat. And here, she holds a card between two fingers—an invitation from someone she barely knows. She tosses it aside. A statement from her banker goes unopened; it's only more bad news, she's certain. Besides, she cannot think clearly. Her head hurts, thanks to Colette. Perhaps she took too much of the medicine last night.

One last envelope on the table shows no return address. She picks it up to toss it aside, too, but something stops her. Her name on the front is scrawled in a heavy, unfamiliar, spidery hand; the sharp letters cutting deep into the paper. Strange. A frisson runs through her as she studies the bizarre handwriting.

How foolish she is this evening with her schoolgirl's superstitions.

Coco quickly slits the envelope open. Two sheets are folded inside. As she pulls the pages out, one slips to the floor. Ignoring it, she unfolds the other. And her eyes grow wide. She drops the sheet faceup on the table, stepping back, her eyes riveted on the drawing, the caricature.

Stunned, she picks it up again, holding it out at arm's length first, then moving it close, afraid to take it in as a whole. There's no escaping the fact. This is a crude sketch of her. The eyes looking out are hers, and the thin arched brows, the wide distinctive mouth. The short dark curls are hers, and there, the spiny ligaments etched in her thin arms—she hates her arms—and even the same striated muscles in her thighs and calves are there.

Now her eyes freeze on the sketch as she takes in the entire drawing at once and the horror registers. She is looking at a caricature of herself splayed naked to the world.

And crucified.

Her eyes drop to the words beneath the drawing: *For France.*

Crumpling the sheet, she flings it to the floor, and then quickly stoops to retrieve it, along with the second page, still folded. No one else should see this picture. Not Alyce. Not Spatz. She reaches out, touching the wall for balance as she makes her way to her chair near the window. Her chest feels tight and she struggles for breath, as if someone has bound her with a tight leather strap. She sinks into the cushion seat, leans back, and closes her eyes. Crucified! Who would send such a thing?

She takes a deep breath, then, with trembling hands unfolds the second page.

Her heart races as the words leap at her:

COLLABO-WHORE.

TRAITOR.

WE WILL COME FOR YOU.

Part Four

Chapter Forty-One

Paris
Winter 1942

The unexpected hustle and bustle in the hotel today surprises Coco. She's spent most days in her rooms since receiving the news that her claim against Pierre was denied. And then, there were those threatening notes.

At least the grim holidays are over. With America joining the war and Spatz still in Berlin and German men dying in Russia, music and laughter seemed to have been officially banned from the Hôtel Ritz. Arletty says the high command have lost their sparkle. Officers are solemn, moody. No more bothering with polish, like holding doors for the ladies. No longer will a flirty little laugh slip you past the guards when they're asking to see your papers and you've forgotten them in your room.

Today, Coco sits in a corner of the grand entrance hall, near the stairs, with Arletty and Laura Mae St. James. While they engage in a game of bezique, Coco smokes, looking off at the comings and goings of officers. The ones departing are weighed down with briefcases and baggage. Where are they all going?

Watching the green-and-white cards fly across the table, she takes note of the ladies' tricks for future reference. Arletty is particularly sly; the woman is an actress and almost impossible to catch at cheating.

At her side, Arletty nudges Coco. She flips up her top card, gloating, "La-di-da! Ten points for the seven."

Laura Mae pouts.

Coco gazes at the military stream pulsing down the grand entrance hall toward the Place Vendôme. "I wonder what's going on." Neither Arletty nor Laura Mae look up from the game. She walks to the concierge desk where Géraud stands at attention. She stops at the desk and lifts her brows.

He ducks his head in her direction. "They've been called to Berlin," he says.

The elevator door slides open just then, and Reich Marshal Göring strolls out, followed by Horst Eckert. She watches as they head for the hotel entrance door, these men who think they will take No. 5 from her.

"Has something gone wrong?"

Géraud lowers his voice. "So I hear. Russia. And you are looking at the reason right this moment."

"General Göring?"

"Indeed, the Reich marshal. Word in staff quarter is his Luftwaffe has failed again, this time on the Eastern front. But just watch, he won't bear the blame; the Führer will find scapegoats. They say Herr Goebbels issued an order last night that for every soldier dying on Russian soil this winter, one hundred of those responsible for sending them off without winter wear will be executed in Berlin, starting from the top."

Coco smiles slyly at Géraud, nods, and turns to stroll back to the card game. When Arletty and Laura Mae pounce, she tells them the news in strict confidence. Arletty nods. "My Hans was not called this time. But he says the entire command in Berlin is seething."

Laura Mae looks up. "Is General Göring leaving too?"

Coco nods. "Along with more treasure."

"Good." Laura Mae studies her cards, then pulls out two and tosses them onto the table. She's avoided the general since he had the armoire she so loved removed from the Imperial Suite.

She's not heard another word from Colette about Maurice. It is time to visit, to comfort her. Evan has the night off, but Géraud arranges for a driver to take her to the Palais-Royal near the Louvre, where Colette lives. The driver pulls up to the entrance on rue Saint-Honoré. "Wait for me here," Coco instructs. "I won't be long."

The night is cold. Shivering, she turns up her fur collar, walking through the darkened arcade, past the bare, abandoned gardens, past the antique shop, the bookseller's shop, the baker, the bistro—all closed—counting the arches overhead until she reaches the door to the stairs leading to Colette's apartment. She knocks on the door, waiting, then knocks again.

When the door opens, Colette's maid, Pauline, peers out. "Ah, you frightened us, mademoiselle. We thought perhaps the Boche had returned."

"It is only me," Coco says, brushing past. "Have you heard anything from Maurice?" With a glance toward the back of the apartment, "How is she?"

Pauline shakes her head, and Coco follows her into a small room with a single window facing the Louvre. The beamed ceiling here is low. Colette sits at a table beside the window, writing. Except for an amber circle of light from a lantern near Colette, the room is dark. In the distance, from the river Seine a foghorn sounds.

"I thought I recognized your voice," Colette says, setting the pen into a holder. Leaning back in the chair, with a longing glance at the writing tablet on the desk, she hugs herself. "You've pulled me back into the world." Her tone accuses Coco.

Coco tosses her purse onto a table and, turning to Colette, throws up her hands. "I thought I'd find you frantic." Colette frowns. Without removing her coat, Coco sits in the only chair in the room, a large cushioned chair covered in worn blue fabric. The chair smells of Maurice. "How can you write with Maurice gone missing?"

"I am never completely frantic, however I can accommodate, if you wish." Colette smooths her hand over her hair. "Just now I was caught up in a new story with my little Gigi. It's scheduled for publication in two months."

Coco lights a cigarette. She understands. Once, she was like Colette, absorbed in her work, in her art, in creating something new while her worries faded—at least for the time. But that was before this war. She realizes how bereft of life and drained she feels without her own work, invisible—like the missing flowers in the Tuileries.

Colette rests an elbow on the little table and her chin in her hand. "And Maurice?" Coco taps cigarette ash into a small glass bowl beside Colette. "Have you heard anything yet?"

"Susanne finally telephoned. The ambassador made some calls." A visible shudder runs through Colette. "Maurice is held in a prison camp in the Compiègne." After a pause, she adds, watching Coco, "At Royallieu."

Coco's cigarette hovers midair as visions of Étienne's château rise. Seconds pass while she takes in Colette's words. She sees herself racing over the fields on Flost. She thinks of the lovely forest of Compiègne, the deer and flowers and streams. The very thought of Maurice a prisoner there stains the memories. Colette must be wrong.

"This is not possible," she says at last, releasing a stream of smoke. "Étienne would never allow Royallieu to be used as a prison."

"The prisoners are in barracks, in the fields," she says. Colette's tone is arch. "Do not be concerned, Coco. I am certain the chalet is reserved for officers." She swipes a tear from her cheek. "Susanne said it's the fault of the Resistance. For each German the Resistance kills, ten Jewish hostages will be shot."

A pain rips through Coco. "But why Maurice?" she cries. Good, sweet Maurice.

"Because he is a Jew." Colette's voice is sharp. "Jews disappear every day in Paris." Colette holds her eyes. "Have you really never noticed?"

Coco stiffens. She does not care a sou if Maurice's blood is Jewish.

Colette gives her a look of pity. Her voice is resigned. Her smile, weak. "Poor Coco." She looks to the door. "I will call Pauline and we will have some cake and cognac. Let me read for you a bit from my little tale of Gigi. You will feel better. The real world is not so pleasant, *n'est pas?*"

Chapter Forty-Two

Paris
Winter 1942

She is almost asleep when a siren shrieks. Coco starts, sits up, and grabs the quilt, pulling it up around her shoulders. By the time Alyce rushes in from her small sleeping room, Coco is standing in the middle of the bedroom in her nightgown.

"It's a raid." The shrill siren whirls around them, almost deafening. Alyce runs to the armoire, pulls out a dress—one Coco does not favor—and turns to her. "We must go down into the cellars at once, mademoiselle."

The noise seems to be diminishing, the wailing not as loud as at first. "Not that one," Coco snaps, pushing past Alyce to the armoire. If she's going down to the cellars in the middle of the night, she will be comfortable. Grabbing a warm robe and some slippers, she orders Alyce to do the same. At the dressing table, she runs a brush through her hair, then finger flicks the curls framing her face.

Just then the siren winds up again, and with a cry Alyce runs to the windows, throwing open the curtains and peering up at the sky. "Airplanes, mademoiselle! Hundreds!"

"Close the curtains at once! And stop that noise. Really, Alyce, you are worse than the siren." Alyce obeys, stepping back. The sirens are driving Coco crazy.

Suddenly the building rumbles, shaking, and Alyce freezes. With a sigh, Coco digs another robe and a pair of fur slippers from the armoire, handing them to her maid. "Put those on, now." Between the noise overhead and the sirens, she is forced to shout. Now she stands, waiting, hands on her hips watching Alyce throwing on the robe over her nightgown, slipping feet into the slippers.

Alyce looks up at her, beaming. "Did you see them, mademoiselle? They call them fighter planes."

"Hush." Coco scoops two pillows from the bed, handing them to Alyce. Then, turning, she strolls through the sitting room toward the hallway door. Alyce follows with the pillows. In the hallway, Alyce turns right toward the stairs at the end of the hall, and Coco turns left, toward the elevator.

"This way, mademoiselle!" Alyce cries. "The stairs are this way, this way!" Coco looks straight ahead, pressing the call button for the elevator. Please, mademoiselle." A glance toward Alyce reveals her tears. "I am certain Madame Giror is already in the cellar."

"Who is Madame Giror?" Coco stabs the button this time.

"She is the elevator operator."

"Ah." Turning about, Coco strolls toward the stairs where Alyce waits, shifting from one foot to the other. As Coco takes the stairs at a measured pace, Alyce runs ahead, halting at each landing, looking back with pleading eyes.

Géraud is waiting at the foot of the stairs when they arrive on the ground floor. Every light in the hotel is turned off. He hands over two gas masks and Alyce places them atop the pillows. "This way," the concierge says, tugging on Coco's arm. "It is the RAF.

We are not safe up here. You are the last resident to arrive; you must please hurry."

The concierge stops at the top of the stairs leading to the hotel cellars, letting Coco and Alyce descend, and he follows. Halfway down the steps, Coco grabs the railing when a nearby explosion rocks the building.

The wine cellar is dark and cool. Her eyes are not yet adjusted to the darkness, but Géraud takes her arm, leading her through tall racks of stored wine bottles, past several rooms crowded with hotel guests. They are in the small tasting room near the back of the cellars, and she hears Arletty's voice: "This way, Coco. Come, turn to your left, this way. Turn left."

At least in the cellar the siren noise is slightly muffled. Coco turns a corner and suddenly a candle glows before her. Géraud steers them toward the light, where Arletty sits on a bench near an old plank table, waiting. "You must snuff the candle, please," he says when they arrive. "The hotel is under blackout orders, mademoiselle."

Arletty tosses her head. "This is the only light left in Paris; we must guard it. Besides, there are no windows here, and I can see nothing without it."

"That is the point."

She waves him off. Alyce takes a seat beside Coco. "You certainly took your time."

"What a nuisance," Coco murmurs, looking about.

"Géraud has provided sleeping bags, if necessary. They are made of Hermès silk, he says."

Coco frowns, looking at the hard, tiled floor. Arletty lets out a laugh. "He's also brought fur rugs."

Coco sighs and leans back against the table. "Well it could be worse. Colette's husband is trapped in a prison camp. The Gestapo took him in December."

"Colette, your friend the writer?"

"Yes. Madame Goudeket. Her husband Maurice is a Jew. He was taken as a hostage, or some such thing."

Arletty sighs. "I wish I had a cigarette. Do you have one?"

Coco looks down at her robe. "Of course not. But we must remember to bring provisions for the next raid."

Arletty huffs and props her elbow on the table, chin in hand. "Actually," she says, leaning forward, "I think I remember hearing that Maurice Goudeket was released from that camp a few days ago. Even though, so far as anyone knows, he's still a Jew." With a look at Coco she adds, "Haven't you heard?"

Coco freezes her expression, feeling Arletty watching her. Maurice, free? This cannot be possible. She must be wrong. Colette would have called if Maurice was released. Surely she'd have called.

A day passes and still Colette has not telephoned with news of Maurice's release. How is this possible after all Coco's done for Maurice and Colette—begging favors from Susanne for her friends to help them. For the tenth time she mulls this question over. And for the tenth time she tells herself that Arletty's gossip was wrong. She must have been thinking of someone else.

But the next morning she's woken abruptly by Alyce. "Mademoiselle!" Coco opens her eyes and rolls over, groaning. "Mademoiselle, are you awake?"

She shades her eyes with one hand. "I am now. What do you want?" The medicine makes her groggy, she knows, but she can no longer sleep without it. Propping up on one elbow, she glares at Alyce standing in the doorway.

"You have a telephone call. Madame Goudeket is asking for you. She says to wake you. She says it's urgent."

Coco glares at Alyce. "All right." The words come out a growl. She motions to the phone on the table by the bed. "Go ahead. Hand it to me."

Alyce scrambles while Coco slides up to a sitting position, plumping the pillow behind her. "What time is it?" Coco drawls into the receiver as she slumps back, watching Alyce hurry away. A click tells her Alyce has hung up the sitting room extension.

"Maurice is here, Coco! He is back and safe." Colette's voice sings through the wires.

"Really! When did he arrive?"

"Ah. Well, a few days ago."

Coco grips the phone. Arletty was right. But she must forget this slight for Maurice's sake, even though she longs to cut Colette dead. Though she lets a few seconds go by before speaking. "This is wonderful news, Colette! He was released?"

"Yes, thanks to Susanne and Ambassador Abetz, and … you, Coco. But he's not well. He's very thin, and has a fever, and …"

"He's ill!" But of course, this explains everything. Colette was distracted, worried about her husband. Coco falls back onto the pillows as relief flows through her. "Listen, Colette. I will send a doctor at once."

"No. Please." Colette's voice hits a high note on the last word. "Please. It's nothing, really. Why he'll be well in no time. Imagine this, Coco. He arrived in the back of an open trailer covered in mud." She's almost breathless as she speaks. "But now he's home and safe."

Coco smiles. "Otto Abetz has a long reach. This is wonderful news. All right, I'll wait until tomorrow to visit, Colette. I must see Maurice then, if only to welcome him back."

But instead of a response, there is unexpected silence on the other end of the telephone.

Alyce walks in with the breakfast tray, setting it across Coco's lap. The usual breakfast of hot tea and lemon and buttered toast. Coco squeezes a slice of lemon into the tea. "Are you there, Colette?"

"Yes, yes, I'm here." But Colette's tone is strange. Coco waits while Alyce moves around the bedroom, straightening the little quilt at the foot of the bed, picking up a pair of shoes. And then, Colette says, "But you must not come this week, Coco. Maurice is not well."

Coco clucks her tongue. "Nonsense. I will cheer him up."

"No." Colette's tone turns hard, sharp, cutting through the line, and through Coco's sleepy fog. She sets the teacup down on the tray, intent now, listening. "Maurice is not ready for visitors yet. You must understand he's just come from hell."

There's something off in her voice, like too much musk in a sweet perfume. Colette continues, talking in that strange low way, speaking carefully. "Maurice says that we must take care. We must not take any risks."

"Risks? What does that have to do with me?" She waves Alyce from the room. "Certainly Maurice trusts me."

She hears the sigh from the other end of the telephone. "Please understand, Coco. Maurice trusts you, of course. As do I. But do not come. You live among the German high command in your hotel. We cannot see you now. The Americans will come soon, and then we'll resume our friendship. But it's not safe now; not until Paris is free."

As Coco sets the receiver down into its holder, in her mind she sees the threatening note: COLLABO. She is on the Free French blacklist and the Resistance list, she's heard. But Colette and Maurice are not rabble. They are not the Free French, nor are they Resistance. And yet Colette has asked Coco to stay away from them now, even after all the help she's given them. Do Colette and Maurice also see her as a collaborator—as a "collabo"?

And if so, how many others view her in that light? She thinks back, struggling to recall the last invitation she's received from an old friend. But she cannot. It's been that long.

A hot flush burns her face. How much must she endure? She pounds her fists on the mattress at the very thought of Colette's ingratitude. Would Colette even try to help her if things were the other way around?

She shivers. Even Colette and Maurice see her as the enemy now. Setting aside the tray, she pulls the sheet and blanket up over her shoulders. If the Americans and British free Paris, the Free French—with their blacklist and hunger for revenge—will also come. They'll demand justice for those who were warm during the winters, those who lived as the rich have always lived in Paris, while everyone else suffered. Already bills nailed on posts all over town boast the Resistance will bring down every single collaborator. Police tear the papers down, but they reappear the next day.

Here at the Ritz she has lived with the German high command for over two years, from the beginning of the war. No excuse will be acceptable to the Resistance, she realizes. Nor to the Free French. To them, she is a collaborator, or worse.

Chapter Forty-Three

Paris
Spring–Fall 1942

Arletty sits down and leans close to Coco. They sit at their usual table near the marble staircase in the grand entrance hall, as they do every afternoon these days. Except for daily trips to the Maison across the street, Coco stays close to the hotel since those threatening letters came. Time passes slowly, but no one knows who or what waits outside now that she's branded a collabo. She lifts her cocktail, a sidecar for this time of day, and raises an eyebrow at Arletty.

"Listen." Arletty speaks sotto voce. "You will never believe what I heard this morning." Without waiting for an answer, she goes on. "Laura Mae is under arrest. They came for her yesterday."

"What?" Coco sits up straight.

"Yes." Arletty's brows shoot up. "It's because she is American. All Americans in Paris were rounded up yesterday, Géraud says. The men are held in the barracks at Royallieu, in Compiègne. But the women …" Then, with a little shrug, she adds, "Well, she should have left long ago."

Coco sips her drink. Then, "Surely Géraud can do something? He is a concierge. He has many friends."

Arletty straightens. "Well, he's found her, but, so far, he says he is unable to help. He visited her in prison this morning, against the rules though. You will never guess where the American women are held!"

"Where?" Coco asks, her interest piqued.

Arletty lets out a strange little laugh. "They're all in the zoo— the Jardin d'Acclimatation, in the Bois de Boulogne."

Coco scoffs. "Impossible!"

"It's not funny, I know. I tell you this is true. At the Prefecture they told Géraud there was no place else to house so many women." Still, Arletty's eyes dance. "They emptied the monkey house at the zoo and the ladies moved in."

"That cannot be!"

She crosses her heart and holds up her hand. "The police captain came right out with it, Géraud says. No visitors were allowed."

"So what did he do?"

"He says as Laura Mae is a guest at this hotel, he had an obligation to find her." She spreads her hands. "He went to the ticket office at the zoo. For five francs he purchased a ticket. Then he says he merely walked around to the front of the monkey house where there's a big glass window—do you remember that? Yes? Well, that's where he spotted them. The crowd of American women inside the monkey house behind the glass, and rows and rows of sleeping cots. He finally caught Laura Mae's attention. She was sitting with Sylvia Beach. Do you know her? The bookseller on rue de l'Odéon?"

"Yes! Well, I'm speechless." Coco's eyes are wide. "Was he able to talk to Laura Mae? How is she? Really, Arletty! Must I pull out every word?"

Arletty sweeps her long hair back over her shoulder and lets it fall. "They spoke through the grills in the animals' play yard, until a policeman came around. Géraud says Laura Mae was calm, although she said the place is freezing."

"There's probably little heat in those cages." Coco makes a face.

"She asked for blankets, and also food, and he'll see she gets them. The Hôtel Ritz won't let down a resident, even if our other German guests refuse to help."

"Perhaps your Hans can do something?"

She shakes her head. "He says there is not one thing he can do. He says they're lucky not to have been sent to Germany as hostages."

Spatz returns from Berlin with dark news. Hitler intends to extend the occupation to Southern France. The Wehrmacht will move into the unoccupied zone of France immediately. The demarcation line between the occupied north and the Vichy south will be erased.

Coco closes her eyes, seeing the sun shining over La Pausa, the glittering water below. She sees the flower fields in full bloom, can almost inhale the fragrance. All that will disappear, trampled under German tanks and boots. The flowers will die of neglect. And what will happen to La Pausa?

And yet, Coco wavers. She turns to Spatz, seeming nonchalant. "Why change plans now?"

"Because," Spatz says, "it's clear the Americans are coming."

Coco thinks of the threatening notes she received, but says nothing. She's never shown them to Spatz. Not that she wouldn't trust him. But she cannot tell him that she's frightened, that she's been branded a collaborator and now fears an American victory. It is treason to even mention the possibility of a German defeat. But if the Americans free Paris, what will happen to her after?

They stand together before her windows, looking out over the Place Vendôme. The plaza is filled once again with armored cars and strutting officers and rows of gray-green Wehrmacht soldiers standing at attention in rigid lines of eight. Heavy armored tanks churn past the hotel. Behind the Ritz on rue Cambon, they shake the very walls and foundations of the building.

Today the sun hides, like the rest of Paris, under a veil of gloom. The low clouds are flat, dark, and ominous. Coco shivers. She is warm inside, but she can almost feel the icy wind blowing out over the plaza. On the other side of the street a brass band plays German songs, and despite the cold, three young girls wearing short, springtime dirndls struggle to smile as they sing along.

Beside her, Spatz is silent. At least Göring has disappeared. He has fallen out of favor with the Führer and is bunkered in his château outside Berlin, Spatz has said. The Luftwaffe failed in the Battle of Britain. Their blitz bombings failed in London. In the siege of Leningrad the Reich Marshal's air force has failed yet again, at least so far. With Wehrmacht soldiers caught at the frozen front, Göring is lucky to be alive, Spatz says.

Officers in the Ritz are surly when she passes them these days. The hotel staff wear smiles on their faces that say they believe any day the Americans are coming. The RAF strafes the suburbs of Paris most nights, driving Coco and Alyce into the cellars.

Spatz is gone most of the time, back and forth to Berlin, he says. The days are long. The city is on edge. Coco's world shrinks to her rooms, and the apartment in the Maison across the street, where she lounges, longing for the old days, the days before the war. André has not yet written from the sanatorium in Zurich, and she's heard nothing from his doctors.

She aches to work—to use her hands, to cut cloth, to design, to create new perfumes. She must have something to occupy her mind, to sweep away thoughts of this war. She will not allow herself to stagnate, nor to fall victim to fear. She will rebuild the House of Chanel to its former glory as soon as this war ends. Her life will have purpose again.

Pacing the length of the sitting room one afternoon, Coco spots two large military vehicles racing toward the hotel. She watches the trucks swerve, skidding to a stop before the hotel entrance. Several officers emerge, followed by fifteen or twenty soldiers in uniform. They storm toward the hotel entrance in their nailed boots, flying past the sandbag barriers and duty guards without so much as a salute.

Coco rises, heading for the doorway, curious. The elevator is filled with officers when Madame Giror pulls the doors open. The men shove aside, making room as Coco enters. As she exits the elevator, the soldiers she'd seen emerging from the trucks rush in, until Madame Giror is forced to shout that there is no more room, that the rest must wait, sliding the grill closed with a crash.

Coco strolls to the concierge desk where Géraud stands, his hands clasped before him on the desk. Uniformed officers cluster together speaking in low tones, their expressions grim. An electric current seems to grid the large room, connecting them.

"What is this commotion, Géraud?"

Géraud looks at her, his chin dipped, his eyes half closed. His voice is a whisper. "We are blessed with good news today, mademoiselle."

"Oh, yes?"

"Yes." He bends toward her. "BBC reports the Allies, the Americans, are pushing back General Rommel's forces in Africa." He holds up one hand before she can speak. "Do not smile, mademoiselle; do not smile right now."

The thought had not crossed her mind, but she says nothing as he goes on. "Our friends have their hands full." He gives her a sly look from the corner of his eye. "Do you admire how I have mastered the language of war?"

Coco sweeps her eyes over the nearby officers. "I've never seen them all so tense."

"Yes." He ducks his head and lifts a fountain pen from the holder, pretending to write on a notepad. "And do you know why?"

"No, but I am certain you will tell me."

"Yes, mademoiselle." He continues scribbling and lowers his voice. With his head down, a small smile flicks across his face. "It is because they are afraid. This time, the Americans are truly on the way."

She looks at the large hotel windows and glass doors, so vulnerable without the guards. She imagines the hotel without these officers, filled perhaps with officers of other armies— American, British. She thinks of the upstart general over the English Channel who no one knew before this war, Charles de Gaulle, and the men who call themselves the Free French—she calls them the Fifi. And the words of the anonymous note—*we will come for you*—train through her mind.

Chapter Forty-Four

Paris
Winter 1942–Spring 1943

Like the streets of Paris, the Ritz is generally a hotel without men, but for Géraud and the staff. In the dining room are only women alone, like Coco—the women left behind. Arletty's Colonel Soehring is somewhere in the south of France, so this evening, Coco beckons her over as she enters the dining room.

They are both prisoners of the hotel, they agree. Nightlife has ended. The streets are not safe to walk. It's no longer even safe to visit a café on a sunny afternoon. Throughout lunch they remain silent, each sunk into her own thoughts.

Coco taps her lips with her napkin as she finishes her soup. It seems she has no appetite for food these days. She looks over at Arletty. "Have you any news of Laura Mae?"

"She's still a prisoner, but at least she's no longer in the zoo."

"Where's she held?" Coco waits, hoping the answer is not once again Royallieu.

"The women were moved to a cluster of hotels, somewhere

around Bordeaux, I believe." She smiles, pushing her half-empty plate aside. "I imagine she's more comfortable now, than in the monkey house."

Coco remains at the table as Arletty takes her leave. Lifting a cup, she sips the last of the tea and sets it down. As she rises from her chair, she turns at the sound of shouting from the Place Vendôme. She leans forward, peering through the window, watching a small group of disheveled young men running toward the barricades and guards outside the hotel entrance.

She hurries to the grand entrance hall and the concierge desk, but the expression on Géraud's face freezes her. Following his eyes, she turns, looking through the front entrance door where the boys outside are fighting with the guards—she counts them, there are three—and a guard jams the butt of a rifle against one's head, knocking the fellow to the ground, so now there are only two and they're running off, heading across the open plaza. The fools, the little fools! And then her heart pounds as two of the guards take a knee and raise their rifles, sighting the running boys. Without thinking Coco moves toward the door, her arms outstretched, reaching. Two hands grab her from behind, stopping her. She turns, meeting the eyes of a young Wehrmacht officer. He shakes his head. "They were attempting to enter," he says.

She nods, and he releases her.

Coco stands very still beside the soldier, watching. The hurt boy struggles to crawl, but a few hard kicks from the guard fell him right away. Her eyes dart to the two kneeling soldiers and as she covers her ears with both hands and shuts her eyes, the rat-tat-tats burst forth from the long guns.

"*Mon Dieu!*" Géraud blurts.

Coco turns to see the concierge picking up the telephone on the desk, his voice urgent. Out on the plaza the two youths tear across the broad, open space. "Monsieur, come quick. Yes, yes, I know the guards are on duty, but ..."

Gunfire drowns out the rest of his words, the guards' rifles swinging from side to side, spraying the running boys—sons, brothers, lovers—lifting them off the ground, backs arching, arms flailing, both seeming suspended in the air for an instant before they drop, dead weights to the ground.

Slowly Coco looks to Géraud. The concierge's face is ashen, his eyes fixed on the scene as he replaces the telephone in the holder.

She blinks back tears. Why should she care? She cannot afford to care. The boys were probably members of the Resistance. If they had lived, perhaps one day they'd have come for her. Coco turns to the elevator, where Arletty waits. As she presses the call button, Arletty's eyes meet hers, mirroring the budding fear. Ah, so Arletty, too, has received the threats.

A sudden wave of sheer terror hits Coco as the elevator rises—she is vulnerable even here in the Hôtel Ritz with guards posted. What will happen to her if Paris is liberated and the guards desert their posts outside? A thought strikes. She presses her lips together and lifts her chin. It is past time to act. She will take control of her own fate.

As Coco walks down the third-floor hallway, a plan begins to form. She turns it over in her mind. She will not allow anyone to see her fear of the Resistance and the Free French. She is Chanel. And this plan might just work. If nothing else, it will buy time in the event the Allies do free Paris, precious time that she can use to reach her old British friends for help—perhaps Churchill or Westminster, even Sam Hoare.

In her rooms, with new resolve she picks up the telephone and orders Géraud to locate Evan. The next call is to Director Prudone at the Maison—he is to travel to the factory in Neuilly immediately. He is to requisition—or, if he must, he will pay for—every bottle of No. 5 left in stock.

That afternoon, with Géraud's assistance, Evan is given a hotel supply truck to drive Director Prudone to Neuilly.

Coco waits in her apartment at the Maison for the truck full of No. 5 to arrive. Colette believes that she is weak, that she does not understand, because she does not want to know. That she does not see, because she does not want to see. Colette is wrong to believe that she is weak.

She merely avoids looking at those things over which she has no control. Situations which she is helpless to change.

Part Five

Chapter Forty-Five

Paris
Spring-Summer 1944

One warm afternoon Coco sits gazing through the window at the deserted Place Vendôme. Four years ago, the plaza was filled with people fleeing from northern France as the Germans approached—gentry, workers, families with children, the elderly, rich, poor, farmers, aristocrats.

And, three years ago the Hôtel Ritz and plaza still bustled with people—but the hotel guests were German officers and their visitors, and the ladies in residence. The orchestra still played in the dining room back then, and the food and wine were excellent. The officers were gentlemen, charming—excepting Göring and Horst Eckert. The ladies still looked their best, wore lovely dresses and jewels. Of course, since she'd closed her couture at the Maison before the war, she wasn't surprised some of their dresses were a bit dull, compared to her own designs. But there you are—fashion is another war entirely.

But two years ago, after America joined the war, life flipped upside down. The Americans landed in Africa, and brave, bold General Rommel beat a retreat to Tunisia, to Spatz's utter surprise. In the Hôtel Ritz, the orchestra vanished and the guest rooms slowly emptied. Some of the Ritz's German officers were ordered to the south of France. Others, less fortunate, were sent to Russia. Back then, as the officers abandoned the hotel, she'd not really understood what was coming. She had not realized the full extent of danger to herself that could come out of this war.

Only a year ago American fliers joined the RAF, circling and bombing towns and cities in Europe, although, while they hit the suburbs of Paris, the center city remains so far intact. Spatz says the year 1943 will go down in German history as one of hell in his country. Not much was spared. The Axis planes burned Hamburg to the ground. And Spatz warned American ground forces were on their way to Europe—no one knew where or when—just that they were coming. They took Africa, they landed in Italy.

And now they're here—on Europe's soil. The Americans landed at Normandy in June, taking everyone by surprise. Each day they're coming closer—they've taken Caen, they're threatening Chartres, and already their fighter planes pound the suburbs of Paris. What will happen to her now?

Paris is in turmoil. Rumors of a failed attempt on Hitler's life are whispered by the hotel staff. It is true, Spatz finally admits. A group of military officers tried and failed to murder the Führer. Worse, Admiral Canaris was one, and he's now missing. Spatz is unusually quiet these days—pale and withdrawn.

The sound of a key turning in the lock startles Coco from these thoughts. She turns her head, silently watching Spatz walk in. He's early today. He says nothing as he yanks off his hat and sets it on the telephone table. Then, wearing a solemn expression, he walks to her and sits down in his chair, facing her over the little glass table between them.

"The Allies are near Paris, Coco. Word is Leclerc's Free French are moving ahead with General de Gaulle. BBC says they will enter Paris first." He hesitates while she stares, unmoving. "We're leaving. I'm going home to Berlin." He swallows as he says this, looking off across the Place Vendôme, avoiding her eyes. "It's not safe to stay, Coco. Already the rabble are barricading streets in the 6th arrondissement. Things will get worse as the Allies get closer."

So soon! She cannot think. Spatz leans forward, clasping his hands between his knees. His expression is sorrowful. "Do you understand? I must leave." He pauses, then, "And you must come with me."

She'd been dreading this day for months. But now she thinks of the bleakness of Berlin. Spatz lifts his eyes to her, and she shakes her head.

"You are not safe here," he urges. "You *must* come with me. Violence is erupting from the very sewers of Paris. All through the city the Resistance rats and communists and students are rioting, looking for blood, seeking revenge. They're searching for victims—the Ritz will be one of their first targets. Our forces are in disarray; we can't protect you." He rubs the back of his neck, watching her. "You cannot count on our help, Coco. Only our worst will remain, the SS. And take my word on this: they will not leave Paris without a slaughter."

He stretches out his hand. "Please. Come with me. We'll go back together."

She takes his hand, lifting her eyes to his. "I cannot leave." They have lived together for the most part of four years. She cares for Spatz, but she does not love him. And truth is, she cannot live in the gray stone city of Berlin, hunkered down under a dome of gloom. Berlin is now a city with no light, no music, no laughter. "This is my home. This is where I must stay."

Besides, Chanel is Paris. Despite the threatening notes, despite the Resistance and the Fifi, she tells herself that she will remain safe. Because if the Americans and British come, her plan will work long enough for the rabble to burn through their rage, until the city settles down under the new authorities. And then, she will appeal to the British.

Spatz packs his bags while Coco sits, staring through the windows. When he returns to the sitting room, Coco hears Alyce calling downstairs for someone to come pick up his luggage.

He stands before her, saying nothing. At last, he reaches for her and she rises, letting him draw her into his arms. She closes her eyes, resting there, leaning into him, and Spatz rests his chin on her head. How she wishes he would not leave, this old friend. But when she voices the words, he pulls back, holding her at arm's length, looking deep into her eyes.

"I cannot stay. I am German, Coco, and Abwehr."

"Yes, I know."

"Then, this is goodbye."

"No." She touches his lips with her fingers. "This is au revoir. We will meet again."

Street by street they fight—the Resistance and stubborn remainders of the Reich's army. The Luxembourg Gardens are now a Wehrmacht fortress. On the roof of the villa in the gardens they've installed a battery of canon and machine guns. Sometimes at night she hears the booming cannons from across the river. Again, the city air is filled with smoke, and the stench of danger.

Citizens of Paris are ecstatic, drunk with victory, and yet

hostile, vengeful. Ration cards are tossed away as people rush the markets; but fighting on the roads outside Paris only increases shortages. Angry mobs form. The people say they will rule now. Things will come right again, when the people take charge.

When the Wehrmacht tanks leave the Luxembourg, rolling down the boulevard Saint-Michel still firing away, citizens riot. Riots turn to looting. That evening Coco dines with Arletty in the hotel dining room. Gunfire erupts from a rooftop across the plaza. Silenced, they watch bursts of fire from the darkness.

Coco places her fork down carefully on the edge of her plate, looking about. The dining room is empty, except for Coco, Arletty, and the maître d' standing at his post. The hotel is eerily silent. She longs for the old, ordinary sound of bustling waiters and music, of guests in the dining room and automobiles rolling up to the doors. A glance through the windows confirms her fear. She swivels toward Arletty.

"The guards are gone."

"Yes." Arletty lifts her eyes to Coco. There's a touch of bitter in her voice. "Everyone is gone. My Hans, your Spatz. The guards. Everyone. The last of our German guests disappeared this afternoon, Géraud says." Her face is resigned. "And the sandbags are also gone. Géraud says Resistance fighters came for them after the guards left. They use them for barricades. He says he could not stop them."

Still chewing, she gazes off. "I'm not certain that I believe him." Shifting her eyes back to Coco, "I think our concierge is waiting for General de Gaulle to arrive. He will celebrate Germany's defeat."

Her eyes reflect Coco's fears. At least the German boot had insured order in the streets of Paris. Neither one of them had really thought this moment would come, she reflects. Furiously she lights a cigarette. "Someone's shooting from the rooftops on the Place

Vendôme and we have no guard. Surely the police will come." Turning, Coco motions to the maître d'. Hands clasped behind his back, he hurries over at once and bows.

"Yes, mademoiselle?"

"Did you hear the gunfire just now? Where are the police? You must call the police at once. Hotel residents require protection from the street mobs, monsieur."

His brows draw together and the corners of his mouth curl down. "I am sorry, mademoiselle. But there is nothing we can do. The police have declared a strike. They are barricaded in the Prefecture."

The Free French are first to arrive, wearing their GI khakis and red pompom hats. Alyce wakes her at noon with a breakfast tray, excited, bubbling as she describes the parade in great detail while Coco nibbles on her toast. First came the Fifi, Alyce says, followed by the great general returning home. They came down the Champs-Élysées, from the Arc de Triomphe to the Place de la Concorde.

"They say he followed the exact route down the boulevard the Boche took when they first arrived. The Fifi trampled over the occupiers' very footsteps. The general has liberated our city, mademoiselle! The Boche have fled—at last, at last they are gone!" She dances a few steps around the room.

Alyce has lived with her for almost six years, since before the war. When, after the workers' strike, she'd arrived at the Maison looking for work, right off Coco had known the girl knew next to nothing about invisible seams or needlework or fabric. Besides, she had no need for a seamstress back then, since she'd closed her couture. But something about that earnest young face convinced her to take a chance on training Alyce as a lady's maid. And she was right.

Observing Alyce now, she realizes she knows nothing of her life. Nothing about her family, or whether she has a beau, or her real ambitions. So she asks whether Alyce has family in the city.

"Oh, no," Alyce says. She's kneeling before the armoire in the bedroom, sorting pairs of shoes. She falls back onto her heels and turns her head, looking at Coco. "Maman died when I was young."

Just as Coco's. "And your father?"

She lifts a shoulder as a flush rushes to her cheeks. "He left not long after Maman passed on. I haven't seen him since." Again, just like Coco. And then, ducking her head, Alyce turns back to the shoes.

"But, have you any brothers? Sisters?"

"No, mademoiselle." Busily she moves the shoes around.

"A beau?"

"No, mademoiselle."

Evan is gone. She has not seen him in a week. Coco watches her little maid now, understanding that soon Alyce, too, will leave. A surprising melancholy feeling comes over her. With André all but withdrawn from her world, she realizes she's come to think of Evan and Alyce almost as family.

Soon after the great parade down the Champs-Élysées, the Americans and British enter Paris. Géraud gives her the news with glee. She nods, attempts a smile. She stands very still—she must not faint. She must not faint.

Collabo. Whore. We will come for you.

Opening her eyes, she looks at Géraud, and she's never before felt so alone.

On that night of August 25, at exactly twenty-two minutes past eleven, as Alyce injects Coco's medicine, the bells of Notre-

Dame ring out. It is the F-sharp Emmanuel, Coco realizes—the largest, deepest, most beautiful bell of Notre-Dame. They have not tolled since the moment the first Germans arrived in Paris on July 14—four years ago. The medicine enters her mind riding on the musical bells. Rainbow colors swirl through Coco's head as Alyce dances from the room and the great bells toll on and on, out over the city and through the suburbs, singing that Paris is liberated.

Paris is free.

Chapter Forty-Six

Paris
Fall 1944

The mob demands retribution for the long cold years of German occupation. With the Fifi looking on, ragged youths with dark eyes and shaggy brows, with blade-thin bones, carry knives and guns, prowling the streets seeking revenge while leaders of the provisional government avert their eyes, arguing amongst themselves. They seek the collabos.

This is the time of the purge.

From behind the heavy silk curtains at her windows, Coco peers down at the youths, the mob of angry citizens, now gathered in the Place Vendôme before the hotel. They shout for retribution from those who lived well during the occupation. Between the tall bronze column and the Ritz, a space is cleared. In the open space, two men hold a woman sagging between them. The woman is naked, stripped of her clothes. There are more women down there too. They are tied together by a rope.

A man with a pair of scissors stuck in his pant waist holds

up a long razor as he emerges from the crowd, strutting up behind the naked woman. While the crowd roars, he grabs a thick handful of her hair, and yanking back her head, saws with the razor. The woman struggles, twisting one way then the other, while the two men hold her arms, and everyone around them laughs, shouting obscenities. When the handful of hair is held high, a deafening cheer rises from the crowd, the obscene noise pulsing in waves out over the plaza, crawling up the hotel walls where Coco watches and waits.

This could be her. Coco forces herself to watch. They cut off all of the woman's hair. They shave her head. They yank her arms behind her back, so that one shoulder juts up at an angle. And while she's held immobile, another man steps up to her and lifts his hand to her face. When the woman sees the flame, she shrinks back. Coco suddenly realizes—the new weapon is a cigarette lighter.

The crowd closes in so that Coco cannot see, and the woman screams—an inhuman sound that comes over and over, agony repeating and repeating. For an instant the crowd parts and Coco sees the woman still fighting, rearing back. Her heart races but she cannot move; she cannot look away. She's riveted to the scene until the cheering crowd closes around the poor woman again, blocking the view.

Coco releases a shuddering breath. Dropping her head, she presses a hand over her eyes. When she looks up again, she stares, her lips parting. Then, doubling, she wraps her arms around her waist, feeling sick. The woman's shame is marked forever on her forehead with a large black swastika branding her flesh.

But here now! Just when the woman's screams have died, another is dragged forth from the rope. Men pull her through the dancing, jeering crowd, stumbling into the circle. Coco gasps, pressing a hand to her mouth as two men hold her, while a third cuts off clumps of her long, curling hair. No, it cannot be.

It cannot be Arletty. She twists, flinging back her head, fighting while others tear off her clothing.

Coco grips the windowsill, her heart pounding. *Please don't let this be Arletty.* It's so difficult to see; she cannot tell. Falling onto her knees and retching, she sobs. *Please don't let that be Arletty.*

Minutes later, hollow inside and with the raucous crowd still cheering, Coco grabs for a leg on the dressing table, and straining, pulls herself up from the floor. When at last she's standing, she sinks into the chair before the dressing table, gripped by terror and pity. And, knowing that, if she is right and that was Arletty out there, they will soon come for her.

She, too, is on their lists.

Wildly she calls, "Alyce?"

But no one answers.

Voices rise in song on the plaza—they are singing the Marseillaise. She must run. Breathing hard, Coco hurries to the armoire where her valise waits, packed days ago. Picking it up, she rushes through the sitting room. But at the hallway door, she hesitates. Turning, she gazes over the room which has sheltered her for the last four years. Who knows when she'll return.

A piercing scream from the plaza propels her through the door. She stops only to lock the door behind her, as she always has. Dropping the key in her skirt pocket, she strides to the elevator and pushes the button. When Madame Giror slides the door open and greets Coco, she forms a tight smile and calmly steps inside. She is silent during the descent, grateful she cannot hear the screams in here.

As she exits the lift, she stops at the sight of a wave of khaki uniforms bursting through the entrance door. Some wear camouflage shirts and wide-brimmed hats, and they rush forward, charging down the grand entrance hall. Coco shrinks back against the wall—she is too late. They've come.

A big ruddy fellow enters behind them, standing alone at the door and brandishing a gun. Halting just inside, he lifts the weapon high over his head. "Have no fear!" he shouts. "We've come to liberate the Ritz!"

From the corners of her eyes Coco glances at Géraud. Surely there's something he can do. But a surprising grin spreads across his face. Throwing out his arms, Géraud comes around the desk, calling, "So you've arrived at last, Monsieur Hemingway. Welcome home!"

Hanging onto the valise, Coco turns, striding toward the corridor to the rue Cambon entrance of the hotel. Once outside, she picks up her pace, running, running until she reaches the Maison. The door is locked; she presses the bell, looking about as she waits. Minutes pass before the shop girl arrives to unlock the door. "It is the mob, mademoiselle. I was afraid."

Coco nods, lifting her chin as she steps inside. She greets the girl with a calm smile.

She is here, and she will emerge from the Maison untouched. The purge won't last long. The crowd will soon turn its attention elsewhere. She has survived worse—Maman's death, Papa's disappearance from her life, and an impoverished childhood. She has survived Boy Capel's treacherous love and giving up her son, and Pierre's theft, and powerful men and their ambitions. She has survived the war, despite regrets. And now, with her strength and wit, she will survive the purge.

Here in the Maison she has prepared her own guard. They will arrive soon. At least she has a plan. Here she will be safe. She is Chanel.

Chapter Forty-Seven

Paris
Fall 1944

Two days pass, and still the purge continues, raging. While the new provisional government assumes office, violence increases in Paris. Mobs rampage—they hunt collaborators, those who ate well and kept warm in the last four years while their own children and elders starved. Fierce fighting breaks out in the regions south and west of the city and food remains short.

But the Maison on rue Cambon is searched out by mobs of a different sort. Word has spread. Her plan is working, as it should. American and British soldiers crowd the narrow street before the House of Chanel day and night, pressing to get inside. In the shop window Coco has posted a sign: "In appreciation—free to American and British soldiers in uniform: one bottle of Chanel No. 5 to take home to your sweetheart."

Her shelves are heavy with bottles of No. 5. Director Prudone obtained the entire remaining stock of the perfume from the plant at Neuilly. On the evening she'd assigned him the task, he'd found the factory deserted, except for the night watchman. The man was easily won over by a gold coin the director always carried in his pocket. He'd even assisted Prudone and Evan in transporting the bottles to the truck. That gold coin served as security, always in his pocket in the event of an assault in these uncertain times, Prudone later told her. Nothing enrages a man set on robbery like a victim with an empty pocket, he'd said. Coco had replaced the coin with one of her own at once.

At least Director Prudone remains loyal. He followed her orders exactly. She smiles at the thought of Pierre's face when he learns of her turnabout theft of all Neuilly's No. 5.

Now, as she had hoped, with the free gifts of her premier perfume, mademoiselle is every foreign soldier's sweetheart. Her own guard swarms in the street below. No dirty resistant or *les Fifis* will break through this crowd. She's survived here for days, and she will be here long after the purge is forgotten.

In her apartment over the salon in the Maison, Coco rests on the beige sofa this afternoon, while the shop girls handle the crowd below. She's neither seen nor heard from Alyce since she fled the hotel. She will miss the girl. But she will not allow herself to become sentimental. She will not worry about the little maid. Alyce knows the streets of Paris. Like Coco, she will survive.

Still, she misses the girl.

Laughter and cheers come from the salon as the shop girls downstairs hand out the free perfume. They work in shifts, giving the bottles to soldiers day and night. This day is warm and sun shines through the open windows. From below she hears the soldiers thanking the shop girls, and outside, calling to their friends—holding up the sweetheart gifts in triumph. Neither the Fifi nor any mob will reach her through the crush of soldiers in the street below. To the cheerful sounds downstairs, Coco closes her eyes, drifting off.

The sun has disappeared when a knock on the door startles Coco. Glancing at the clock on the desk across the room, Coco is surprised to see the afternoon has slipped away. She's slept for hours. Rising, stretching her arms overhead, she fluffs her hair and walks to the door. When she opens it, Minette, the Maison's senior shop girl stands before her.

The girl looks flustered. "I'm sorry to disturb you, mademoiselle, but the perfume is almost gone—we've no more than perhaps one hundred bottles left, and yet hundreds of soldiers are still waiting outside for their gifts. What shall we say?"

"This is impossible, Minette. We have several thousands of bottles in stock."

Minette lifts one delicate shoulder. "Thousands of soldiers came for them." With an uncertain smile she adds, "I am certain they will remember the gift and this day forever, Mademoiselle Chanel."

She hesitates only a moment. "As will I," Coco says. She works for a steady tone. "When the perfume is finished, you must close the shop. Apologize to the remaining soldiers. Lock the grill over the front door and pull down the shutters before you leave. Make certain the shutters are also locked."

"Yes, mademoiselle."

As the girl starts off, Coco adds, "Best take the sign out of the window too. The Maison will open tomorrow as usual. Ten o'clock. Do not be late."

"Yes, mademoiselle."

So this is how it ends. She closes the door and leans against it.

She waits, perched, at ready on the sofa in the dark, remembering the women on the Place Vendôme. Now the crowd will jeer and laugh at her. Even now, she hears the women's screams. When they come for her, she will walk with her head high and her back straight, looking neither right nor left. She is Mademoiselle Chanel and they are thugs.

Still, trembling, she draws her knees up to her chest. Gazing around the comforting room, her eyes stop on a Coromandel screen, one Boy had given to her, long before he'd married. Regarding the screen, she sees instead her early days with Boy—the forest near Royallieu where they first made love, sitting on the terrace, talking of the stars, and what may be beyond. Caught in moments of the past, she smiles, remembering how Étienne and Boy had bartered her between them, and how angry she'd become. She thinks of holding André just after birth, a sweet, soft bundle of new life in her arms.

She pulls herself from the soothing memories. She must focus. She must be ready when they come for their revenge. She will not give in now to fear, nor—thinking of the past four years—to regrets. Except for one: André.

If only she could have told her son the truth before she's taken.

They come at two thirty in the morning, as the Gestapo always did. She hears them banging on the downstairs doors. She hears them ripping shutters from the windows; smashing the glass. She hears their heavy boots pounding up the spiral stairs, and now they come running down the hallway and they're pounding, pounding on the door of her apartment and her heart pounds too. Slowly she rises, moving toward the door feeling almost weightless, as if none of this is real. As if she's floating.

They are Fifi of course. Three have come—young and crude, unshaven. Their pants are torn; their shirt sleeves rolled, with armbands identifying that they're Free French tied above the elbows. Long, lanky hair falls over their eyes. She says that she will need her purse and a wrap, but two reach out, grabbing her arms. Enraged, with every ounce of strength in her body, Coco jerks free, catching them off guard.

Then, with a look of contempt for the little group, she lifts her chin and, without a word, walks past each one and out into the hallway while they follow. She walks down the spiral stairs free, but the hands snatch her again as she reaches the ground floor. They crowd her. She holds her back straight and her chin high, looking neither right nor left, in silence forcing them to work to increase her steady pace as they pull her along between them through the shattered window glass. They taunt, but she says nothing. Not even when they shove her into the back seat of a sour-smelling car while calling her the worst names, nor when they slam the door.

They taunt her all along the way, laughing—*Coco, coquette, collabo-Boche whore*—around the Place de la Concorde with bursts of gunfire flashing from the dark Tuileries, over the bridge jammed with revelers, through streets barricaded with sandbags and broken furniture piled one piece atop the other. At last the car stops before a plain, three-storied building not far from the Hôtel Lutetia.

"Please come into our office, mademoiselle," one of the Fifi says in a mocking tone as he opens the car door. She looks up at a crude sign over the entrance: "*Forces françaises de l'intérieur.*" Yes, these are Fifi.

They try to drag her—they do—but she's too fast. She will not allow herself to be dragged through the hallway and up the stairs. The room they push her into at last is small and square, with one window and one bare electric bulb. An older man, several days unshaven, sits at a wooden desk with his stocking feet on top, crossed at the ankles. The bottoms of his socks are black. Chewing on a cigar in the corner of his mouth, he looks her up and down, then jerks his thumb. One of the boys pulls over a straight ladder-backed wooden chair, placing it before the desk.

Robespierre, the revolutionary, lover of the guillotine's sharp blade, points at the chair.

Coco sits, placing her hands in her lap, regarding him. He lifts his feet from the desk, dropping them onto the floor with a thud, and opens a file. The rude boys are silent now, sulking against the wall behind her. Minutes pass in silence while Robespierre hunches over the file, reading. She hopes he cannot hear her pounding heartbeat. She presses her hands together, one atop the other so as not to fidget while she waits.

"Gabrielle Chanel, known as Coco." He chews on the cigar as he looks up. "This is you?"

"Yes, of course. I am Mademoiselle Gabrielle Chanel."

"And you reside where—at 31 Rue Cambon? Or the Hôtel Ritz?"

"Both."

His eyes hold hers. "But for the past four years during the occupation, you have resided in the Hôtel Ritz with the German, Baron Hans Günther von Dincklage. Correct?"

"I do not believe he is German."

"No?" His smile is grim. "But Baron Hans von Dincklage's nationality is well-known. How could you not know?"

"I never thought to check his passport."

The smile vanishes. "You would be smart to answer my questions carefully."

"May I have a cigarette?"

He snaps his finger toward one of the young boys. The boy hands her a half-smoked butt from his mouth. Robespierre studies her. His tone is reflective when he speaks. "Do you know, I did not have a real cigarette for four years during the occupation."

She clamps the cigarette between her lips and inhales, tasting the rude boy's spittle. But the familiar smoky warmth relaxes her a bit.

"Von Dincklage lived with you at the Hôtel Ritz."

"On and off. When he was in Paris, that is. He's an old friend."

"An old friend, charged with espionage, mademoiselle."

She takes the cigarette from her lips and looks at the grand inquisitor. "I know nothing of that, monsieur. I am a fashion designer, a perfumer. So far as I am aware, Baron von Dincklage is in the business of importing and exporting fabric."

He glances down at the file. "His dossier says otherwise. Von Dincklage was quite at home in the Paris Abwehr offices. And currently he is SS."

"I know nothing of spies." Pinching the cigarette between her lips again, she takes a long draw, inhales, and lets out a stream of smoke. "Certainly, if you are correct and I had known, our friendship would have ended."

"But you lived in a nest of spies at the Ritz."

"The Ritz was my home long before the Germans arrived."

And suddenly, as she's answering these questions, it comes to her—the dossier this man is reading from is Spatz's Abwehr file, not hers. Perhaps they've not found hers yet. They hate her for collaborating, for living in the Hôtel Ritz along with the Reich high command. But it seems they know nothing of her trips to Berlin and Madrid. Nothing, so far, she prays, of her bargain to spy.

As the thought forms, she grows calm. Tossing the cigarette butt to the floor, she grinds it under her toe. Robespierre's eyes follow the cigarette. Hours pass as he continues the questions— sometimes, the same ones just put in different ways. The chair is hard, hurting her back. The air in the room is stale. The boys who brought her here smell of the sewer. But she answers each question one after the other in an even, measured tone.

And then, as Robespierre's questions turn more menacing and a flutter of new fear builds in her chest, the door behind her bursts open. The inquisitor glances up and Coco turns her head. A man hurries toward the desk, handing a note to Robespierre, who snatches it from him. The room is silent as he reads. Then, he regards the fellow, frowning. Ignoring Coco, he stands, and with an irritable gesture to the messenger, moves toward the door, followed by his minions.

Taking a long breath, Coco slumps, glancing at her watch. She'd thought she had been in this room for ten or fifteen hours, and yet the watch says the time is only six fifteen in the morning. *Madonna, pray for my worthless soul; pray this messenger has not brought the Abwehr file to Robespierre.* And they cannot yet have Schellenberg's file—the Allies haven't reached Berlin yet. Clasping her hands together, she squeezes them. If they have found her file, then perhaps at least she'll go to prison, instead of being mauled by the waiting mob.

Minutes pass. And then half an hour. And then the door slams open behind her, hitting the wall. A Fifi struts in, looming over her. "Get up," he says.

She stands, turning to him, and he jerks his chin toward the door. "This way."

A rush of terror almost makes her stumble, but she rights herself and walks to the door. Where are they taking her? She's heard of tricks like this—ask the easy questions first. Get what you can. Then the hard part begins.

The real interrogation.

The only sound in the hallway is the sound of her shoes and the boy's hitting the wood plank floor. He leads her down the same stairway they walked up, on down through the same ground floor hall. He stops before the painted wooden door they'd first entered, a lifetime ago, it seems. There, standing aside, he says in a surly tone, "Go on off, then. You're free." He spits on the floor near her feet. "For now."

And suddenly the nightmare is over. For now. Coco stands at the foot of the steps on the pavement, dazed as she looks about. The area is deserted this time of day. But there is the Hôtel Lutetia, one block away. She stands without moving, gathering her wits, orienting herself by the hotel. She has no purse, no money. She has no baby-blue Rolls Royce and driver, and the Maison is more than a mile away, across the Seine. But she can walk, and she will walk to the Maison and think of what comes next.

Coco lifts her head, in case they are watching from inside, and begins to walk. For now, at least, she is free.

Chapter Forty-Eight

Paris
Fall 1944

Minette is standing before the shop door when at last Coco turns the corner onto rue Cambon, one block down from the Maison. The sun is high and hot. Coco long ago removed her shoes and blisters burn the bottoms of both feet, especially on her toes. Who would think toes could be the worst? She longs to call down the street to the girl for help, but her throat is dry and her muscles strain from sitting in that chair. Her neck is in a vise. If only she had one sip of water, then she could call.

"Mademoiselle!" Minette flies toward her now, with a flurry of exclamations. Minette takes Coco's arm. Her voice is soothing as they walk, Coco leaning on the shop girl. But at the Maison, Coco stops, staring at the glass scattered across the pavement. She looks at the shattered windows and the front door of her shop, the grill now ripped from the frame, the door smashed open, and she fights back tears.

"Step carefully here, mademoiselle," Minette says, sweeping

glass aside with her shoe and guiding Coco through a pathway. As they enter, Coco sways. Minette steers her to a chair.

"Water," Coco whispers. "I need something to drink." Then she leans back in the chair, closing her eyes.

"Yes, mademoiselle. Right away."

Eyes closed, Coco listens as Minette hurries off in the direction of the small kitchen in the back of the shop, wondering if even now the Fifi are hunting for her Abwehr dossier. Visions of the women on the Place Vendôme rise, haunting. Was that Arletty she saw? She shudders—was Arletty's beautiful face scared forever by the swastika brand?

She shakes her head. She cannot stay in Paris. Perhaps, La Pausa?

She opens her eyes. Of course. Yes, that is the place. She will leave immediately for La Pausa, her refuge. There she can rest.

Minette returns, and while Coco gulps the water, the girl moves toward the doorway, kicking aside more glass. The sound of the glass on the tiled floor grates Coco's nerves. But the water, and thinking of La Pausa, revives her spirit. Already she feels better. "Take the broom from the closet behind the stairs, Minette. You will cut yourself that way."

La Pausa is the answer. Thinking of the serene villa on the cliff over the sea almost makes her smile.

"But what is this?" Minette's stooping, picking up a piece of paper from the floor. With a glance at the handwriting, Minette hands a note to Coco. "I believe this is meant for you, mademoiselle." Her brows rise, her eyes grow wide as Coco takes the paper, recognizing the concierge card with the embossed name of Hôtel Ritz across the top.

"You are not safe," Géraud has written. "Please come at once, mademoiselle." He has underlined the words "at once" with a thick stroke of ink.

She groans. Crumpling the note, Coco tosses it on the floor. Perhaps already they are learning of her work with the Abwehr and this is Géraud's warning. Perhaps they know her code name—Westminster—how stupid that name sounds now. And what would Bendor, Duke of Westminster, think if he found out?

"Fetch my purse from the apartment," she says to Minette, who stands before her, gaping. "Hurry, please. And fetch my pearls too. They're in a box in the bottom desk drawer."

She must flee to La Pausa. Turning, she looks up the stairs for Minette, and here she comes, hurrying down with Coco's purse and the strings of pearls.

"Thank you," Coco says, slipping the pearls over her neck. "I have decided to close the Maison for a few weeks. I think we all need a little rest, don't you?" A look of surprise crosses Minette's face. The girl is silent. Coco opens the purse and pulls out several reichsmarks. "This will have to do for now," she says. The amount is considerably more than Minette's wages for a few weeks.

Minette stammers her thanks.

"Géraud, in the hotel, will exchange them for you into francs if you wish."

With the exception of Géraud, who is at his desk as always, the grand entrance hall is deserted when she enters from the side corridor. The concierge looks up, and his eyes snap as he sees Coco. He beats his hand over his heart. "Ah, such a relief! At last you've come."

"Yes. I must leave this morning for La Pausa, Géraud. Please have my car brought round. And I'll need a driver."

He looks at her. "The south is not yet safe, mademoiselle. There's still fighting throughout southern France. But the Hotel Palace in Lausanne wired this morning, confirming your reservation."

"Lausanne?"

"Yes. The wire arrived early this morning." He juts his chin toward the hotel doors. "And your car is waiting." Coco turns, following his eyes. The blue Rolls is parked just outside. A uniformed driver—not Evan—lounges against the hood of the car with his arms crossed, smoking. Géraud clears his throat, looking strangely sad. "I thought ... I thought they'd taken you."

She frowns, turning to him. "Is he your man?"

"No. But you will be safe with him, mademoiselle." She sees it in his eyes. He knows, somehow, as concierges always do; he knows everything. "The hotel is pleased to vouch for this driver." He lowers his voice. "We will miss you. But Lausanne is pleasant this time of year. And the Hôtel Ritz will always be here, waiting for your return."

"I've made no plans for Lausanne." She glances again at the automobile outside. She must leave. Remembering the note, she makes the decision. "Well then, with your guarantee." He nods. "I suppose I must go upstairs and pack."

"We've taken that liberty, Mademoiselle Chanel. Your bags are in the car."

She gives a firm shake of her head. "Oh no, I cannot leave like this. I must make certain everything's in order in my rooms. And if Alyce has returned ..."

For the first time ever in all the years she has resided at the Hôtel Ritz, Géraud steps from behind the concierge desk, comes to her, and puts his arm around her shoulders. "They have come twice, mademoiselle; last night, and again earlier this morning. They will be back, you may be certain. You have no time." He draws back, still speaking low. "They are Resistance, part of the mob out in the plaza each day."

She shudders. "You are right, I must leave at once." Despite the rising terror, the urge to flee, something stops her. Alyce. She cannot abandon Alyce without making arrangements for her safety in the unlikely event the girl does return. The Hôtel Ritz was her only home. She really has no one else but Coco. She clutches the pearls. She is terrified, but she cannot leave just yet.

Trembling, Coco looks at Géraud. "First, I must make arrangements for my maid. She's young. Have you seen her, my Alyce?"

Géraud's face changes and he glances toward the door behind his desk. Coco follows his look. Stepping back, Géraud heaves a sigh. "Yes, mademoiselle, I have. I had hoped to spare you yet another worry. We have your maid in hand and will do all we can." Gently he nudges her toward the entrance and the car.

Coco turns about; Alyce is behind that door. As she whips around, hurrying toward the door, Géraud runs behind her. Flinging it open, she stops just inside.

Alyce lies on a sofa, limp. Her arm is bandaged—vivid colors of her dark-red blood soaked through the white cotton bandage threaten to overwhelm Coco. Alyce, so young, so obedient. So loyal. The girl's other arm hides her face, but Coco can see her hair is cut short, uneven, as if sawed with a razor. And her dress is torn. Coco turns to Géraud, eyebrows high. "What's happened?"

"They'd started when we got there," Géraud says. "They accused her as a collabo. The hotel staff gathered, stormed out onto the plaza for her." At Coco's look, he adds, "She is one of ours, mademoiselle."

"The mob calmed when they realized. It was our uniforms perhaps. We said it wasn't fair; that the girl was only your maid."

This was her fault. Alyce was punished for her. As Boy had always warned, actions have consequences, and Alyce is now suffering because of Coco. The girl bursts into tears as Coco kneels beside her. Coco brushes hair back from Alyce's forehead, even as fresh blood streams down one side of her bruised face and into her hair.

Raging anger, and an emotion she cannot yet name, fills

Coco. Every part of her own body hurts, but she aches more for the young girl stretched out before her.

"You must go," Géraud says from behind. His tone is urgent. "There's no more time. The people will soon come. If they see your car …"

Coco holds Alyce's eyes. "Move it around to rue Cambon."

"Yes, yes," Géraud mutters. "I will tell the driver," and he hurries off.

"I am sorry, Alyce. They did this to you because of me." She touches the bruises on the girl's flesh. Alyce attempts to lift her hand, but it drops instead onto her chest.

"It happened yesterday, in the evening," Géraud says, rushing back to her side. He hands a handkerchief to Coco. "There are no doctors, so we did what we could."

Tenderly, Coco wipes the tears and blood from Alyce's face. "Little one, I am sorry you were hurt in my place. I will take care of you. You'll be safe with me."

Alyce closes her eyes.

"She is harmed, I'm afraid." He stutters over the words and his face flushes red. "She is lucky to be alive. Antoinette in the kitchen wrapped her up; with seven boys, she's practically a physician. The arm is broken—and, I think, her heart." Coco gives him a quick look. His eyes drop. "No telling what they did before they took her out onto the plaza. But the arm is good enough for now, Antoinette says."

Shouts rise from the Place Vendôme—a few voices, some together, some alone, sinister sounds from different directions outside. "Is the car ready?"

"Yes. At the rue Cambon entrance." He touches her shoulder. "Mademoiselle Chanel. You must go. You must leave right away."

Coco looks down at Alyce. "I cannot leave without her," she says.

A strange sound comes from the back of the concierge's throat while Coco strokes Alyce's hair, whispering now in her ear. Alyce will come with her to Lausanne. Coco will care for her. Coco will see her well and strong. They—the two of them—will stick together. Alyce can think of everything else later. Now she must come; she will be safe with mademoiselle.

As she whispers, Géraud goes to the door, opens it a few inches and looks out, then turns to Coco. "Hurry, there is little time. Quick! They are gathering out there again. Paris is no longer safe."

"Alyce, will you come with me?"

The girl's eyes open. She nods, with an almost imperceptible smile.

They help her up—Coco bracing one side and Géraud the other. As Alyce limps toward the door, emotions swell in Coco's chest. Robespierre's inquisition is forgotten as they reach the door.

She cannot change men and wretched wars. But this is a problem which she can control. She will protect this girl. She will keep her safe. The thought flashes through her mind—if Colette were here, perhaps she'd understand that, indeed, Coco has a heart.

You see? I do have real blood pumping through my veins. And, I do feel the sting of a bee, and rejection.

As Coco and Géraud help Alyce down the corridor toward the rue Cambon entrance of the Hôtel Ritz, Alyce moans. The car is waiting, engine on. The driver comes around, lifting Alyce into the Rolls, and Coco says au revoir to Géraud. Already she feels strength flowing back through her limbs.

Chapter Forty-Nine

Lausanne
Fall 1944

Weeks later, on the promenade along the shore of Lac Léman at Lausanne, as on every other day since she's arrived, Coco sits alone on a bench. Alyce is resting in the rooms at the Hotel Palace. Slowly, she's recovering.

The water is still this afternoon. Snow on the mountaintops across the lake shimmers in the hazy sun. The autumn temperature is pleasant—not too warm, not too cold. Coco wears a simple skirt, a crisp white blouse, with a light sweater thrown over her shoulders, dark stockings, her comfortable walking shoes, and a straw boater. But in weather like this, she's ditched the gloves.

She sits on the bench, grateful for the solitude and fresh air. Unlike Paris, everything in Lausanne is clean. The entire city climbing the hills behind her is clean, the shops and cafés, the gardens she passes through while walking to the promenade each afternoon, the shore along the lake. Her rooms in the Hotel Palace are white, spotless, filled with light. Here in Lausanne the air sparkles and the earth is sanctified, like the abbey at Aubazine when she was a girl.

Thinking of the abbey days no longer makes her angry. It no longer pains her to think of the girl she'd once been. Day by day in the solitude here, Coco has come to realize that young girl from the abbey is alive and thriving inside. Gabrielle and Coco—the old and the new—they are one.

She is a woman who has walked alone through fire and survived, despite the war, despite Papa's betrayal and Boy's and Pierre's, despite Göring's greed, and most of all, despite André's withdrawal from her. She is a woman who has had to struggle each day of her life just to survive.

Now they say the Jews taken from Paris were sent to prison camps in Germany, beaten, starved, and they seem to think she should have known. They say the Americans and British have found graves in those prison camps—mass graves and skeletons piled high. Although no one seems to know for certain what has happened.

She blinks, looking out over the lake. How could she have known? And if she'd known, what could she have done? None of it had anything to do with her. She did what she could—when Maurice was treated badly, she stepped up to help Colette without hesitation. And now she's taking care of Alyce.

No. She can think of nothing more that she could have done. Besides, she was forced to fight her own wars during the last four years. She leans her head back and closes her eyes, letting the sun warm her skin, forcing away the unwanted thoughts.

Soft fur touches her ankles. Coco starts, and looking down, sees a small yellow kitten resting at her feet. Reaching, she scoops it up, placing it on her lap. The kitten is soft, happy, new. It knows nothing of war. She smiles now, scratching behind its ears, stroking its furry haunches. "Are you an orphan too?" In reply the kitten curls in her lap, purring.

Eyes still half closed, stroking the kitten, the pleasant feeling returns. She watches the ferry from Montreux rising from the mist. The steam whistle blows as the ferry approaches Ouchy, the port of Lausanne, and the various fishing wharves located along the shoreline. She watches the old steamboat pull up to the dock as it does every day at this time. From the distance she watches the passengers disembark, then she looks out again over the blue-silver water, across Lac Léman to the snowy mountains over there.

The cat purrs. Perhaps Alyce would like to have a kitten. Coco gathers the kitten in her arms, preparing to rise. But as she moves, a voice from behind speaks her name.

She knows the scent, the smell of the man—leather, pipe tobacco, wool tweed. The dust of the big city. Slowly she sits back, clutching the kitten, fixing her eyes on the mountains. The kitten struggles from her grasp, curling again in her lap. Footsteps come from behind; a shadow slants toward her.

Just out of sight, he stops.

She does not turn around. "Was it you who snatched me from the Fifi, Pierre? And the warning note—yours too? And the driver?"

He walks around the bench, looking older, but still slim, still handsome. He wears a light overcoat, buttoned, and his old black homburg. Removing the hat, he sits down on the bench beside her.

"Yes," he says.

She hides her smile. "Well, do not think I will credit you in my memoirs. I shall say it was Churchill who saved me."

He chuckles.

"I hear you are selling my No. 5 in America, still using my name. Worse, I hear you're selling it even on military posts."

"PXs, they're called." After a pause, "Sales are good. Besides the PXs, we're everywhere in North and South America. Anyplace we can ship."

She strokes the kitten behind the ears. "I suppose you're degrading the perfume with synthetics."

He looks out over the lake. "No. We were lucky enough to obtain the jasmine absolute."

She tightens her lips. "Yes, I heard."

Pierre drops a piece of paper in her lap, and, without thinking, she picks it up. "What is this?" She looks down at the page filled with rows of numbers.

"Take a look."

"You know I cannot read this small print without my glasses. Just tell me what this says."

He crosses his legs and rests the hat on his knee. "It's a statement of a deposit into your Geneva account, and a breakdown of your share of perfume sales over the last four years." He points to a line on the page. "Here, this one in particular. This very high number is the total figure showing your portion of sales of No. 5."

She looks at the numbers squinting. As he said, it is a large number, bigger than she'd ever dreamed.

If this is real, she is rich again. Very rich.

Beside her, Pierre says nothing.

She folds the page, fanning her face with it, even though the air is crisp and cool. "You are still a thief, Pierre."

"Is that all you have to say?" He throws up his hand and drops it. "Well, I suppose I've been called worse. But it was impossible to transfer the funds into your account in Paris during the war, you know."

"It was also impossible because you lied about who owned the company, and now you are stuck with the lie." With a glance from the corners of her eyes, "According to the law, Félix Amiot owns the company, not you."

He waves off her words. "Forget all that."

"No. 5 is mine. It is my only security."

"That's not true. You may always count on me. I thought you understood that. Despite our differences, we've somehow managed to remain friends from the day we met." He crosses his legs and leans back. "I can still see you there in Deauville, at the races, pretty as a picture in that blue dress and your straw boater with ribbons."

She is silent for a moment. Then, "I'd thought we were friends too. But when you left France in the beginning of the war, and sent Alain back to steal my formula, my name." Her voice lifts a key, "Well, what else could I think but that you were a thief! That you planned to cut me out of the business."

"Well, about that. I've been thinking about our long relationship." He pauses. "You are a difficult woman to please. So, I've arranged a new agreement …"

"Ah, you are dictating terms?"

"No. Just listen." He pauses, then continues. "In addition to your existing shares in Société Mademoiselle, you will receive an increase of two percent on total Chanel perfume revenues, worldwide."

Stunned, Coco says nothing. Silence is sometimes best when one is listening to an offer.

"I am giving this to you." When she says nothing, he adds, "It is a gift."

She clucks her tongue against her teeth.

Pierre sighs. "You must stop worrying about security, Coco. I am here to make an offer. A one-time offer to my friend."

"Oh, yes? Is there more to this offer?"

"Yes, in fact. I've come to a conclusion—it's time for us to stop fighting one another over business." He turns his eyes to her. "The big war is over. Now ours must end. I'm willing to guarantee your security forever, Coco, in exchange for peace. I'll pay all of your expenses from this life into the next, if we can call a halt." He smiles and she looks off.

"Everything?"

"Yes, everything."

She strokes the kitten, feeling the purring vibrations. "For my lifetime?"

"Until you finally kick the dust." After a moment, he covers her hand with his. She looks straight ahead, avoiding his eyes. "But I must have your promise we shall never again meet in court," he says.

She almost smiles. "André is ill, in a sanatorium near Geneva. His expenses, and for his wife and my nieces, are mine. I must purchase a house here in Switzerland for André, for when he's released from the sanatorium. Soon, I hope." She gives him a sideways look. "In Swiss francs, of course."

He nods. "Just let me know. I will cover it." His big hand, curled over hers, is soft and warm. "The papers are already drawn up. Your Paris attorney, René de Chambrun, has a set of my signed copies. He will send them to you to sign."

With three whistle blasts, another ferry comes in sight. The mist has cleared. Lac Léman mirrors the blue of the cloudless sky in the autumn sunshine. A warm mellow feeling spreads through Coco while Pierre holds her hand, and a little smile finally breaks through. Security—Pierre is offering to his old friend this great gift. And with this thought comes another—strangely, she feels loved.

They sit together in silence, watching the ferry glide to the dock. The kitten snuggles against her, sleeping. Life is strange. After all that's passed between them, who would have guessed that in the end their friendship would have withstood all this time, unlike the lovers who disappeared.

It is a kind of absolution between them.

Ah, yes, the future is suddenly bright. She is free from all those worries—rich again, and secure. A surge of energy runs through her as she thinks of returning to Paris soon. She will remodel the

Maison, sweep away dust of the past. Most memories are short, and she's done nothing wrong. She will create, design, resume her couture. After all, she's still Chanel.

Pierre squeezes her hand. "Give me a kiss now, Coco, before I go. You have worn me out."

She peeks at Pierre. His eyes are closed. Well, he does look older. And tired.

But really, it's not her fault.

Note from the Author

Coco was questioned by the Free French in 1944, and luck gave her a pass as they'd not yet unearthed her military or intelligence files. She fled to Switzerland in the aftermath. There, generally in disgrace, Coco Chanel remained in a self-imposed exile in Lausanne, until February 1954. She presented her first postwar couture collection at a show in Paris on February 5, 1954 and Paris yawned. The French had long memories. Still, at Pierre Wertheimer's encouragement, she kept working, and received warmer reviews for her collection in 1956. But Coco's real comeback caught fire in the United States. In the mid-1950s, Americans, distanced from Coco's reputation during the occupation of Paris, loved everything Chanel.

For this story, I have taken creative liberty in changing names of the companies involved. The company manufacturing No. 5 and owned by Pierre, his brother, and Coco is given the fictional name Société Mademoiselle. Pierre owned several other companies in which Coco held no interests. I've referred to the one which she mistakenly thought was producing No. 5 in the United States by the fictional name Lenthal.

Despite her failed attempt to use the Jewish laws against Pierre in their battle for the company during World War II, Coco and Pierre remained friendly during the remainder of their lifetimes. I have utilized dramatic license in imagining the actual court procedures governing Chanel's claim under the Jewish laws against Pierre, and also with reference to the timing of Pierre's offer after the war to pay all Coco's expenses during her lifetime. Although she received No. 5 revenues after the war ended, the latter arrangement for paying her expenses was formalized between Coco and Pierre later in 1954, after a few more disagreements.

Because of Pierre's friendship, in the end Gabrielle "Coco" Chanel spent her last days living in luxury at the Hôtel Ritz. Some might say, she won her war with Pierre. She died on January 10, 1971. Mass was held, in accordance with the dictates of the card she always carried, at the Madeleine Church in Paris, just steps from the Place Vendôme.

She is buried in Lausanne.

Published documents evidence Chanel's cooperation with German military intelligence on two missions to Spain. In the book *Sleeping with the Enemy: Coco Chanel's Secret War* by Hal Vaughan, photographs of some of the fifty pages of military records evidencing her enrollment as an Abwehr agent are reproduced and described. As in this story, Chanel was recruited by the Abwehr as agent F-7124, code name Westminster. Her name and acquaintances with such people as Winston Churchill; Sam Hoare, British ambassador to Spain; and the Duke of Westminster, Hugh Grosvenor, unknown to them, provided good cover and contacts for the missions. Evidence also shows that after the first mission, André Palasse, ill and near death, was freed from prison in Germany. In the interest of simplifying the complexity of the two missions, I have taken the liberty of compacting them into one. Details of the missions are vague, so I have used history, logic, and poetic license—my best guess—for what happened in the shadows in between.

The rumor that André Palasse may have been Coco's son rather than her nephew is fascinating, and is mentioned in several Chanel biographies. The dates surrounding the birth of André are fuzzy, and it appears that no birth certificate for him has ever been found. Although, it is known that Étienne did procure a letter claiming paternity from a lover of Julia-Berthe. Over the years, Boy Capel appears to have treated André almost as a son, financing his expenses growing up, and enrolling him in Boy's old boarding school in England. Regardless, son or nephew, it's clear that Coco loved André as she'd have loved a son, and also Catharina, and his children, Gabrielle and Helen. After the war, André remarried and lived in Switzerland in a home purchased for him by Coco.

The story of the German attempt to kidnap the Duke and Duchess of Windsor to Spain is related by many historians and biographers and appears to be generally true. The imprisonment of American women in the zoo in Paris after the United States joined the war is written in the fine book *Americans in Paris: Life and Death under Nazi Occupation* by Charles Glass.

Hans Dincklage was imprisoned after the war. Once free, he lived for some time with Coco in Lausanne before returning to Germany. He died on March 24, 1976, in Germany. Admiral Canaris was murdered for his part in the attempted assassination of Adolf Hitler.

Walter Schellenberg was sentenced to six years in prison at the Nuremberg Trials, but fell ill with liver and gallbladder disease and was moved to Nuremberg City Hospital. Not long before he died, he was released on a medical pardon. Schellenberg worked on his memoirs during those years. Before completing the book, he asked Chanel for, and received, financial assistance. Coco delivered the money to him in person, in Swiss Francs. Perhaps that is why she was not mentioned in his memoir, which omits their association described in official records.

Coco Chanel was known to be an anti-Semite and a controversial and secretive woman, with emotional layers as difficult to differentiate as the various scents in the compositions of her perfumes. It is often said that jasmine from Grasse is the top note in No. 5. It's difficult to pick out the true "top note" in Coco's own life, the events that formed her. But my guess is the most important factors would not derive from her childhood troubles and Aubazine, which she kept for the most part well hidden, but rather from her own struggles to survive, and deep sorrow over André.

But, dear reader, I leave you to judge.

Acknowledgments

I want to thank the amazing team at Blackstone Publishing for turning my story of Coco Chanel into a beautiful book. First, thank you, Rick Bleiweiss, for acquiring *The Queen of Paris* and welcoming me into the Blackstone Publishing fold. Thanks also to Jeff Yamaguchi, Greg Boguslawski, Lauren Maturo, Megan Wahrenbrock, and Mandy Earles for their creative work in publishing and marketing, and for introducing the book to readers. And to Josie Woodbridge who welcomed me to Blackstone with open arms and pointed me in the right direction in her cheerful way time after time.

Readers are the reason writers write. More thanks to Lauren Ash and Binnie Syril Braunstein for also assisting me in reaching out to readers, all of you, with this book.

A good book cover evokes the essence of the story at first glance without giving it away. It is a mere glimpse of the secrets inside. Thanks to the talented cover artist Alenka Linaschke for achieving exactly the right touch.

Special thanks to editor Corinna Barsan for her patience and encouragement throughout the editing process, and her magnificent expertise. Corinna was an amazing partner in this important task. I felt that we were both on the same wavelength throughout. Thanks also to Deirdre Curley, copyeditor, for her work polishing and shining the final manuscript.

Julie Gwinn, my literary agent with the Seymour Agency, is also my longtime good friend. Julie has a passion for the written word which encourages and motivates writers lucky enough to work with her. Thank you, Julie, for your friendship, loyalty, and for placing *The Queen of Paris* in a wonderful home.

Readers, as you must know, a manuscript goes through many early drafts before it's finished. When my brain would turn groggy from writing and my eyes were blurred from looking at the same pages of type day after day, friends Debbie Intravia and Cheryl Schleuss were always there for me, reading the words I'd written with fresh eyes and alert brains. Their resulting ideas and gentle truth-telling were invaluable and I thank them both.

Finally, I thank my husband, James Lott, for his unwavering love and great patience. He is also my best friend, and has been since we were children. You are my true love and my rock, Jimmy.